The Grand Manor

A Novel By

Dee Cohoon-Madore

DEELIGHTFUL READING

Copyright 2014

Self-published by: Dee Cohoon-Madore Self-Publishing

Digby, NS, Canada

Visit DEELIGHTFUL READING on the web at
http://deelightfulreading.com

e-mail: dee@deelightfulreading.com

The novel The Grand Manor is fictional. Any similarity to actual persons either living or dead is completely co-incidental.

The Grand Manor (print edition)
 ISBN 978-0-9869507-5-9

The Grand Manor (e-book edition)
 ISBN 978-0-9869507-6-6

About the Author

Avivacious young senior, Dee lives in Digby, Nova Scotia. Being retired, she is free to escape into endless hours of writing.

Dee Cohoon-Madore

Dee grew up in a relatively poor family, in a rural community and was born fifth of ten children. She came from a seriously dysfunctional family, which made her childhood a very unhappy place to be. Her parents separated when she was eight years old leaving her mother with a brood of kids to raise on her own. There never was one place they could call home for very long. They moved from place to place every few years or sooner if called for. She can remember her mother wrapping dishes in old newspapers and packing them in a barrel. There was not much to move once you got past the dishes and linens. The furniture was scarce, and they had only the bare essentials. Sparse living room furniture, beds, table and chairs mostly made up the household furnishings. Life was far from easy for the family.

She married her childhood sweetheart at twenty and moved to Toronto for several years. Although the marriage could have been a good one, it lasted for only seven years, but it brought her two beautiful children. It seemed she had already come full circle since now she was the single mom. Living on a shoestring budget, she managed to see both her children graduate from high school and begin new lives of their own.

Because of the empty nest syndrome, she focused on pursuing further education. With an entrepreneurial spirit, she formed a company and operated a successful business for several years. It was during her business years that she met her future husband.

After she remarried, she began to focus seriously on her writing. She had notebooks and scraps of writing, but nothing really materialized until she wrote her first novel, '*Gifted.*' Her second book, '*Tidbits, Tips & Treasures*,' a self-help book meant to have something for everyone and '**Gypsy Heart**' took on a more personal side.

All of Dee's books are available on her website, deelightfulreading.com.

Finishing '*The Grand Manor*' she is ready to turn her attention to her next two adventures, '*From Then, Now and Forever*' and '*JOY.*'

Dee hopes that you will let her know your thoughts after settling in with any of her novels, by leaving a comment at her website. She reads and personally replies to every bit of correspondence so, don't be shy.

Dee thanks everyone for their love and support, and hopes you enjoy reading her works as much as she enjoyed writing them.

Dedicated to:

My God, who is my source of words, and without
His constant presence in my life, this book
would not have been written.
His guidance and everlasting love,
have led me to this place of
Peace, Tranquility, and Creativity I now enjoy.

Acknowledgements

I spend many hours with my head buried in my notebook writing notes and ideas for my books. Once that process is 'done,' relatively speaking, it must be transferred from paper to laptop. This is where my stories begin to come to life. I take those notes and expand on them to create my characters into what I want them to be and hopefully into people my readers can relate to and fall in love with.

So, for all the time I spend buried in novel notes and at the keyboard, I'd like to thank my husband, Jim. Your patience and your good-natured spirit are second to none. Thank you for being my 'go to' guy for answers to the many questions and for explaining things that would help give me another perspective.

I wish to extend a heartfelt thank you to my editing team, cover artist and web designer at Cedar Springs, for being there for me, giving of your time and going above and beyond to get **The Grand Manor** to print.

Lastly, to my dedicated readers, thank you for your patience, your welcomed comments and especially for requesting to be on the list for my next books. Your excitement and anticipation for *The Grand Manor* is appreciated and makes this all worthwhile.

My life consists of two kinds of Time

The Time when I am with you

And the Time when I am waiting

To be with you again

Words from my friend and mentor

Everyone has their own path. Walk yours with integrity and wish all others peace on their journey. When your paths merge, rejoice for their presence in your life. When the paths are separated, return to the wholeness of yourself, give thanks for the footprints left on your soul, and embrace the time to journey on your own.

Author Unknown

The
GRAND
MANOR

Prologue

She swayed beautifully to the music that flowed out from the speakers that were hidden inside the walls. 'Dance like no one is watching' they say, so she did, but someone was. She did not see anyone at first as she swung her arms and moved her hips to the rhythm of the music. She caught a glimpse of herself in the mirrored wall as she twirled and curled to the beat as gracefully as any ballerina. As the music ended, she arched her back, raised her hands to form a circle above her head, then to an arc and brought her feet together. Raising her eyes to the mirror, she caught sight of a shadow ducking quickly out of sight. Her first thoughts went quickly back to a time when she had noticed her aunt leaning against the door frame of this same loft watching her with sheer pleasure. As she encouraged her to continue, she danced there before her. But it was not her aunt who was watching, and fear gripped her at the thoughts of an intruder inside her home!

"Who's there!?" she yelled, as she raced to the door. She stopped short in her tracks as she came chest to chest with the intruder. Umph! The sound escaped her lungs as they collided.

"You!? What are you doing here!?"

He knew, in his mind what he wanted this piece to say to him. It was indelibly imprinted in his mind. He swiped the canvas with four quick, black strokes, two long verticals, and two shorter horizontals, resembling the frame of a full-length mirror.

He pictured her reflection as she danced in her loft. Her body slim, beautiful and lithe. Her arms were long and lean as she positioned one over her head and the other toward the floor, resembling an awkward arc. Her fingers perfectly pointed. Her skirt flared and wrapped around her knees as she twisted and twirled to the music.

'God, she's beautiful,' he thought. He could feel the excitement build as thoughts of her flashed through his mind.

He laid the brush down and stepped away from his work. He rubbed his stubbly face and paced the loft. He could still feel her chest against his when she came rushing through the door.

He had passed that loft numerous times and had never seen the door open. It was totally unexpected, and of course, human curiosity caused him to look in. He just did not expect to see her there nor did he expect to be caught watching her dance. It was accidental in every way. He stopped when he caught a glimpse of her. Once he realized who it was he could not help himself, he had to pause and watch as if mesmerized. He nearly stopped breathing when he saw her dancing alone. 'How graceful she is,' he thought, as he began to wonder if she was a professional dancer now or was she just caught up in the moment. He remembered her in his arms all those years ago.

1

Summer vacation had arrived, and the sisters had packed their bags for another visit. They loved to go and spend their vacation with their great aunt Evelyn Roma, their grandfather's youngest sister, on their mother's side of the family. She lived on the outskirts of Kanyon Cove on a magnificent estate called *'The Grand Manor.'*

Deanna was Evelyn's niece and she and her husband Ben Coleman, along with their two daughters Darla and Dawn, were yearly visitors at the manor. The sisters were born just eleven months apart and were very close to each other. In fact, outsiders thought they were twins, but in their minds, they were more like best friends than sisters.

Deanna and her family were the only family members who continued to make the trip to the manor each summer, and they had been for as long as the girls could remember. The family had considered it their vacation house, and Aunt Evelyn had looked forward to their visits. There were several occasions throughout the year when they would holiday there, but it was only for long weekends. Summer was their favorite times.

The sisters grew up in a beautiful, peaceful, medium size town called Kanyon Cove. Life was simple there, and they enjoyed spending their time together. Their favorite times were those spent at their aunt's beautiful property at the edge of town. Evelyn lived there alone except for a few servants, so having family around for several weeks in the summer had meant a lot to her.

They thought their great aunt had been the most beautiful and graceful lady they had ever known. Even as children they both dreamt of being just like her when they grew up.

Evelyn had inherited 'The Grand Manor' from her father, the great Samuel Roma. He had been a wealthy investment banker in his hay day and worked and played among the elite. He invested his money wisely, and all of his assets were placed in his daughter's name. Evelyn was his only child, and she was a millionaire before she was out of her teens. Except for her boarding school years, she spent her entire life at 'The Grand Manor.' Along with her father, she led a life that most could only imagine. Unlike her father, she was a modest spender, although she did what she wanted to. She traveled to different parts of the world, shopped in foreign boutiques and returned home with great memories. She donated to her favorite charities, which were mostly her father's choices and volunteered her time on several community boards.

Evelyn had lost her mother when she was just an infant, so it had always been just her and her father. She remembered that he enjoyed hosting parties, and when she was old enough, she was always there to help coordinate them. It gave the kitchen staff something to smile about as she practiced giving instructions for when she was old enough to host her own.

She also remembered her father entertaining his investor clients on the front lawn. The corners of the white linen tablecloths would gently blow in the breeze as guests gathered. The women were dressed in long gowns made of expensive fabric and lace and wore matching wide brimmed hats, carrying a parasol for extra shade from the hot afternoon sun.

The grounds were abuzz with servants and maids. Each was dressed in black and white and carried a tray. The man servants' jackets were short and fitted at the waist with tails at the back. Their starched white shirts had standup collars, and a few frills poked out from between the lapels. The maids wore black dress uniforms with frilly bibbed aprons and stiff white lacey caps that were pinned onto the top of their heads. They were instructed to always keep the guests satisfied with food and drinks.

In Evelyn's prime, 'The Grand Manor' had been a hot spot for friends and family. In that era, there were maids and servants who resided there and were at their beckon call. Friends would gather for Evelyn's weekly afternoon tea parties. It gave them a chance to catch up on weekly gossip, news events and to plan shopping trips.

Several times a year, she and her father hosted a gala that took place inside the manor where after dinner the women gathered in the living room for tea while the men gathered in the den for brandy and cigars.

When the Coleman's arrived for their summer vacation, the girls leapt from the car and chased each other around in the wide-open spaces. There was so much freedom here even though the property was surrounded by security fences.

There was a grand pool in the backyard that seemed to spread out for miles to two young girls that lived in a limited space in town. They spent hours around the pool, roaming the grounds and playing on the beach. There was a stone patio under the elm trees where a table and chairs sat, along with a double seated wooden glider swing. It was like a private cove under there with a walking path that took them to the pool house and then on to the edge of the property. It was there that they could look out over the ocean. It was another one of their favorite spots. The stars in the night sky were endless, and one could gaze into the darkness and listen to the crashing waves against the shore. If they needed to light their way, they carried either a flashlight or a lantern, and it was quickly turned off when they reached the spot.

Darla and Dawn would lie on a blanket and try to count stars, make wishes on them and point out the different constellations they had learned in science class. Each summer just got better and better for them because as they got older, they had more freedom to roam and explore.

Evelyn had a mixed breed dog, named Dodger who followed them everywhere they went. Darla thought he was probably so happy to see young people arrive that he did not let them out of his sight for a minute. He was a mixture of Little River duck tolling retriever and sheltie with colors of brown, tan, blond and a bit of black. He had the black patch on his tail that is known to shelties. He was a fabulous, well trained and well behaved dog. He knew his boundaries, and he never ventured far from the house.

One afternoon, the girls were playing in the pool, and Dodger was lying under a lawn chair out of the sun. He never took his eyes off them as they splashed and played in the water. Hour after hour he faithfully watched and never tried to sneak in a nap. Once when Dawn stayed under water a little longer than he figured she should have, he reared out from under the chair and barked as if he was calling 911. It was a game the sisters played to see who could stay under longer. But Dodger was having none of it.

There was a fabulous cabin on the property. They loved playing there and, to their knowledge, no one had ever lived in it. It was beautiful. Now that they were older and had more freedom, they had permission to stay in the cabin from time to time for a sleep over but never without Dodger. A circular staircase led to the loft where there was a mattress for them to sleep on. Using a mattress allowed them more space as opposed to having a bed with legs. They just climbed up the stairs and crawled onto the mattress. At the head of their 'bed' was a floor to ceiling window with sliders on the bottom. On still nights they would lie up there with the sliders open and imagine the waves as plainly as if the beach was just below the window instead of some distance away. They spent many hours in the cabin. It was their playhouse, and Dodger was always there with them. While they were up in the loft, Dodger laid by the front door. To protect the girls, he likely would have torn an intruder limb from limb.

They did a lot of art work in the cabin, especially on rainy days. They painted pictures, wrote stories and doodled to pass the time. All of the pictures had their signature on their work in order to identify each piece. 'Darla Coleman' and 'Dawn Coleman', and each piece was tacked up on the loft walls.

Summers were indeed their favorite time of the year. Sadly though as each summer passed and their lives changed into teenagers, their interests changed. There were teen dances, parties to have and attend, clubs were formed, and life became full. Their love for the manor had not changed, but life had.

2

Darla Coleman married Craig Harrington when she was barely out of high school. They met in her last year, and he proposed before she graduated. Since he insisted they get married before she had a chance to go to college, she had hoped that he would provide assistance or at least co-sign for a student loan to further her education, but he refused. As it was, Craig had already finished university, but the selfish part of him did not care whether or not she went to college. He was of the mind-set that women did not need an education to be a wife.

She felt absolutely useless in the marriage. There was no real intimacy to speak of, and it left her feeling empty, alone and neglected. But Craig was holding onto a secret, and he had no idea that it would be his own wife who would eventually figure it out.

Darla and Craig were married for only one year when things began to change. To say it went from bad to worse would be an understatement. Since it had already started out as 'worse,' it should never have begun. Hindsight, as they say, is twenty-twenty.

Try as she might, Darla was unable to land even a part time job to earn extra spending money. To say she was paranoid was not quite beyond the truth. She began to suspect that Craig had paid businesses not to hire her so she would be at home most of the time. She put nothing past him. Every cent that she needed she had to ask him for it. It was not only embarrassing to her, but she felt it was also degrading. It was a rare occasion that he offered her money for personal items. He earned the money, and it was his to do with as he saw fit and it was none of her business. The sad part was that Craig was quite well off. He owned a bar, in a part of town that she had never been, but he basically lived off his father's money. He lived the high life while keeping her penniless.

They had a great penthouse apartment, and everything she could ever ask for was in it, but she did not feel as though she ever had him. He was never home and rarely told her where he was going or why he kept such late hours. Whenever she complained about it, he basically told her that if she did not like it, she could make other arrangements, so she stopped asking. She was between a rock and hard place because she had no other place to go and no money to get there. He made sure she was broke and seemed to have her right where he wanted her.

It was their first anniversary, and he tossed her a few bills and 'told' her to make herself look nice, he was taking her out to dinner. She had just enough money to get her hair trimmed and shaped which was a luxury she could not afford without his say so.

With her blonde hair done to perfection, she dressed slowly knowing Craig was ready and waiting for her. She wanted to look her best since this was their first time out together since they were married. She stepped into a green print dress that she loved but had never had the occasion to wear since she bought it. She slipped her arms in place after wriggling it up over her shapely hips. Shifting her body to settle the dress in place, she then reached behind her and zipped it up, then sat on the bed to put on her sandals. *'There, done,'* she thought, as she moved to the mirror to examine the results. She was pleased to see that the dress molded perfectly to her tiny frame. Examining the reflection, she twisted to the left and then right, running her hands down each side from her waist to her hips. *'Perfect.'* The green in the dress accented her already beautiful sea green eyes. Finally, she applied a bit of mascara which only made her more ravishing and draped a shawl over her arm. She was ready!

Craig gave a low whistle when she walked into the living room. "You are one gorgeous, sexy lady!" he said, walking up to her. He kissed her cheek so as not to smear her make-up, which was always his excuse. It was a rare occasion that she got a compliment or anything else for that matter, but tonight she was not going to be petty.

"Are you ready?" he asked, raising his arm to her.

"Looking forward to it," she said, taking his arm as she smiled back at him. She was going to allow herself to enjoy this evening, come hell or high water because she so totally deserved it.

Their table was ready when they walked into the restaurant. To her disappointment, they were seated promptly upon their arrival. She had been looking forward to hanging around the bar for a few minutes to show herself off but that was not going to happen. She was escorted to their table, and it was there that she stayed.

They were served two glasses of champagne within a few minutes.

"This is lovely, Craig."

He raised his glass to her, and as she picked up hers, he said, "Happy Anniversary, Darla." *Not 'honey' or 'Babe' or 'My Love,'* just 'Darla.'

"Thank you, Craig," she said, past the lump in her throat. *'Why should this night be any different than the other three hundred and sixty-four days of this year?'* She was not going to let it get to her though, she was out for an evening, and she was going to have fun.

"I hope you don't mind, but I took the liberty and ordered for us."

The words barely escaped his lips when a waiter sat a plate of appetizers down on the table between them.

The waiter left the table and Darla had just reached for a small piece of food when she heard her husband's name.

"Craig! Hey man! It's good to see you again!"

"Well, hey yourself, long time no see, man."

Craig stood up to shake the man's hand, and they gave a quick 'man-hug' and then sat back down. "Join us for a minute," he said and pulled out a chair next to him for his friend to sit down.

Darla was so used to being ignored that she did not even look up.

"It looks like I might be interrupting something special."

'Interrupting something?' she thought as she nibbled on an appetizer, *'I hardly think so!'*

"Nah," Craig said, raising his hand and giving it a downward flop, "sit down, we've got a few minutes before our meal arrives.

Connor looked at his hand and thought, 'Some *things never change*.'

Let me introduce you to Darla. Darla, this is Connor Barnes a buddy of mine from university."

"Nice to meet you, Darla," Connor said, reaching his hand across the table as he half rose off his chair at the introduction. She looked up as she heard her name, saw his hand and automatically reached out. She felt the flame as soon as they touched.

Darla had been instantly attracted to Craig when they first met, but not like this... this was like nothing she had ever experienced. She squirmed in her chair as her entire body became heated with excitement. This instant attraction sent shivers through every inch of her existence. '*Oh my God!*' she thought, 'what *is wrong with me? Who is this man and why am I hot flashing all over the place?*' She could not move her eyes away from this Adonis as they continued to grasp each other's hand.

Connor was searching his own feelings at the same time. '*Where has this beauty been hiding out?*' he thought, '*where did Craig find this one?*'

Locked in a mutual gaze, they both suddenly realized that Craig was asking a question. "I'm going to the bar; can I bring either of you anything?"

Darla suddenly awoke, instantly yanking her hand back. Realizing what was happening, she composed herself into an air of innocence and said, "Sorry... what did you ask?"

With Darla's sudden movement, Connor looked back at Craig and tried to shake it off as well. He was still trying to take in as much of her beauty out of the corner of his eye when he responded, "Uh, no... I'm good thanks." Darla confirmed that she was happy with her champagne and off Craig went.

Once he was away from the table, Connor asked, "What was that?"

"What?"

"That, that spark between us!"

"Spark!? I was thinking more along the lines of flames!" She gushed and pretended to fan herself.

"Where did Craig ever find you?"

"Right here in Kanyon Cove," she replied, tilting her head a bit in flirtation.

He grinned at her playfulness and came back with a question that surprised her.

"If you and Craig are not in a serious relationship, I would really like to see you again."

"Seriously?"

"Hell ya!"

She tilted her head slightly and raised an eyebrow just as she raised her left hand and with a sinking feeling said, "Craig and I are married."

"What? Why didn't he introduce you as his wife?"

"Maybe because he doesn't want to admit to anyone that he is married?" she shrugged, "I don't know."

Conner felt he knew why but he let it pass. "You are absolutely ravishing."

"Thank you," she blushed.

"So, what do you do besides being Craig's wife?"

"I'm a stay-at-home wife if you can believe that."

Really? Why is that?"

"For reasons beyond my control, I'm afraid, and I'm not happy about it."

To shift the focus off herself, she asked the same question. "What do you do when you aren't being Craig's college buddy?"

"I'm in town for a few days with a group on a seminar."

Darla realized that she was instantly comfortable with Connor. In giving her his undivided attention, he seemed genuinely interested in what she had to say, definitely something she was not accustomed to.

"What goes on in this town anyway?" he said, tossing it back to her.

"Depends on what your interests are."

"My 'interest' at the moment is totally in you, and I want you to know Darla, that I do not ever come on to women like this, especially at first glance and absolutely not to married women. But, I am very attracted to you, and if I may be so bold, I believe that you feel it too."

He got his answer when she did not deny it. She just lowered her eyes for a few seconds, and when she looked up at him, he nearly came unglued. He ran his hand over his face and said, "Damn it you're driving me crazy and I've only known you for a few minutes! This can't be happening."

The words barely left his lips when Craig appeared at the table.

"Are you sure I can't get you guys a drink?" he asked.

"I'd love a cold drink, Craig, ice water and lemon would be great, please."

"Connor?" he asked.

"Yeah, a beer, please, whatever is on tap."

"I'll be back in a few," he said, totally unaware of what was unfolding before is eyes.

"I'm sorry Darla, I can't leave this alone," Connor said picking up where he had left off. "I know I should but I can't. Do you have a cell number, so we can stay in touch, maybe?" He sat back and put both hands up in front of his chest and said, "If I am out of line here, just tell me, and I will go away."

The thought of never seeing him again was not an option for her. She glanced over at Craig, who was still at the bar. She looked at Conner, bit her bottom lip and asked if he had a pen.

He passed her a pen and his bar receipt. She quickly jotted down her number and tossed it across the table. It was in his pocket in a flash. Her heart was nearly pounding out of her chest as her passion returned. She was not certain if it was the fact that she and Connor were openly flirting and getting away with it or if she was just craving attention. Either way, it was exciting and made her feel sexually alive.

"Thanks," he said, winking at her, "I think it would be best if I got the hell out of here before I give myself away." He reached over and wrapped his fingers around hers and gave them a tiny squeeze. She held onto his hand for a brief moment as they gazed into each other's eyes. He got up from the table and walked over to the bar to where Craig was. She saw him shake Craig's hand, slap him on the back and then he waved at her before he disappeared through the door and into the night. She felt strangely alone as she realized how much she missed having a normal conversation with someone who would actually listen to her. She hated it now that he was gone and she wished for him to come back. She did not believe in wishes coming true, at least not for her, so she knew she had to let it go.

Connor took his cellphone out of his pocket, programed her number in and then threw the receipt in the trash can. *'Can't take any chances on someone finding that!'* he mumbled to himself.

Her phone chirped from inside her purse as she sat waiting for Craig to return with her drink. Thinking it was her sister; she got it out, opened it and pressed Message. *'Good night sexy lady, CB.'*

She took a quick scan around realizing it was Connor's initials but did not see him. She sat there in a daze trying to wrap her mind around the text. Finally, when it sunk in, her head shot up and her eyes darted around again trying to find him.

The phone chirped again. *'I'm outside at the window taking in the beautiful view.'*

She peered at the window, but she did not see anyone. She had not given it a second thought that he would be standing outside looking in at her. She thought that he would be long gone. Relief spread over her body when he walked closer to the tinted glass so that she could see him. He waved and then backed away before drawing attention to himself.

Chirp once more... *'Chat soon, btw, email, cbarnes@gmail.com, nite.'*

She replied as fast as she could, *'wait!'* and she flipped her phone shut just as Craig returned with her water. Conner saw her talking to Craig, so he waited as she asked.

She was clearly flushed by the time Craig got back to their table, but he was too distracted to notice. Someone at the bar was obviously getting more of his attention than she was. She took a long gulp of water to moisten her dry throat before she spoke. "Do you mind if I make this an early night?" As she swallowed, she thought, *'Oh my God, what am I doing?'*

"Are you feeling alright?"

"Uh huh, why?"

"You seem... rattled?" he said, frowning.

"I think I would just like to go home."

"Would you like for me to call you a cab, I'm not ready to go yet."

"Yes, I figured you weren't ready to leave and thanks, I'll call a cab from outside." She opened her handbag and took out her phone.

"Are you sure?"

"Yes, I'll be fine," she leaned in to peck him on the cheek and left. When she reached the door, a thought crossed her mind, *'careful what you wish for, you just might get it.'*

She was relieved to see that Conner was still there, waiting for her. She guessed him to be approximately six foot one or two. His blond hair was longer than she was used to seeing since Craig got a trim every few weeks, whether he needed it or not. Connor's was not quite shoulder length, and it was not scraggly looking. He was dressed in jeans, a white tee shirt, and a sports jacket. Her knees weakened at the sight of him. *'What now?'* she wondered. She just wanted to wrap herself around him and never let go.

When Connor saw her walking out the door, he nearly lost his mind. Her beauty took his breath away. He inhaled deeply trying to compose himself as if he had just seen an angel. He thought she was the greatest thing he had seen in all of his entire life. He had not felt this strongly toward anyone in his few years of dating. He could not help but notice how perfectly her dress fit, and those legs! He had only seen her from the waist up at the table, but now he got a full view and was deeply aroused with what he saw. "Hey," he said softly walking up to her and reaching for her hand. He never took his eyes off her for a second. "Is everything ok?"

"Yes, everything is fine, can we go somewhere?" she asked nervously as she did a quick scan around. She looked into the restaurant window where she could see Craig at the bar talking to the friend who had been the one holding his attention.

"Where would you like to go?"

"Let's just walk for now and get away from here before someone sees us."

"That's a great idea," he said, do you have any particular place in mind?"

"I'm not too familiar with this area, but we'll look for a place."

He was in awe of the fact that she wanted to spend more time with him and before he could realize it, he said the first thing that came to his mind. "You are so beautiful."

"Do you think so?" she asked, watching his expression change. His face sobered as he replied, "Oh, I'm very serious." They were both lost in the moment and had forgotten that they were still in front of the restaurant as he gently pulled her into his arms. "I just want to hold you right now," he whispered to her as his breath quickened. He slid his hands up along her back and into her hair which was now intertwined around his fingers. He tugged on it just enough to bring her face to his. He gazed into her eyes for a few seconds and then lowered his eyes to her lips which were so close to his that he could feel her breath. He lowered his head until their lips met and they kissed passionately there on the sidewalk. He flicked his tongue inside her mouth, and she welcomed it with hers. Somewhere in the deep recesses of his brain, he became aware of their surroundings. He picked her up off her feet as if she were a China doll and backing up a few feet he made a half circle with her still in his arms, stepped into an alley and flattened himself against the building. "We must stay out of sight," he breathed, Craig is just inside. He lowered her gently until her feet were back on the ground.

"We should go for a walk and get away from here."

"Yes," and grasping her hand, they walked away from the restaurant.

They had only walked a few blocks when they came to a park. In the middle of the grounds, they came upon a covered gazebo.

"This is perfect," Darla said, "let's stay here for a while."

"It is nice here, but it's a little chilly, would you like my jacket?" He was standing in front of her, and before she had a chance to answer, he had it off and placed it around her shoulders."

'Oh,' she thought, '*he is so hot in that tee shirt!*' She ran her eyes over his chest, down to his tight abs and up to his face. She could not help herself as she reached out and placed both hands onto his chest. She spread her fingers and began to move them across his body and down to his waist.

He could hardly breathe as he watched her facial expressions turn serious. He placed his hands on each side of her face and drew her in for a kiss. She accepted his kiss with the same passion. They were both lost in the moment as his hunger matched her own. She breathlessly pulled away and looked at him. "What are we doing, Connor?" She turned away briefly and put the back of her hand up to her mouth as if to wipe the desire away. He put his hands on her shoulders and turned her back around to face him. "We don't have to do this if you are uncomfortable. We can just sit here and talk," he said, pointing to the bench behind them.

"You don't understand," she said, "this is all new to me."

"What is?"

"This is," she said, pointing from him to herself, "you, me, us, all of this! It's confusing, it's beautiful, and it's what I have dreamt of for myself since I was old enough to date. You are free to do this, but I am married, Connor." Tears of frustration nipped at her eyelids as she stood there trying to explain herself, but she wasn't doing a very good job.

He reached out, pulled her gently to his chest and held her close as he laid his cheek on the top of her head. He closed his eyes and drew her presence deep within.

He knew he was falling in love with her; he had no doubt about it.

"I'm sorry if I made you uncomfortable in any way Darla. I don't want you to think that this has to go any farther than it already has."

"It's not you Connor, it's me." She tried to find the words to tell him but she could not. She was embarrassed enough as it was and this was something she could not share with him, not yet anyway.

"Whatever it is, it's OK, and I won't push. I just want to spend some time with you. I would like to get to know you better, and the only way we can do that is just what we are doing. I am very attracted to you, and I would like nothing more than to make love to you right here and right now but that's not what this is about. It must be mutual or nothing at all."

She moved away so she could look at him. "I feel the same way as you do. My entire being is screaming out to 'seize the moment,' but not here on a park bench."

He could not help but smile at her words. Her face glowed in the moonlight as he looked at her and cocked his head. "Any suggestions?"

"Only one."

"Well, let's hear it then," he said, playfully, hoping he would not be disappointed.

She pressed her lips together as if gathering up courage. "It's chilly here in this gazebo, can we go somewhere?"

"Where would you like to go and please don't say you want to go home," he said shaking his head back and forth. "I'm not ready to let you go just yet."

Suddenly she felt very brave and very determined. If this was only going to be a one-night stand, then she had to take the leap.

"Where would you like to go?" he repeated.

"Anywhere where there is a bed," she said barely audible.

He pulled her back into his arms and kissed her. He fell madly in love with her right there on the spot. She wrapped her arms around his neck and moved her hands to the sides of his head. "Where can we go? We can't allow the passion we are feeling to disappear," she breathed, pressing her body into his.

"My God, you are driving me crazy. There is a motel just a few blocks over; I have a room there while I'm in town. Shall we go there?" he asked, almost to the point of begging.

"Yes, let's go!" she said excitedly. "Just a second though," she said, gripping his arm for support. She reached down, took her high heeled shoes off and slipped the back straps between her fingers. "OK, I'm ready, let's get out of here."

They ran the entire few blocks and laughed like a couple of school kids and for the first time in a long time, she felt free, wanted and loved.

The motel was U-shaped and pretty much the same as all motels in the area. There were planters scattered along the edge of the walkway for color and even in the evening shade they looked attractive. The parking lot was empty of people, so they were quite certain they had not been seen. He slid the motel card in the lock, opened the door and they hurried inside before they were noticed by anyone.

She felt exhilarated by all the cloak and dagger antics and started to relax slightly, knowing that she had lots of time. Since Craig stayed out half the night anyway, what he did not know would not hurt him. She was exactly where she wanted to be. This was the opportunity that she had missed growing up and marrying so quickly. She suddenly craved someone who wanted her too.

"That was exciting!" she giggled.

He laughed, agreeing with her.

Reaching for him she put her hand behind his head, stood on her tiptoes and drew his lips down to hers.

He put his arms around her tiny waist and walked her over toward the bed. "Are you sure you want to do this?"

She knew why they were in his motel room. "Positive!"

She turned slowly, tipped her head down and quivered as he unzipped her dress. He slowly slid it from her shoulders and watched it collapse to the floor. She could feel the heat of his words as he whispered into the back of her neck. "My God, you are so beautiful."

She turned toward him slipping her hands up inside his tee shirt, lifting it as high as she could. When she could not reach any higher, he finished removing it, exposing his broad chest and six pack abs. His hands worked their magic as he drew her closer as if trying to get inside her skin.

Their eyes were locked as she gently moved both hands down to tug him closer to her. He was now absolutely crazy at her touch as they stood for what seemed like hours, locked in each other's stare, the lust they were feeling intensifying.

She wanted him so badly that it was too painful to have to wait for time to unfold. She felt her body burn with every movement he made.

Connor was lost in the pleasure and could have stood there for hours. He had envisioned having her since the moment they touched hands in the restaurant. He reached down, slipped his hands into hers and drew her up, reclaiming her mouth. Placing one arm around her back, he lowered her onto the bed by lifting her with the other, all the while kissing her passionately. She arched her back, becoming weightless with her feelings.

The heat they felt for each other was something neither one had experienced before, especially her. The depth of their passion and newness of their love caused them to shiver like children playing doctor for the first time.

They had been clutching each other for several minutes to take in the emotional sensation they were both experiencing when Darla broke the silence, "This is right Connor. It can't feel this right and be wrong."

Conner sighed deeply, acknowledging her by nodding his head. He started gently kissing her neck. She was breathing so hard her fingers tips were beginning to feel tingly. She felt as if she were hyperventilating. "Conner? Come to me, my love."

This was not how she had imagined sex. In fact, she realized at that instance that she really did not know what to expect. The intensity she was feeling came to a crescendo beyond anything she could have dreamt. She could feel her entire body stiffen with pleasure like an over-wound watch.

Connor suddenly felt Darla's crush, but their first encounter, their shining moment was over all too soon, and he felt devastated for not having more control. "My God baby! I'm so sorry. It was so intense I couldn't hold back. I... I've never experienced anyone like you before."

Seconds passed in silence. Breathlessly she said, "Neither have I," and after a brief pause she whispered, "literally."

He paused in thought for a moment, "Literally?"

"She smiled at him and said, "yes, literally."

All of the heightened parts of their bodies started to relax, but they tried desperately to maintain their locked position. He propped himself up on one elbow, smiled down at her and, looking into her eyes asked, "What do you mean 'literally'?"

She hesitated for a few seconds, bit her bottom lip and relaxed her grip letting him go. She then moved from underneath him to reveal her secret. He looked down and saw blood on the sheet and looked back at her in a stunned hush. She could see the questions forming in his mind.

"Wh...wh..," he started again, "what?"

"You are my first, Conner; you are the first man to ever make love to me."

"My God... are you serious?" he said, the pitch of his voice rising in disbelief.

"Yes I am," she said shyly, "that's what I wanted to tell you when we were in the gazebo. I just couldn't get the words out."

"But you're married," he said softly reaching out to touch her face.

"Yes, I am, but Craig has never touched me. He has never even taken an interest in me as a woman. I was a virgin when I met him, and I still was," her sparkling eyes lit up the room as she added, "until you."

He wrapped her up in his arms like a delicate flower, and he could not have loved her more than he did at that moment.

"You are also the first to call me 'baby' and 'sweetheart,' and I like it."

She melted into him again for a few minutes and finally pulled away. She looked at the bedside clock and said, "I have to go."

"Go? Where?"

"Home silly before Craig gets there ahead of me. I doubt very much that he will because he never gets home until the wee hours, but there is always a first time."

"I'll go with you then, to see that you get home safely."

"I live just a few streets over so I suppose we can get that far without being noticed."

They dressed quickly and headed out walking hand in hand, chatting about nothing in particular, but the conversation never stopped. She did not have this since Craig was not much of a conversationalist when he was home, but she knew he was a social butterfly when he was out. Finally, he had to ask the question that had been dangling in the air since they left the motel.

"Can we see each other again?"

"I don't know Conner, we took a big chance tonight, and we are bound to get caught if we press our luck. I don't even know where tonight came from. As you witnessed, this is surely not my thing to make love to a perfect stranger."

"Well, I'm hardly 'perfect,'" he said, smiling down at her." He stopped her there on the sidewalk and kissed her. She could feel the flames growing inside her again.

"You are perfect to me Conner, and I want you to know that tonight meant everything to me."

"It did to me too, I can't imagine not seeing you again though."

"I will have to think about this before I make my mind up. It's dangerous; to say the least. I don't know what would happen if this ever got back to Craig. He has control issues for sure."

"I will leave it up to you, you have my cell number, and my email address and I will wait to hear from you."

"Thank you, Conner, we'll figure it out. I will be thinking about you, and I know already that I love you, but I want to think about it. Promise me you won't call."

"I promise, I won't call, but you must promise me that you will call me when you have a chance to think about this or at least email or text me, please."

He put his finger under her chin and turned her face up to his, he looked her in the eyes and said, "I love you too, baby, don't ever forget that."

"I won't, I have to go inside now. I don't want to leave you but I must. It's late, and Craig could come home."

"I'm in town until the day after tomorrow, call me if you can."

She reached up to kiss him one more time and walked away. She walked up the steps to her building and looked back once. He was so gorgeous that she could not help herself. She ran back down the steps and right into his arms. He scooped her up and held her tightly as he nuzzled into her neck. He held her so tight she could barely breathe. He lowered her so that her feet were back down on the sidewalk. He kissed her deeply and knew that he would never get enough of her no matter how long they stood there in the dark.

"I'd better go inside," she whispered, "I miss you already Conner, and I love you so very much."

He pressed his forehead to hers and closed his eyes not wanting to let her go but knew he had to. She moved away from him enough to look into his eyes. She pressed her finger to his lips and turned away. When she got back up to the top of the steps, she turned toward him one more time, waved and saw him wave into the darkness. She blew him a kiss as her lips quivered in sadness and went inside.

When she closed the door, her heart was breaking, and tears slid down her cheeks. What she did not know was that Conner was doing the same thing right outside her door. She got into the elevator and pushed the penthouse floor and waited for the doors to open. She unlocked the door, and the apartment was still in darkness. Breathing a sigh of relief, she made her way to the living room and sat down in a lounge chair. Slipping off her shoes she drew her legs up and wrapped her arms around them and laid her head down on her knees.

She was still sitting in the dark when Craig arrived home. It was very late, but she was very much awake. She was still fully dressed and was just sitting there in the dark.

"Darla? Are you alright? Why are you sitting in the dark?"

She nearly jumped out of her skin at the sound of his voice. She had not heard his key in the lock or the door open and close. She had relived the evening with Connor over and over again. She was lost in her thoughts of how this evening had unfolded. She had gone to their anniversary dinner with Craig and ended up in bed with another man that she had fallen madly in love with. She knew she would never forget this night.

"Umm, sorry; I didn't hear you come in."

"I was especially quiet as I thought you'd be well into a sleep by now. What's wrong, you are never up this late?"

"I'm fine, I guess it's just the heat, it's very warm in here, don't you think?"

Craig had not put a light on yet, and she prayed that he would not hit the switch. When he did not, she closed her eyes against the darkness and took a deep breath. *'Relax,'* she told herself, *this won't likely go beyond tonight so just forget about it for now before he gets suspicious.*

"I...um...I just wanted to stay up to" *'to what?'* she thought, thinking fast on her feet, "... thank you for tonight, Craig. It was nice to go out," she stammered, feeling guilty for her actions but, as usual, he was oblivious to her nervousness. He began to piss her off when he did not care enough to even notice how nervous she was. Not wanting to waste her thoughts on him she used it to her advantage. Grinning to herself she thought, *'Hey that was easy, it might not be so difficult to get out again after all.'*

"Yeah, sure, you're welcome," he said with a wave of his hand like it was no big deal to him. "It was nice to see Conner tonight."

Just the mere mention of his name sent flames to all the wrong places!

"I'm going to take a shower and go to bed," she said.

"Yes, its late Darla, I'll sleep in the guest room so you won't be disturbed again." He half flipped her off as he picked up the remote to find a ball game. She rolled her eyes as she left the room and she so wanted to say, *'what else is new,'* but she resisted the urge. She was lucky to get that, he never notices when she leaves the room anyway.

She went into the main bath, where there was a larger shower stall and turned the shower on full blast. She felt the temperature of the water before stepping in, then set the handle to 'cool' hoping it would ease the flames that were still attacking her body. *'My God, he is so handsome and so damned hot!'* Her body was on fire at the thoughts of him and their romp in the motel. She stepped in the shower stall to a less than warm splash of water on her body causing her to inhale deeply and shiver slightly. It felt good, but Connor had felt better. She leaned against the tiles and let the water run over her. It did not help. *'There is nothing that is going to put the fire out,'* she thought.

She went from the shower to the bedroom wrapped in a towel and on the way past the living room she noticed that Craig had indeed found a game after all.

She finished drying herself off and applied deodorant and lotion and climbed into bed. Her face was still flush as she settled down to go to sleep.

"Hello beautiful," he said, walking over to her. "I know I shouldn't be here, but I had to see you."

"I've wanted to see you too, but I didn't know how I was going to do it, but I'm so glad you're here!" She slipped her arms around his neck, and he held her tight. She could barely breathe, she wanted him so badly. He pulled away and looked into her eyes then drew her face to his lips. She gasped for air as she tried to kiss him deeper and deeper. *'Those flames,'* she thought. "We weren't going to do this again," she said to him.

"I want you so badly; please don't ask me to leave."

"I want you too, Conner."

He laid beside her on the bed and began to caress her skin. "You are so beautiful," he whispered; breathing in her freshly showered scent while kissing her body and nibbling at her skin. She arched her back as he drove her almost to the brink.

"Darla," he whispered, "baby, I love you."

They were both more than ready when she heard a door slam. Startled, she drew in a deep breath and sat straight up in bed. "Conner?"

Craig opened the bathroom door and looked at her strangely. "What's that? I thought you were asleep? Sorry if I woke you."

He looked at her in a questioning way. "Are you alright? You're perspiring."

She looked around the room as if looking for Conner. Orienting herself, she licked her lips and tried to speak. "I'm fine," she croaked, "I just need a drink of water." She threw the covers off and went to the kitchen. She got a bottle of water from the fridge and took a long drink. *'This is not good!'* she thought as she pressed the cold bottle against her forehead.

She heard Craig close a door. As she made her way back down the hall, she noticed that under the guest room door, the light was still on. *'He could have used the bathroom in there,'* she thought, *'why did he have to rob me of my dream!?'* The thoughts she had towards Craig caused an adrenalin rush, and she was wide awake. *'He is even taking my dreams from me too.'* She tiptoed swiftly and silently to the living room and picked up her handbag and made her way quickly back to the bedroom. She closed the door without a sound and unzipped her bag. Her cellphone was in the pocket, and she pulled it out and switched it to 'vibrate only' mode. She flipped it open and began to type. *'I can't believe how much I miss you! I just had the most awesome dream about us.'*

She pressed send and climbed back into bed and barely got the covers over her when her phone vibrated. *'You must be reading my mind! So good to hear from you, I didn't think I would.*

Tell me about your dream.' She smiled when she read his words as it vibrated again. *'I miss you too baby. R U sure we can't get together B 4 I leave?'*

She replied, 'Probably, *I'll text you tomorrow,'* She waited for the phone to vibrate and she knew it would.

'Nite my love, hope to see you tomorrow, thanks for texting me, I love you.'

She smiled again, *'I love you too, nite.'* Her phone vibrated again.

I love you more! And I still wanna hear about your dream!' He made her smile, and she loved that. She was happier than she had ever been.

She settled back down to wait for sleep to come, only this time she was smiling. Still, she laid awake for most of the night thinking about her evening with Connor. She was conflicted as to how she was going to see him again. She did not know where they could meet that would be safe. *'Maybe his motel room again,'* she thought. She would have to think about it before she decided for sure.

3

In the morning she heard Craig leave earlier than he normally would, but she did not care anymore. Their first anniversary had meant nothing to him except another day as usual. *'Take the little wifey out to shut her up, and life goes on.'* Little did he know that it was the best night ever for her! She got out of bed and went in to brush her teeth before going to the kitchen. He had not even taken the time to have a pot of coffee ready for her when she got up. *'Why was he always in a rush to get out of the apartment? Where does he go and what keeps him away from home anyway?'* she wondered. She was already having terrible thoughts this early in the morning, and she told herself to focus on more pleasant things instead.

She poured fresh coffee into a mug and sat on a stool at the island counter. She set her cellphone down on the countertop and stared at it for several minutes. She twirled it and spun it around while trying to decide what she wanted to do with it. She had told him last night that she would probably text him about meeting him, but now she was not sure if she should. She sat her mug down and leaned back hooking her foot on the rung of the stool. Bouncing her leg nervously for a few minutes she picked up her phone and opened it to 'messages.' Connor's was the first number to pop up since he was the last one she had texted last night. She scrolled to 'add,' and his number automatically went into her address book. Then she went back to 'messages' highlighted their entire conversation and hit 'delete.' *'That was the safest way,'* she thought since she did not feel comfortable having them in her phone. Accidents happen, and people get nosey when a mixture of suspicion and curiosity is thrown into the mix. *'Who was she trying to kid,' she thought, 'Craig was not the least bit curious or suspicious. In order to be suspicious, you first have to give a rat's ass, and he did not'.*

She scrolled again, stopping briefly at Connor's name. She looked away from the phone and chewed on her lower lip for a few seconds. She knew for sure that she wanted to see him again and all she had to do was give in. She had butterflies in her stomach thinking about him and with every minute that passed, she was closer and closer to relenting. Quick thoughts of Craig and his treatment of her soon gave her the justification she needed.

She quickly decided that she was going to see Conner one last time before he left town, come hell or high water. She had almost changed her mind a dozen times, but the thought of never seeing him again was more than she could bear. Turning her attention back to the phone she sent him a one word text. *'Hey.'* She already knew that when he received it, he would be overjoyed since he had made her promise that she would contact him. She pressed send and waited.

'OMG! I was hoping against all hope that you would contact me!'

Getting right to the point she replied, *'Can we meet?'*

'Sure! When and where?'

Just reading his words made her heart pound and she smiled at his quick reply.

'Motel?'

'Sure, come on over!'

'OK, give me a few minutes, got to get dressed.'

'Not for me, lol.'

She giggled like a schoolgirl when she read her screen and replied, *'U R bad, C U soon.'*

'Hurry!' he pleaded.

She quickly showered even though she had had one only a few hours before, allowing her time to plan her next move so she would not be recognized. At the top of her closet, she found a crate that had been stored since she moved into the penthouse. Pulling at it she got it to drop into her arms. Inside was a stack of old clothes from her life before Craig. That was the one, and only time he gave her his MasterCard and insisted she get a new wardrobe. He thought she was way too outdated in her choice of clothing. She could not help but roll her eyes while thinking about it.

She found a pair of old blue jeans and a tee shirt with *Aerosmith* written across the front, remembering that she had found it in a thrift shop once, and wished she could have afforded to go to the actual concert. She began to dig deeper into the crate until she found her old *Mickey Mouse* cap.

She pulled on the jeans and tee shirt and then stepped into a pair of flats. Next, she found her old jean jacket and slipped it on. She shrugged her shoulders and shook her arms to settle it in place, then shoved the sleeves up to mid arm. She looked like someone out of Grease, 'oh ya...,' she thought, 'this'll work!' She twirled in the mirror approving once more at what she saw, grabbed her sunglasses and keys then, tucked her phone into her jacket pocket and headed out. As she locked the apartment door, her heart was racing. All this James Bond stuff surrounding seeing Connor again was really turning her on and smiling she mused, '*Uh huh... I'm going to make love to this guy a-l-l d-a-y l-o-n-g.*'

She looked up and down the empty hall and made a beeline for the elevator. She stepped inside and silently prayed that no one else would get on. She floated all the way to the lobby. Slipping on the sunglasses she carefully hid her face as she ducked outside. She tipped her head from side to side so as not to run into anyone on the sidewalk and quickly made her way to the corner. *'Just one more block and I'll be safe in his arms,'* she thought.

She had just walked into the motel parking lot when a car whizzed past her. It was so close it nearly touched her jacket. She jumped to one side, and when she lifted her head, she saw Craig's Mercedes pulling into a parking spot in front of one of the rooms. She froze in her tracks! *'Oh my God! He knows about me and Connor, and he has followed me after all! Now what!?'* she thought, backing up until she got behind a hedge and waited. *'How did he know, what tipped him off, I was so careful.'* She was sure he had seen her. She could hear her heart thumping in her chest as she waited for him to call her name or come around the hedge to question her. She had not heard his car door open or close. She was not sure if she could have heard it with her heart beating inside her ears. From where she was she could not hear or see anything.

With shaking hands, she pulled her cellphone out and sent Connor a text. *'I'm here, but Craig is in the parking lot!'*

'Where R U?

'Behind the hedge at the sidewalk.' She was shaking so badly she could hardly type.

'Wait there, I'll be right out.'

She was near to hyperventilating when she heard Craig's voice yell across the parking lot. "Hey Connor, what's going on?"

'That's it,' she thought, *'he definitely knows something.'*

"*Oh, hey'*, he said, sounding as if he was surprised to see him there. *"I'm just going out for breakfast, what are you doing here?"*

There was dead silence, and Darla silently parted the branches slightly to see what was happening. Craig looked like a deer that was caught in someone's headlights while Connor brazenly stood there waiting for him to answer. Craig looked behind him and pointed with his thumb at the motel door behind him and began to stammer that one of his clients was in town and he was picking '*them'* up for a breakfast meeting. He did not commit to 'he' or 'she' but referred to his breakfast date as 'them.'

"Where is a good place to eat in this town anyway?"

"Darla looked from Connor to Craig as they spoke back and forth and she was watching Craig's reaction at being held up by Connor now. He was acting nervous at the thought of running into Connor, of all people, at the same motel. He watched the motel door, and she could almost feel him wishing it would not open. Whoever was in the room, she could tell that he hoped 'they' had enough sense to stay inside. She was nervous, but she loved the fact that Connor was making him squirm.

"Where do you want to eat? A diner? A restaurant? A café maybe?"

"A diner or café, whichever is closest. Just want to grab something before I head out of town," he lied. He was not leaving until the next morning.

"There is a small café just up there on the right," he said, making finger swirls in the air for directions, "called 'Morning Brew,' you should find what you need."

"Do you ever eat there?"

"No, never been there."

"OK, thanks man, maybe I'll see you the next time I am in town. Say hello to that gorgeous wife of yours, Dora."

"Darla," Craig corrected him.

"Oh yes, Darla, take care and have a good one," he said, waved into the air and headed for the hedge.

Darla had scurried off to the café when she heard Craig's directions and knowing that it would never be one of his haunts.

She had never been there before either, but she felt a little safer there than behind the hedge.

Her phone beeped, *'Where R U?*

'Café.'

'Be right there.'

At the counter, she ordered a latte and found a small table by a window and waited. Her heart leapt from her chest when he came into view. Just knowing he was coming to see her, and only her filled her entire being with love for him. She had never had anyone who wanted to be with her as emphatically as Connor did.

He walked in and searched the room. She waved when she saw him, and he had to look twice to be certain it was her. Squinting his eyes and smiling, he made his way over to her moving between tables. She got up from her chair and walked into his arms.

"What's with the outfit?" he whispered into her ear.

She could feel herself blushing as she whispered back. "I was trying to be incognito, and it's a good thing I was! He nearly hit me with his car, and he still didn't know it was me, freaked me right out!"

"Yes, I was surprised when he spoke to me, but I know his games, and I put him on the spot deliberately."

Darla did not bother to ask for an explanation she was just happy to be with him again.

"I like the outfit," he teased, "you didn't happen to run into John Travolta on your way, did you?"

"Very funny."

"I don't think I would have known you if you had made it to my door, but good for you for being inventive. It pays to be careful."

"We certainly can't go back to the motel now, Connor," she whispered.

"Ah, no, at least not that particular one."

"What do you have in mind?"

"This town has more than one hotel and motel in it, so I'm sure I can find one for us."

The next morning as she lay in bed waiting for Craig to leave the apartment, she was amazed that she could not muster up even an iota of guilt for deciding to meet Connor again. Reliving her time with Connor, she smiled and allowed their last day to linger in her memory.

They had spent the entire day and evening together. Between walking, talking and making love, the day was prefect. It had been close to noon before they began to look for a place to go. They had had breakfast at the 'Morning Brew' then took a long walk along the waterfront. There was no one in the neighborhood that knew Connor, and even though it was only a few blocks from the penthouse she did not know anyone, so she felt quite safe.

When he finally got around to asking if they might meet again before he left, she declined. She had already gone against her better judgment and met him again so before anything happened, she knew she had to refuse.

It saddened her to think he was leaving, but she was not going to allow it to ruin her mood. She was glad she had decided to see him again, but it grieved her knowing she might never see him again. They had talked about everything except when he would be in town again.

She had spent another sleepless night as she had the night before. Her body was weary, but her mind was wide awake, and she ached for him.

She finally heard Craig leave and she got out of bed and did her morning routine before making her way to the kitchen for a fresh cup of coffee.

To keep herself from texting Connor she needed to keep her mind occupied.

"Hello?"

"Hi Dawn, how are you?"

"I didn't sleep well last night, so I got up, it was either that or continue to toss and turn. What are you up to today?"

"Not much, my shift doesn't start till three, so I have part of the day to put in. What about you?"

"Why don't you come over and waste your day with me and I'll cook you breakfast?" she teased, trying to lure her in.

"Sure! You're on! I'll be there in a jiffy, See ya!"

Darla was very grateful that she had such a close relationship with her sister. Only this time she had to keep a secret from her. It did not sit well with her, but this is one of a few things that she could not share, even with Dawn. The other thing she had not shared with anyone was her sham of a marriage. The only person who knew about that was Connor, and since nobody knew about him, it made it easier to keep the secret.

She began to prepare breakfast for her sister and tried to think about more pleasant thoughts that did not include Craig as it made for a brighter day. She always felt negative, horrible thoughts when it came to him. They had nothing in common, nothing special to share, no special occasions or exciting getaways, nothing, period.

She had come to the conclusion that she was not going to call or contact Connor again. At least for now since he was leaving anyway so what would be the point. She loved him, and he loved her, and she guessed that that story had come to an end. She did not know where he lived, what he did for a living if he would ever be back in town or even what brought him to Kanyon Cove in the first place. She did not ask him and guessed he did not think to tell her. Perhaps he actually thought he would have more time with her, but the thoughts of being caught in public with him creeped her out.

Craig had a lot of clout in this small town, and she did not want to be on the other end of his wrath. That was the one and only reason for the decision she had made not to see Connor again. It saddened her to even think about not seeing him again, but she would, however, hold on to the beautiful memory of their two nights together. No one would or could ever take that away from her. She thought perhaps if he had not told her he was only in town for a few days she may have taken the chance. She did not think it was worth the risk of being caught for another meeting. This town was way too small and with too many people with nothing to do but look for something to gossip about, so she could not do it. She finally knew what love was, how it felt and how it lasts, long after everything else is over. This was her secret and hers alone to bear.

So, with that out of the way, she prepared herself for a quiet day with her sister.

Connor Barnes had waited until the very last minute, hoping his phone would ring but he already knew it would not. She had already told him she could not see or meet with him again and as disappointed as he was, he had to keep his promise not to call Darla. He had left it up to her and hoped that he would hear from her but he was mistaken. He threw his bag into the trunk of his car and headed out for the drive back to class.

He was living out his dream of being an artist. After college, he managed a few odd jobs to save enough money to take art classes. He was in Kanyon Cove on a three day seminar for up and coming artists. His art teacher had told the class that going to seminars and other art shows would be beneficial to their careers and encouraged them to go. Connor counted his pennies to see if he could afford to go, with the price of gas, food, and motels. There were a few dollars left in his college fund, but he wanted to keep it. He knew that someday, down the road, he would need it. He did not know what for yet, but when the time came, he would.

He could not describe, even to himself how horrible he felt having to leave Kanyon Cove without seeing Darla again. Disappointment was an understatement.

He met Darla on his first night in Kanyon Cove. His heart ached whenever he spent too much time thinking about her, so he had to throw himself into his painting. He remembered the smell of her skin, how she felt in his arms and when she told him that he was her first lover; he could not have loved her more.

On his first day back in class, he had to force himself to concentrate on his work. Darla was on his mind day and night, and every dream he had was of her.

He had his paint colors spread out on the floor on a sheet around his easel. Paint cans were everywhere. He had always painted this way so when he needed a color they were close by. Standing in front of the easel, his phone rang. Certain that it was Darla, excitement got the better of him. Hurrying to open his phone, it slipped from his hands and into one of the cans of paint. "Damn it!!!" he shouted as he watched it slowly sink to the bottom. His hands went up into the air, and he wanted so badly to kick that can of paint across the room. He stood there looking down into the can in disbelief. "Now what?" he said as he paced back and forth in front of the paint cans with both hands on top of his head. His only thought was that Darla's cellphone number was programed in there and he had not used it enough to memorize it, and now it was gone! He was sick at heart. As long as he had her phone number he felt connected to her somehow. He had not asked for her email address since he had her number programed in the phone and now he did not even have that! He was furious with himself. There was no way he could ever concentrate on work. He jammed the covers back on the paint cans and decided to go out for a drive and maybe stop somewhere for a beer and cool off.

When he left the class, he noticed a phone kiosk across the street. He went over and looked through several of the glass display cases at the phones and chose an updated version of the one he lost. He asked the tech if it was possible to retrieve his number. He asked if his account was with them and he told him no.

"If the number is with another company and still activated, I can't give you the same number. But I suggest you contact your cell provider and have it deactivated, or you will continue to get a bill from them."

"How can it still be active when it is at the bottom of a can of paint?"

"It doesn't matter where it is, if you haven't called to have it deactivated, it is still an active number. Would you like for me to issue you a new number?"

Connor was frustrated to the core and had no choice but to accept what had happened. He got his new phone and left.

Shortly after their anniversary dinner, Darla's life returned to normal. She had made peace with her decision not to call Connor on his last day. Craig still ignored her and continued on with his late nights, coming home whenever he felt like it without an explanation. She had not seen Dawn since their breakfast date and was ok with that. She thought about Connor night and day. She relived their nights over and over in her head until she was dizzy. She dreamed about him night after night. It was the same dream and in the same context as the very first night when Craig took the ending from her. That was as far as the dream would go no matter how she longed for it to continue.

One day Dawn showed up for a visit, and Darla buzzed her in. She had several items to take to the dry cleaners and asked her sister to tag along. The cleaners were just down the street, and it was a nice day for a walk.

"Yes. Sure, I'll go." Dawn agreed, "it's a beautiful day, and the walk will be lovely, and besides, we haven't had time together since our breakfast, like what...weeks ago?"

'Time flies doesn't it? Give me a few seconds to go through this stuff, and we can get out of here." She quickly ran her hand through each pocket to be sure there was nothing left in them like Kleenex, change or anything to be kept. She pulled out a business card with the name of a club on it. She flipped it over a few times reading each side. "Have you ever heard of this place?" she asked and passed the card to Dawn.

"Um, maybe, but I don't think it is a place that Craig would hang out."

"Well, ok, if you say so, let's go then." She shrugged it off but slipped the card into her pocket just the same. Something was just not sitting right with her.

When the errands were done Darla invited Dawn home to have lunch with her. While they were eating, Dawn made a comment that surprised Darla.

"Is there something you'd like to tell me, Sis?"

"Like what?"

"You seem different, are you ok?"

"What? Yes, I'm fine, why do you ask?"

"You've changed somehow, and you look like the cat that swallowed the canary. What's up?"

"I have absolutely no idea what you are talking about!"

"Darla, I have been watching you all day, and I know you well enough to know there is something different about you, now fess up!"

"Don't be silly, Dawn, I'm the same as I've always been!" She chuckled a little, and Dawn caught the nervousness in her laughter. Darla had never confided in her sister the truth about her marriage, and the fact that it was never consummated was beyond embarrassing, so she had never told anyone else except Conner. She and Craig had been married for fourteen months and all the days and weeks were the same routine.

"Are you pregnant, Darla? Are you and Craig trying to have a baby?"

"What!? Are you serious?"

"Well, you're glowing for a reason, Sis."

"Shut up and eat your lunch!" she said and tossed a piece of roll over at her playfully, but inside the very thought had made her heart begin to pound. She felt as if she had been punched in the gut. She was shaken beyond words as she made light of the conversation. She tried to eat, but nothing would go down. Her throat was dry so that the food seemed to gag her and she laid her fork down and pretended to chew. She put her elbows on the table, locked her fingers together and rested her chin on them. When Dawn was not looking she closed her eyes for a few seconds and tried to remember.

Relief struck when Dawn spoke up, and the mood changed.

"I have to go and get ready for work, this has been great. You know I enjoy spending time with you, and I love that you cook for me, but duty calls."

"We'll do it again soon, Dawn, thanks for coming over, it sure breaks up my day." She gave her a hug, and as soon as she closed the door, she thought she might faint. She put her back against the door to orient herself and then pushed away and ran for her handbag. She got out her pocket calendar and began to count the days. "Oh My God!!!" she said aloud. "Two periods!? No way!" Panic set in. "I've missed two periods! SHIT!!!" she screamed. Biting down hard on her bottom lip she scratched her head and began to pace up and down the hall. She felt like a caged animal. She counted again and again and still got the same results. She had to get a grip before this blew up in her face. She reached for her wallet and began searching for money. She went into the spare bedroom to see if Craig had any lying around the dresser. Luckily he had. She grabbed it and began to count again. How much did she have? She had about twenty dollars to her name. Jamming the money back into her change purse she headed out the door. She walked a few blocks to the pharmacy and then became paranoid. *'Everybody knows,'* she thought, *'they are all looking at me.'* She stopped on the sidewalk to take a few deep breaths and then she realized that the people on the street were all going about their business and she was just as ignored here as she was at home. But today, that was a good thing, that was what she wanted, to be ignored.

She went into the store and walked up and down the aisles until she found what she was looking for. She took one off the shelf and began to read the side of the box. She was certain this is what she wanted so she made her way to the check-out counter and as she waited in line, she prayed she would have enough money to pay for it.

"I can help someone over here!" came a voice from the next check-out. "Miss? Miss? I can help you over here, dear."

Darla came out of her daze, moved over and placed her item on the counter.

"Did you find everything you were looking for today?"

"Yes, I did, thank you," she all but croaked the words out, and she had to clear her throat.

Numbers were poked in, and a tally rang up, and a voice spoke.

"That'll be nineteen dollars and twenty seven cents, please." Air escaped her lungs when she realized she had been holding her breath. She pulled out her change purse and dumped everything on the counter, and the cashier began to count out what she needed and pushed the rest back for her to collect. Her hands were shaking so badly she could barely pick up the few pieces of change. The cashier put her item in a bag and tore off the receipt and handed it to her.

"Have a nice day and thank you for shopping with us."

Darla gave her head a nod in thanks and left.

Once out on the sidewalk, she began to run. She ran until she was breathless. Her heart was racing as if she had just robbed a bank and had out run the police and that was exactly how she felt too, like a criminal. Who was she running from? Herself!?

She knew she had lots of time before Craig got home to complete her task as he would not be home for hours. She allowed herself a few minutes to settle down before she proceeded.

"I gotta get this over with; I can't stand it any longer." She was talking to no one except herself. She removed the item from the bag and ran her thumbnail along the edge to break the seal. Her hands were shaking as she removed the instruction sheet from the inside of the box.

"Well, that's simple enough! Pee on the stick and wait for three minutes." She kept reading aloud; "Check for a plus or a minus. Plus - your pregnant, minus - you're not. Sounds pretty simple to me. OK then, we can only hope for a minus sign!"

She laid a triple thickness of paper towel down on the edge of the bathtub for later. She sat on the toilet, stuck the stick between her legs and concentrated on peeing. She was so nervous she could not muster up even a dribble. Taking deep breaths, she relaxed, turned the tap on and soon, with the sound of running water, she got enough of a dribble out that mercifully hit the stick. She sat the stick down onto the paper towel and washed her hands.

She went into the kitchen and set the timer on the microwave for three minutes. She began to pace up and down the hall again as she waited for the microwave to finish. Her palms were moist, her throat was dry, and she could feel herself wanting to faint. 'Breathe,' she told herself, 'just breathe.' She ran her fingers through her hair like a mad woman, and when the timer finally went off, she nearly came unglued. She walked slowly to the bathroom like it would be her last walk, but she could not go in. She clasped her hand over her mouth as tears sprang to her eyes. "I have to go in," she whispered. She chewed on her thumbnail and looked at the tub. She took a few steps inside the bathroom and slowly moved over to where the stick lay on the tub's edge. Tears ran down her cheeks as she whispered, "*Damn it!*"

She was so overwhelmed that her stomach flipped upside down. Nausea overcame her as she made a leap to the toilet bowl. '*Oh my God!*' she thought, '*this cannot be happening, we were only together twice!*' She flushed the contents and rested her head on her arm until she was certain she was finished. She picked herself up off the floor and washed her face. She rinsed her mouth, brushed her teeth and rinsed again with mouthwash.

She gathered up the box and crammed the stick, instruction sheet and store receipt inside the bag and grabbed her keys and headed out to the elevator. She got inside and pushed 'B' and waited. It stopped, and she stepped out. She opened the door to the garbage room and tossed the bag and the contents into the dumpster and went back up to the penthouse. She would figure this out, she had to.

4

Darla could not get that business card image out of her head or the comment that Dawn had made. *'I don't think it's a place where Craig would hang out,'* and she wondered why she would say that. *'What did she mean by that anyway?'* It bothered her that he would have a business card for a club that he would not hang out at. She sat down, pondered her thoughts, and she knew she was not going to let this go. She had to know one way or the other. It had taken her several minutes of thought but got nowhere, so she took out her cellphone and called Dawn.

"Hey, Sis, what's up?" Dawn said when she answered her phone.

"Can you come over later?"

"I sure can, I'm off tonight, and I'm glad you called."

"When you come over, please wait in your car until Craig leaves, I will meet you outside and oh, park facing north."

"Sure, but what's going on?"

"I'll tell you later, he'll be home soon. I'll see you around seven, gotta go, bye." Just as she tucked her phone back into her purse, Craig unlocked the door. He grunted his usual 'hello' and went straight to the main bathroom to take a shower. *'He is so habitual,'* she thought. She pretended she was watching TV when he came out of the bathroom. He went into the bedroom, and she went to the window. She saw Dawn pull into a parking spot at a safe distance from the underground parking driveway. '*Great!*' she thought. She took out her phone and texted Dawn. '*Pretty sure he'll be heading north but watch to see which direction he goes, don't text me back, he is right here.*' She put the phone away.

Craig was dressed to the nines and ready to leave. He gave her a slight wave, grabbed his keys and left. Darla grabbed her keys and purse and headed out into the hall just as the elevator doors closed. She walked toward the elevator and watched the numbers drop. When it lit up 'B,' she gave it only a few seconds and hit the down button. She got in and pressed 'M' for main and waited for it to stop. She stepped out and hurried out to the foyer just as Craig's Mercedes passed by. She rushed out the door, down the steps and jumped into Dawn's car.

"What's going on, Darla?"

"Follow him."

"Why?"

"Go! Before we lose him!"

"OK, OK!"

"Where do you think he is going?"

"I can almost bet he is going to that club that I asked you about weeks ago."

"No way!"

"Yeah, well, we'll see. All we have to lose is a little gasoline."

Craig's signal light came on, and Darla touched Dawn's arm. "Pull up over here," she said, pointing to an empty spot a few car lengths away. She noticed his head lights flash, figuring it was a signal, she waited and watched. Sure enough, from the opposite side of the street, another set of lights flashed several times. It was sort of like a private signal. Craig's was, flash once, and the other was, flash several times. It was a signal alright. Darla never missed a thing.

Craig opened his car door and got out. Darla heard the '*tweet,*' and his lights flash so she knew he had locked his car. Across the street, the car door opened, and by instinct, Darla reached inside her bag for her cellphone. She was sure a woman would be getting out of the other car, and she wanted the goods on him. She opened her phone and scrolled to the camera and waited. "Come on you bastard, make my day!" She had to wonder if she was not cutting it for him then who the hell was! "What the hell is this place anyway?" Darla asked.

"I don't know, to be truthful, Sis, I've never been to this district before."

A man stepped out of the other car and Darla said, "This place must be one of those high fluting clubs where men gather for business meetings." Darla was feeling a little embarrassed at this point, but still, she waited it out. The men walked toward each other, and it looked like they were going in for a man-hug. Darla raised her cellphone and zoomed in. 'Click.' They unlocked from their hug and seemed to be chatting as Darla watched every move but still something ugly stirred inside her.

"What is keeping you out every night?" Darla spoke in low tones and almost to herself.

Dawn knew enough about her sister to trust her instincts, so she just watched and waited and said nothing except to respond to her sister's last statement.

"Every night?"

"What...the...hell!?" Darla drawled out. 'Click" once...'click' twice. Dawn saw the look on her sister's face as she turned just in time to witness their next move.

'Click' three times and then a series of clicks as she saw her husband and the other man go in for a long kiss right there on the street! She got it all on the cellphone camera.

The sisters looked at each other in disbelief, more so for Dawn than Darla because she knew that something was not right since the day they were married.

"That fool is gay! No wonder he has been cold and unfeeling towards me, I'm the wrong gender!"

"Darla? What is going on here?"

"I'll explain later, let's get out of here!"

"Where do you want to go?" Dawn asked.

"Home," she said, shaking her head, "to pack."

Dawn watched as Darla packed her bags and her personal items. She did not know what Darla was going to do and she did not ask her any questions. From what she saw, she had plenty of reason to want to flee this penthouse. She figured that Darla would tell her when the time was right for her. Before Dawn got that thought processed, Darla began to speak. She told her sister about the farce of a marriage she had been in for the past fifteen months.

She knew Darla was angry, so she did not interrupt her until she saw her sit down on the edge of her bed and put her hands up to cover her face. Dawn put her hand on her sister's arm, pulled her in for a hug and said, "I had no idea, Sis, I'm so sorry." She reached for a tissue and passed it to Darla and just held her while she cried. Darla was not feeling sorry for herself or the fact that her husband was a cheating rat. It was sheer relief that she could finally get out of this mess with a good reason. '*This reason,*' she thought as she touched her tummy. Darla blew her nose, stood up and said, "Let's get out of here."

Darla got her cellphone out, dialed and waited.

"Hello?"

"It's Darla, I'm sorry to bother you at this time of night," she said, speaking in low tones, "can you please come and pick me up?"

"You know I will, where are you?"

"I'm at Dawn's apartment, but I will wait for you outside, this must stay between us, please."

"I'll be there as soon as I can."

"Thank you," she said as her voice cracked.

"Hold on, I'll be right there!"

She hung up her phone and looked around the apartment for a note pad.

Dawn,

Thank you for being there for me tonight. I couldn't have gotten away from Craig without you. I can't tell you where I am going, but I will be in touch. You can call or text me but please give me some time, and I will contact you when I am ready.

I found your old cellphone and charger in a drawer, and I am going to take it with me. In the morning, please call the company and have it re activated. Get a new number and text it to me to your old phone. I am turning mine off, and we can stay in touch on your phone and the new number. You know that you will be the first person that Craig is going to call. This is where you will give a performance of your life time. I know you will do your best to cover my ass. You are the best sister ever! I love you.

~Darla~

On the back on her note, she wrote out instructions as to what to say to Craig when he called, and she knew that Dawn would not let her down.

She picked up her stuff and quietly closed and locked the door, went down to the street and waited.

She began to tear up again as soon as she saw the car pull up. The door opened, and she saw the figure get out. Darla looked around, and when she had a clear path, she ran into waiting arms.

'Get into the car, darling, I'll take you home."

"You don't know how great it is to see you. I have so much to tell you."

"We have lots of time."

"Thank you for coming for me."

"You're welcome, honey.

Darla welcomed the touch on her hand as the reassurance she needed. They proceeded to the outskirts of town and pulled up to a gate, a button was pushed, and they drove up the long lane. When the car stopped, Darla looked across to the driver and spoke softly. "Thank you, Aunt Evie."

"You just had to ask, Darla, you just had to ask. Let's go inside."

When they went inside *'The Grand Manor'* Darla stood in the foyer and looked around. She had always been in awe of this place. "I love it here," she said.

"I know you do, you and Dawn were such a delight whenever you'd visit."

"I'm sorry I haven't been here in a while, Aunt Evie, I don't have a car, and I had to depend on Dawn, and her schedule, to go anywhere."

"I know all about your dilemma, my dear. I know it is late but would you like a cup of chamomile tea?"

"That sounds great." Her aunt's remark had escaped her.

"I'll make a pot, and we can talk, or would you rather unpack first."

"No, that can wait," she said, giving her hand a flip towards the suitcase.

"I'll be right back then, make yourself comfortable."

This house took her to places of the heart. She truly loved this Manor and had since she was a child.

Evelyn came into the room carrying a tea tray. She had a few small party size sandwiches and a few sweets next to the tea pot. Darla thought her aunt might miss entertaining when she saw the tray and its contents. Her belly was telling her that she could use a sandwich or two since they were only small.

"Come over here darling and sit down."

Darla loved that her aunt called her 'darling.' Her elegance and high society ways had always put Darla in awe of her.

"Would you like to tell me what is wrong or would you rather wait to get your thoughts organized?"

"No, Aunt Evie, I'm fine, and I'm ready. I want to make myself perfectly clear though, this must stay between us. No one else must ever know about this conversation. I haven't even told Dawn. Please, promise me."

Evelyn looked her straight in the eye, knowing she was already taking mental note with plans to break this promise, but she said it anyway.

"Of course, darling, your secret is safe with me."

Darla got up from her chair and sat next to her aunt on the loveseat. Evelyn reached out to Darla and took both her hands in hers. She saw tears well up in Darla's eyes as soon as she touched her. "It's OK darling, we have lots of time."

"I'm pregnant," she blurted out.

"Well, that's wonderful news, Darla, but why are you here and not at home sharing this news with... what's his name?"

"Craig," she smiled through her tears realizing that he had never met her aunt. In fact, she could not recall ever mentioning her name to Craig nor did she know if he knew she even existed. *'Come to think of it, this could be a bonus,'* she thought.

"It isn't Craig's baby." The words were out of her mouth before she realized she was going to say them.

Evelyn raised an eyebrow but said not a word to allow Darla to continue.

"When Craig and I got married, just over a year ago, there was something important that I did not know about him."

"Oh, and what was that?"

Darla hesitated for only a few seconds and realized that she had to be truthful about everything if she was expecting Evelyn to help her. She took her cellphone out of her handbag, opened it and passed it to Evelyn. "Press here," she pointed to the arrow, "to see the others."

"Oh dear! This is Craig?"

"Yes, this one," she pointed him out. "Turns out he is gay, just a little something he forgot to mention. We never consummated our marriage, and now I know why. I was beginning to think it was me but now I know it wasn't."

"Then....if you and Craig haven't had sex then how did you end up pregnant?"

"Oh God Aunt Evie," she said, covering her face with her hands for several seconds. She brought her hands down into her lap and began to speak. "I met the most amazing guy. We were only together a couple times, and the last thing I expected was to get pregnant. Living with Craig has been awful. He has a great business, we live in a beautiful penthouse, but there's nothing else. No love, no togetherness, we have never had a conversation to speak of, and I was alone most of the time, except for Dawn's visits. It's been a very lonely year. I tried to get a job but it was impossible, no one would hire me. I began to think that Craig paid people off to not hire me. Call me paranoid, but there must have been a reason why every business in town declined my resume. He gave me very little money, and if I wanted anything for myself, I had to ask him for the cash to buy it. It was very embarrassing.

"I can see why!" Aunt Evie butted in.

"He is very selfish, speaks very little to me. When he comes home it is only to shower, change clothes and he is gone again and always with no explanation what so ever. I can't, for the life of me, figure out why he asked me to marry him in the first place. He has no interest in being married and not once has he ever introduced me as 'his wife' to anyone. Why bother? What was his intention? Why not just live as a bachelor? Why, why, so many 'whys'! I don't have any answers."

"Well, it's quite simple, darling, it seems as though he was using you to hide being gay. Perhaps he has more to hide, who knows. I'm glad you called me, we can work on this together."

"Anyway," she continued, "a few months ago, Craig took me out for our first anniversary. We went to a nice restaurant downtown where I had not been before. It was nice to get dressed up and actually have him take me somewhere. The only other times I got out were when Dawn was available, and we'd take walks or sit around and catch up on our news. There was never cash lying around for a cab or to go shopping. Anyway,

I'm digressing. A college friend of Craig's stopped by our table, and Aunt Evie I swear, I fell in love right then and there. It was mutual for sure. We had spent a few hours in his motel room that night, and for the first time, I was actually made love to. He took my virginity Aunt Evie but I never once thought he'd leave me with a baby!" She was unaware that she was cradling her tummy, but her aunt noticed. "We met the next day too because he was only in town for a few days. He gave me his cell number and his email address, but I haven't tried to contact him since our last night together."

"Why not?"

"Because, he told me he was only in town for a few days, so why prolong the inevitable?"

"Did he ask if he could call you?"

"He did, but I asked him not to until I had time to think about what we had just done. I did not want to have an affair. This is a very small town, and people talk. I had to figure stuff out."

"And, did you?"

"No," she groaned, "but all this happened before I found out about Craig."

"Are you telling me that it has taken you over a year, in a sexless marriage, to figure out there was something wrong?"

"I know, Aunt Evie, I was between a rock and a hard place. He made sure I was penniless and had no place to go."

"No place to go? Are you serious? Where are you now and why did it take a near crises for you to call me? I've always been here."

"I'm sorry Aunt Evie, perhaps it was fear of failure or too embarrassing but yes, I should have asked for your help a long time ago."

"Indeed, you should have. You certainly did not have to stay in that situation, Darla," she said patting her on the arm. "Come here," she said, opening her arms to her.

Darla moved in for a hug and tears sprang to her eyes. "I'm really in a mess, Aunt Evie."

"Well, I'm here to help you do whatever you feel you must do. We'll do it together."

Darla clamped her lips together and looked at her aunt. "Does that mean I can stay here for a while?"

"Of course you can! I told you I have always been here. I'm glad you called me. But I think, for now, you should go up to the west wing, where you've always slept, and get some rest. It's been a horrible time for you, and you need to relax. I asked Emma to get your room together while I went into town to pick you up." She put her finger under Darla's chin and drew it up to look her in the eyes and said, "OK?"

"Thanks," she said, and then added, "Is Emma still here?"

"Yes, she is such a gem."

"You are correct, I am tired; thank you again for rescuing me."

"I wouldn't call it rescuing my dear. We are family, and you my angel are very welcome. We'll talk more tomorrow."

"Good night, Aunt Evie." She pulled the handle up on her suitcase and wheeled it across the foyer then carried it upstairs. When she got into the bedroom, she closed the door. Tossing her suitcase up on the bed she dug around for Dawn's cellphone and plugged it in to charge it up.

Evelyn went to the foot of the stairs, waited for the door to close and reached for the phone. "Sam? I'm not calling too late am I?"

"Not at all, my dear, what can I do for you?"

"I have to see you as soon as possible."

"Sure, come anytime?"

"Is it too late to come now?"

"You know it isn't."

"See you in a bit then, thanks, Sam."

Evelyn entered Sam Logan's office. She walked straight into his arms as he greeted her and kissed both cheeks. "Thank you for meeting with me on such short notice and at this hour. If it weren't important, I would have waited until another time, but I feel that I must confide in you and ask for your help."

"Please, sit," he said as he held the back of the chair for her. It's great to see again, but before we get too involved in conversation, Evelyn, how have you been?"

"I'm fine, Sam, but I must get down to business and get back to the Manor before anyone knows I'm gone."

"Anyone? Isn't there only yourself and Emma at the Manor and since when do you have to sneak around?"

"This is about my niece. Remember when I hired your firm to check up on my nieces for me? Well one of them needs my help now and what I am about to tell you was told to me in the strictest of confidence. I certainly do not feel good about betraying her trust, but I feel it's necessary. I know I can trust you to see this through with me or I would not be here. I pray to God she never has to find out that I am betraying her."

"You have my word, Evelyn, always."

"I'm asking for your help in a situation that needs to be dealt with quickly and discretely. Basically, it's this; my niece, Darla Coleman-Harrington, called earlier this evening and asked if I could pick her up. For her to ask me that, I knew something was wrong since she has never asked for my help, ever. It seems she has been living in a sham of a marriage, with a fellow named Craig Harrington, for the last fifteen months. I believe he is a club owner in downtown Kanyon Cove. She insists they never consummated their marriage, which to me, in itself, is grounds for an immediate annulment, no muss, no fuss. So, in case he has any bright ideas about coming after her, I need papers drawn up for Darla's name to be changed to Roma. It's our family name, and she has a right to use it. When the name is changed, I need for you to delete her last name from any file with Harrington or Coleman attached to it. I don't trust her husband not to have her tracked down. From what she said, I'm assuming he is a bit of a control freak. Apparently, he kept her in complete dependence of him, and I doubt that she even has a bank account in her name. Since she has nothing legally attached to her name, this should be fairly simple, am I correct in assuming this?"

"Yes, you are, but what is the urgency? What are you not telling me, Evelyn?"

"Darla is pregnant, Sam. She saw another man on a couple of occasions, and it led to a baby. She is three months along. She has a few decisions to make, but I am almost certain in saying that I believe she will likely keep the baby. There are too many strong feelings attached to the father for her to give it up. I would also like for you to start a fund for this child. It can always be changed if she decides on adoption but for now, I need a fund to commence immediately. As you know, my father founded, and the estate continues to fund, private schools, which are also named after him. He has one for boys and one for girls, so whichever gender this child is, it will be able to attend either school. They are called the Samuel Roma Schools and are on a private road in Lando County so the child will be close to home and well cared for. The child's tuition will be taken care of through my estate and at your direction. Since you are handling my estate, I will sign whatever is needed for permission for your office to handle this matter each and every year. I know I am jumping the gun here and the child won't be able to attend the school until he or she is five years old. But during those first five years, I would like to be able to help out my niece. I'll need a bank account opened in her new name and monthly deposits put in it as soon as this is handled. I will figure out an amount and let you know."

Sam was taking notes while Evelyn talked and he smiled on occasion. "Samuel Roma, eh?"

"Yes, and it is purely coincidental that you have the same first name, the only difference is, no one ever called him 'Sam.'"

"So, is this everything I need to know?"

"No, there is something else. Darla showed me pictures on her cellphone that she took tonight of Craig in a compromising situation. It seems he is rather gay, unbeknownst to Darla, and we may be able to use it to our advantage. It isn't something he wants out in the open, obviously, or he wouldn't have used my niece as a cover. So if he wants to keep his secret hidden, he has to play nice."

"Do you think you might be able to forward a copy of those pictures over to me without causing suspicion?" Sam asked.

"I might be able to, I'll let you know. I must get back to the Manor. Thanks so much for seeing me on such short notice, Sam, I really appreciate it."

"Don't give it a second thought, Evelyn; I am always here for you, my dear." He walked around his desk and held out his hand for her to stand up. He kissed her on both cheeks again along with a gentle hug and walked her to the door. "Call me if you need me, and I'll get this paper work started first thing in the morning."

5

Craig stumbled into the penthouse in the wee hours of the morning. He did not open the bedroom door to check on Darla he just went straight to the guest room. He undressed and fell into bed and was asleep as soon as his head hit the pillow. He awoke the next morning with a slight headache and got up to find some aspirin. He did not find any in the main bathroom, so he tiptoed in to look for some in the master bath cabinet. When he opened the bedroom door, his face sobered. The bed was empty and made up. He found that unusual since Darla never liked to get up early. He liked that because it gave him time to shower, have a cup of coffee and be out the door before she even got out of bed. He immediately left the bedroom and went to the kitchen to see if she was there. When he did not see her, he went to the living room and back to the bedroom. He was half hoping that she would magically appear, but she did not.

"What the hell?" he mumbled. He was worried now. His mind was running overtime and realized that he had not seen her since he left for the restaurant last night. He had not called her nor had she called him. That was not unusual though since they did not make it a practice of keeping in close contact while he was out. He checked the clock on the dresser, and it was just past six o'clock. He picked up the phone from the night table and dialed her cell phone. It went straight to voicemail. He did not bother to leave a message. He did not want to give her the impression that he cared he just wanted to know where the hell she was. He began to dial again.

"Hello?" came the sleepy voice that answered the phone.

"Dawn?"

"Yes, who is this?" she pretended to stifle a yawn, but she had been up for a while.

"It's Craig."

Dawn had already been apprised as to what to say when Craig called, and they both knew she would be the first one he would call.

"Craig? What's wrong? Is Darla ok?"

"I'm sorry to wake you up so early; I was hoping you could tell me where Darla is."

"Where she is? Isn't she there with you? Craig, what's going on?"

"I don't know, when I got up this morning she wasn't in her room."

"Her room?" She knew she had him now. "What do you mean by 'her room'?" she asked. "Wasn't she in bed when you got home from the club?"

"I, um, I, er, I don't know," he stammered. "I got home late and didn't want to wake her, so I slept in the guest room."

She had taken the heat off herself and placed it squarely back on him. She felt that he believed her since it was he who had something to hide.

"I'll try other ways to find her."

"Have you called her?"

"Yes, and the call went to voicemail."

Dawn already knew he could not get hold of her since she had told her she was keeping her phone turned off. A few days before, Dawn had bought a new cellphone and had tossed her old one in a drawer. She was given instructions to have it reactivated so Darla could use it.

"Would you let me know what you find out, Craig?"

"Yes, I will Dawn, sorry to have to wake you with this kind of drama. I'm sure she is ok."

"Well I'm sure she is too Craig, just give it some time maybe she is visiting a friend."

"I never thought of that," he said.

"She does get pretty lonely there alone Craig with your schedule and all."

"That is true, being a club owner does have its downfalls," he admitted. "I suppose you're right, I do keep late hours." He was just realizing that he had never given her feelings a second thought until this moment.

"If I hear from her I will let you know Craig."

"Thanks."

She had won this round. Now all she had to do was wait a few more hours to make the call to activate her old phone and text Darla with the new number. She had already asked her not to call and that she would contact her at some point. She had to respect her sister's wishes. She hoped that her sister was alright and in a safe place. It surprised her somewhat that she did not confide in her as to where she was going. But she knew she would know when the time was right for Darla to talk to her.

The next morning Darla was up earlier than she was used to. She slept but not very well. She missed her familiar surroundings and her own bed, but it was equally comfortable here. She just had to get used to being away from feeling trapped in that penthouse. She took a long shower, got dressed and went downstairs.

"Good morning Darla, did you get any sleep at all? I know what you must be going through since all this is so upsetting. Just remember that I am here for you, darling. By the way, can I ask a favor of you?

"Sure Aunt Evie, what can I do for you?"

"Would it be possible for you to download those pictures from your phone to my laptop? It's ok if you say no, I'll understand."

"I am only keeping them for collateral damage in case Craig gets any smart ideas so, sure I'll give you a copy. I brought my laptop as well so how about if I just email them over to you?"

"That would be lovely, dear, thank you. Now, what would you like for breakfast and I'll have Emma bring it to you."

"Just a couple slices of whole grain toast and a cup of decaf tea, if you have it, please."

"I'll go check with Emma and how about you send me over those pictures while you wait."

"Sure."

Darla went back upstairs to get her laptop. She unplugged Dawn's cellphone and slipped it into her pocket, grabbed her own and headed downstairs with the laptop. She sat it on the dining room table, took out her phone and turned it on. She connected it to her laptop, loaded the pictures over to her laptop and turned her phone off immediately. When she finished the process, she then copied and pasted them to her email account and sent them over to her aunt's email. When Evelyn came back into the dining room, Darla told her she had finished with the pictures.

"Well, that was fast!"

It isn't a difficult concept, especially when you have all the time on your hands that I had. I learned a lot through the internet.

"Thank you, Darla, I appreciate you doing that for me."

Emma came out with her breakfast, so the subject was dropped since they were keeping it between themselves, or so Darla thought.

Evelyn excused herself and told Darla she would be back in a jiffy. She went into the den and opened her laptop to check her mail. She watched as the download came in and she checked the door to be sure she was alone. She opened the email and the pictures that Darla had showed her last night were all there. She clicked on, 'forward,' and then Sam's name and quickly typed out a note. *'These are what we discussed last night,'* and she hit 'send.' She left the den and returned to the table.

Before Darla finished her breakfast, she heard a familiar cellphone ring tone. Realizing it was Dawn's old phone; she took it out of her pocket and looked at it. A message was waiting from Dawn. *'Got you cover with Craig and your new number is 387-7793, text when you can, I love you!'*

"Sorry about that, how is your breakfast? Did Emma have what you wanted?" Evelyn said as she reentered the dining room."

"Yes, she did, and I want to thank you again for letting me stay here."

"There is no thanks needed darling, I'm glad I can help. While we were talking last night, you mentioned that you were in a 'real mess' as you put it. What do you want to do about this baby? You have options, dear. Abortion, adoption or keep it. It's quite simple really, and I can help with all three, but it's your decision."

Darla had not given herself time to think about any of those three options that her aunt just put before her. She touched her stomach as if she were just realizing there was a baby in there. She had only called it 'pregnant' since she peed on the stick. But now, as she spoke the words aloud for the first time, it was real! "I hadn't really thought about it in terms of 'baby,' Aunt Evie because I've had no one to share this with. But now that the words have been spoken, I know that I definitely do not want an abortion."

"Ok then, that only leaves two options, and you have time to think about those two." She smiled over at Darla to show her support, which meant a lot to her. "Who is this guy darling? What's his name?" Evelyn could see her tense up. Her back went poker straight, and panic sobered her smiling face. "Relax, darling, there is only you and I in the room, no one else."

"I know, but I haven't spoken his name since that night. I think about him day and night, but I refused to say his name out loud."

"And now?"

Darla took a deep breath, looked around the room as if in deep thought. She finally looked at her aunt who was waiting patiently for her to answer. "Connor Barnes." It felt strange to even say his name aloud. It made him real again, and it also made her heart beat faster just tossing his name out there in the room.

"And what does this Connor Barnes do for a living?"

"I..er..I really don't know," she answered with a furrowed brow. "I don't have a clue what he does, we never talked about it. Perhaps if I had stayed in touch with him, I may have found out more about him. That's neither here nor there, he is gone, I don't know where he is, and it's done. I can't go back for a do-over, and he has likely moved on by now anyway. It has been three months."

"You have no plan to tell him he is going to be a father? Do you think that is fair?"

"I don't know what is fair anymore, Aunt Evie. This is all new to me, and I don't know yet what I'm going to do. Dawn doesn't even know where I am. I will, eventually, have to text her before she starts going crazy with worry."

"I suggest you give yourself time to unpack, settle in and try to relax. Tension and stress is not good for the baby. I will make an appointment for you to see a private doctor friend of mine. We'll see this through together Darla." She excused herself again and told Darla she was going to take a shower. She left the room and went upstairs to her bedroom and picked up the phone. "Hello, Sam, it's Evelyn. I just found out that the father's name is Connor Barnes but Darla has no idea what he does for a living nor does she know where this fellow lives or where he is from originally. I don't know if we should try and contact him or not, what do you think?"

"If you are asking for my advice, and I assume you are, I suggest we leave that up to your niece and let her decide whether or not she wants him back in her life. However, I do have the paper work started as per your requests from last night, and I have also received your email. They will be quite useful if this young man gets out of hand."

"Thank you, Sam, I appreciate the rush. I will wait for your call to come in and sign whatever is necessary."

"Good talking to you again and thanks for the information, it's gives us a starting point. I shall call you personally when I have the papers drawn up. In the meanwhile, I suggest you come up with an explanation as to why you are changing your niece's last name. She needs to be informed in order for the documents to go through with her signature. You have a great day."

Evelyn called and booked an appointment with Dr. Rayburn for Darla's checkup. They had to wait for two days in order to get in. In the meanwhile, she took the opportunity to broach the subject on the name change.

She came back downstairs from her shower and found Darla sitting quietly in the den with her laptop. "There you are. Is this a good time for a chat?"

"Yes Aunt Evie, I'm just scrolling through stuff on the laptop, nothing that can't wait. I did get a text from Dawn earlier though, and she has set me up with a new cell number on her old phone. I haven't had mine turned on except to download and send those pictures to you. Did you receive them by the way?"

"Yes I did and thank you again for sending them; I'll look at them again later." She jumped on the opportunity to broach the subject and felt it was the perfect time."

"Do you want to talk about something? Is everything ok with me being here?"

"You're beginning to sound paranoid darling about being here. I wish you wouldn't because I love having you around. You'd better get used to it since you'll be here at least until after you deliver this child. So, can you please relax and enjoy your stay?"

"I'd like that; it's just that I don't want to be a burden to you and I have no way of repaying you for your kindness."

"Now, now, we'll have none of that kind of talk. You are not here as a charity case. You need my help, and I have offered it to you, but you must be willing to accept it gracefully and without guilt. Are you willing to do that?"

Darla nodded her head because she knew if she spoke she would cry.

"Fair enough. Now I have to speak to you about something important. You've told me that while you were with Craig, he more or less kept you penniless and dependent on him. Am I correct in assuming this?"

Darla swallowed and nodded, again trying to control her feelings. *'Damned hormones!'*

"Ok, so, I am also under the assumption then that you did not have a bank account in your name or other documents of any kind?" She waited for a response from Darla.

"Yes, that's true. All I have is a driver's license, but I don't have a car."

"Now we are getting somewhere."

"Why all the questions Aunt Evie?"

"I'm getting to that, but first I have to ask you a serious question, and I need an honest response from you." She saw Darla nod again, so she continued. "Do you think that Craig will try and find you? I mean through a private detective, computer or a GPS device of some sort?"

"It wouldn't surprise me Aunt Evie, he certainly has the means. That's why I am keeping my cellphone turned off and using Dawn's. In case he tries something, I really do not want him to find me, ever!"

"That's what I wanted to hear! How would you feel if I make arrangements with my private lawyer to have your name changed to our family name, Roma?"

Darla sat up and took notice now, with interest.

"I thought that might get your attention," she laughed. "Would you like to hear more?"

"I sure do! Tell me what you have in mind."

"Wonderful, I was hoping you'd see it this way. Since you have no bank accounts or other legal documents floating around out there, it'll be pretty difficult for anyone to track you down since you aren't that deep into the system. So, if you give me your driver's license, I can have my lawyer draw up papers for your signature to change your name to Roma. Once that is done, we can delete any documents, including a marriage certificate, with the name Coleman or Harrington. You will be provided with a new driver's license, birth certificate and there will be nothing for Craig to use to track you down. I'm assuming he knows nothing about me either so he will not be able to connect our names. Is this of any interest to you at all?"

Darla jumped to her feet and went over to hug her aunt and told her what an amazing idea it all was and asked if it could be done.

"I assure you it can be done and all I need is your permission."

"Yes!!! You do have my permission!"

"There's one more thing, Darla. Since you and Craig never consummated your marriage, you are entitled to an annulment. You won't have to go through divorce proceedings since there was no marriage to speak of."

"Really? How do you know all this?"

"I've lived a lot longer than you my dear, and these things are commonly known to anyone who is interested. You are still practically a child and would not have given it a second thought. So, are we in agreement? Shall I call my lawyer?" She did not share anything else with her and besides now was not the time.

"Yes, Aunt Evie, I think we should get this started as quickly as possible. Thank you so much!" She reached into her handbag and found her wallet and flipped through a few sections and pulled her license out and passed it to her aunt. "This is all I have with my name on it except for the marriage certificate."

"We can find that document in the court system. I'll call my lawyer and ask his advice, and I'll let you know what we find out. You're doing the right thing, Darla. Oh, by the way, we have a doctor's appointment in a few days for your first checkup and examination but don't fret about it, I'll be with you."

"Thanks." It was all she could say. She was overwhelmed with all the information that her aunt had just dumped on her. She also felt a lot of relief knowing that it was possible that Craig would never be able to find her. That in itself was a load off her shoulders. She was wishing she had Dawn to talk to, but that would come when she was ready.

Evelyn went into her den and made another call to Sam. When he answered his private number, she told him that she had spoken with Darla and explained the situation to her and everything was a go. Sam was glad to hear from her and told her that most of it had been taken care of already. She told him that she was in possession of her license and would drop it off to him as soon as she could. He suggested that she use a courier service and that way she would not be seen coming and going from his office. She thought it was an excellent idea and agreed with him.

"I will courier the papers over for Darla to sign and the documents you requested pertaining to a bank account. Now that she is in agreement I will go ahead and clear her name off the system, the faster, the better in this case." They hung up from their conversation, and she called the nearest courier company.

In less than an hour, the courier arrived to pick up Darla's information. The driver bagged it and gave Evelyn a receipt after writing down the address for delivery. The van was not out of the driveway when another courier service arrived with a large envelope. She called Darla to the foyer and asked the driver to wait for a return delivery, so he went to the van for an envelope. She opened her envelope and found the documents to be in order. She knew Sam well enough to know they would be done to perfection.   She gave Darla hers to sign, and she quickly signed her own.   She asked the driver to please deliver them to the same address as where he had picked them up.   He in return bagged them and gave her a receipt.   Before he left, he reassured her they would be delivered promptly.   Time was of the essence in this case.   She wanted to have all the bases covered before Craig got any ideas of his own.

As they drove out of Kanyon Cove, Darla was nervous, and Evelyn reached across the seat and touched her arm for comfort.

"Everything will be perfectly fine honey, try not to fret, we've got this covered."

Darla looked over at her and said, 'we'?"

"Well...yes 'we,' you and I darling." Evelyn hoped she had taken that as an answer to her question as she tried to concentrate on the road.   Darla would be disappointed in her if she knew the truth.   She had had no choice but to betray her niece's confidence. 'It'll all work out,' she told herself. She had a pang in the pit of her stomach knowing that she had betrayed her niece by breaking her promise.   She was still of the opinion that she had done the right thing for Darla.   If she had to do it over, she would do it exactly the same. *'We all have to make choices,'* she thought, and she had made hers.

They drove in silence, each in their own thoughts, doubts, and fears while trying to hide it from the other.

Darla was reading road signs when all of a sudden she realized they were out of Kanyon Cove. "Lando County? Where are we?"

"Almost there my dear, not to worry."

They turned into a private road called Sluice Point, and as they passed many beautiful manors and estates, they finally pulled into one equally as grand. Evelyn shoved the shift up in park, turned the engine off and sat back against the seat as if relieved that at least this part of the drive was over. "We're here Darla. Are you ready?"

"I have to be I guess; I don't have a choice, do I?"

"Yes, you certainly do. You can decide to see your own physician and risk being seen or we can do this privately. What would you like to do?"

Her shoulders slumped as if in defeat and agreed that this was her only option and that her aunt was right.

"Can I just sit here for a few minutes? It seems rather scary. I've never had an examination before, and it's making me feel uncomfortable."

"Take as much time as you need, just remember that from now on, until you have the baby, this is going to be a monthly occurrence. Perhaps there won't be an internal examination every time, but certainly, the monthly appointments are inevitable."

"I guess, I never thought of that!"

They got out of the car and walked into the office. The receptionist was waiting for them, and she spoke to Evelyn as if she were a close friend.

"This is my niece, Darla Roma," she said as Darla looked at her.

"Dr. Rayburn will be with you shortly, please have a seat."

"What?" Darla asked. "Roma?"

"This is going to happen so you may as well get used to it now as later," Evelyn spoke in low tones so as not to be overheard. "Roma will be your name soon enough so relax and let it go."

The doctor appeared and spoke to Evelyn. She introduced Darla to him, and he showed her into one of his rooms.

"Well, that was embarrassing!

"I'm sure it was, but it was necessary Darla."

"Maybe I shouldn't have ruled out an abortion after all. At least it would be over with on this first trip!"

"Well, my dear, you still have that option, as long as you don't wait too long. Plus, you have to consider what is involved if you decide to keep it."

"I know Aunt Evie, I don't believe I am ready to raise a child alone. I also don't want to believe that I can give up a child that was created with a man that I love so much. How could I ever walk away from Connor's and my baby? This is so hard!" Tears sprang to her eyes as all the reality of the pregnancy was flooding her mind. She was tired from the trip, and her back ached from the drive.

Evelyn patted her arm. She did not know what it was like to be pregnant since she never had been, but she felt compassion for her niece. She certainly was in a difficult place, mentally. The decisions she had to make would take its toll on anyone. Evelyn now thought she might be leaning towards adoption, but she doubted it. She certainly understood her reasoning behind not wanting to give up a child made with the man she loved. If there was anything she could do for her niece she definitely would, but she prayed that she would not find out what she has already done.

Now that Darla had been to the doctor, this baby was first and foremost on her mind. The doctor had told her that she was about thirteen weeks along. Connor was on her mind as he always was, but now it was worse. They were having a baby, and she wanted to see him so badly. His phone number and email were indelibly imprinted into her memory, and she still had it in her cellphone. She turned on her phone and looked it up. She kept it charged up since all her information was still in there. Her heart was pounding as she programed it into Dawn's phone. Her instinct was to call him, and she did. She had to sit down, she was shaking so badly. *'We're sorry, the number you have dialed is no longer in service,'* came an automated message. She could not believe her ears. She hung up and dialed again, just in case she had misdialed. *'We're sorry...'* she closed her phone; she'd heard enough and began to cry. Great sobs ripped from her body. Now she knew for sure that he has moved on, and it was killing her. If he would go so far as to change his number he was definitely moving on. She was heart sick and just lay down on her bed and let it out. She cried until there were no more tears. She got up, washed her face, applied cream and went downstairs. She walked around the house and looked at items that she failed to see as a child. Beautiful paintings and ornaments that looked as if they had come from many different parts of the world.

She and Dawn had made several trips here to visit on their own. Aunt Evie had a driver at that time, and he would pick them up and drive them here to see their aunt. But, at that time, they never felt as if they could just walk around on their own and snoop. The visit was usually held in the den or the living room and after they had a snack, a beverage and conversation they were driven back home. She had such great memories of this place, and she hoped one day to have one just like it.

"Hello dear. Are you reacquainting yourself with the Manor?"

"I hope you don't mind. I don't remember seeing most of this stuff before. It's quite fascinating, actually."

"Of course I don't mind, this is your home for the time being feel free to wander around at your leisure."

Darla turned to look at her and Evelyn sobered in concern. "You've been crying! What's wrong, Darla? Are you alright?"

"I am now, thanks for asking."

"Tell me what happened," she said as she walked over to her.

Darla looked at her for a few seconds, and Evelyn instantly felt guilty and wondered if she somehow found out about her betrayal. She waited with a lump in her throat until she began to speak.

"I tried to call Connor today." The hurt was still in her face, and her voice broke as she spoke.

Evelyn felt relief as she listened to her speak. "And what happened?"

"His number is no longer in service," she said with a shaky voice. She did not want to break down again, so she stopped talking, '*damned hormones!*'

"I'm so sorry to hear that darling. That must sting. What do you think happened there?"

"Just as I figured, he's moved on of course" as she threw her hands up in the air. "I should have called him before now. I should have called or texted him the next morning before he left. I should have called him instead of calling you. I should have involved him while I still had the chance." She was crying again, and Evelyn went to her and held her while her heart was breaking. "All the 'should haves' is not going to fix anything my darling." She felt so sorry for her. Her niece was definitely feeling rejected, and nobody does rejection well, no matter who it is. Evelyn was thinking that if Craig could not find her, then certainly neither could Connor. It was a foregone conclusion that Sam had wiped her out of the system days before. Darla Coleman-Harrington was wiped off the map and replaced with Darla Roma.

6

Several days had already gone by, and Craig still had not heard from Darla. His control factor was kicking in, and he was anxious to know where she was. As far as he knew, she had no friends, and the only other person he knew of was his sister in law, Dawn. He had called her several times since the morning he had noticed her gone, but she insisted she had not heard from her either, which he thought absurd. They seemed pretty close, but right now he could not be certain of anything. He had not taken the time to ask her about friends, family or her interests. He knew absolutely nothing about her and was beginning to realize how utterly selfish he had been, never once giving thought to her feelings. He was out every night of the week, and she was home in the penthouse alone. Dawn's words to him had hit very close to home, and it played on his mind. He just wanted to find her to know for himself that she is alright.

He was beginning to feel like a caged animal. '*Where is she?*' he thought, '*Where would she go?*' He knew he had to do something, so he got the phonebook out and flipped through the yellow pages until he found the listings for Private Detectives. Running his finger down the page, he rested at one and read up on the ad. He picked up the phone, made the call and asked for an appointment.

He sat outside of the office for several minutes looking at the sign. *'Holden Montgomery, P.I.'*

Gathering courage, he got out of his car and walked in. There was no secretary, as he had envisioned. No dumb blonde with a skirt up to her ass filing her red fingernails and chewing gum. He realized that he had watched way too many 'Columbo' reruns late at night! Instead, he was greeted with a rough looking, red neck type guy sporting a shoulder holster, with his head buried in a file folder.

He stood up from his desk when he heard the door open. "You must be Craig, I'm Holden Montgomery." He offered him his hand, but Craig refused it. *'So much for a handshake,'* Holden thought, he pointed to a chair across from his desk, but he refused that as well.

"Thank you, but I'll stand."

'Oh, here we go,' he thought, *'one of those!'* "Suit yourself." He already did not like him. "What can I do for you then?"

"My wife is missing, and I'd like for you to find her. Her name is Darla and here is a picture of her. I have no further information. The only address I have is her sister's, and she insists that she has not heard from her either. Here is her address. If she is not hiding out there, I have no idea where she is."

He was angry, and Holden saw the veins protruding from his neck as his nostrils flared. He knew 'control' when he saw it. This fellow was losing it, and he was not happy.

"Where is this address located?" he asked.

"Google it, asshole!" he said, raising his voice. "Do I have to do all the work for you or can you at least do that much!"

Somewhere deep inside, Holden resisted the urge to reach across his desk, jam his fist all the way down this guy's throat and rip his lungs out through his neck. Instead, he kept reminding himself that his guy was loaded and was spending a bundle for him to find his wife. Big Bucks! If he had not been so desperate for the money at the moment, he would have dropped him for a dime.

Craig tossed a bulging envelope of cash on his desk and shouted, "Find something I can use!" He turned on his heels as he glared at Holden, squinted his eyes and left. Holden winced as the door slammed and was full of distain for this poor excuse for a human being.

'Who is the unlucky gal who caught this one?' he thought.

Holden Montgomery was one of several Private Detectives in Kanyon Cove. When Craig Harrington made an appointment to see him, he had no idea what kind of a man he was. He had agreed to see him because he knew he was one of the most influential businessmen in town, and he also knew he could benefit from him as a client. Business in Kanyon Cove was slow, and he had bills to pay, rent coming due and he welcomed the call, or so he thought he did until he met the guy. Now he wished he had never answered his phone or agreed to see him. He picked up the envelope and ran his thumb under the seal. Ten thousand dollars, the agreed upon amount for retainer fees, stared back at him. He dropped the envelope into his top desk drawer and opened his laptop. He hit 'Google Search' and entered her name. 'Darla Coleman – Harrington.' *'Geez, I hate these kinds of jobs!'*

He rubbed his chin and then ran his hand through his hair and down across his face in frustration. "There's nothing here!" he said aloud. "Who is this person?" The only one he had to talk to was himself, and he did that a lot. He could not find one single thing with her name on it. He searched with what seemed like hours as he crisscrossed her name using it several different ways and still there was nothing. He even tried to use her name as an attachment to Craig's, and she was still nonexistent. There was not even a bank account with her name on it anywhere in the entire town. It was like she did not exist. He clicked out of that page and entered Dawn's name. At least she has an address. It was a place to start.

7

Craig was in the foyer of his building checking his mailbox when a man walked in. He was looking through the names on the board when he noticed that he had pressed his penthouse number. "Excuse me, I'm Craig Harrington, can I help you?"

"Oh, ya, I have a delivery for you, sir, sign here please."

After Craig signed the paper on the clipboard, he passed him an envelope, and he left.

He took his mail and the delivery up to his suite and opened the envelope first. The return address was from some lawyer's office... Sam Logan, Attorney at Law. This raised his curiosity as Craig didn't know him and he had not been expecting any legal work to do with his business. He could not believe his eyes when he read the contents. There was a document notifying him of an annulment of his marriage to Darla Harrington, nee, Coleman. It had been signed, stamped and notarized. In the accompanying letter, he was put on notice not to try and locate Darla. The letter continued to say that the contents in the smaller envelope were copies and that the original images were safely stored in the lawyer's office, and would be used if he were to force the issue. He opened the envelope, and there was a half dozen or more pictures of him and his friend on the street in front of a not so popular night club. *'Oh My God'* he thought, '*where did these come from?*' He picked up the letter again and began to read.

'An account for Darla has been opened in an undisclosed bank. For the next five years, you will send' he read the amount of money 'to my office, on time and without fail, at which point I shall deposit it into her account. You will be promptly notified of your release from further payments at the conclusion of the five year period. This amount shall be considered as restitution for pain and suffering you have caused during your year of marriage.' The letter went on to dictate, 'You will have absolutely no contact whatsoever with Darla Coleman. She is no longer your legal wife. Any attempt to find and/or contact Darla Coleman shall constitute a breach of the terms of the annulment on your part, at which point further action will be taken to expose your indiscretions.' It was blackmail, but at this point, Craig knew he was not going to win this one.

He began to pace around the apartment. He was sweating profusely, and after rereading the letter, knew what he had to do immediately! He picked up the phone and made a call.

"Holden Montgomery, how may I help you?"

"This is Craig Harrington."

"I'm sorry man, but I have nothing to report yet, it's like this woman does not exist. She doesn't even have a bank account man."

"I'm calling to ask you to stop the investigation, immediately."

"But..."

"I mean now! Don't worry about the retainer, it's yours, just close the file." He hung the phone up in his ear and began to pace again. Holden's words echoed in his ear. *'She doesn't even have a bank account, man.'*

'What the hell have I done?' He was only now beginning to realize what he had put her through. He could have given her everything. If not his love then certainly he could have been more generous with her and bought her a car to use and put money in an account for her to spend. He had put her in an awful position, but it took this for him to figure out what a selfish slug he was. He did not even dare to call her cellphone and apologize for his behavior. He realized that if he did call her, it may apply, to this warning. *'The letter sounds pretty emphatic,'* he thought, and he could not take a chance on being arrested. So he figured he had better not even try. He could not run the risk of these damned pictures going public. He had to do what was expected of him and bow out gracefully for his own

good. Stupidity had, not gotten him this far in life, but he knew that ignorance, arrogance, and selfishness had.

8

Time was passing quickly, and Darla still had not made a definite decision. She had done a lot of thinking about her options but as far as adoption or keeping it was concerned, she was definitely stuck in a rut, and either one made her cringe. She already knew if she raised it alone she would struggle. She did not think that she could pay for an apartment, utilities, and babysitters. *'What would happen if I can't find a job?'* she thought. She did not have a car or a job. How could she feed two people when she did not know how she was going to be able to feed herself. She knew she could skip a few meals if money was tight but she could not allow a child to go hungry. It was looking like adoption was going to be her only alternative, and that made her sick to her stomach just thinking about that. It saddened her and kept her in a funk for days. She wanted nothing more than to raise her love-child that belonged to her and Conner. She loved her baby already, and she had to make sure it was taken care of. He or she deserved a chance at a good life, and if she were to go on her own selfish thoughts, she would only bring her child up in poverty.

Darla spent a lot of time walking around the property, down the path to the water's edge or just sitting on a little park bench that had been there for decades. The water always calmed her and helped her to think in a sane and rational manner. She wanted her child to have some of the fun times at this peaceful place that she had experienced when she was a child. She had nothing but great memories from spending her summers here. She could not remember one single time when there was ever sadness here. Every trip was a blessing, and the freedom that she and Dawn had was something she would never forget. She began to miss her sister and thought maybe she should text her or even call to hear her voice. Then she thought perhaps she should wait since this whole thing would soon be over anyway. There was plenty of time to involve her. But still, she missed her sister, her friend. She realized it felt great not having to look over her shoulder and find Craig standing there. That was a blessing in itself. If she never saw him again, it would be too soon. She would never allow that to ever happen to her again. She may be just a little older now, but she was whole lot wiser. She strolled over to the cabin, Dodger in toe, and just sat out on the front porch and listened to birds chirp, squirrels chatter and the occasional silence. She never went inside. She cupped her eyes and look in the windows, and everything was exactly the same. She loved this cabin and thought it a pity that no one ever lived in it. A waste of a perfectly great spot for someone who preferred a peaceful existence. She made a mental note to ask

Aunt Evie about that. It always was in the back of her mind but was never brought up.

She thought about Connor every second of every day, not having much else to do in her solitude. She was carrying his baby, his and her baby, and she loved this child with all of her heart. He was still very deep inside her heart and soul that she lived and breathed for the day she would see him again. She somehow doubted that would ever happen, but she always lived in hope.

Evelyn left Darla alone as much as she could to give her time to think about her options. She knew that when she was ready, she would come to her. They saw each other at the table but other than that, she noticed that Darla spent a lot of her time walking the property with old Dodger at her side.

Darla sat by the pool, took walks to the cabin and spent time looking out at the water. She began to feel the weight of the baby now, so she did not venture down the steps to the beach anymore because of the long climb back up. She figured it was safer to stay up on the look off.

Evelyn kept a close eye on her for the most part and wanted to be sure that she was safe at all times. Dodger always gave a tug on her sleeve or wherever he could grab with his teeth if he knew she was too close to danger. He loved to walk with her along the paths, and when they got to the cabin, he would find a stick for her to throw. He was not a young dog now, but he could still fetch a stick.

To Evelyn's relief, Darla walked into the den.

"Can we talk Aunt Evie?"

"Yes darling, sit down and tell me what is on your mind."

"Nothing, except my baby." She waddled over to the loveseat and sat on the edge of the cushion.   Her back ached, and she was very tired.

"Have you come to any decisions, my dear? Is that why you're here?"

"Yes, it is. Aunt Evie, I would love nothing more than to keep my baby but I don't think I can, financially. I can't even wrap my head around adoption. Just knowing that I wouldn't be able to see my baby every day is killing me. I can't keep it for selfish reasons, and I can't possibly give it up. I want to keep my baby but how can I?" She broke down at this point and began to cry.

Evelyn went to her and sat down beside her. "There is something I must tell you, now that I know how you truly feel. It sounds as if you would like to raise your child, am I right?" she said, passing her a tissue.

Darla nodded her head and blew her nose.

"Fine then, if that's what you truly want we'll make it happen."

"I can't raise a child, I don't even have a job or a place to live," she sobbed.

"Yes you do, there is so much that you don't know. But I had to wait for you to make your own mind up without any interference for me. Mind you, it hasn't been easy watching you in torment, but this type of decision could only have been made by you."

"What are you talking about Aunt Evie?"

"There is something you must know and now is as good a time as any to tell you."

"It sounds serious." Darla frowned.

"I think it is and I owe you a huge apology.

"An apology? For what? You've been nothing but kind, patient and gracious to me since the night I called you."

"Maybe so Darla but I betrayed your confidence when you first came to me with your dilemma."

"What?" she asked, furrowing her brow.

"I'm so sorry, darling, I know there is no excuse for betrayal, but I had good reasons.

"OK, tell me what you did and also what betrayal are we talking about?"

Evelyn began her confession. "I contacted my lawyer immediately to keep him apprised of all this the first night you arrived and confided in me. I needed him to know so we could protect you from Craig. I instructed him to begin to process an annulment, getting your name changed and flushing you from the system. He contacted Craig months back to inform him of the annulment using copies of the pictures that you gave me as leverage. I had him make provisions for you and your baby. Craig does not know about the baby, but he has been making regular payments into a bank account for you. We'll call it 'pain and suffering' for the year he stole from you. He has agreed to make payments for five years. You did not need to know before now, because I have been providing for you thus far. You will soon be out there on your own again, and his money will give you a nice start.

"Really? Craig agreed to this? ...Craig Harrington?" Darla asked, stunned.

"Yes he did, I have a very good lawyer. It was 'do this or be exposed,' and he doesn't want that. He has agreed not to contact you in any way or try and find you. So, we have him out of your hair for good."

"Wow!" was all she could say to her aunt.

"I knew, from the beginning, that you would not, and could not give up on your baby but I had to let you come to your own conclusions darling. Finally hearing from your lips that you want to raise your baby, I want you to know that you will have the funds with which to do so. The money from Craig would have been there regardless but knowing you wanted the baby even when you were broke, that makes all the difference in the world. In conclusion, I must tell you this, and then I will be done. I have arranged with my lawyer to start a fund for your baby."

"Aunt Evie, I can't..."

Evelyn put her hand up to stop her from saying anything more. "Yes, you can accept it, and you will. It is my gift to your child. Now, I have a condition to put before you, if I may."

"Sure, go ahead," Darla nodded.

"My father's estate has been funding private schools. They are named after him, and I have arranged for your child to attend one of them once he or she turns five years old. One is a school for boys, and the other is for girls. Since we don't know the gender yet, we have it covered. Once you give birth and recuperate here, we can find a house or an apartment for you and the baby. Are you ok with this so far?"

Darla just sat there stupefied. "I... don't know what to say, except, thanks!!! I had no idea about any of this. I've been so torn between either bringing my baby up in poverty or giving him or her a fighting chance with new parents. It has been first and foremost in my thoughts since I've been here. The thought of adoption absolutely broke my heart."

"I'm sure it did, and I can certainly understand why. I couldn't have done it either, but for now, there is no need for you to think about a job or where your next meal will be coming from. The money will be there for you in an account under your new name, Darla Roma. When the time comes, you will have all the necessary papers, bank card and a new birth certificate for your new beginning. It can be here in Kanyon Cove or wherever you choose. I hope you stay around though so I can be a part of my great-great niece or nephew's life. Surely you wouldn't deprive me of that would you?"

"How could I possibly Aunt Evie, I can never leave this town, I love it here. It makes me want to stay even more now knowing that I don't have to be watching over my shoulder waiting for Craig to show up."

"That will never happen my dear. He knows the consequences of his actions so he will stay away, guaranteed."

Darla flinched, and her face sobered. Evelyn caught the look on her face and immediately spoke. 'Is it the baby?"

Darla was trying to catch her breath after the stabbing pain ripped across her tummy. "I think it is; I've been having pains in my back for most of the day, I thought I just needed to rest. That's why I came back to the Manor, and I'm glad I did."

"What! Why didn't you say something, darling! You are in labor! I'll contact the doctor, and he'll meet us at the hospital." She went to the foyer and called for Emma. When Emma appeared, Evelyn asked her to please go up to Darla's room and get her suitcase. Evelyn heard a crash coming from the den, and she ran back to see what was going on. Darla was standing in the middle of the floor, doubled over in pain and standing in a puddle of water. She had reached for something to hang on to, to ride out the pain but she missed, and an ornament tumbled to the floor and broke. Evelyn ran over to her to help her to sit down, but she was in too much pain.

"Oh my Gosh, Aunt Evie, I think the baby is coming! The pain is unbearable! It feels as if the baby is coming." She winced with pain and Emma came running into the den. She looked at the situation at hand and ran out of the room. She returned with several sheets and pillows and spread them out on the floor. "We have to get her to lie down," she said to Evelyn. "Help me to get her down on the sheets and then I will call her doctor and tell him what has happened."

"I think it would be best if we use the chaise lounge, it has no arms, and it will be more comfortable than the floor.

Emma picked the sheets up off the floor, spread them out on the antique lounge and propped the pillows up on the curved end. Emma then began instructing her to move over to the lounge, and they would help her to sit down. We have to do this, and we have to do it now! Are you ready?"

Darla was whimpering softly at this point, and it was plain to see that she was in a great deal of pain. She was giving quick puffs of air to work through the labor pains that were coming fast and furious. She knew she had to get herself to the lounge and she was doubled over with a hand on her back as she slowly scuffed across the floor.

"Yes, I'm ready."

Emma said, "Ok, on the count of three your aunt and I will hold you steady so you can keep your balance as you lower yourself down, do you understand? First, I think it would be easier if we undressed you while you are standing Darla, is that ok with you?"

She was perspiring and all but screaming in pain as Emma removed her footwear and asked permission to remover her clothing from her waist down. At that point, she could not have cared less what she did to her. She just nodded her permission and puffed through another pain. Emma reached up and pulled her slacks and underwear off, and when she stepped out of them, Emma covered her with a sheet.

"Ok, ready?"

Darla backed up until she felt the lounge touch her legs.

"Yes," she said and nodding at the same time.

"Ok, on the count of three, one...two... and three, lower yourself to the lounge, it's directly behind you. Here we go."

She squatted and moved backwards until her bum touched down, with great relief.

"Good girl darling," Evelyn said softly, "now, turn yourself and I'll lift your legs onto the chaise, and we'll help you to lay back."

"Give me a second please Aunt Evie. The pain is so bad!"

"Whenever you're ready, we're here, just breath Darla."

"Ok, I'm ready," she said, and she rolled to one side Emma help to lift her legs up and over onto the chaise. They helped her to lie back onto the pillows. She let out a sigh of relief. "Thank God for small mercies," she said half-jokingly, but it did not last long when another pain gripped her. Evelyn was beside herself, trying to stay calm and not upset Darla any more than she already was. While Emma had been tending to Darla, she had called the doctor and asked him to come as quickly as he could, it was an emergency.

Evelyn was sitting on an ottoman next to Darla, holding her hand. Emma had brought in a basin of water in so Evelyn could keep Darla's forehead cool.

"I'm so scared Aunt Evie, I'm so scared," she whispered.

Evelyn wiped her face and neck with a cool cloth and told her she was there with her and that the doctor would arrive soon. Darla had a hold of Evelyn for dear life and made her promise not to leave her.

"I'm not going anywhere darling, I'm staying right here."

They heard the doorbell, and in unison, they both said, "Thank God!"

Emma ran to answer it and showed the doctor to the den.

"What do we have here, young lady?" Dr. Rayburn asked.

"It's really good to see you and thank you for getting here so fast, it's really bad."

"I'm sure it is, but I have something to help with the pain." He pulled a syringe out and got it ready. "This will relax you Darla, I know you have been in a bit of a panic stage, and this will help."

"What is it exactly? Will it hurt my baby?"

"It's a systemic analgesic, a pain-relieving medicine if you will. It will act on your entire nervous system rather than just a certain part of your body. The pain will be dulled, but will not be eliminated completely. Also, it won't slow down your labor or interfere with contractions. It may cause drowsiness to you and the baby. This will make it easier to cope with labor, and it will help you to relax. So, Darla, are you ready?"

"Yes, I am."

He wiped her arm with an alcohol swab, flicked the syringe a couple of times and slowly injected the needle. Bit by bit she watched it leave the syringe, and she began to relax. She did not know if the injection was working already or if it was the fact that he was here to take over. Either way, she felt better.

9

Darla looked down at the bundle in her arms while tears of love and joy overcame her. "She is so beautiful."

"She certainly is," her aunt agreed, "you did a great job my darling, I'm so proud of you. You did this on your own, you were very brave."

"Liar," she said jokingly, "I was scared to death!"

"Maybe so, but wasn't it worth it?" Evelyn asked.

"She is perfect, Aunt Evie," she said, as the baby curled her fingers around hers as if claiming her mommy.

"Have you thought of a name for her yet?"

"I was thinking Evelyn Grace Roma-Barnes, but I'd like to call her Grace."

It was Evelyn's turn to tear up when she heard the words. "Oh, darling, really?" She had her hand over her mouth so as not to cry aloud, but Darla could see that her lips were trembling.

"Are you ok with it? We can change it if you'd like."

"I think it is perfect, but I never dreamt you'd name her after me! I can't believe it!"

"I love you Aunt Evie, and you have been here for me very step of the way throughout this ordeal, I can't think of a better way to show our appreciation," she said nodding to her bundle.

"May I hold my namesake, please?"

Darla lifted the baby to her aunt and watched as Evelyn struggled to get it right.

"I've never held very many babies and especially one this small! I think it is a wonderful idea to give the baby her father's name. She is so beautiful darling."

"She certainly is Aunt Evie, I can see Connor's features in her too."

"She looks as if she is going to have your blonde hair though," she added.

"Darla smiled and said, "yes, but Connor is blond too."

"Oh, I didn't know that. I wish you had a picture of him." "Yes, me too! But looking at Grace is the same as looking at Connor," she said in a sad voice.

"I'm going to sit just over here and rock her for a few minutes. Why don't you get some rest, I won't leave the room." "That sounds wonderful, thank you Aunt Evie, I am tired." As she dozed off, Evelyn just stared at the bundle in her arms. Just a few hours ago she had watched her being born. "You are a little miracle, Miss Grace. I'm your Aunt Evie, and I promise that I will always take care of you. I may not get to see you grow up, but you my darling will carry my name and my love with you always.

Darla smiled at her tender words as she drifted off to sleep, knowing her daughter was in very good hands.

It had been a while since Darla called or sent her sister a text. Now that this was all over, she was the first one outside of the Manor that she wanted to talk to. She opened her phone and dialed her number.

"Hello?"

"Hi Dawn, how are you?"

"Oh Darla, I'm so happy to hear your voice! It has been ages since your last text, are you alright?"

"Yes, I'm fine, but I would like to see you."

"Yes! Where are you and where would you like to meet?"

"Can you come to me? I am at Aunt Evie's."

"Aunt Evie's? Great, I promised that I wouldn't ask you any questions so, yes and when?"

"Now, would be a great time, if you are free."

"Yes, I am free. I'll be there soon. I can't wait to see you."

Darla did not know why she had not included Dawn in her ordeal, other than to make sure that Craig would not follow her. Now that things were over and done with, she really wanted to see Dawn. She was still recovering from the birth but was getting around by taking things slowly. She had a shower and dressed with care. She was not quite back to her normal size, but Evelyn made sure she was taken care of when it came to clothes. She chose a loose fitting, powder blue floral print dress that came just above the knee, along with a pair of white flats. Her hair had grown over the last months, and it was now a shoulder length. Tying it back in a blue ribbon at the nape of her neck, she went downstairs to wait for Dawn.

Watching from the front window, Darla ran out to greet her when her car pulled up. The two embraced, thrilled to see each other again. Dawn had missed her sister a lot over these long months and was coming to realize just how much.

"It's so good to see you, Dawn. I'm sorry it took me so long to call you."

"Never mind that, I know you must have had a good reason, and I totally understand. I only had a few calls from Craig, and then they stopped completely, which was fine by me," she said, flipping her hand, "because I had nothing to tell him."

"That's partly why I kept you in the dark, so you wouldn't have to lie for me. Anyway come on in, you haven't seen Aunt Evie in ages."

"Yes it has been a few years since we were here together, hasn't it?"

"Dawn!" Evelyn said as she sashayed through the foyer to the door and held her arms out for a hug. "Come in! It's so good to see you again."

They went into the den and sat down as Emma came in with a tray of tea and snacks. She poured them each a cup and left the room. As they sipped tea and chatted, there came a little squeal over the monitor that sat on the table. Dawn jumped slightly at the sound and looked around the room. Just as she opened her mouth to ask what it was, Emma came in with a pink bundle in her arms. Dawn's mouth fell open as Darla got up and went to take the baby from Emma. She whispered 'thanks' to her for bringing the baby in and walked over to Dawn. Dawn stood up with an absolute expression of surprise on her face.

"Dawn, I'd like for you to meet Grace, your niece," she said as she held her out for Dawn to hold.

"Grace? That's Aunt Evie's middle name isn't it?"

"Yes, her legal name is Evelyn Grace." She conveniently left 'Roma-Barnes' off the end because she had not told Dawn anything that has been going on.

"She is beautiful, Darla. Does Craig know? No, wait; it can't be Craig's...?"

"Just relax and acquaint yourself with your niece, I'll explain it all to you in due course."

Just then, old Dodger waddled in to smell Dawn. When he realized who she was, he began to whine in excitement. Evelyn explained that she would soon have to put the ole boy down. He could barely hear, and his eyesight was so bad that he was beginning to bump into anything that was out of place around the house. He knew the house inside and out from memory but got confused when something got in his way. He has been with Evelyn since he was a puppy and he had been a good and faithful companion to her.

Between Darla and Evelyn, they explained just about everything to Dawn. Darla neglected, however, to mention Connor's name as she was not ready to talk about him. Aunt Evie knew about him and obviously her lawyer, whoever he was, and she wanted to leave it at that for the time being. Connor's name was on the birth certificate, and she wanted Grace to have his last name, but it still wasn't something she was ready to share with Dawn.

10

As time passed, life moved forward, and Darla found an apartment for her and Grace. It was close to Dawn, and soon the sisters were back to their old selves again, only there was another girl in their group. They decided to raise Grace together, but Dawn knew when not to interfere. Darla bought a car when she left the Manor, and it allowed her to make frequent visits to see Evelyn.

The years had begun to take a toll on her aunt and Darla was beginning to see more signs of aging, even if it was gracefully. She was still a very attractive woman for her age.

Grace was the light of Evelyn's life, and she adored her great-great niece. She would be turning five soon, and Darla was not looking forward to sending her off to boarding school. She and Evelyn talked about it almost every time she visited. Evelyn had Darla convinced that it was still the very best thing for her daughter. She reminded Darla again that she would be well taken care of. She would get the life experience that every girl needs and deserves. "The best part is my dear, she won't be that far away. Some parents send their children abroad for their education. Can you imagine seeing your child once or twice a year? That's absurd! That's the reason why my father founded these schools in the first place. He wanted me to have the very best education but wanted me close to home. He could not imagine me being that far away from him so, before I turned five years old, he had made arrangements to have a school for girls built so that I could attend when it was completed. He then made arrangements and funded a school for boys. It only made sense to build two. They are very prestigious schools, and I'm happy to know that Grace will be one of their students. I can't even imagine her attending any other school except for the 'Samuel Roma Private School' that he, her great, great," she waved her hand in the air and squinted her eyes while thinking far enough back in the generations .... "great uncle had built." They laughed at her trying to figure out that her father and Darla's grandfather had been brothers.

But still, it saddened Darla to think about not being with her daughter. She had not spent one day away from her since her birth.

"I'd like to change the subject for a bit Aunt Evie if it's OK with you."

"Sure, what's on your mind dear?"

"I've been meaning to ask you about the cabin."

"Of course, what about the cabin?"

"Would you tell me about it, I mean its history, why no one ever lived there, at least that I can remember."

Evelyn was pensive for a few seconds as if she were gathering her thoughts before she spoke. "Shortly after my father acquired The Grand Manor, he had the cabin built. It was built specially for my mother actually, and it became their special place. She was originally a country girl, and she had sacrificed her home, family, and friends when she chose to marry my father. My mother was never comfortable living in a grand house so to give her back her familiar surroundings, he built her the cabin. The cabin is where they went to be alone, to have a few drinks, and just be away from the household staff. Evie chuckled as she went on to explain, "In fact, it seems that the cabin is where I was conceived, and when I finally came along, the only thing that father wanted was to honor my mother Grace, by naming his only child after her."

"Darla's eyes welled up with tears. "And now my Grace is named after your mother."

"Yes, dear she is."

"Why didn't I know this before? I guess I have to familiarize myself with our family tree! I'm sorry for interrupting Aunt Evie, please go on."

Darla listened intently as her aunt went on about the cabin.

"According to my father, even though they had the entire twenty-five room Manor, most of their time was spent down in a four or five room cabin. He loved her more than life itself, and he would have done anything for her. There was a house full of maids and kitchen staff, but at the cabin, she could cook and clean for her husband. She had promised him that she would go to the Manor before she had the baby because he secretly did not want his child to be born in a common cabin. When the time came, she went up to the Manor sounding alarms that it was time to call a midwife. One of the maids had already been instructed to have a room prepared for the occasion. Mother climbed the stairs and prepared herself for the birth of her first child. It was awful for her. Neither a mid-wife nor a doctor had shown up even though they had ample notice to be at the Manor. With the maids' assistance, I, Evelyn Grace had been delivered, cleaned and wrapped before anyone arrived to help her. She had her baby in the company of her staff and had gained a great amount of respect for them, and told them so. Unfortunately, my mother did not survive my birth," Evelyn said sadly.

Now that Grace was at boarding school, Darla had lots of time on her hands. She decided to look for a job but was struggling to find a decent one. There was not much to choose from on the job-line, but she logged into it every day to keep current on what was being posted. She finally saw a job that interested her and applied for it. She hand delivered her resume to the 'Kanyon Cove Book Store/Internet Café.'

A few days later she received a call requesting an interview. The owner was impressed with Darla and interested in hiring her on a three month trial basis. This would give her time to decide whether the book store would be the ideal job for her. She agreed to take the job on whatever terms were offered. She needed something to keep her occupied or at the very least, from going insane.

She loved the job and also the people who wandered in off the street. They were interesting, and some were very curious about books, authors and loved being able to relax and read while having a cup of coffee. The Café was full almost to capacity every day, and the owner gave most of the credit to Darla. She was great at customer service and learned as much as possible about the business, and kept up with current events so she could be helpful when asked her opinion.

Her three-month trial basis was long over, and they asked her to stay, with a raise in pay. Darla felt proud of herself as she knew she had earned this position.

11

From the time he left university, Connor Barnes was a struggling artist. He did not know anyone in his class that was not in the same boat as he was. He had always thought that the 'Struggling Artist' title was just a cliché for those who loved to paint but hated being tied to a nine to five job that they hated. He loved to paint, but his hard work was going nowhere.

His friends teased him unmercifully about being gay. They knew that he was not gay, but he had not dated anyone since they had all taken the trip to Kanyon Cove on a seminar a few years ago. He put all his time into painting, and he would join them now and then for a beer, but he would not go bar hopping, girl chasing or clubbing. He had absolutely no interest in any of it. He had met and fell in love with the woman of his dreams and lost her as fast as he had found her. His heart still ached for her, and he thought about her and missed her every day. Every blonde haired woman he saw made his heart stop beating until he realized it was not Darla. He wondered every day where she was, how she was and if she had moved on with or without Craig, and forgot about him. He could have told her a thing or two about her husband, but it was not his business. He was sure that Darla would eventually see through Craig and get the hell away from him. He had heard rumors back in college about him hitting on a few of their classmates but chalked it up as just that... rumors. He had never gotten those vibes from him, but he knew something was up when Darla told him that she and Craig had been married for a year, yet it was he who had taken her virginity. There was something wrong with that picture! There would not be a man alive who would not give her a second look.

He had not been back to Kanyon Cove since they first met and shared that precious time together but he was sure that she would have moved away by now. Since he had not heard from her, he felt that she did not want to continue with their affair and he had to let it go. He did not live that far from Kanyon Cove, but circumstances beyond his control may take him back there.

He still had a few dollars in his 'college fund' so when he saw a sign for a loft to sublet he decided to check it out. It was on the outskirts of Kanyon Cove, and he liked what he saw. He was told the lease was for eighteen more months so, with a few mental calculations, he figured if he was careful with what money he had left, he could afford the rent. If things worked out as he hoped, perhaps he would have a few paintings sold by then to off-set the rent, and maybe he could eat as well. If not, then he was screwed. He would definitely have to consider closing up shop and go job hunting. Even the mere thought of it made him shiver.

He hated to even think about not being able to paint but he also had to consider providing for himself, and he did not like the thoughts of starving to death either. Until then though, the loft would provide him a place to live and paint, so he had months down the road to get a collection together for a gallery display.

He spent hours in his studio catching the morning light and moving around with the sun as it moved from window to window. He was doing what he absolutely loved; there was nothing else like it... well, almost nothing. There were those passionate encounters with Darla he would love to revisit. He could not get her out of his mind no matter how hard he tried or how many hours he stood at his easel. He just had to close his eyes, and he could see her before him as he envisioned her naked body. He could still feel her next to him as they made love and as they held each other afterwards. He still remembered how her hair felt wrapped around his fingers as he kissed her. He clenched his fist, and it was as if he could still feel it; he shook his head and began to focus on his work. *'Darla, where are you, after all this time?'* he thought. Memories of her still haunted him, made him half-crazy at times and still made his heart race.

He had painted the perfect likeness of her from memory. He did not have a picture of her, but he had a great imagination along with a good memory and every line, every detail was done with loving strokes. When the painting was finished and dried, he had it framed and hung it on the wall for inspiration. He would never love anyone like that again, and he knew that she was irreplaceable, so he did not try.

Over the next year and a half, he worked on several pieces. He advertised his work in a local newspaper, his website and on a Kijiji site. He had lots of interested parties, but it seemed it was not what they were looking for at the moment. He was disappointed, but not discouraged, so he kept at it.

The count down to the lease was looming, and he still had not sold any of his paintings. He placed more ads and resorted to spending close to all his remaining funds on flyers to mail out in home delivery in the area.

The day came. With a saddened heart and a busted ego, he began to pack up his art supplies, easels, and belongings. He was nearly broke. He had no idea where he was going, but he guessed it would be away from Kanyon Cove. He was not looking forward to living in his truck either, but it looked as if he had no choice until he could find a regular job and right now he was desperate.

12

Evelyn arrived home from the veterinarian finding it empty to not have old Dodger make his way to the foyer to greet her. It broke her heart when she had to have him put down, but it was something that needed to be done. He had been with her for almost twenty years, and she figured she was lucky to have had him that long.

She had sent Darla and Dawn each an email explaining that it was time to have old Dodger put down. She told them it was best if they remembered him as he was and asked them not to come out to the Manor to say their good byes.

They both replied that they were broken-hearted but also knew it was time. They wished her good luck and sent their love and support. That was enough for Evelyn.

The veterinarian, whom she took him to, reminded her that Dodger's first family was still breeding and that the owners had new puppies. Not from the same mother, of course, but from another one from Dodger's lineage. He asked if she was interested in one and passed her a card for the kennel. She was a bit surprised that it was still at the same location as where she had gotten Dodger from.

She sat with him while the vet injected him. He licked her hand as she patted him and she knew he was thanking her for the good life she had given him and also that he knew that she loved him. He slowly closed his eyes as his heart stopped and the vet left her alone with him for a few minutes.

It was difficult for her to leave him there but she had made arrangements for cremation and for his ashes to be delivered to her. She already knew the spot where he was to be buried. It only took a few days when a delivery truck pulled up. When she answered the door, a man passed her a clipboard for her signature. He handed her a box containing Dodgers ashes, and she placed them on her mantle for the time being.

It had taken her several weeks to decide to go to the kennel to take a look at the puppies. As soon as she got out of her car, she could hear the familiar yips when someone was near. It was a sound that she missed and excitement began to build inside her as she became anxious to see them.

The kennel owners greeted her as she walked toward them. They introduced themselves and chatted for a few minutes to give the puppies time to settle down. When they walked inside with her to see them, Evelyn's heart swelled up. The very first dog to waddle up to her was the spitting image of Dodger. She was certain it was Dodger's puppy. Knowing full well it was impossible, she began to see how strong his bloodline really was.

"This one," she said, bending down to pet the puppy, "I'll take this one."

"Really? But you've only seen one!" the owner said.

"Yes, I know, but this is the one. Is it male or female?"

"It's a male."

"Perfect! May I take him today?"

"You certainly may, all we need is a bit of information, and we are good to go! We provide you with a collar, leash, food bowls and a bag of food."

"That won't be necessary; I have all I need at home. Give it to someone who may need it. I brought my own leash and collar as well, but thanks. May I put them on him?"

The owners looked at each other in complete surprise, smiled and just nodded their heads as they watched her. Evelyn, as old as she was, got down on her knees and the puppy sat in front of her as if he knew her. She opened her handbag and got a small collar out. She let him sniff it, and when he did, he seemed to know whose it was. He just sat there while she buckled it around his neck. When she finished, she brought out the leash and connected it. When the dog heard the clasp snap, he stood up. The owners where amazed at the connection the two had already made. The puppy smelled the leash and its familiar scent and accepted it as his own. Evelyn reached her hand up for the male owner to help her up, thanked him and walked into the office, dog in toe.

Evelyn answered all the questions to their satisfaction, and she wrote out a cheque. They accepted it and wished her luck with her new friend.

"By the way," the owner asked, "do you have a name for him?"

"Yes, I do" she replied. "His name is Dodger."

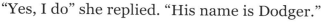

Months after she brought Dodger home, Evelyn planned a trip abroad. She figured it would likely be her last trip, so she wanted to make it a special one. She called her travel agent and explained what she wanted and asked them to call her when they had something that would interest her. Several days later she got a call from the agency, and she accepted what was brought before her. She made a call to the local boarding kennel and took Dodger there.

Before she left on her vacation, she drove into town and had a visit with Sam. He was pleased to see her but was painfully aware that she should not be taking this trip. He noticed that she was wearing down and although she was still quite striking, there was something wrong.

She asked him if all her papers were in order and also if her last requests about her nieces were taken care of. He assured her that everything was done to the letter and that she should enjoy her trip worry free. He advised her to get some rest and sunshine while she was away. They made dinner plans upon her return. He kissed both her cheeks, hugged her tightly and showed her to the door.

Before she left, she had sent Emma off on a vacation too. Since she was nearly Evelyn's age, she felt that she had been loyal enough to her over the years and thought that she should offer her the retirement package that Sam had been instructed to draw up for her. She would give her the option to stay or go.

A few weeks later, Evelyn arrived home from her trip and discovered that her mail had not been put on hold at the local post office as per her request, but had been delivered instead. When she opened her front door, her foyer was strewn with pieces of mail. Evelyn set her suitcases aside and stooped down to gather up the many pieces of accumulated envelopes and flyers. She had a bunch stuffed into one hand that she had to take into the den and then come back out for the rest. One particular flyer caught her eye. She read it with curiosity and immediately recognized the name. She had no choice but to go and check it out.

He had the last of his belongings in the back of his truck and was tying down the last corner of the tarp to protect his artwork from the elements when he heard a car pull into the driveway.

'Probably someone lost and looking for direction,' he thought.

A Rolls Royce pulled up with a woman driver. She unbuckled her seatbelt, turned slightly and picked up a sheet of paper from the passenger seat. Conner watched as she stepped out of the car. He looked her up and down from behind his sunglasses and noticed she was still quite attractive and guessed her to be in her late sixties. What did he know; he was not good at guessing ages anyway.

He recognized his flyer in her hand as she approached him.

"Mr. Barnes?"

"Yes, I'm Conner Barnes, how can I help you?"

"I just returned from an extended trip, and I found this circular among my pieces of mail. I'd like to see your paintings. I hope I am not too late."

"I'm afraid I can't do that right now, Ms....?"

"Roma," she said, "Evelyn Roma," she offered him her hand.

He extended his hand and said, "It's very nice to meet you, Ms. Roma."

"I don't understand why you aren't showing your work Mr. Barnes, why the advertisement if there is no show?" She held up his flyer in protest.

"Honestly Ms. Roma, those flyers are weeks old. I've run out of time, and I'm just about to leave town." He tapped the tailgate of his truck and continued, "I'm packed up and ready to go, you just caught me tying up the loose end, so to speak."

"If you don't mind me asking, why are you leaving?"

He laughed at her question and thought she was a bit too inquisitive. But he indulged her and gave her an honest answer. *'Why not?'* he thought, *'I won't see her again.'*

"Mr. Barnes, I asked you a question."

"Yes, you did, and you deserve an answer." He smiled at her and nodded his head to the side, "come inside and sit down."

She followed him inside the huge building. He removed his sunglasses and showed her to a chair and helped her to sit down.

Once she got a good look at him without sunglasses, she knew instantly.

'*My word!*' she thought, '*there is no doubt what so ever that this man is Grace's father. This Connor Barnes is indeed one in the same.*'

He noticed a change in her facial expression, but he smiled again as he sat across from her. "Ms. Roma, this place," he said pointing around the vast space, "has been my home for the last eighteen months. The lease is up, I haven't sold a painting since I moved in and now I have to find a job so I can live somewhere besides in the cab of my truck. What bit of money I have left, I need it to feed myself. So how is that for a struggling, starving artist's story? Contrary to popular belief, it is not every artist's dream to be homeless and broke, and it certainly isn't mine either. Never mind having to look for a job that I will likely hate while the work I do love will end up in a storage locker while hunting down my next meal. So that Ms. Roma, is why I am leaving town."

She pierced her eyes at him and asked another question. "What kind of 'job' are you looking for Mr. Barnes?" she asked, her fingers accented "job" in quotations.

Before he answered, he ran his hand over his face and back up across his hair, gave his head a scratch and winced. "I'm not sure, I've always been an artist, you know, so I don't really know what else I can do or what I am good at, but I am going to have to find out now, aren't I."

"Perhaps I can help you Mr. Barnes."

"Oh? And how is that?"

"If I can provide you with a place to live in exchange for your services, would you consider staying in Kanyon Cove?"

"Well, just what exactly do you mean by 'services' Ms. Roma?" He made a clucking sound as he cocked his head to one side as if to tease the lady.

"Oh my God!" she blushed, "I'm so sorry, that came out wrong!"

He laughed and waited for her to explain.

She could not help but giggle at the mistake she made, but she pulled herself together and continued with her proposition. "I own The Grand Manor just on the outskirts of Kanyon Cove. It is a very large estate, and I am currently alone. Since my housekeeper accepted her retirement package, it is becoming increasingly difficult for me to keep up with everything that needs to be done. I mean the lawns, gardens, pool maintenance, and all-around grounds keeping. Not that she or I was very good at that sort of thing." There is a cabin on the property that is suitable for a single guy, like yourself," she continued, opening her hands up to indicate him. "I'm only assuming you are single since you live in a loft," she waved her hand around and smiled. "I'm not trying to be pretentious, Mr. Barnes I'm trying to be helpful, so how does that sound so far?"

"It sounds good, but a cabin hardly leaves me room to set up a place to paint."

"Don't you worry about that Mr. Barnes; I have a solution for that as well. There will be a steady pay cheque along with free rent, and you'll be in total charge of the grounds. There will be no 'list of things to do' or a schedule to keep. You will familiarize yourself with the property, and what needs to be done, it will be up to you to take the initiative and do it without my direction or interference. I just don't want to have to think about that part of estate anymore, if you know what I mean. Do we have a deal Mr. Barnes?"

This conversation sounds like a scene from the movie, 'African Queen,' where Katherine Hepburn kept referring to her costar, Humphrey Bogart, as Mr. Allnut throughout the entire movie.' Conner thought; as he listened to her describe his duties.

He looked at her for several seconds, and she cocked an eyebrow expecting an answer. He held out his hand and said, "I believe we do Ms. Roma."

"Evelyn," she said. "Call me Evelyn."

"I'm Connor."

"Yes, I know who you are, Connor Barnes."

He looked at her, squinted his eyes and wondered why this petite, blonde stranger looked vaguely familiar.

"Would you like to follow along behind me and I'll show you to your new residence?"

"Lead the way," he said as he put his sunglasses back on. He followed her to her car, opened the door for her and went back and closed and locked the loft one last time. She waited until he was certain the loft was securely locked before she spoke again. "By the way Connor Barnes, I'd like to have a look at those paintings once you get them unpacked."

He gave her a pretend salute, got into his truck and followed her as she drove slowly out of the driveway.

Conner could not believe his eyes or his luck as he pulled up to the gate behind the Rolls Royce. He saw her raise her hand and the gate opened. He drove up the winding lane behind her and rounded the corner to the front of the house. "What the...?"

Evelyn got out of her car and motioned for him to get out of his truck. He stepped out and closed the door.

"You have got to be kidding me!" he said.

"Well, I did warn you that it is a large property."

"It's beautiful!"

"Thank you, Conner, it's lovely, but if it doesn't get the TLC it needs, it won't be. I'm going to ask you to take a look around," she said, digging into the bottom of her handbag. "Here, take these, they are keys to the pool house, tool and maintenance shed, and this one with the red on it is for the cabin. Come back to the house when you are finished, and we will have a beverage, and I'll make a sandwich for you. The cabin is down there," she pointed. "Why don't you start there? The path is around the back, go past the pool and follow the stone walkway."

He nodded his head, took the keys that she offered and told her he would be back. He followed her directions and went around the Manor where he saw the pool. Opening the gate, he entered into another world that he could never have imagined, let alone being offered to live and work here. No one would have guessed this area was here from looking at the front of the house.

The in-ground pool was enormous with blue-green tiles along the sides and white tiles on the bottom with different patterns including an impression of a huge turtle in the center. Wooden decking surrounded most of the back-yard pool where off to the left was a huge gazebo, a table, and six chairs. Out on the landing in full sunshine, were loungers and beverage tables under umbrellas. Attached to the pool house was a remote controlled, fifteen foot wide canopy that expanded ten feet out for more shade. It was aqua in color and matched perfectly to the colors in the pool.

All along the edge of the property beyond the pool area, there were plant beds, flowering shrubs, and trees of every description. It was well laid out but had not been properly cared for except for what was closest to the house. He figured that was all that Evelyn was capable of managing for the size of the gardens. Looking around, he quickly assessed that nothing could be done overnight to return the property to its beautiful state. He continued on, doing a little gardening in his mind as he calculated how long it would take.   Continuing down the path, he came across the tool shed. He found the right key, unlocked it and looked inside to find everything imaginable including the biggest, bad-ass lawn tractor that he had ever seen. *'Riding this machine will get the lawns done in no time,'* he thought. He walked around and picked up a few tools, made some mental notes and left.

Behind the shed was the stone path that Evelyn had mentioned. He followed the path that did indeed lead to a cabin. "She wasn't kidding when she said there was a cabin! This is a genuine log cabin, the real deal!" he said, even though he was alone. I've been alone way too long," he muttered to himself for the umpteenth time. He no more than got the words out of his mouth when something wet and cool gently touched his hand.

He looked down, and there sat a beautiful dog with the most beautiful eyes. Conner knelt down on the grass and stuck out his hand, and a paw went into it immediately. "Well hey there fella, and who are you? Are you lost?" The dog shook his fur, and he heard dog tags rattle. He felt around the dog's neck and found a tag, and on it, he read 'Dodger.' He flipped it over and on the back was an address. He frowned for a few seconds and then smiled at the dog. "You're not lost, you live here too! Hey Dodger, I'm Conner." Dodger offered his paw again as if he understood every word that Conner spoke. "Pleased to make your acquaintance Dodger." Dodger went a few feet away and came back with a stick and dropped it at his feet.

"Are you serious? You want me to throw this for you?"

He gave a gentle 'woof' in acknowledgement.

Conner picked up the stick and tossed it gently a few feet away. Dodger trotted off to get it and brought it back and barked with more authority this time.

"OK buddy, you're on!" Conner picked up the stick and hurled it across the lawn. Dodger's toenails spun the grass up as he ran across the lawn full out. Conner stood there shaking his head and smiled as he watched him gallop back and lay the stick at his feet again. "Good boy!" he said as he patted his head and scratched his neck. "Let's go inside and have a look around, OK Dodger?"

"Woof," was the reply.

He searched for the red tipped key on the ring, slipped it into the lock and opened the door. After stepping inside, he just stood there and looked around. He was trying to take in the beauty of this magnificent cabin. He figured when she said 'cabin' she meant a guest house or bunk house at best, but this, this is perfect. He just stood there in amazement looking around the room. To his left was a floor to ceiling beach rock fireplace taking up most of the wall. On one side of the hearth was an old brass log holder and on the other, a matching set of brass fireplace tools. Straight ahead of him across the room, he could see part of a kitchen. There was a door way on the left, and one on the right side that lead to a small dining area, completing a circle. In the middle of the living room, in front of the fireplace, was a huge comfy looking leather couch and glass top coffee table. To the left sat the matching leather chair at an angle facing the hearth. To his right was a dining table. Between the couch and dining area, a large winding staircase rose to a bedroom loft. As he stood in the doorway taking in the details of the room, he looked up at the railing that spanned the width of the wall in front of the kitchen. He took a step inside and made his way to the loft. He climbed the staircase as

Dodger waited by the door. When he got to the top, he saw a mattress that had been placed on its side against the wall. He smiled as he took a close look at the pictures, paintings, and drawings that filed the walls. "These are kid's drawings," he said aloud. Moving along his stomach took a flip when he read the names on the bottom of several of the works. 'Darla Coleman, Dawn Coleman... no way. Darla Coleman... it can't be, it just can't be. Na, it's just a coincidence.' He tried to shake it off but just couldn't shake the feeling in the pit of his stomach. He looked at the signatures again and shook his head as he headed down the steps. 'Too strange for my liking,' he grumbled. With his mind still focused on the art work, he totally missed the detail in the kitchen as he wandered through another door. He suddenly realized he was in a bathroom where there was everything he would ever need. He noticed a door off the kitchen and thinking it was a back entry he opened it just to check out the size. "Whoa!" he said aloud. "Would you take a look at this!" He was looking out at a lanai type sun room that was attached to the outside kitchen wall. It ran the entire length of the cabin, was glassed in on all three sides with full screens for summer breezes. It was fully furnished with two matching, beige leather loveseats on either side of a coffee table. At the other end was a glass top dining table with four rattan chairs, perfect for evening dining. Up along the wall was another floor to ceiling fireplace that sat between the living and dining area. There was a huge white rug near the hearth and two white, over stuffed leather chairs in front of the fireplace. He could not help but wonder who had benefited from this romantic setting. Satisfied with what he saw, he made his way back through the cabin, hesitated at the front door and looked up at the loft. Thoughts of the drawings and the artists' names played on his mind. He tried to shake it off as he left and went back up the path to the main house. He knocked on the front door and waited with Dodger by his side. Evie opened the door and ushered them inside.

"I see you've met Dodger, he's a lovely boy."

"Yes, he is and full of energy too."

"He is. I've only had him for a short while, but he fit right in as soon as we met. I suppose he found a stick for you to toss?"

"Yes he did," he laughed.

"He seems to need to run off some pent up energy every now and then." She petted the dog lovingly. "His ancestor was part of the family for nearly twenty years, and he was quite fond of my nieces. His name was Dodger. This young one looks identical to the old boy, so he is Dodger as well.

"Your nieces? Would they be Darla and Dawn?"

His questions startled her momentarily and she swallowed before she spoke. "Yes, that's correct, do you know them?"

"No, I don't know them, but I saw childhood art work on the walls of the loft and thought they might be family. I have known only one other person named Darla, but it would be purely coincidental at best to be the same person."

Evelyn saw him flinch, as if in pain as he spoke her name. "Who is this Darla that you speak of if you don't mind me asking?"

He looked at her, and she could see that he was upset even at the mention of her name. He cleared his throat and tried to talk, but he had to swallow the lump in his throat. Speaking her name was not something he was used to doing and to hear it spoken aloud only made him miss her more. 'She's...er..." he put his hand up to his mouth to clear his throat, "someone very special to me."

Evelyn knew enough to let it go and changed the subject.

So, what do you think? Still interested?"

"In Darla?"

"Connor, what do you think about the job I offered you?"

"Oh, sorry, I guess I'm a little rattled. I think this place is amazing except for one thing."

"And what might that be?"

"The cabin is beautiful by the way, and I love it already, but I didn't see a place to set a studio."

"Oh that," she said with a wave of her hand, "follow me."

They went up the front staircase and across the hall and up another flight of stairs to the third floor. Evelyn opened a door and went directly down the hall through another. "There you go; you have two lofts here to choose from. Look around and decide on one." She waved her hand at one room and then the other.

"Seriously?" he asked.

She nodded her head once.

He stepped into the second door since they were standing in front of it. He admired the skylights and thought it would provide perfect light for him to paint. "Well, this is perfect, but I'd like to see the other one as well before I make up my mind."

She stepped aside to let him pass and followed him back down the hall to the first room. She just watched and held her breath as he looked around.

"I don't think I will need anything with hardwood floors and mirrors," he said, 'so, the one down the hall will be great." He thought he heard a sigh of relief escape her lungs. "Don't you think it will be awkward for me to just come up here and do my thing? I paint at all hours of the day and night you know, whenever the urge strikes me, and I wouldn't want to disturb you."

"I have that covered already. Come with me."

He followed her a few feet down the hall, and she opened another door that led down a back stairwell. She began the descent down the first staircase, across the hall, and down the last staircase to the bottom floor. All he saw was a wall and a back door and nothing else. There were no doors leading into the main house, at least none that he could see.

"You will have complete privacy here. You can use this back door to go to your loft anytime of the day or night, and you won't disturb me. Do we have a deal?" She smiled smugly, knowing full well that she had met all of his wishes and expectations to his satisfaction

"We sure do!" he beamed.

"Good enough then, I'll leave you to unpack that truck of yours. There might be a few cobwebs in the cabin though; it hasn't been used since my nieces where here last."

"That's not a problem at all Evelyn."

"How do I get my truck around back to unload the painting?"

"Go back out the main gate, and the first driveway on your right will take you to the back of the property. Here is a fob for the main gate to keep in your truck and you will find a good size dolly in the shed to move your paintings across the deck to the back entrance. On the key ring that I gave you earlier, there is a green key next to the red one. That one will get you in the back door. Just remember to keep it locked at all times whether you are inside or outside, please."

"That will not be a problem, Evelyn."

"Thanks."

"Thank you, for trusting me."

She gave him that nod again and said, ""Here are the keys to the back door and loft. I'll leave you to unpack and look forward to seeing your work soon."

Are you okay here to get back to the inside of the house? There are no doors leading back in," he said looking around the large entrance.

"Don't worry about me. Go on and get your stuff and when you are finished, we'll have dinner."

"Right then, I'm off," he said, as he opened the back door and disappeared.

When she was sure he was gone, she locked the door, cranked the lever under the steps, waited for the wall to open and went inside. She pulled the lever under the piano leg, and the wall closed, then went to the kitchen to prepare supper.

13

Connor Barnes is blond, handsome, and ruggedly built. His employer has graciously given him permission to set up a studio in one of the gorgeous lofts at The Grand Manor. It had possibly been part of the servants' quarters back in the day, and now that he had chosen which loft he wanted, he began to carry his boxes up to the third floor.

As he walked by, he admired the other loft but felt it was more than he would need. He wondered if anyone would ever benefit from such a spacious area; it had so much potential. He had chosen the room with a rougher, not so polished floor because of his work. Besides, the room he chose was perfect with the huge skylights which let in lots of natural light, which he needed for his work. Plenty of the outside streamed in from the abundance of large windows that filled the walls. He was very thankful to his landlord for giving him this opportunity. Free rent at the cabin plus a pay cheque, in lieu of odd jobs around the property, running errands, a bit of gardening and as far as he was concerned he thought she would enjoy having someone on the property.

Once he had all his art supplies and paintings up the back stairs, he began to organize his space. He had lots of space in the other loft he had leased, but this was something else! It was perfect!

The first painting he unpacked was the one he had done of Darla a few years back. He opened the legs of an easel and placed it towards the back wall. He put the painting on the ledge so the light from the front window would catch it. He stood back with his fingers wrapped around his chin in thought. *'This is a perfect spot for you my love,'* he said, as he walked over to it and touched the face on the canvas.

It did not take him long to get organized. He was used to dragging his stuff around, and as long as he had it all close to him, he did not really care how perfectly positioned it was. His cans of paint were on the floor; his brushes were handles down in a wide necked ceramic jar, the paintings were leaning against the wall. Several unfinished works were perched on easels while his palettes, knives and paint rags were on a table close by. He stood back, admired what he had accomplished and decided to go downstairs and have supper with Evelyn, having finished for the day.

After he ate, it was still early and cool enough to mow grass, so he made his way to the maintenance shed. He took the mower out of gear and rolled it down the ramp onto the grass. *'From now on this puppy will be backed into the shed,'* he thought.

After checking the fluid levels, he turned the key in the ignition and started it up.

Dodger bounded around the corner when he heard the mower start up. He chased it around for a little bit until Connor clued in to what he wanted. He stopped the mower, and Dodger jumped on and sat with him until they were finished. It was a breeze since he was driving a zero-radius- turn model with a 50-inch cutting deck. To make it even easier, it mulched and bagged everything up. It was so efficient that there was very little left to trim. He finished the entire grounds in less than two hours and still had lots of daylight left. He cleaned and hosed the tractor down then backed it into the maintenance shed. "Now, it's my turn to clean up," he said to Dodger. "Want to come with me to the cabin?" he asked. Dodger nearly turned himself inside out at the invitation. As they walked down the path, Connor kept throwing a stick, and Dodger kept fetching and dropping it at Connor's feet to be tossed again. They were very good companions. Dodger followed him inside and laid down by the door. Connor got a drink of water for him then went off to have a shower.

"It's time for me to go into town and get a few groceries for this place. Come on and walk me back to the house." They did their usual of toss and fetch back up to the Manor. Connor walked to his truck, and Dodger nearly went crazy. He barked so loud that Evelyn came to the front door to see what was going on.

"What's up, Dodger?" she asked.

"I think he wants to come into town with me, I'm going for a few groceries. Is it ok to take him?"

"Sure it is, just be sure he has ventilation while you're out of the truck."

"No problem then," he said as he opened his truck door, "get in Dodger."

Evelyn watched and smiled as they drove down the lane knowing her dog was in good hands.

Darla was busy in the bookstore. There were so many customers wanting her attention and advice she hardly had time for a break. Finally, a helper came along and insisted she escape for a bit. She poured herself a cup of coffee and went to sit at a table by the window. She checked her phone for messages and found a couple from Dawn and several from Grace. She answered Grace's immediately knowing she had only certain times to use her cell phone and then called Dawn. As they chatted, Darla was gazing out the window at nothing in particular when she saw a dog's head sticking out the passenger window of a passing truck.

"What the hell?" she half whispered, but Dawn heard it.

"What? Dawn asked."

"You aren't going to believe this, but I just saw a dog that looks exactly like Dodger! I just caught a glimpse as a truck passed. This dog had his head out the side window. It just gave me the creeps since it wasn't that long ago that Aunt Evelyn had Dodger put down."

"That's weird, but poor old Dodger was around for a long time," Dawn added.

"Maybe I'm just over tired or something," Darla said, "I have to get back to work anyway, we'll chat soon. Come for dinner on Saturday."

"Sounds good!"

Darla had a weird feeling about the dog. *'Was it an omen, maybe?'* she thought. *'I suppose it's time I give Aunt Evelyn a call.'*

She could not help herself as she opened her phone and sent Evelyn a text. *'Aunt Evie, I saw a dog today that looks exactly like Dodger, and it's creeping me out. Maybe I should have come to the Manor to say good bye to him when I had the chance.'*

Evelyn's phone was in her handbag, so she did not hear the beep of the incoming text.

14

Connor invited Evelyn up to his loft as she had asked. She saw several pieces that interested her and offered to buy them. She particularly adored the painting of Darla that sat alone at the opposite side of the room. She commented on it and asked if it was for sale. She knew it would not be, but she asked anyway knowing it would be perfect hanging in the other loft.

"No, I'm sorry, that one is not for sale."

"I see, how about all these other ones then?" she asked.

"Any of the others are for sale."

"I'll take this one," she pointed, "and this one. And I would like for you to hang them for me, please, in the living room downstairs. I have a painting over my safe at the moment, and I'd like to replace it with this one, and I'll show you where to hang the other one. If that is alright with you, I will go and prepare a cheque for you."

"Great! I'll be down shortly with your purchases, thank you."

"You're very welcome; see you downstairs."

When Connor finished hanging her paintings, she asked him if he would do her another favor. "I have the ashes of my dog on the mantle, and I would like it if you would bury them. Could you do that for me please?"

'Sure, you just have to tell me where," he said.

"Have you ever noticed the burial grounds some distance behind the cabin? It has a chain-link fence around it."

"Would that be the one with the head stones," he teased and cocked his head to one side and grinned at her.

She was quick to jab him in the arm and laugh with him. "Yes, my dear Connor that would be the one. I would like to have old Dodger buried in that plot with the rest of our family. He always loved being around the cabin when my nieces visited, and he often wandered down there by himself even though they weren't there."

"I'll get it done now if that's alright with you," he asked.

"That would be great Connor and thank you so much. Come with me."

He followed her to the den, and she took the container off the mantle and handed it to him.

"If it's Ok, I'll make a cross to put with the ashes."

"I would appreciate that very much, thank you."

A few days later she made her way down the path to the grounds behind the cabin. The first thing she noticed was that Connor had the grounds perfectly manicured. Then she saw the freshly turned earth and the white cross with Dodger's name painted in black. She finally felt as though she had put him to rest.

Connor saw from the cabin that she was standing at the site, so he went out to say hello.

"Does it meet with your approval?" he said smiling at her.

"Yes it does, it's a great job, thank you again." She looked at him as if she wanted to say something, so he helped her along.

"Go on, say what you're thinking," he coaxed playfully.

"Alright Connor, I will. Walk with me dear," she said taking his arm as she led him to the large head stone. "This is my father, the great Samuel Roma and next to him is my mother. I don't remember her at all, but he wanted to be buried beside her. One of these days my ashes will be delivered here."

"I am asking if you would do me the honor of burying my urn in my father's plot, with him. He was my world for a lot of years, and I was his, and it only seems fitting that I be buried close to his heart. Will you do that for me?"

Connor felt sick to think about what she was saying and to think that someday she would not be here.

He folded her up in his arms as he choked back tears. She felt his chest lurch as he stifled a sob and she rubbed and patted his back. He grew to love this woman so much and now she was asking him to bury her. She pulled away to look at him, and he rubbed a fore finger and thumb across his eyes and brought himself under control. "I will Evelyn. For you, I will do anything."

"I'll hold you to that Connor."

He noticed that she had an envelope in her hand but did not want to be too inquisitive, so he waited for her to mention it. *'Maybe it was none of my business,'* he thought.

"Connor," she began, holding the envelope up, "I had these papers drawn up for you shortly after you moved here. This gives you full rights to the cabin for as long as you live here. It means that if you want to remain here as grounds keeper, this cabin is your home until you choose to do otherwise. Once you decide to move, then this becomes null and void," she said holding the envelope up again and passing it to him. "Read these pages at your discretion and then put them in a safe place. Did you know there is a safe in there?" she asked pointing toward the cabin.

"No, I didn't notice one, where is it?"

"Come with me, and I will show you," she said taking his arm again.

They went into the cabin, and she walked over to the side of the fireplace. She pulled a false piece of rock from the fireplace and behind it was a safe. She punched in a few numbers and opened it up. "There," she said, "the numbers are 8 4 9 7. It will come in handy if you want to keep certain items, like those in your envelope, safe."

"Well I'll be damned," he said. They both laughed, and she asked if he would walk with her back to the Manor. He offered her his arm and they, along with Dodger, headed back up the path.

The more time Evelyn spent with Connor, the more she understood why her niece had loved him so much. He was a great man.

15

Evelyn's health was weighing heavy on her mind. She felt tired all the time and felt it was time she saw the doctor. She made the call, got an appointment and waited for the date to arrive. Realizing that age was not necessarily kind to everyone, she took every day as a blessing.

In the meanwhile, she thought about calling Darla and telling her about Connor, but something always got in the way.

He had been with her now for almost a year and knew that she could not live there without him on the property. She depended on him more and more without realizing it. He was a Godsend to her, and she felt safe with him so close. He came in every day to check on her to make sure she was alright. He too had noticed that she had failed a bit just since he moved there.

Evelyn drove herself to her appointment in Lando County. Dr. Rayburn was the same doctor she had for years and the same one who had delivered her namesake, Grace Roma. The doctor was quick to ask her how she was feeling when he saw her. She was honest and told him exactly how she felt; tired, listless and just generally awful most of the time. He took her blood pressure and told her it was rather on the low side and gave her a requisition for blood work.

'Do I have reason for concern?"

"Your blood seems to be low but let's wait until the results are in before we jump to conclusions,"

It did not make her feel any better hearing those words, but she had to accept the fact that whatever the result revealed, she had had a great life.

Only a few days had passed when she got a call from the doctor's office asking that she come in for her results. She did not expect to hear anything for a few weeks, so this gave her cause to worry a little bit. Especially since the receptionist gave her an appointment for the next morning. This filled her mind with all sorts of scary thoughts, and it consumed her mind. It took a lot out of her, so she went to bed earlier than usual. Getting up early for the appointment, she was already tired out due to the fitful night's sleep she had gone through. She forced herself to eat a slice of toast with a cup of tea before heading over to Lando.

"They have done very extensive testing of the blood work, and I'm afraid it isn't good news Evelyn," Dr. Rayburn said, flipping through sheets of paper. Her heart almost stopped. She thought she had herself prepared for anything, but she surely did not like the sound of his voice."

"Ok, what are we looking at here?" she asked, pressing her lips together."

"As you remember, your father was a patient of my father's, and when I learned of your blood tests, I pulled his files to do a comparison. It seems as if we are looking at late stage leukemia, my dear. You've inherited this from you father Evelyn, it's the same thing that he died from."

Evelyn seemed unusually calm now that she had answers and she listened to every word.

"We did not know much about it back then, but over the last several decades we've learned more about this disease. The symptoms that you've described to me usually only show up at the very last minute, so to speak. Which is why, you've been feeling so sluggish, of late. There are treatments, of course, sometimes they work and sometimes they don't, but we always give you choices."

"I don't believe I will opt for treatments Dr. Rayburn. I've actually done a bit of research online about my father's disease, and I believe that treatment would not necessarily prolong my life. So with what life I do have left, I prefer to live it without radical treatments that will only make me sick."

"I have to agree with you Evelyn. It's a very wise decision my dear." He reached over and touched her hand and smiled at her as if to say he was very proud of her decision.

"Thank you, doctor, I appreciate your honesty." She left his office with a feeling that she would never be back again.

16

Evelyn made plans to meet with her nieces to tell them about the serious nature of her health. She did not want them to hear the news at the Manor for fear of creating sad memories of the place they both loved. She invited them to have lunch with her in a restaurant in downtown Kanyon Cove. Darla and Dawn sat with Evelyn as she explained her prognosis to them. They were both shaken up upon hearing her words and could not imagine what their lives would be like without their Aunt Evie.

"I've had a good and long life, and I don't want any undo sadness from either of you. This is a process that we all must go through, and I'm just going through mine now. I have made arrangements with my lawyer about my funeral so there will be nothing for you to do. I have requested no funeral, and my ashes will be taken care of. So let's enjoy our lunch and each other while we can. Darla, tell me about Grace. How is she doing in school?"

Darla tried her best to talk past the lump in her throat, and after a few words, her voice evened out. "Aunt Evie, she absolutely loves being at the school. I selfishly hoped she would hate it and give me an excuse to bring her home, but she is happy. I'm so glad you talked me into sending her there and also for providing funding for her, thank you again."

Evelyn reached across the table and took her hand in hers. "You're very welcome my darling girl. I do not want you to worry about Grace's education. It has been taken care of since before she was born."

"None of this would be possible if I had tried to do this on my own. I don't know what kind of life I would have been able to provide for Grace if I hadn't called you that night," she said squeezing her aunt's hand.

Evelyn smiled at her and said, "I'm so glad that you did and so blessed to have been a part of Grace's life. I will always be here as long as Grace is around." She smiled at them both as they tried to eat but they were not hungry. She wanted so badly to mention Connor, but she had made a decision long ago not to interfere with their lives. She was going to leave that alone and let nature takes it course. *'It would happen soon enough, and she felt it would be best if it happened on its own rather than her trying to play cupid. That usually gets screwed up when people try to interfere and match make.'*

Evelyn called down to the cabin and asked Connor to come up to the Manor. When he got there, he knew immediately that something was wrong. She asked him to call 911. She had a phone number on a piece of paper in her hand when she passed out. He sat with her until the ambulance arrived but she was gone before they got there. One of the ambulance attendants called the police, and they contacted the coroner.

Connor called the number on the piece of paper, and when Sam Logan answered the phone, he knew what the call was about. Evelyn told him to expect the call and to set things in motion as soon as time permitted. Sam contacted the coroner, who was a personal friend of his, gave him Darla's phone number and asked if he would give it to the police so they could contact her.

Darla answered the knock at her door thinking it was Dawn but instead there were two officers standing there, a male and a female; her heart sank.

"Oh my God! Has something happened to my daughter?"

"Are you Darla Roma?"

"Yes, I am, why are you here?"

"Ms. Roma, I am Detective Mary Sturgis, and this is Constable Joanne Wheaton. I'm afraid I have some bad news about Evelyn Roma. We understand that she is your aunt?

Through nervous tears, Darla replied, "Yes... yes, she is my aunt. What's happened?

If we could come in, we can explain the circumstances.

Darla led them inside, and the detective sat down beside her and began to speak. "Is there is someone that you'd like us to call to possibly come and be with you?

"Yes, my sister Dawn; her number is on the list by the phone; what happened?"

The constable took the number and dialed Dawn, explained who she was and asked her if she could come to her sister's side.

"We can wait for your sister if you wish?" the detective continued.

"Frantic for an answer she replied, "No, tell me what happened, please."

A knock came at the door before the officer could answer and Dawn came rushing in. She ran pass the officer, who was standing by the door and went directly to her sister's side. "What's going on?" she asked, as frantic as Darla was. She quickly sat down beside her sister and waited for someone to speak.

"It's about your aunt, I'm sorry to have to inform you that she passed away this afternoon. Darla sat in a daze trying to take in what she had just heard. She buried her face in her palms and cried broken-heartedly.

Several minutes had passed, and the detective asked if there was anything else she could do for them. Darla was too upset to answer so Dawn thanked them for calling her and told them there was nothing else. She left Darla's side only long enough to show them out and went straight back to her sister.

Dawn had been able to hold herself together until she returned and saw how upset Darla was and she hugged her sister and cried with her. She knew that Darla had always been closer to their aunt than she was but she would miss her too.

Not being able to sleep, they spent the rest of the night talking about their aunt and all the fun times they had as children. The more they talked, the more the tears ran until finally, they had begun to feel that their last visit with Aunt Evie made perfect sense. She had gone through her life-cycle and was OK with that so now, they have to be OK with it too. They both had beautiful memories. Darla, in particular, is comforted knowing that her daughter is her aunt's namesake. Aunt Evelyn will always be with them through her daughter. They all resembled each other by being blonde, petite and strikingly beautiful.

Darla's next thoughts turned to Grace. She thought, 'she has to be told; but how?'

17

One night, while Darla was visiting with Dawn, she could see how depressed her sister was. "I hope someday you will be able to afford a decent car sis," Darla said touching her sister's arm. "I'll help you out if I can, Dawn, but I'm pretty low on cash myself. Craig's payments stopped long ago, and I'm on my own again too."

"Thanks sis, but if something doesn't happen soon, I've been thinking of filing for bankruptcy. I may not have a choice. I'm making payments on a car that I can't drive and can't afford to fix, and my rent is due in a few days. It's so slow at the bar. I haven't been called into work for like four days. The pay is crappy, but tips are usually good enough to cover my expenses. It seems that people aren't bar-hopping much since drinking and driving is so strict now. Most people are just staying home to drink and party. Thanks for your offer though, I know your heart is in the right place, but your pockets are almost as empty as mine."

"Well, I have a few extra bucks at the moment so how about we go out and get some dinner; I don't feel much like cooking tonight. Wanna come with me?"

"Are you paying for dinner?"

Darla laughed and said, "Yes, I'm paying for dinner, would I invite you out if I weren't?"

"Sure, why not, I'd be a fool to pass up a free meal."

While they were eating, both of their cell phones went off at the same time.

"Who is texting us at this time of day?" Darla asked as she squinted over at Dawn. "I don't recognize the name or the number," she added.

"Neither do I," Dawn said as she frowned at her phone.

"That's very strange, don't you think? Both of our phones getting a text at the same time. Do you think it's a hoax? There are so many of them these days," Darla continued in a half-hearted voice. "Should we open them?"

"Maybe we shouldn't. But what if it's important?"

"Well, then maybe we should open them in case it is," Darla shrugged.

They both dropped their heads at the same time and opened the incoming message . At the same time and right on cue, they both said, "Who the hell is Sam Logan?" They looked up at each other and gave a nervous laugh before they became serious again.

"How did this guy get our numbers," Darla mumbled.

'Appt. My office, 2 p.m. tomorrow. 1400 Upper West Blvd, suite 201. Sam Logan.'

They looked up at each other, and again Darla said, "Who the hell is Sam Logan and what does he want with us? Does this sound a bit scary to you?"

"Kinda, but very official," Dawn said wrinkling up her nose, "do you think he is a lawyer maybe?"
"I have no idea and why would a lawyer want to see us anyway? This is all very strange, don't you think. There's no reason why we would both be summoned to an office without us making an appointment ourselves. Should we go?"

"I think we should but give me a sec... I'm Googling him first to see who he is," Dawn said. "Geez Darla, you're right, he is a lawyer."

"OK so... I don't know why a lawyer would want to contact us, but I am thinking we should go. How about I pick you up and we go together since this guy," she pointed at her phone, "wants to see us at the same time."

"Sure, my car is dead so, yeah, I'd appreciate the ride. I don't think I'll get much sleep tonight thinking about this impromptu appointment." Dawn said.

They were more than a little nervous when they determined that they had both been summoned to a law office. When they pushed open the glass door the receptionist looked up and smiled, "You must be Darla and Dawn, please take a seat," she pointed to a pair of overstuffed leather chairs off to one side of the reception area. They settled into the buttery soft chairs and looked at each other. Darla lifted up one eyebrow and nodded as if to say, 'nice chairs!' Dawn widened her eyes and nodded in agreement.

"Mr. Logan will see you now, ladies."

They rose up at the same time and looked at each other.

"This way, please."

They followed her, like two lost puppies into a magnificent office.

A man rose up from behind his elaborate desk and came around to shake hands with the sisters.

"Hello ladies, my name is Sam Logan."

"Hello, I'm Darla Roma, and this is my sister Dawn Coleman, and we are both confused as to why we are here and why you want to see us," she continued.

"Thank you, I know who you are, please," he paused, thinking how much Darla resembled Evelyn, and pointed to the two chairs, "have a seat." When they were seated, he returned to his chair on the opposite side of the desk.

"Why are we here?" Darla asked again.

"You sound a little impatient, Darla," he laughed, "please, allow me to enlighten you both.

"Thank you," Darla said, as Dawn nodded in agreement.

"I've asked you both here today for the reading of the Last Will and Testament set in place by your great Aunt Evelyn Roma."

"OK, right, so why are we here?" Darla asked as she sat forward, "and where are the others?"

"Others?" he asked, with a furrowed brow and spreading his fingers widely in question.

"Yes, 'others', as in Aunt Evie's family."

Raising his fingers in quotations, he replied, "There won't be any 'others' here today."

"Really?" Darla asked now furrowing her own eyebrows.

"If you will allow me to continue," he said, raising an eyebrow, "it will become clear soon enough."

"Sorry," she apologized and sat back in her chair.

"This will was dated just a few months ago. Ms. Roma came to me with a few last minute changes once she realized the end was near."

"You are Aunt Evie's lawyer?"

"Yes, indeed I am, have been for years actually."

"I always heard her speak of her 'lawyer,' but she never mentioned a name. So, you are the one..." She realized just how well he did know her; he had been the one her aunt had confided her secret in!

"Yes, I am, shall we continue?"

"But..." Darla said, leaning forward.

Sam Logan raised his palm at her and said, "No buts, please allow me to finish."

She sat back again and waited.

"Ms. Roma's transcript clearly states that you, Darla Roma and you, Dawn Coleman," he paused looking from one to the other before he continued, "are the sole beneficiaries of her estate."

"What!!?" they both said in unison as they came forward in their chairs.

Sam held his hand up again as he continued to look at the papers in front of him. "Please, let me finish." He loved this kind of situation. Here were two ladies sitting in front of him totally unaware of what was coming. It was obvious that there was no greed involved and they clearly wanted nothing in return for loving their aunt.

They sat back in their chairs again, and neither one took their eyes off him for a second. They both took a deep breath and let it out again, but before Sam could open his mouth again, Darla had a question.

"I'm sorry to keep interrupting you Mr. Logan, but I have one question. Dawn was tugging on her arm for her to sit back but she snatched it from her grip.

Sam put his elbows on his desk and touched his fingertips together and worked them in an open and closed motion. It reminded Darla of a spider doing push-ups on a mirror.

"Go ahead Darla," he nodded, watching her over his hands.

"My sister and I came here today at your request so please, tell us this isn't a joke. It would be very cruel indeed to find out otherwise."

"I assure you both ladies, this is not a joke. I can see why you would think it might be but if you would please allow me to proceed, it **will** become clear."

Darla took another deep breath and sat back in her chair as Dawn touched her arm, nodded and smiled at her as if to say, *'let him finish.'*

"So, are you ready for me to continue..?" he asked looking from one to the other for approval. "Right then, let's move along, shall we. The estate consists of, the Grand Manor property, including the cabin, her Rolls Royce and vintage Mercedes Benz in the garages". Pulling his desk drawer open, he reached in and brought out a large, royal blue velvet bag and placed it on the desk in front of him. "Her jewelry." Reaching into the drawer again, and came out with a grey, oblong box and opened it up in front of them. "Three strands of pearls." Yet again, he reached in the drawer and produced a smaller jewelry box this time, lifting the lid and sliding it into view. "Her cherished diamond ring, worth over a quarter of a million dollars."

They were both gasping for air as they were being smothered in disbelief.

"One moment," he said as he reached for a manila envelope. "In here is a portfolio of stocks and bonds in both your names and a bank statement showing a balance of over four million dollars..."

"Wait a minute!" Darla said tearfully, shoving her chair away as she stood up. "What the hell are you telling us!?"

Sam was struggling not to crack a smile and maintain his judicial demeanor. He then continued, "Well, if you would let me finish... please sit-down Darla, I'm almost finished here, and once I am, I will answer any and all questions you have.

He passed her a box of tissues, and she took one and handed them back to Dawn who in turn said, "I don't understand."

"You will in a second, shall I continue?"

They both nodded, wiped their eyes and blew their noses.

"In the envelope, besides the bank account information is the deed to her property which is also in both of your names. Also, in here," he raised the envelope and continued to read, "is a separate account with ample funds for maintenance, repairs, taxes, etc. for you to use for those purposes, instead of the money in the bank account.

There is, however, a condition in the deed that you must abide by. It reads, "The cabin on the property known as The Grand Manor currently houses an occupant and, as long as said occupant wishes to maintain a presence, the occupant shall enjoy full use of said cabin without cost for rent nor maintenance. Further, said occupant shall enjoy the unencumbered use of an attic loft in the Grand Manor house which may be used as a studio, again, without cost for rent nor maintenance.

Sam went on to explain that the occupant had been a groundskeeper, Evelyn's driver and friend for the past two years. I have spoken to him, and he has agreed to maintain his occupancy of the cabin and continue to undertake the grounds-keeping responsibilities and, as the deed stipulates, as long as he chooses to live there, the cottage will be his. Upon his departure, the cabin will be yours to do with as you see fit.

Last, but not least, Darla, I am in charge of the fund your aunt set up for your daughter Grace. So there is no mistake, I assure you it is now and always will be in place.

Now, ladies, what are your questions?"

"What are our questions? Are you serious right now?" Dawn spoke for only the second time since entering the room. "What is this all about? Aunt Evie has relatives out there, where are they? Why is it that only my sister and I are here today?" she said pointing back and forth from herself to Darla.

"Yes," Darla said, "what is up with that?"

"Well, that's a fair question." Sam was finally able to let his feelings show. His tone moved from his official lawyer voice to that of a confiding friend. "There hasn't been anyone in Ms. Roma's family who she deemed worthy of her inheritance. It has always been you," pointing to the two girls, "you have been there for her over the years. Whether it was visits, phone calls, emails or letters. You both always remembered her birthday by mailing her 'real' cards and not an obligatory e-card. You both visited her either together, or separately, you remembered her on each and every holiday, while no one else acknowledged her existence." He sat looking at them admiringly with his fingertips together again.

"How do you know all this?" Darla asked.

"Yes," Dawn chimed in, "how **do** you know all this personal information?"

Sam leaned back in his chair and clasped his fingers together and rested them on his chest. His voice broke when he began to speak. "Well... you see... I was very close to Ev... er... uh, Ms. Roma. She confided in me her thoughts and feelings. You two were most highly regarded and she loved you dearly."

"How 'close' were you and our aunt, if you don't mind me asking," Darla asked.

"We were very close for the last few decades. We dated occasionally. We were companions if you will, an escort if we needed one, opera buddies and really good friends. I loved her a lot." His voice broke again when he uttered those last words. He leaned forward again, folded his arms in front of him on top of his desk, shrugged like he had just confided his lifelong secret and asked, "Is there anything else?"

"Yes, there is, I...er...we... are very sorry for your loss. We had no idea."

"Thank you ladies, I appreciate that and I too, am deeply sorry for your loss," he said looking from one to the other again.

"Thank you so much and again, I am sorry for all the interruptions this afternoon," Darla said. "You can only imagine our surprise here today."

"I certainly can, and I can certainly understand why Evelyn loved you." He stood up and walked around the desk. He placed the items into a box, locked it and placed it into an oversized briefcase. He locked it as well and passed it to Darla along with the keys. "Everything you need is in the briefcase. Enjoy! These are yours to do with as you wish. She has the name of a collector, in the envelope, in case you are interested in selling the jewelry."

"Sell her jewelry!?"

"Yes, she felt certain that you would since they are decades old. There are a few really good pieces in there," he said pointing to the briefcase. "If you do decide to sell, then perhaps the money could be donated to either your or Evelyn's favorite charity. I can help with that too if you wish. It's totally up to you both, and by the way, the keys to the estate are in the envelope too."

"Thank you," they said with a nod of their heads.

As he had always done with Evelyn, Sam rounded his desk as the girls stood up and offered each one a sincere hug.

Once outside on the sidewalk, Darla stopped, put her back against the building and said, "What the hell was that!? Is this a dream, Dawn?"

"I don't think so Darla! My God! Do you know what this means? We are freaking millionaires!!!"

"I know! I can't believe this! Let's go to my place since it is the closest and let this sink in. We can have a look at all this stuff and try to figure out what it all means. My head is spinning with all of what he said in there, and it's going to take a while before it becomes real."

Dawn asked, "This is real isn't it?"

"Let's get out of here and find out!"

She agreed and followed Darla to her car.

"Would you look at all of this stuff!" Darla said as they stared at the contents on her coffee table. "I would never have believed this in a hundred years. Both of us have struggled for years and lived in our crappy apartments because it was all we could afford. We've both lived from paycheck to paycheck, week after week, month after month and year after year. I know I am pointing out the obvious here but Dawn, we've both tried so hard to get ahead only to have different circumstances knock us back on our asses. Dawn honey, it's over! Look at us! Look at this stuff!!" Darla said waving her hand over the strewn mess on her table.

Dawn, sniffed, blew her nose, tossed the tissue into the waste basket and reached for another one. She wiped her eyes, cleared her throat and took a deep breath. Reaching for the manila envelope, she said, "Let's go ahead and check out what's in here." She pinched the two tabs together and drew them out from the hole in the flap. Pushing some of the jewelry aside, she dumped the contents out on the coffee table. She lined them up as Darla watched from her hunched position as she gaped over the contents too.

- Two bank statements to a joint account

- One bank statement to the household maintenance account

- One deed to the Grande Manor Estate (in both their names)
- Two complete sets of house keys
- Two complete sets of car keys
- Two single keys (with a note attached)

Darla reached over and flipped the attached note over and read, *"For the safe; must have both keys inserted to open outer door."*

Darla reached for the certificates to see what they were. She read for a few minutes as Dawn watched her face. All of a sudden the papers slipped from her fingers onto the floor. She touched her fingertips to her lips and stared at Dawn.

Dawn's eyes widened. "My God Darla, what's wrong!? She gathered the papers up off the floor and began to read. "Darla, what does all this mean? I don't understand stocks and bonds, do you?"

"No, neither do I Dawn." Darla looked almost shell-shocked as all this information overwhelmed her. "Oh wait! There's a note attached. It says, *'monthly interest will be deposited into your joint account,'* and it is signed by Aunt Evie."

"What!?" Dawn stood up and paced around Darla's cramped living room. She pulled her hair straight back off her forehead, held it there looking more like a mad woman and stared wide eyed at her sister. She opened her mouth to speak but closed it again and then began again. "There are ten stocks and ten bonds here. They are dated decades ago. What are these worth to be depositing interest every month?"

Darla leaned forward, put her elbows on her knees and dropped her chin into her palms. Her mind was whirling as she had no answers for her sister's question.

"Darla? Are you alright?"

"Uh huh, I'm fine," she said softly.

They were both quiet for several minutes as they tried to absorb the events presented to them earlier today.

Darla stood up slowly, and Dawn stopped pacing when she saw her sister stand. As they looked at each other, Darla broke into giggles, causing Dawn to giggle. Their giggles turned into laughter. Dawn wasn't sure why she was laughing except that Darla's laughter was contagious.

"We're rich!!" Darla croaked between fits of giggles and wiping her eyes so she could see her sister's reaction. "We're rich, Dawn! We are millionaires!!"

Dawn sobered, put her hands to her face and stared at her sister as if she had not heard correctly. "We are?" she frowned. "We are millionnaires?" She just stood there to let the moment and the words sink in. "We are! We are millionaires! Oh my God Darla, we are rich!" She moved slowly toward her sister, and they hugged each other as tightly as they could and just absorbed the moment in silence. They were both thinking the same thing. They had been struggling for so long and counting pennies for years to make ends meet, they just had to let it sink in for a bit. Finally, Darla released her hold on her sister. She held her at arm's length, rubbed her hands up and down the tops of Dawn's arms and smiled, "Let's go home," she whispered.

"What?" Dawn whispered back, we are home, well your home anyway."

Smiling, she said, "No honey, I mean... let's go home... to The Grand Manor." She dropped her sister's hands and walked over to the coffee table and picked up a couple of items. She walked back over to Dawn and stretched her hand out. She held a set of keys by her fingertips. She shook them a few times and said, "These are for you." She held up her other hand with keys dangling and raising an eyebrow and an evil grin she playfully said, "And these are mine!"

Dawn slowly reached up and took the set of keys that were meant for her. When her fingers touched them, she wrapped the keys into her palm and agreed, "Yes, let's go home!"

"Yes let's, we can figure this out as we go along but right now, I just want to go to the manor. I'll put a few things in a bag, and then we will go to your apartment to pack a bag for you."

"Are we really going to do this, Darla? Are we really moving?" Dawn was so excited that she could hardly contain herself. It was as though a huge load was gradually falling from her shoulders to the floor as she began to comprehend this wonderful news.

"Yes we are, and I'm going to pack! Can you put all this stuff back into the briefcase? she asked, waving at the coffee table.

"Sure, go ahead; well actually, hurry up!" she giggled. Darla disappeared into the bedroom, and Dawn busied herself by straightening up the legal papers, returning the jewelry pieces to the bag and packing it all into the briefcase, but not before finding something they both had missed. She took a few minutes to look around the small cramped spaced and wondered what life would be like for them once they leave this place.

Darla appeared with a skimpy bag and said, "There really isn't much here that I want; I have enough in here for now," she said raising the bag a little. I think we can afford new stuff, don't you?"

"I'm so used to going to the Goodwill store for something different to wear; I can hardly remember what it is like to afford new stuff. I never thought I would ever be able to say this, but yes, we can buy new stuff now."

"Let's go to your place."

"Before we go I have something to show you."

"What is it?"

"I found this while I was packing up. She handed the sheet of paper to Darla, and she began to read aloud.

Dear Darla and Dawn:

I remember fondly, how much you both loved Dodger. I have recently purchased a puppy from old Dodger's lineage. I chose one who looks identical to our Dodger. He was so much like him that I called him Dodger also in honor of the ole boy. He is not quite a year old and has been a great 'replacement' so to speak, for our beloved Dodger Sr. Dodger Jr is in the 'Paws-a-tively Pets Kennel' on Shoreline Blvd. You can pick him up on your way home. Darlings, I hope you have a wonderful life at the Manor. Make it 'yours' and do with it as you wish. Enjoy your new found inheritance and remember, it is only money and if you take care of it, it will take care of you.

Darla, I am honored that you called on me to help you with my namesake, Grace. She will always be taken care of.

I had hoped, many times, that I could have been of some help to you girls.

Dawn, you never came to me, you never asked me for anything. I would have gladly given you anything I had with no questions asked or obligation on your part. It showed me how strong you girls really are, but now that burden is lifted.

Thank you for your kindness to me over my lifetime.

I love you both.
Aunt Evie xo

Tears were streaming down their faces when she finished, and when Darla looked up from the note, she smiled through her tears and hugged the note to her chest and whispered, "Thank you Aunt Evie."

I think we have somewhere to go after we get a bag packed for you!"

"We sure do! Another Dodger! Who would have guessed?"

They pulled into the parking lot of Dawn's apartment building. Normally Dawn would have been depressed to go in there, but this time it was different. This time could very well be the last time she would have to stumble around her shabby place. Her apartment overlooked the parking lot, and when she looked up at her small Romeo and Juliette balcony, she actually smiled. "Let's get this done." She slipped her arm through her sister's, and they walked together up a flight of stairs. She unlocked the door and walked in. "It is really small in here, isn't it?"

"Yes it is, so go pack a bag and let's get the hell out of here. By the way, when is the last time you cracked opened a window in here sis?"

"Are you serious? These windows haven't been open in years, they are painted shut! It isn't bad enough that it is small, hot as hell and stuffy but to not be able to open a window is downright insane and should not be allowed. It's amazing what landlords can get away with these days; how they can take advantage of people like us. They know it is all we can afford so we have to either take it or leave it. But not anymore! We are out of here!" By the time she finished her rant, she was packed and ready to go. Like Darla, she did not want or need much either, so she packed lightly as well.

They pulled up in front of the kennel and turned the engine off. They heard a roar of dogs barking at the sound of an intruder. Going inside and up to the reception desk, they were greeted by an energetic young woman who looked to be no more than seventeen. Upon inspection though, they figured her wedding ring tossed that theory out the window.

"Hello, welcome to Paws! How may I help you?"

Her voice had that sing-song tone that Darla really detested.

"We are here to pick up a dog name Dodger."

"Dodger? Really?" she said as she her voice went from highs to lows in that singy tone as she cocked her head to one side.

Darla tilted her head to one side too in a mimic fashion. "Yes, really."

"Oh no! That's too bad!"

"Why? What? Darla asked.

"It's just that we love Dodger! We'll miss him!" she whined. "I'll go and get him for you." She tilted her head again as her voice continued in that sing-song tone.

"Thank you!" Darla let her voice 'sing' along with the receptionist's. It was all Dawn could do, not to giggle. When she disappeared into the back of the office, Darla said, "Don't you just hate that? The way these younger people sing their words!"

Dawn had to agree, it was annoying.

They looked up when they heard dog tags jingling on a collar. "Oh my God! Dodger!" They both said it at the same time.

When he heard his name, it was as if he had been waiting for them. He ran over to them as they both went down on their knees to his level. They both expected him to run over them, but when he got to them, he immediately stopped and sat in front of them. He offered a paw to whoever wanted to take it. He was identical to his dad's lineage! He was another Dodger dog! The same kind and gentle dog as they had known and loved for all those years when they visited Aunt Evie.

"Dodger?" Darla cooed, and when he heard his name, he twisted his head to the side. She wrapped her arms around his neck and hugged him tightly. In a little corner of her memory, she remembered a dog riding in a truck not too long ago, that had creeped her out.

It was Dawn's turn. His tail wagged, and he whimpered in delight sensing he was going home.

"Do we owe you anything?" Darla asked.

"No Miss, his bill was taken care of when he was brought in."

"Thank you, does he have a leash?"

"No, you won't need one, he's a good boy. See you Dodger, come back and visit us. She looked at both girls and said, "Feel free to use our services at any time."

"Thank you, he looks well taken care of. Do you mind if I asked who brought him in?"

"Ms. Roma gave instructions for him to be brought here shortly before her passing. A man brought him in but was very hesitant to leave him behind. He found it hard to leave him with us, but he said he had to honor his boss's wishes."

The sisters looked at each and shrugged, not knowing who it could have been. The only one who came to mind would be the groundskeeper.

They opened the door, and Dodger trotted out behind them. When he got to the car, he sat and waited until the door was opened for him. The sisters looked at each other and smiled, "Just like the old Dodger!" they chimed.

They rounded the corner and stopped at the gate that hung on two huge pillars. Dawn got out of the car, flipped open the lid to the control box and pressed several buttons, just as she had done for years whenever they came for a visit. She wondered if the numbers had been changed, but the fence immediately began to open. Darla drove in, and Dawn closed the box, pushed a button and walked through the gate as it began to close. "There must be a remote somewhere in the house for the gate," she said getting back in the car.

"Yes, probably on a keychain, to one or both cars maybe!" Darla added. "And we thought you needed a new car!" They both laughed. They became silent as they drove up the long winding, tree lined lane, except of course for the happy whimpers coming from Dodger.

"This is so unbelievable Darla. This morning I woke up poor and wondering how I was going to pay my rent and fix my old car and this afternoon we are millionaires! How did this happen?" Her voice caught, and Darla touched her arm as Dodger whined from the backseat.

"He has the same protective instinct as his forefathers had," Darla said. "Here, take this," she said, passing her a box of tissues. "I know this is very overwhelming, but we will do this together, ok?"

"Ya, sure, together," she sniffed.

"Here we are," Darla said quietly as she rolled to a stop in front of the Manor. "My God," she whispered, "we own this." Her own voice caught when she said the words. They sat in the car for a few minutes, neither one making the first move. Dodger brought them out of their trance by whining again. He was looking in the direction of the cabin, which was not visible from the house. Dawn got out and opened the door for him. Knowing he was home, at last, he bounded up the steps to the front entrance. Dawn already had her keys out, so she went ahead to let him inside. Darla just sat for a few minutes absorbing it all when Dawn appeared at her window.

"Together," she said, reminding her of her own words and holding her hand out to her sister.

"Indeed, together." She got out, took her sister's hand and together they ascended the concrete steps to the front door, their front door.

Dawn put a key in the lock, no luck, then another one and voila! She pushed the heavy door open to reveal the Manor's magnificence.

Dodger barked as he galloped through the house at lightning speed as if looking for someone.

"He must be looking for Aunt Evie," Darla suggested. He put his paws up on the window sill and barked several times and then ran to the door. Dawn opened it and watched as he tore off towards the cabin.

18

Conner wondered what all the commotion was about. This place was usually graveyard quiet. He laid his brush down and went to the side window to look out, but he couldn't see anything from this angle. "Can't see much out of skylights either," he mumbled, so he went out into the hall where he could get a better look. He saw the car in the driveway. "That must be the new owners, so I'd better get my ass home and out of the way." He was still mumbling to himself. He gave his brushes a quick rinse and dried them off. "Better take the backstairs and the path back, so I don't end up scaring anybody. I spend too, much time alone; I really need someone else to talk to besides myself." He quickly cleaned up the rest of the mess and left. He closed the door and locked it for the first time since he had come to live on the property. Giving the handle a tug to confirm it was secure, he headed off down the back staircase. "For an old house, these steps do not have one squeak in them. Shut up man, there's no one listening to you," he mumbled. He let himself out the back door, locked it as well, went around the pool house into the woods and home.

"Hey boy! Where did you come from?" He knelt down, and the dog eagerly and excitedly licked his face as Conner scratched the dog's neck and back and gave him a big hug. "I missed you too young fella, how did you get back here?" Conner picked up a stick and threw it into the air across the lawn. Dodger immediately tore after it leaving blades of grass flying behind him. He scooped it up mid stride and brought it back to Conner, dropping it at his feet. "Good boy! I can tell you missed this too. This is just like old times, eh boy? It's nice to see you Dodger," he said ruffing his fur, "Let's get you a drink of water."

Dawn saw Dodger tear off after a flying stick and wondered for a moment who the occupant of the cabin was.

Darla wondered off on her own to get a feel of being back here again. At that point, she was not interested in who was sleeping where she just needed to walk around. It was seven years since she had stayed here and had her daughter. If her memory served her correctly, there were four bedrooms, each with its own ensuite bath plus, there was a main bathroom at the top of the stairs. Her mind was active as she climbed the staircase to the second floor. She was not on a timeline, and as she ambled around, she remembered a lot of things she had forgotten. The house was massive with each bedroom in somewhat of a separate wing, making each bedroom very private. She chuckled as she realized that her apartment could fit in the span of the hallway. Each room had a king size, four poster bed with a matching eight drawer dresser and highboy. Over the dresser was a huge wooden matching framed mirror nearly the size of the dresser. There were two matching night tables, each with a touch lamp. There was a loveseat at the foot of the bed, and across from that was a fireplace. A chair sat close to the fireplace with a throw pillow on the seat, and a soft plush lap rug lay casually across the back. Above the fireplace hung a beautiful oversized framed mirror that made the room look double in size. On brackets on another wall, hung a flat screen TV that to Darla's estimation it looked as if it were a fifty two inch. So far the only thing Darla reached out to touch was the lap rug; she loved the feel of softness. Behind the chair, there was a door, and when she opened it, she walked into a closet that was nearly the size of the bedroom itself. She was certain she could put the contents of her apartment in the closet. Over by the bed, there was another door behind which she found an elaborate bathroom. "I remember this being Aunt Evie's quarters," she found herself saying out loud. Darla entered the closet lifting pieces of clothing to her nose. The fragrance of her aunt's French perfume brought back memories filling her eyes with tears.

To stave off her melancholy feelings, she walked out into the hall and down to the next bedroom. It was the same layout except for a different choice of furniture and fabrics. King sized beds, oversized dressers, walk-in closets, wide screen TV and a huge bathroom. The next two bedrooms were just as large and beautiful as the others.

Darla was in awe of it all and decided right then and there that she was not going to bring any of her junk here. It would either stay in the apartment, or she'd take it to Goodwill, but it was definitely not coming here; that much she was certain of. She stuck her head in the main bathroom and looked around. It was equally as elaborate as the ensuites were, but just a little less personal since it was only used by an occasional guest.

She got to the door at the end of the hall and opened it wide. "Oh, I remember this!" she mumbled to herself as she made her way up the stairs. She opened the first door and saw that it was for storage, remembering how she and Dawn used to get permission to come here and play dress up, and search for treasures and old jewelry. Aunt Evie had everything to dress up with. She had the greatest stuff! There were generations of fashion and styles from all over the world and several old travel trunks, boxes, totes, and wardrobes full of clothing. "It'll be fun to go through this retro stuff!" she laughed, "and there's nobody to stop me!" She wondered if any of this gorgeous stuff was back in fashion.

She walked across the hall to another door, but when she pushed on it, it would not open. She rattled the door knob thinking it was stuck but then she realized it was locked. *'Huh, that's weird,'* she thought and made a mental note to see if there was a key somewhere. She made her way down the hall again to yet another door. She gave the knob a quick turn and a push with her shoulder expecting it to be locked also but it swung open, and she nearly tumbled through the entrance.

"Wow," she said aloud, "I remember this, this is a gorgeous loft. This will be a perfect place to escape and do my own thing." She was taking it upon herself that Dawn would have no interest in it. Then again she thought, perhaps if they could find the key to the other room, she too could have her own studio.

Something was coming back to her mind after all they had taken in. She realized that Sam Logan had told them earlier that someone was using a loft which was emphatically one of the stipulations. She brought herself back to the moment and turned slowly in a complete circle looking around the room. "I love it," she breathed with a broad smile. It was bare except for a huge mirrored wall on the opposite the door. The mirror was almost floor to ceiling, and she wondered why it was there. She also wondered how anyone was able to obtain a mirror this size and who could have hung it? A brief flashback came to her. *Music was playing from an old phonograph record. She could see herself as a little girl in this room in front of an oblong mirror that was no bigger than one she had behind her bedroom door in her apartment. She remembered dancing in front of it and looking up to see Aunt Evie leaning against the door, with her arms crossed, just watching her dance. When she saw her, she stopped in embarrassment.*

"Don't stop sweetheart, you are very good you know, continue for me please."

Shyly, Darla began to dance for her again. She swayed and swung her body back and forth in waves and before long, she was dancing like no one was watching. As the music came to a close and Darla went into her last pose, Aunt Evie clapped and clapped as if she were at a recital. "You're very good darling. I hope you continue with your dance lessons and if you do, then you could use this as your dance studio one day."

She walked across the floor and hugged her grandniece, and Darla's memory came to an end.

"I haven't thought about that in years," she whispered to herself. 'There are so many memories here in this old Manor. Perhaps this would make the ideal spot to write down some of those great memories.'

She wondered if Aunt Evie had done this room over for her knowing she would live here one day. It only made sense that she would, or why else would it have been redone. It did not look like this when she was a child.

There was no furniture in the room except for a lounge chair, a desk with a stool and a small bar fridge. Out of curiosity she opened the fridge door, and there were several bottles of water, so she grabbed one. On the desk next to the fridge was a remote which she picked it up and pressed 'play.' Music escaped through almost invisible speakers. It was the same tune that she had danced to all those many years ago. *'I wonder if this was a dance studio at one time?'* she thought. She took the cap off the water bottle and took a long, slow swallow as she walked to the side window. It faced the cabin, and she could see Dodger. She could also see part of the cabin's roof, but the rest was secluded by the trees that had grown up over the years. She loved that cabin. *'I wonder who the tenant is?'* she asked herself since no one else was there with her. Behind the cabin, she saw part of the Roma Family Cemetery and what looked like freshly overturned soil. That would be something else to check out once they got settled. She saw an arm go out as a stick went flying through the air, and Dodger on the run to retrieve it. She smiled to herself as she watched. *'So that's why he wanted to go out so badly. It's probably some old guy that Aunt Evie gave a place to live; she was so sweet that way. Well, we'll find out soon enough.'* She walked over to the desk to set her water bottle down, and she saw the corner of a piece of paper sticking out from under an old ink blotter. She put a finger on it and slid it out.

My dear Darla, welcome to your studio. I know this room will never belong to anyone except you. When I watched you dance all those, years ago, I knew I had to do something special with this loft.

My beautiful niece, dance like no one is watching because I will be!

Love,
Aunt Evie xo

She choked up as she read her aunts' words and tears sprang to her eyes. '*I guess this answers my question,*' she thought. She wasn't, crying out of mourning for her aunt but for her aunt's undying love for her and her sister.

She left the loft and went back out into the hallway.

'*What's this?*' she found herself mumbling her thoughts, '*where does this go?*' as she pushed the door open. '*Hmm, I don't remember these stairs.*' She followed them down two flights, and at the bottom, she saw a door, nothing else, just a door. She felt around the wall as if looking for another opening but there was nothing. She began to think that the upstairs might have been staff quarters at one time; the maid's chambers maybe. It was weird that she had never heard a conversation about that over the years. If it was, then there should have been access to the main house without going outside and around to the front door. *'That would be ridiculous,'* she thought. She made another trip around the wall with her hands, and she found nothing. She went in behind the staircase and touched everything she saw and felt around for stuff she did not see. Suddenly, she looked up and saw a tiny lever. The wheels began to turn in her head. *'Should I or shouldn't I?'* she thought. She stood there for a few minutes thinking about it, and finally, she said, "Well you know you are going to pull it so go ahead! When did you ever mind your own business?" She answered her own question as soon as she asked it. "I never did." She reached up and pulled on the lever, and the entire wall slid open like a huge pocket door. When it opened, she heard a scream. Dawn was standing beside the wall when it opened, and she freaked out. Darla stepped out from the hall so Dawn could see her.

"What the hell!?"

"I know!!" Darla said. "Now we have to figure out how to close it up. I really don't think anyone else knows about this wall, Dawn, and we are going to keep it a secret. Help me look."

They went all over the walls and up and down as far as they could reach and nothing.

"There must be something here to close this wall back up!" Darla said. "We have to find it; we can't just leave it wide open like this. Let me show you where the lever is, Dawn." She pointed out where it was, and Dawn pulled it once to try it. The door began to close, so they ran through in time as it closed behind them.

"Well that works for now but if it opens from out there," she pointed towards the wall, "then it must also open from in here as well. We'll keep looking."

"Yes, there has got to be another switch or lever," Dawn said.

Darla began to tell Dawn about her tour. "I was upstairs, and I had forgotten how massive this place is. Of course, when we came here with mom and dad, we weren't allowed to snoop except for around the cabin, but for now, that is off limits. I love that cabin! By the way, I saw movement over there so I guess that must be the reason why Dodger wanted out so badly. Those back stairs, they come down from the top floor, it's huge up there!"

"You're trying to say too much at one time sis, slow down. Tell me, did you choose your bedroom then?"

"No not yet, but I did realize that none of my junk is coming here."

"What will we do with our stuff, Darla?"

"Leave it there, junk it, give it to Goodwill, I don't care, I don't want it."

"That's a good idea, sis."

"One of the loft doors on the third floor is locked." "Didn't Sam Logan say the occupant of the cabin also has a room in the attic?" Dawn answered.

"Yes, I remember that he told us about the stipulation. Well now, mystery solved."

"Darla, while you were upstairs, I went through the downstairs. I don't remember this place being this enormous. Along with the kitchen, there is a pantry, laundry room, bathroom, and back entry, and this is just in close proximity with the kitchen. Then there is the living room, dining room, and den, plus a glassed-in sun porch. I think Aunt Evie must have replaced the entire wrapped verandah recently because all the wood looks new. Did you see the gazebo that has been added out by the pool?"

"Wow, no I didn't see that. I will look around a little later, but right now, I am famished. I wonder if there is any food in this place."

"Let's go check the fridge and cupboards, I'm hungry too."

The cupboards and fridge were both adequately filled, and there was a little note propped up in the middle of the bread box.

'I instructed Sam to arrange for groceries to be brought in a day before he was to contact you. If you are reading this, I'm glad you are here. Welcome home girls!'

Aunt Evie, xo

"She has thought of everything! I still cannot believe she chose us to inherit all of this," Darla said, as she made a complete circle with her arms out. "Why us, Dawn? Why did she choose you and me to have everything she owned in the world? It makes no sense to me."

"To me either sis. I have been thinking of nothing else since we heard Sam Logan actually say the words."

"Me too. We should grab a quick bite and go into town; we have some things to take care of. The first of which is to give up our crappy apartments, pack up our personal belongings and never look back!"

"Sis, nobody can take this away from us, can they?"

Darla reached for the manila envelope on the table, opened it and pulled out the papers. She flipped through them and passed a legal sheet to Dawn. "Read this."

"The deed to our house?"

"Yes, that's right, our house, our property, our names. According to Sam Logan, this is all ours. Are there any other questions?"

Dawn smiled and said, "No there aren't. I guess I'm going to have to get it through my head that we actually can live here."

"Dawn?" Darla asked, "did you see this when we were going through the envelope? It has our names on it."

"No, what is it?"

"It's another envelope, and it is still sealed."

"Open it up!" Dawn said excitedly.

Darla turned it over and ran her thumb under the flap. She pulls out a single piece of paper, read it to herself and then said, "Follow me."

Dawn followed behind her as Darla headed for the den. Darla stopped, read the page and looked around the room seemingly counting art pieces.

"What are you looking for, Darla?"

"Sec," she said, placing herself as if she were looking at a treasure map. She began to turn as she counted, almost to herself. "One," she pointed, "two, three, four, she turned on an angle, "five, six, right here she said, and walked over to a painting. On the bottom right corner she saw a signature; C.

Barnes. *"What the...? ... It can't be,'* she thought as a brief memory came to mind. *'Don't be absurd,'* she told herself. She tugged on the right-hand side, and it moved outward. When it moved, she turned to look at Dawn and nodded. Dawn walked over to her where they both looked at the wall safe, and then at each other.

Dawn said, "What next?"

"Wanna do the honors?"

"Sure! Well, what is the combination?"

'First, we need the two keys to unlock this first door, and then there is a combination inside."

Dawn went to get both keys and when she returned they each put a key in the slot and turned them to open the outer door, and again Dawn asked, 'What's the combination?"

"Simple, it's the same as the front gate."

Dawn pressed the number buttons on the combination just as she had done a few hours ago at the main gate. Poke, poke, poke, poke and a click, the safe door opened.

"OK! What's in there, sis?"

Dawn reached in and gathered up the contents that were lying in the safe and laid the items out on the coffee table. They sat on the couch side by side and pushed the items this way and that way until they were all separated. There were two car remotes for the main gate and several envelopes. Darla picked up the largest one and opened it. "This is the original copy of the deed to the house. Look at this! The deed has been in our names for a long time! Look at the date on this! It has been years! She never said a thing, ever!"

"I can't believe this, Darla," Dawn said quietly, "I never even thought Aunt Evie was all that fond of us to be truthful. Yes, she was always very gracious and loving when we arrived for extended visits, but aren't all people usually nice and polite anyway when guests arrive?"

"It feels good though to know how she felt about us when she had so many other family members to choose from," Darla added softly.

"What's this?" Dawn asked as she picked up another, smaller envelope. "It says, 'Every girl needs one,' written on the front." She flipped it over and opened the flap. She pulled out two credit cards, one in each of their names.

"Oh my!" she said, "I've never had a credit card before."

Darla piped up and said, "Well I did, and the bank cancelled it on me when I couldn't make payment. I worked my ass off to put every possible cent I could spare on that puppy until I got it paid. The interest was crippling me, and I ate a lot of Kraft Dinner, but I did it!" They both laughed.

"The rest of this stuff," Darla said waving her hand over the items, "is what Sam had in the envelope this afternoon. What we were given are copies, and these are the real deal. How about we try these cards out and go out for a nice dinner, with a bottle of wine."

That sounds good Darla. Hey, look at this, it's the address of several of the most expensive dress shops in town and Aunt Evie signed it with, *'Treat yourselves to a new wardrobe, and if you have gotten this far, then you have found all of my notes. I thought maybe Darla would like the front East Wing bedroom and Dawn would likely be comfy across the hall in the West Wing. A note to Darla, look under the right front leg of the piano. I love you both, always. Enjoy the credit cards, 'Every girl needs one.' xo*

"Well, let's go see!" Darla said jumping up.

"Yes, let's!"

Darla pawed around the piano leg, up and down until she found it. She gave the lever a yank, and the wall slid open.

"Shut up!!! How did she know!?" Darla said.

"I guess it doesn't matter how she knew, I'm glad that _we_ know!" Dawn laughed, and her sister pulled the lever to close the wall.

At that moment, they heard a slight roll of thunder, and they sensed that Aunt Evie's work was done here, and she was saying her final farewells.

"Let's go to dinner," Darla said, wrapping an arm around her sister's shoulder.

19

They had been living in the Manor for just over a week and nicely settling in while getting use to their new surroundings. The space they had, compared to their small apartments was like being released from prison.

It was different when Darla stayed here during her pregnancy. It was like an extended vacation for her, but Aunt Evie had been mistress of the Manor while Darla was her guest.

Now that Darla owned this entire property along with her sister, nobody could make them leave. How things change, only this time it was for the better, for both of them. Although Darla enjoyed her job, she decided to give it up to allow someone else to have a job. She did not need it, but she was certain someone else did. Dawn had given up her job at the bar as soon as they found out about the will.

They both just took a few things from their apartments and passed in their keys to the landlords. They explained that they did not want or need the contents of the apartments and gave them an extra month's rent for the inconvenience their short notices may have caused.

The day had come for Darla to visit Grace at school. She had not had the opportunity to share the news with her about inheriting The Grand Manor. Visitation rules were set in stone, and there was no room for exception. That was why the school was popular. The children were learning rules and how to follow them, and if they did not follow them, there were consequences.

She knew Grace would be excited with the news because she too loved visiting there. Aunt Evie had always made her feel like she belonged at The Manor and in hindsight, she realized that she did. She and Aunt Evie had told Grace the story about her being born in the Manor, and it became a big deal to her. From then on, she referred to the Manor as her birth house. It cemented her attachment to her great, great aunt and also to the estate.

Once the hugs and the excitement of seeing each other diminished a bit, they began to share their news. Grace babbled on about her weeks away from her mother and when Darla could get a word in she told Grace that they had inherited the Manor.

"What does 'inherited' mean?" she asked.

'It means that when Auntie Evie went to Heaven, she gave the Manor to us, and now we live there!"

"That is so cool, mommy! I love it there!"

"So do we. I mean Aunt Dawn and me. The Manor belongs to all three of us.

Once Grace heard the entire story, they began to make plans for her first visit home. Their visit was over way too soon, but they were excited about their upcoming weekend together. It gave them something to look forward to.

Darla always felt the same way when she had to leave Grace at the school. It had not changed since the first day she enrolled her. It usually took Darla a few days to shake the feeling of abandoning her child. Her only solace was, she knew how happy Grace was at the school.

The sisters were sitting at the breakfast table having pleasant conversation when they heard the doorbell. Surprised by the sound, Darla looked Dawn and asked, "Are you expecting anyone?"

Shaking her head, Dawn replied, "Nobody really knows that I live here."

Darla's face lit up when she opened the door. "Margaret, Donna... ladies, how are you?" There on the deck stood the four maids that Evelyn had employed for years cleaning the house.

"Why we're fine Miss Darla, how are you doin?" Without skipping a beat, Margaret went on to add her condolences. "We were awful sorry to learn of Miss Evie's passing. She was a fine woman and a good friend to all us girls over the years. We are sure gonna miss her."

"Yes, she was a treasure." Darla agreed.

Moira, the third member of the quartet, chimed in, "We hear that this is now your home Miss Darla? Now you can be the Dame of The Grand Manor!"

Through slightly teary eyes she replied, "That's very nice of you Moira but, we will never be able to replace her."

Margaret looked over Darla's shoulder and asked, "You must be Miss Dawn? We heard about you from your aunt and are pleased we now get to meet you."

Before Dawn could say a word, Darla explained, "These lovely women worked for Aunt Evie forever. They are the reason why this place was so perfect whenever we came for a visit."

Dawn confirmed to the ladies, "this house was always spotless when we were here as children. You probably cursed when you came in after we were here." Everyone laughed which helped to lighten the atmosphere.

"Now Miss Darla, we have to set to work. We haven't been here for a few weeks now, and the old house will surely need a good scrub. I'll bet we are here all day."

"Oh my goodness," Dawn said, "we will have to arrange payment for you."

"No, no," said Louise, the last woman, who now took charge of the situation. "Mr. Sam told me that arrangements are all made for us to continue on just like Miss Evie was still here. We'll get paid, don't you fret yourself about that."

Donna declared, "OK girls, let's dig in," and with that, the foursome headed off to the cleaning closet, which was really a well-organized room with every tool and supply they would ever need to carry out their tasks.

"We'll stay out of your way." Darla laughed as they marched past.

"How about we hang out around the pool for a bit then?" Dawn asked.

Darla briefly thought about the idea and then said, "I think I am going to take a walk on the beach for a little while before it gets too hot." She searched for Dodger but he was nowhere to be seen, so she grabbed her wide brimmed hat and sunglasses. On the way down the path, she covered her arms with a long-sleeved shirt for protection. She made her way down the steps to the beach and walked out to the edge of the water. She bent a bit and slipped her shoes off to keep them dry from the incoming tide.

Connor sat on a rock at the top of the beach near the embankment. He watched her walk to the water's edge. There was something about the way she slipped off her shoes. He rose to his feet and took a few steps as he went back in time to the night Darla held onto his arm for support when she took her shoes off before running all the way to his motel. He continued to watch her. *'She looks familiar,'* he thought, *'but from where, I don't know!* He had not made friends in the area, but even still, she had an air of familiarity about her. He could not tell much from the wide brimmed hat and sunglasses. She could have been a famous actress incognito for all he knew. He had heard that this area was being looked at for several movies, but then again, this is a private beach, so he doubted that idea as soon as it passed through his mind.

It was then that Darla looked around and saw him. *'Damn it!'* she thought, *'who is that now!'* She raised her hand to shade her eyes, pretending to look out at the water from another angle but she was looking at the stranger on her beach. *"Who the hell is that?"* she mumbled, *'this is a private beach.'* She was not certain if people could actually 'own' the beach fronts but what she was sure of was that this section belonged part and parcel to her aunt, which now belonged to her! She was too far away to see who it was or even if she knew him. She could only distinguish a baseball cap, jeans, and a white tee shirt. *"Oh*

God!" she moaned, "*not the jeans and tee shirt type,*" she said through clenched teeth as thoughts of Connor grabbed her. '*Don't even go there!*' she scolded herself. Her mind went directly to the time when they yanked his tee shirt over his head, and she twisted the button on his jeans... '*Oh, no don't go there, please,*' she whispered, as she closed her eyes trying to block out the vision. She remembered the many times she thought she had seen him over the years, but not once had she ever run into him. '*Why didn't he ever come back to Kanyon Cove?*' she thought. '*He said he loved me no matter what, but he never came back.*'

He wanted to go over to say hello but he was remembering the many heart flips he'd had over the years every time he saw a petite woman with blonde hair. He could not see the color of this woman's hair from where he was because of the oversize hat, but she made him think about Darla anyway. '*Why?*' He saw her make her way up the steps and he remembered back to when he watched her climb the front steps of her apartment building. It was the last time he saw her. "Hey!" he yelled. But he was too far away, and the sounds of the sea and the wind muffled his voice. She gave a quick look at him as she neared the top of the stairs, but before he could get his hand up to wave, she was gone. De ja vu.

"You're back early," Dawn said when she saw Darla walking up the path.

"Someone is down on the beach, so I came back."

"Did you see who it was?

"No, he was too far over near the underside of the embankment," she said pointing to indicate the spot she was referring to.

"Isn't that, like, our beach?" Dawn asked, "private, I mean."
"Supposed to be but I'm not sure, but he got down there somehow,"

"He!?" Dawn asked.
"Yes, it's a guy, but I couldn't make out who he was."

"You sound as if you *want* to know who it was," Dawn teased.

"No," Darla shrugged, "he just seemed somewhat familiar, is all."

"How familiar? *Grace* familiar, perhaps?"

"What are you talking about!?" Darla bristled.

Dawn lowered her voice and calmly continued with a subject she had wanted to broach for a long time and now was her chance. "It's just that I know you did not have a sexual relationship with that bird brain, Craig. All of a sudden you disappear for six months, without an explanation, not that you owed me one," she said raising her hands up, "then, I'm introduced to Grace, still without an explanation," her hands flying up again, "just saying. So there is a guy out there somewhere that you obviously fell for or you'd likely still be with Craig. There has not been another man in your life, not even a date, and you are only twenty seven. So, I'm thinking that he hit you p-r-e-t-t-y hard!"

"I haven't had time to date! I have Grace to take care of!" she said defending herself.

"No, no, no, I'm not swallowing any of that crap. I will agree that for the first five years, yes, you were busy with Grace but she has been at school for almost two years." Dawn paused for a bit, empathically softening her tone. "Look, you married Craig before you were nineteen, you stayed in a loveless marriage for a little over a year, OK," she shrugged, "fifteen months. All of a sudden you disappear for six months and voila, we have a beautiful baby girl!? She had to come from somebody Darla, and we know it 'ain't' Craig's baby. She's almost seven; Darla, you still haven't dated anyone, why?"

"I can't."

"Why can't you? Are you still hung up on Grace's dad?"

Darla, pressing her lips together, grew silent. She gazed blankly toward the path to the beach as her mind rushed back to the passion she shared with Conner. It was still her secret. Even after all this time, she still couldn't bring herself to tell Dawn, even though she was her closest friend. The words just wouldn't come out.

"Well, I guess that just about sums it up then. I got my answer," Dawn said softly, reaching out to touch her sister.

Darla's concentration was instantly broken by Dawn's comment, and their eyes met as she quickly turned toward the accusing look. Just then, Dodger came bounding up the path giving Darla the perfect release from Dawn's conclusion. She reached out to pet him and found her hand buried in wet fur. "It looks like someone gave you a bath!" she said.

It must be the man in the cabin since he spends most of his time down there," Dawn added. "Maybe it's the man on the beach. I think one or both of us should go down there and introduce ourselves."

"I don't care who is living down there; it's of no interest to me. I'm pretty sure Aunt Evie gave someone a place to live in exchange for grounds work. We'll see him soon enough, it's almost time for the lawns to be cut."

Darla stole off to her room shortly after supper. She was not in the mood for small talk. She sat up and listened with an ear cocked up to the ceiling. She heard something scrape along the floor in the loft above her room. "That's just what I need!" she whined. She had not heard a thing coming from up there in the short time she had been living here. Now all of sudden, just as she wants peace and quiet, he shows up. After a bit, all went quiet above her, so she lost interest and returned to her thoughts of those brief moments on the beach. Her memories only made her long for Connor even more. It had been seven long years, and she still had not moved on. She was certain that he had done so since he never came back, and she still had not gotten over the fact that he changed his cellphone number, or cancelled it, or... something. "Damn him!" she heard herself say aloud as her temperature rose. Her anger swelled as she reviewed their past. "He didn't care for me! He lied! We had sex! He left!" She paced around her room for a few minutes seething. "Men! They are all the bloody same. Some are just worse than others." Her thoughts carried on, '*Why would I want to get involved with another one! They obviously cannot be trusted to keep their word.*' She could still remember his text as clear as if it was yesterday. '*I love you more!*'

Darla became teary as she reviewed the past in her mind. '*He made me smile, made me happy but, it would have been just so complicated.*' She wished she had of had the nerve to meet with him again, but she was so fearful of getting caught. She thought for a moment then scolded herself, '*I suppose I should take some of the blame for him walking away, for him not coming back for me.*' After all, she had asked him not to call her, and now she was blaming him for respecting her wishes! How dumb am I" she said out loud. A few seconds passed as she angrily reconciled the situation in her mind again. '*Just the same, the bastard should have tried harder. He should have pushed me. He should have made me realize that he wanted me to be with him and not Craig.*' She sat deep in thought for another minute or so and then felt her shoulders relax. '*Who am I kidding? It wasn't his fault. It takes two to tango.*' "These thoughts are getting me nowhere," she said aloud. With a passing glance back to the ceiling and turned on the TV.

Connor could not get the image of the woman on the beach out of his mind. Memories of Darla returned in so many ways. He wished he had made more of an effort to meet her so he could get this stuff out of his head once and for all.

He decided that he needed to paint, so he went up the back stairs taking two steps at a time. He still could not get over the fact that none of these old steps had a squeak in them. The house was quiet; as it always was but he thought now that there were new occupants he was expecting a little more commotion. He scraped his easel across the floor, wincing his face as he did, not wanting to disturb anyone below. He picked up a cloth from the floor and placed it under the legs of the frame for a buffer. He began to paint, or at least he wanted to, but the only image that came to mind was the one of the girl on the beach. He wiped his hand across his face as he always did in frustration. There was no use in trying, so he closed and locked the door to the loft reassuring himself that he would try again in the morning.

20

She awoke early, had breakfast by the pool and then headed up to check out the loft again. She opened the door, stood in the doorway and looked around. Stepping inside, she leisurely walked around and around, then made her way to the window and looked out toward the cabin. There was no one in sight. *'Maybe a little music will help to shed this mood.'* She walked over to the desk and picked up the remote, hesitated and hit play. The music began to move her as she closed her eyes and allowed it to penetrate. She moved to the center of the room and just stood there, then all of a sudden, started to move.

She wrapped her arms around herself and began to sway beautifully to the music. She was lost in the rhythm that flowed out from the speakers that were hidden inside the walls. She envisioned herself as a small child and began the dance routine that was still familiar to her. Thoughts of Aunt Evie came to her as she heard her words again, 'Dance *like no one is watching.'* That is what she told her, that is what they say. As she encouraged her to continue, she danced there before her. Those famous words, 'Dance like no one is watching,' so she did, and someone was.

She did not see anyone at first as she swung her arms and moved her hips to the rhythm of the music. She caught a glimpse of herself in the mirrored wall. She twirled and curled to the beat as gracefully as any ballerina. As the music ended, she arched her back, raised her hands to form a circle above her head. Then she bent, moved one foot out behind her and took a low bow. Raising her eyes to the mirror, she caught sight of a shadow ducking quickly out of sight. Her first thoughts went quickly back again to a time when she had noticed her aunt leaning against the door frame of the loft, watching her. But it was not her aunt who was watching this time and fear gripped her at the thoughts of an intruder inside her home!

"Whose there!?" she yelled, as she raced to the door. She stopped short in her tracks as she came chest to chest with the intruder. *Umph!* The sound escaped her lungs, in a rush, as they collided.

Suddenly, she was frozen on the spot, her eyes locked on the intruder's, like a deer in the headlights. "You...? her mouth open in disbelief. "What are you doing here!?"

Dodger was on the step when Connor opened the door. He gave him a quick rub, tossed a stick and told him he had some work to do, but they would play later. With that, he headed off to the loft. There was no one around but saw breakfast dishes left out on the patio table. Making his way to the back door, he unlocked it and went in. As always, he was careful to lock it behind him, just as he had done since he first moved in. Exiting the first stairway, he could hear music coming from somewhere as he crossed the hall to climb the second flight.

"Well, there is life here after all," he said under his breath. On reaching the top, he continued down the hall, but something was different. The door to the other studio was open, something he had not seen since he was first in the room with Evelyn. The light streaming from the entrance made it clear where the music was coming from.

It was totally unexpected, and of course, curiosity got the better of him. Nothing registered as he glanced in on his way by, but suddenly, as if a light bulb had suddenly been switched on, he stopped dead in his tracks.

'Backing up, he took another look through the door and froze when he realized just who it was he was seeing. "What the...?" The words came out of his mouth in a disbelieving hush. He suddenly was searching for breath as he whispered, *'Darla?'* He tried to move, but he could not help himself, he was nailed to the spot in the opening. Still working to catch his breath, he watched, captivated by her motion. *'How graceful she is,'* he thought as he began to wonder if she was a professional dancer or just caught up in the moment. Her movement was hypnotic, and he felt himself swaying to the beat. Her body was slim, beautiful and lithe. Her arms were long and lean as she positioned one over her head and the other toward the floor, resembling an awkward arc. Her fingers perfectly pointed. Her skirt flared then wrapped around her knees as she twisted and twirled to the music.

Her eyes were closed as she danced and swayed to the music, without inhibition. '*God, she's beautiful,*' he thought. He could feel the excitement build as thoughts of her raced into his mind, remembering her in his arms all those years ago.

Awestruck, he suddenly realized the music had stopped. Frantically, he tried to duck out of sight but didn't make it in time. '*Damn it!*' he thought, '*now what?*' He flattened himself against the wall but realizing he had been seen, stepped back into the doorway just as she came running out.

Umph! There they were... face to face. Their eyes were locked together, both in total disbelief at their discovery, too shocked to move.

Finally, Darla realized what was happening. "You...? her mouth open in disbelief. "You!? What are you doing here?"

"I... uh... I live here...?" he blurted defiantly.

"I live here!" she shouted. "This is my home!" There was a long pause then she peered at him through squinted eyes and asked, "Are you the person living in the cabin?"

He just stood there dumbfounded. She was so close he could feel her breath on his face, and his eyes moved down to her mouth. He wanted so badly to kiss her! '*Oh, what the hell,*' he thought, as he put both hands on the either side of her face and pulled her in to his lips. He heard her moan and felt her relax. For about ten seconds, their hearts were home.

She could not believe he was here, and kissing her. For his part, he could not believe he had finally found her. Suddenly she pulled away and looked at him.

"What do you think you're doing!" she seethed, seemingly coming to her senses. She drew back and slapped him across the face. "How dare you!" She was so angry that tears sprang to her eyes.

His hand flew up to his cheek, "Damn it girl, where'd you learn to hit like that?" It did not help that a smile followed the question.

She stood there with her hand up to her mouth in disbelief that she had just slapped him. She took a step back, tears rolling down her face. All the thoughts she had had over the last seven years came flooding back. '*Where had he been? Why did he not come back for her? Why did he lie about coming back? Why did he tell her he loved her if he didn't?*' She could not believe he was standing here in front of her, still as handsome as the last time she saw him.

"What are you doing here?" she said, in barely a whisper. "Where have you been? It has been s-e-v-e-n y-e-a-r-s!" She was blubbering at this point, and he was barely able to make out her words. She backed away and walked back into her studio. She went over to the desk and pulled a tissue out of the box and blew her nose. She kept her back to him as she tried to contain herself.

"Darla?"

"Get out," she said, without looking at him.

"Get out? Are you nuts? I'm not leaving you, I just found you."

"Found me? Was I lost!? How hard did you look for me, Connor? Get out!"

The room was deathly quiet, and she was afraid to turn around. Finally, when she did, he was gone. She began to cry again. *"What have I done!? He was right here, and now he was gone!"* She made her way down the hall and stopped briefly at his loft. Pressing her ear to the door was fruitless. Not hearing anything, she opened the door to the front steps and went down to her bedroom.

He knew she was angry so he backed away and made his way down the hall to his loft. He let himself in and closed the door. He just stood there in silence looking at the door as if she were going to come back and look for him. She did not. After a minute, sadly he gently nodded his head in realization and turned toward his easel.

He took out some paint and poured a few colors onto his palette. He knew in his mind, what he wanted this piece to say to him. It was indelibly imprinted in his mind. He swiped the canvas with four quick, black strokes. Two long verticals and two short horizontals, resembling the frame of a full length mirror. He pictured her reflection as she danced in her loft.

He laid the brush down and stepped away from his work. He rubbed his stubbly face and paced back and forth. He could still feel her chest against his when she had come through the door. He could still taste her lips from the kiss then, rubbing his cheek, he could also feel her response. *'She's angry now,'* he thought, *'but she won't always be.'* He figured it was smart that he left when he had.

He sat down in a chair by the window and stared into space with only Darla in his mind. He still could not believe that he has been living this close to her and did not know it. It finally hit him, *'It was her I saw on the beach yesterday! The movement,*

her shape, how she stood; no wonder she looked so familiar.'
He was that close to her, and he had let the opportunity pass.

Now he felt that he could not leave the loft. If he did, she would surely disappear somehow, and he could not stand to lose her again. He knew she was somewhere on the floor below him, but he had not been through the house to know where any of the rooms were located. He had been in the kitchen several times, hung his paintings up for Evelyn and did odd jobs that she was no longer able to do, but he had no reason to go upstairs. From the back entry, it was a totally different route. It went up a flight of stairs, crossed an empty hall and ascended another set to the third floor. If there was an access to the main house, he did not look for it as he felt it was none of his business. He went to the house when he was summoned and other than that, he went there to paint.

He stood up and looked around his loft. The canvas on his easel stared at him from when he tried to capture her dancing. He was so overwhelmed that he could not get out what he wanted this painting to portray. Looking over at the first painting he ever did of her from memory, he went to mush. She was so beautiful and seeing her today, confirmed that she had not changed at all. Just more mature, in an unhappy way. It bothered him to think that he may have caused her to feel that way.

Her words echoed in his ears, *"How hard did you look for me?"*

'That was a good question,' he thought, *'more of a slap in the face than the real one.'* He reached up and touched his cheek again, rolled his jaw around a few times and grinned at her fiery spirit. Those words came back to haunt him again. *"How hard did you look for me?"* He shook his head in disbelief as he realized he never really looked for her! *'Well, there was that one time...'* He remembered looking her name up online just to see if she was still in Kanyon Cove. He could not find anything associated with her name. The only one he knew her by was Harrington, and there was nothing! He simply assumed that when she did not contact him, it was over and that she was carrying on with her life. It nearly killed him to let it go, but he felt at the time that he had to respect her decision. Now he got the vibe from her that she had been expecting him to find her. *'Where have you been? It has been s-e-v-e-n y-e-a-r-s...!'* he heard her words clearly in his mind. "Boy, she drove that point home."

'What the hell!? Why is it so difficult to figure women out?' He was frustrated to the core. In her mind, he had obviously screwed up somewhere or had missed some vital piece of information. He racked his brain to think about her words to him on their last meeting.

'*I will leave it up to you,*' he told her, '*you have my cell number and my email address, and I will wait to hear from you.*' He was certain that was how the conversation had gone. He relived it many times thinking that he clearly remembered her reply.

'*Thank you, Conner,*' she had said, '*we'll figured it out. I will be thinking about you, and I know already that I love you, but I want to think about it. Promise me you won't call.*'

'*So what did I miss?*' He scratched his head and rubbed his chin as he thought back to their night together. '*She had made herself quite clear that I was to wait for her to contact me!*' he mumbled. He went back to his chair and sat down again. He spent hours thinking about her and wondered why he did not try to contact her instead of giving up so easily. "Damn it!" he said aloud, "I thought I was respecting her wishes." He returned his gaze out the window in deep thought. '*Now she was asking me where I have been all this time! It makes no sense? There is something wrong with this picture! She indicated that she has been waiting for me for seven years?*' He was deeply frustrated at being more than a little confused but softened again as he recalled how she felt in his arms today. Never had he thought that he would ever get to hold her again.

Darla heard a tiny knock on her door. Her first thought was that it was Connor, but after giving her head a shake, she realized he would not have known where her bedroom was. "Come in," she said, knowing it was Dawn.

"Darla? Is there something wrong? You've been alone nearly all day."

"Yes, I'm fine; don't worry about me, Dawn."

"But you've been acting weird since you came back from the beach yesterday. Are you sure everything is OK?"

"Yes, everything is fine; I'm just trying to figure a few things out for myself?" She turned around so Dawn could not see her face. She was upset but had mixed emotions as to why. The guy she had longed for all these years was now living right under her nose in her cabin. Her face sobered as a realization hit her. Without turning around, she asked Dawn if she would give her a few minutes. Dawn obliged, excused herself and left the room.

She sat down on her bed and began to put a couple of things together. Aunt Evie knew who Connor was! Why did she not mention him to her? Darla was remembering the paintings downstairs with Connor's signature on them. *'She knew who he was!'* Now she was pissed. *'She knew how I felt about him. I had confided in her my inner most thoughts and feelings about him. She knew how I felt when I couldn't get hold of him and* she knew I never stopped loving him. How could she do this to me? He must have been living here for more than a year! I can't believe this! What the hell was she thinking?' Now she was angrier at her dead aunt than with Connor. 'He didn't know who she was, but she damned well knew him!' Now she was rambling. "Oh my God! Grace! She knew he was her father and she did not say a word! All this time... and she took her secret to the grave!" She was reflecting in whispers, realizing that Dawn may be close by. She frowned at her next thought. 'She left this house to me, knowing he was living here. Was that her way of not interfering? She never interfered with anything unless she was asked. She knew we would meet sooner or later, living on the same property,' she mused. 'She must have had a reason for bringing him here. Did she want to keep an eye on him? Did she want him close by, so he wouldn't disappear again?' Her aunt was a clever woman, and she did not do anything without reason.

Connor was still in his loft, deep in thought, and still wondering what he could have done differently. He knew that life happens, time cannot be retrieved, and there are no do overs.

He began to think back over his time with Evelyn; their first meeting at the loft, where she showed up with his flyer in hand.

After they introduced themselves and became acquainted, Evelyn had said something that never left him. *"Yes, I know who you are Connor Barnes,"* she had said. "Why would she have said that? How did she 'know' me when we were complete strangers back then? Was it only because my name was on the flyer or was it something else?"

He now knew why she had always seemed so familiar to him. She must have been Darla's aunt as he realized now how much they resembled each other. He wondered why she had never mentioned her niece to him. He had mentioned the childhood drawings and artwork he had found in the cabin loft, and still, she had said nothing. She did, however, say that she had a niece named Darla. She knew the connection, but he did not. He looked across the loft at his painting of Darla, and he remembered that she had asked him if he would sell it to her. It made no sense to him then, but it certainly did now! She had also bought a couple of his paintings and had asked him to hang them for her knowing that Darla would be at the house and might possible recognize his signature. So many things were coming to mind now that he realized he would never have the answers to.

He yawned and swiped his hands over his face and leaned his head against the back of the chair. In no time, he had nodded off. Hours later he opened his eyes and rolled his shoulders around to get the stiffness out of his neck. It was dark in the loft, and he tried to make his way to the wall to flip the light switch. As he crept across the floor, he stubbed his toe on a closed can of paint knocking it over. He stopped his stride in midair and sucked in his breath, hoping he was not heard from below; he was wrong.

The house was quiet and still. Darla had been lying on her bed struggling to stay awake since coming down from the loft hours earlier. Any thought of sleep was quickly extinguished by the encounter with Connor. All of a sudden, she heard the noise from above. Frightened, she sat up to listen. She was going through the layout of the Manor in her mind and realized that Connor's loft was directly above her head. She was wide awake now and knowing he was so close she began to feel the old flames.

It had been a long time since she has had these thoughts and feelings, but here they were again, just knowing he was so close. She walked around her room a few times and kept looking up toward the ceiling. Her heart was pounding, her palms sweating, her mouth completely dry.

She looked at the clock on her nightstand. Five thirty... *'Why is he up there so early?'* She tried to gather the courage to climb the stairs and came to the conclusion that if she didn't do it now, he could be gone again. She knew that while he was this close, she had to make a move.

"*I have to,*' she thought, walking to the door. She paused in the hallway for several seconds continuing to build the nerve to climb up the stairs. *'Should I or shouldn't I,*' she asked herself for the umpteenth time.

Connor continued to creep his way over to the light switch and flicked it on. Squinting against the light, he checked his watch and went back to set the paint can up right. *'Five thirty, I hope I didn't wake anyone,*' he mumbled. He no sooner got the words out of his mouth when he heard a tap on the door. He looked at it realizing that, the only person to ever knock on his door was Evelyn, and he knew it was not her. He went over to open it, fully expecting to be chewed out for making a noise at this hour.

She stood in the doorway of his loft looking like a lost child.

"Darla," he said.

She cleared her throat and whispered, "Can I come in?"

He stepped aside and swept his hand sideways to invite her in. "Yes, come in. I apologize if I woke you up."

"It's okay but why are you here so late," she asked.

"Well, uh... I actually haven't left yet. I... I came up here after we saw each other earlier and I... I just couldn't seem to... to go back to the cabin."

Her heart swelled just looking at him. She had remained silent for several minutes.

He waited for her to speak. He knew she had things to say and he wanted her to say them now, and get it over with.

"Connor, why didn't you ever look for me? I have to know for my own sanity. I just want to know the truth."

"I couldn't look for you... you asked me not to! I waited for you to contact me; why the hell didn't you?" He didn't mean to toss it back at her, but he did and instantly regretted saying it. This was not how he envisioned their first meeting. He pictured in his mind, them running towards each other in slow motion, him picking her up in his arms and swinging her around while they relished in the joy of finding each other. *'Man, I'm watching way too much TV and listening to too many country songs!!'* he mused.

"You could have found me if you had wanted to!" she yelled.

"Did you want me to find you?" he asked, and waited for her to answer, but she did not. "Darla, answer me, did you want me to find you?"

"I can't answer that."

"Why not? You asked me a question, and I answered it, so I deserve an answer from you as well."

"Connor, I...um...it has been seven years, I gave up any hope of ever seeing you again."

"Well, I never gave up hope of finding you." His voice not quite accusing, but very close to sarcasm.

"What... you never gave up?" She was talking very slowly to make sure he heard every word. "You never gave up?" she repeated, her voice dipping sarcastically. "Then where the hell have you been!" she shrieked at him.

"I've been in Kanyon Cove for nearly three years. Before that, I was living in the town next to here after I left university." He had his arm out pointing into the air in the direction he was speaking of. "Where have you been? There is no record of you anywhere, especially nothing under Harrington or Kanyon Cove. I couldn't very well have asked Craig where you were, now could I! That was totally out of the question, and I didn't know you by any other name".

His words instantly floored her.

"Oh my God, Connor!" She was dumbstruck. She closed her eyes and swallowed.

"What?" he asked. "Darla, what?" he asked again.

She opened her eyes to the realization of what these last seven years of hell has been all about. She had been so busy blaming him that she totally forgot the turn of events her own life had taken. She opened her mouth to speak, but nothing would come out. She swallowed again, and Connor could see her struggling. He walked over to her, put a hand on each of her arms and gently asked again, "Darla, tell me what's wrong."

As soon as his hands touched her arms, she stepped into his in a flood of tears. She wrapped her arms around his back and curled his shirt around her fingers as she held on to him. He in return tightened his embrace, laid his cheek on top of her head and waited. He could feel great sobs ripping from her body, and he knew that whatever was going on, was serious.

"I'm sorry," she blubbered, "I'm so sorry." The more she thought about it, the more she cried. All of sudden she realized, this entire mess was her fault, not his. She was the one who had decided not to contact him. She thought it was the right thing to do. *'The right thing for who!?'* she asked herself. She let her dumb decisions overrule her heart, and where had it gotten her, and most especially, Grace? It was time to face Connor with the truth, the truth that she was just realizing.

She forced herself away from the comfort of Connor's chest and stepped back. As his arms loosened from around her and dropped down, she slid her hands down his arms and into his hands. He was a bit confused, but he wrapped his fingers around hers and asked, "What are you sorry for?"

She did not want to say the words aloud, but she had no choice. She had blamed him long enough, and now it was her turn to take full responsibility.

"Connor, I...um...," she cleared her throat and started again. "I had my name changed almost seven years ago. I had it done to prevent Craig from finding me!"

It was his turn to react. "You've been away from Craig for almost seven years!?" He heard himself repeat it, "S-e-v-e-n... years?" still in total disbelief. "You have been free all this time?" He dropped her hands and walked over to the window and just stood there not knowing what to say.

"Connor?" She went into panic mode. His back was toward her, and all she could think of was a worst case senario. '*Was he angry? Did he hate her? Would he forgive her?*'

He looked at his watch again, it was already seven o'clock. "Are you expecting anyone, there is a car pulling up out front," he asked.

"No, I'm not; my sister is home and can see to whoever it is. Connor, we have to talk about this."

"What is your last name anyway?" he asked, turning from the window. "Why couldn't I find you?"

"My Aunt Evie made that happen. She had my name changed to Roma, our family name, shortly after I moved in with her to get away from Craig."

"So, Evelyn *was* your aunt?" he asked.

"Yes, my sister and I inherited this place a few weeks ago."

"Connor, I tried to call you shortly after I moved in here seven years ago with my aunt. Your number had been changed, and I thought you didn't want to be found."

Connor put his hand up and swiped it across his face and shook his head. '*I knew that day would come back to haunt me and here it is!*'

"What's wrong?" she asked.

His shoulders slumped down, and now it was his turn to confess. He sheepishly started, "I... uh... I kinda dropped my phone into a bucket of paint", his voice fading off to an embarrassing whisper as he pointed to a can marked with an X on the floor. Summoning back some courage, he went on to explain, "My phone rang while I was working and I was so sure it was you that I got clumsy and dropped it while trying to get it open." His words were coming out a mile a minute as he wanted her to know that he was really praying that he would hear from her. "When I went to get a new one, I couldn't get the same number. Not only that but when you gave me your number I put it in my cell phone list and threw the paper away, so I wouldn't be caught with it. I didn't have it memorized since I never used it, so when I got the new phone, I couldn't remember what your number was. I still have the paint can and with the phone still in it."

"I've been blaming you all these years for forgetting about me, so I tried to forget about you Connor," she paused for what seemed like an eternity to him, "but I couldn't."

"I never ever forgot about you baby. How could I do that? You were everything to me. I desperately wanted you to contact me, and I waited for any sign that you wanted me as much as I wanted you. I just figured you had settled back in to a life with 'Creepy Craig' and moved on."

She smiled and said, "Creepy Craig?"

He looked at her with a grin on his face and said, "Yes, Creepy Craig. He was the creepiest guy in college."

"Oh, how so?" she asked, trying not to laugh, yet knowing exactly what he was going to say.

He looked at her for several seconds, deciding if he should say anything about Craig since he was not here to defend his sorry ass. "He was just a creep, that's all."

"No, that isn't all, tell me what you know." She knew he was embarrassed because he was blushing slightly. "Connor," she pushed him teasingly.

"He hit on several of my buddies in college, so we just called him 'Creepy Craig' behind his back. We didn't know that he was as gay as a goose until it came out that he was hitting on some of the guys in our group."

"So, you knew this back when we saw each other then, and you didn't think I would be interested?" she asked.

"Well....yeah? It all added up when you told me that I was your...um...er," he was making little circles with his finger trying so come up with the word.

"First? Are you trying to say 'first' Connor?" She was so enjoying teasing him, but he did not know it until he looked over at her and saw her smiling.

"You're enjoying this aren't you?" he asked.

"I so am!" she said and they both began to laugh.

"I was totally shocked when you told me that you and Craig were married. When did you find out?" he asked.

"I not only found out I have pictures," she grinned

"Pictures!?"

"Yes, my sister and I followed him one night when he was meeting up with a 'friend' so to speak. I got them both in a lip lock on my cellphone. My aunt and her lawyer used them as leverage to keep him away from me, and that's when Aunt Evie arranged to have my name changed.

How dumb was I anyway? I never even put two and two together that you'd never find me under a new name!" She was pensive for a few seconds as a recent memory flashed. "Were you in town not long ago with Dodger... in a truck?"

"Yes. He loves the truck, why?"

"When I was at work at the book store, I saw him on the passenger side of a truck, and it looked so much like the old Dodger, it just gave me a start."

His face sobered as he said, "Well this has been one hell of a mess, hasn't it? Both of us blaming the other for circumstances beyond our control," he said, looking at her. "Can I ask you a question, Darla?"

"Yes, sure you can if I get to ask one in return."

"Fair enough. Have you been alone all this time, I mean, are you involved with anyone?"

"Yes, to the first part and no to the second," she said and waited for his response. The look on his face was priceless. He thought back over his question and in which order she was answering it, and he was dumbstruck.

"You aren't...seeing...anyone?" He was having difficulty believing what she had just said, and he shook his head back and forth as in 'no' while he responded.

"Yes, Connor, I have been alone all this time, and no, I am not involved with anyone, is that clear enough for you?"

He saw her smile, and he knew she was teasing him again. Walking toward her he asked, "Seriously?"

"There has been no one before you or since, Connor," she said softly.

He reached for her and wanted so badly to kiss her. When he ducked close to her lips, she put a finger between them and whispered, "Umm, my turn."

He straightened up and nodded at their agreement, "Yes, of course, you get to ask one also, go ahead."

"My question, Connor, is the same as your question," she said as she cocked her head to one side and waited for his answer.

"Well, my answer, Darla, is the same as your answer."

"Really!?" she said, widening her grin and throwing her arms around his neck. He folded her tiny body up in his arms and pressed close to her. This is where they both had wanted to be for the last seven years. She brought her head up far enough for the kiss they both were anxious to get on with.

"Mommy, Mommy, Mommy!!!" they heard, as Grace bounded up into the loft. "I've been looking all over for you!" she said throwing herself into Darla's arms. "It so nice to be back at Auntie Evie's! I love it here!" She was bubbling over with excitement since this was her first time at the Manor since it belonged to her mother. She was so happy to be with Darla that she did not see anyone else.

Connor saw that Darla was beaming with pride as she listened to this little girl jabber away. She was biting her bottom lip with tears in her eyes as she hugged the little girl. Realizing he was still there, she glanced up and looked at him as Grace wrapped herself around her legs. "Grace, honey, there's someone I want you to meet."

"Who?" she said, and her eyes met Connor's as she looked behind her. His heart melted when he looked at her. It was as if he was looking at his own image. Those blonde curls and blue eyes that would melt even the most stone hearted. He looked up at Darla and then back at Grace.

"Grace, this is Connor, Connor Barnes, and Connor, this is Grace."

He squatted down to her level and offered his hand to her. She looked at it and then accepted it as the little lady she was being taught to be. "Hello, Mr. Barnes."

Darla's heart was bursting inside her chest and was nowhere near ready for what came out of Grace's mouth next.

She still had Connor's hand in hers when she said, "Are you, my daddy?"

He stood up, still holding her hand and stared straight into Darla's eyes. He knew in an instant that he was since Darla had just told him that she has not been with any other man. Darla's hand went up to her mouth, and she pressed her fingers against her lips in acknowledgement. Tears welled up in his eyes, and he pressed his lips together trying to contain himself as he drew in ragged breaths. In a few seconds, he knelt back down to face Grace.

"You are my daddy aren't you? We have the same last name! My name is Evelyn Grace Roma-Barnes," she smiled proudly at him.

"Yes, Grace, I am your daddy, and I am so very happy to meet you, my angel. Would you be offended if I gave you a hug?"

She threw her arms around his neck with the same gusto as when she saw her mother. Darla watched as Connor closed his eyes at his daughter's touch and she heard him choke up. He hugged her tightly, and they both acted as if they were making up for lost time. Grace was in no hurry to release him, and he certainly was willing to wait until she was ready. He wrapped his arm around her bottom and scooped her up in his arms. He stood up still holding her tightly and reached for Darla's hand. When she gave it, he squeezed it, happy in the fact that they both were silently agreeing that there is no room for blame here.

Dawn walked in the doorway and stopped in her tracks. What she saw was indescribable. Three faces, all with the same happy smiles, all with tears of joy in their eyes and the feeling of 'home' flooded the room.

"Well, what do we have here?" she said, with her own smile. "I came looking for Grace... and found a family!"

"Dawn, honey, this is Connor Barnes," Darla said reaching for her hand. "Connor, this is my sister, Dawn Coleman. She is part owner here at the Manor."

"It's a pleasure to meet you, Dawn," he said, reaching out his free hand. She took his hand and said, "I don't even have to ask how Grace fits in, all I have to do is look at her. She is your daughter, no question! You make a great looking family."

Grace was still wrapped around Connor's neck, and he put his arm around Darla and smiled in acknowledgement that they do indeed, make a great family, at last.

There was so much lost time to try and make up for. Time, they know they can never get back but what they were sure of was, that it was time to begin to make new family memories. Connor, Darla, and Grace, the way it was always meant to be.

Epilogue

Darla had hoped the rain would hold off just long enough to get through the ceremony. The sky had been threatening and was dark and ominous. There were just enough sunny intervals to give everyone hope.

They were having a poolside ceremony with a reception to follow on the front lawn. Darla had hired waiters to serve the guests when the ceremony was over. Tables were set up under a huge canopy with one table for china, silverware, glasses, and napkins at the front.

It would not be a big gala affair like her aunt would have assembled, but enough to make their day special. Connor had invited a few of his college and art buddies, Dawn had invited a few friends and acquaintances from the bar where she had hosted, and Darla had invited her friends from the book store. It had been nice to see other people show up, but all that mattered to them was having their family there. She had asked Sam Logan to walk her down the aisle. He was delighted to have been asked, and graciously accepted.

At Darla's request, Sam took a walk around the grounds to be certain everything was going as planned. The waiters were in place, the tables were set up, and food was ready. Pool side, there were tables set up for refreshments, and finger food was available while the guests waited.

Meanwhile, Darla, Dawn, and Grace were upstairs in Darla's bedroom getting dressed.

Grace's outfit was an ankle length white lace dress with a satin lining. A mauve satin ribbon tied around her waist at the back with each end of the ribbon touching the floor. Underneath her dress was a crinoline with enough starch to make the dress full and white patent leather shoes. In her blond curls, she had a few violets pinned at the side. She made a beautiful flower girl.

Dawn wore a knee length mauve satin dress with spaghetti string straps, white leather heels, and would carry a bouquet of white baby roses. In her hair, she had a spray of violets pinned just above her ear.

A hush fell over the bedroom. Grace watched wide-eyed as Dawn helped Darla step into her wedding dress. She zipped the back of the floor length, strapless gown. It fit snuggly in the bodice and molded to her tiny frame at the waist where it billowed out over mounds of crinolines. Sitting them down in front of her, Darla stepped into white satin covered shoes which extended her height an additional three inches. Dawn helped her with the veil and placed it around the top of her head in a tiara type band.

Then she reached around and pulled the veil up over Darla's head and down over her face.

Dawn gasped at the site of her sister. "Beautiful!" was all she could say as she choked up. She waved her fingers, fan-like in front of her face so as not to ruin her makeup. Darla never said a word knowing she would be in the same predicament as Dawn. They knew each other well enough to know what each other was thinking anyway, so there had been no need for words. Dawn passed her the bouquet of purple violets and white baby's breath. The three of them stood in the full length mirror matching perfectly. "I think we are ready," Darla whispered. All the while they were dressing; a photographer followed them around taking pictures as another photographer followed Connor around the cabin capturing photos of the groom.

Dawn and Grace left the room, and Dawn sent Sam upstairs for Darla. When she invited him in, he was speechless for several seconds. Thoughts of Evelyn flashed through his mind thinking of how much she resembled her. "You look amazing my dear, and your aunt would be so very proud if she could only have been here to witness this grand event.

"Thank you for agreeing to do this for me today, it means so much to me Sam."

"There is no need for thanks my dear, it is my pleasure, but I'm sure you have a groom waiting to see this vision of beauty so, let's get this show on the road," he said, smiling as he offered her his arm. She wrapped hers around his and headed down the stairs, through the house to the patio doors. When she got close enough to see outside, she stopped to take in the sight of Connor. Sam felt her suck in her breath, and he patted her hand in understanding.

There he was, tall and handsome and waiting only for her. Her heart swelled at the thought of how much she loved him. He was standing next to the minister, in a white tuxedo, white leather shoes, a mauve bowtie, and matching cummerbund. On his lapel was one single purple rose. Dodger was sitting proudly next to Connor's leg knowing he was 'the best dog.'

Connor looked nervously toward the door, waiting for her to walk out. She squeezed Sam's arm to indicate she was ready and they stepped forward in full view of everyone. Connor could not believe his eyes when he saw her walk through the door. A smile of relief spread across his face at the sight of her. *'Seven years I have waited for this day... s-e-v-e-n.'*

Sam walked her slowly around the pool as soft music played in the background. Darla's ear caught the music and realized it was not the traditional wedding march but instead, the music from her dance studio. Aunt Evie crossed her mind and instantly she thought it was perfect that it was being played at her wedding. Her presence was being felt now, and Darla was certain she had something to do with the choice of music, in approval of today's event.

Connor was more than willing to receive Darla's hand from Sam's. He shook Sam's hand and thanked him for being there and together, turned to face the Minister. The ceremony went quickly, knowing they could be rained on at any moment. The reception line went slower than expected and as people stood around sipping on their drinks and eating finger food, a few drops of rain fell. Suddenly the sky darkened, and it began to sprinkle. Darla realized they were closer to the back entrance than to the patio door so, before the advancing downpour, she made a decision. "We are all going inside through the back entrance!" she yells so everyone can hear.

"We won't all fit in there, Darla," Connor said.

Darla looked at Dawn, winked and said, "Yes we will," indicating for her to go ahead and prepare.

Dawn ran to the back entrance ahead of everyone and pulled the lever under the stairs. The wall opened to the den then she went down the hall to open the door to the outside. This was Darla's signal.

She kept her eyes on the door, and when Dawn appeared, she began to move her guests toward the entrance.

"I'm telling you, baby, we are not all going to fit in that entryway," he said, pointing in that direction.

"And I said, yes we will," she smiled. Taking his arm, she led the guests inside.

When they got to the door Connor's face fell when he saw the inside of the house before him. "What the...?"

"Not now my love," Darla said, squeezing his arm as she talked through her smile.

The servers had been instructed earlier to be prepared for the rain, so most of the food had already been brought inside before the skies opened. Thunder rolled, and lightning flashed as the storm settled in. There seemed to be fewer people when they were outside, but now that everyone was inside, it seemed full.

Again, her Aunt Evelyn came to mind. She had known how much she had loved a good party and had enjoyed entertaining in her day. She glanced over at Connor's painting, just as one corner tipped ever so slightly. *'Yes, I thought you were here!'* Darla said to herself. She smiled and latched on to Connor's arm.

Once the food had been eaten, and the cake was gone, the guests found their way to the front door and to their respective vehicles. Darla, Connor, Dawn, Grace, and Dodger had their house back.

Dawn and Grace went upstairs, Dodger laid down in front of the fireplace and, as the servants cleaned up the mess, Connor took his bride's hand and together, made their way down the path to the cabin.

The End

Other Titles by the Author

Gypsy Heart
Available Online & Print

Gifted
Available Online & Print

Tidbits, Tips & Treasures
a Self-Help Book
Available Online

Watch for Dee's future books

J O Y

&

Then, Now & Forever

To remain in touch with Dee,

contact her through her website at

deelightfulreading.com

DEElightful Reading

Made in the USA
Lexington, KY
10 February 2019

SEARCHING FOR TRUTHS

Amidst Expressions
of
Unity and Diversity

by

KARL POHLHAUS

Fogfree Publishing

ABOUT THE AUTHOR

Karl Pohlhaus hails from the East Cost. Born in a Lutheran family and raised in a mixture of Protestant fundamentalism and Lutheranism, Karl's mother saw to it that Karl, who became known as Charlie, attended all sorts of religious gatherings. Her need to understand became infused in his very soul. Having set his sights on a scientific career in engineering Charles/Karl graduated from a top engineering college and went on to a good Lutheran seminary to become grounded in what could never be answered by science in its empirical guise. But initial ministry still posed too many questions and Charles went on to graduate studies to learn all he could of the world religions.

It was in this setting that he sought to find a common ground in what he had learned from Science and what he had learned from Religion. Ultimately, his watchword became the truth and not doctrine. After serving a parish for a number of years he retired from ministry to pick up teaching world religions. His thoughts had jelled to the point where they needed to find an avenue in writing. His search for truth has afforded him many friends from the world of Science and Religion, including well-known figures in each world. He brings a unique perspective, having studied all of the religions currently on this planet, including the various denominations and historical expressions whose shadows still find their way into human consciousness.

Perhaps most importantly, Karl/Charles' love affair with truth and his growing need to share values that seem to get lost in the hue and cry of partisan politics and culturally-derived social views, have permitted him that unique dual perspective that sees and knows enough of reality to bring a prize back from the world of religious philosophy and scientific technique that can benefit those who have not taken that journey.

Charles teaches world religions and religious philosophy and contributes editorials to this local newspaper. He has done a number of things including basic medical research, physics and mathematics teacher, engineer, designer, chef, chaplain, minister, trustee, lecturer and fiduciary. He resides with his wife in the Phoenix area and is a member of Unity along with his lovely wife Judy.

FOREWORD

This book provides an overarching perspective of the world's religions and philosophies, old and new, and provides an integrated view of Truth as expressed by many cultures. From the viewpoint of various religious positions, equally valid, the author distinguishes the key differences between honest inspiration and revelation. He recognizes Truth as being both relative and subjective with the greater reality being related just as much to our connectedness as to our seeming separateness and individual differences all in wonderful contrast in God's garden of life.

As a physicist by inclination and training, I believe it useful to share the general scientific perspective on Truth so that one may see its relative nature.

Humanity is concerned with scientific enquiry because people want to understand the universe in which we find ourselves. People want to engineer and reliably control and modulate as much of their environment as is possible to sustain, enrich and propagate human life. Following this path, the goal of Science is to gain a reliable description of all natural phenomena so as to allow accurate prediction of nature's behavior as a function of an ever changing environment. Science seeks to provide internally self-consistent knowledge of how phenomena relate within a minimum set of assumptions and definitions. Science's minimum set of definitions restricts its activities to relative knowledge rather than absolute truth.

As humans, we perceive events but often we perceive them partially. The total inherent information content or complete reality remains unperceived. That is so because we take from events a convolution of:

(1) the extent of our developed sensory system that has taken in the event, and

(2) our belief structure that selectively filters out and amplifies segments from the original data stream.

As humans, we rely on the extent to which our five senses can register information. Therefore, only a fraction of the information we receive is available to us to use. We make personal observations through a distorted psychological lens defined by our individual mind sets, and not the neutral available data field. That field can be penetrated more completely by specially designed instruments, but even here those instruments become limited to our average cognitive development.

Over the course of the past four to five centuries, we have learned how to conduct scientific investigations; initially under the rubric of Classical Mechanics; more recently using Quantum Mechanics. The human struggle involved in making this investigative paradigm shift falls under the subject of truth.

A century ago, Science developed a rigid position on Classical Mechanics. More recently, experiments have demonstrated strange new discrete quantum packets of change and relativistic couplings of the separate coordinates of time and distance. Thus, space-time was born. But these new experiments violated basic assumptions of Classical Mechanics and consequently were rigorously resisted. Today, they are accepted, but it has taken almost a century of productive work to make it so.

Today, the prevailing truth about nature, via the Quantum Mechanic paradigm, is struggling with modifying its internal self-consistent picture to include experimental observations conducted in the new fields of Psychoenergetics, Extra Sensory Perception or ESP, Homeopathy, and the extraordinary feats of the mind and emotions. Today physicists must either deny the existence of such observations or expand their model of nature to include these phenomena. In time, it will happen as Humankind develops its corporate consciousness to understand the place of observed phenomena.

This fine book by Karl (Charlie) Pohlhaus shows how the general human community has struggled with these types of issues throughout history. I wish for all readers to gain as much joy and insight from reading this book as I have.

Dr. William Tiller
Chair and Professor Emeritus
Material Sciences Department
Stanford University

TABLE OF CONTENTS

Chapter One: Introduction To Truth (1–9)
1. Some historical background
2. The Scientific Method
3. Toward a definition of Truth
4. What are Truths?
5. Is Truth objective or subjective in nature?

Chapter Two: How Do We Know When We Arrive At Truth? (11–19)
1. Arriving at Truth
2. Misperceptions
3. Toward solutions that express Truth
4. How do we know when we have the Truth?
5. Openness to Truths wherever we may find them

Chapter Three: Characteristics Of Truth (21–29)
1. Being authentic
2. Consensus realities
3. The Hebrew prophets
4. Being positive
5. Organic Truth

Chapter Four: Exploring Eastern Religions For Truth (31–39)
1. Some historical background
2. Contrasting Eastern philosophies
3. Commonalities among Eastern religious philosophies
4. Where is my basic identity on the spectrum of Eastern philosophies?
5. The great underlying truths the East has offered humanity

Chapter Five: What Are Scientific Truths? (41–49)
1. Church and Science
2. Moving beyond Newtonian physics
3. Scientific theories and discoveries of this century
4. New insights, from atomic physics
5. Overriding Insights from the New Physics

Chapter Six: Exploring Judaism And Christianity For Truth (51–59)

1. Judaism- the basic theme of returning to God
2. Central to Judaism
3. Judaism and the Holy Name of God
4. Christianity-salvation through a human called Jesus
5. Christianity-The Message

Chapter Seven: The Place Of Inspiration And Revelation? (61–69)

1. Inspiration and Revelation-two sides of the same experience
2. Eastern Inspiration-a closer look
3. Western Revelation-a closer Look
4. Inspiration and Revelation-by what authority?
5. Toward a unified understanding of Inspiration and Revelation

Chapter Eight: Universal/Ultimate/Existential/Personal Truths (71–79)

1. Truths come in many packages
2. The question of evil
3. Factors which have shaped our consciousness
4. The appearance of limitations
5. The Issue of relevance

Chapter Nine: Power (81–89)

1. The reality of Power
2. Power demonstrated in the greater scheme of things
3. Power as it is intended to be
4. Getting from here to there
5. Some conclusions about Power

Chapter Ten: Toward An Integrated View Of Truth (91–99)

1. A cosmological view implicit in religion and philosophy
2. The meaning and direction of our lives
3. Spiritual evolution in keeping with organic evolution
4. Dualism and Monism, both sides of one universe and reality
5. Life is worth living when we reach for the ring of Truth

ABOUT THE BOOK

Do you have a clear handle on what is true? In the light of recent political events, are you confused about truth? Does it seem to you that honesty has taken a vacation, or that people call something true when it seems obvious to most everyone else that it's not? In this book the author discusses a way of defining truth; looking at it from different vantage points, and drawing conclusions that make sense in a time and culture that honors other values more than it honors truth for truth's sake.

Is there a way of seeing the various religious positions that allows each one to have a respectable role in this world? The author draws some interesting pictures of the various religions of the world; how they evolved and why they represent truth. Like a growing number of informed people, the author takes the position that all religions speak true words and reflect honest inspiration and revelation. More importantly, the author takes a bold eastern view while subscribing to a Western faith. Reality is organic; not atomistic. As such, reality is connected. Each electron knows what it's partner is doing. That bold discovery from one of the new physicists reflects a part of what the author includes from the new physics that is just beginning to influence how we see the world around us.

Truth needs to be discussed at seminaries and graduate schools today, perhaps more than it has ever been needed in days past. Exclusive theological and philosophical positions, while practical as training techniques for gaining converts, lie at the heart of the anti religious and social feelings one group has for another. Seeing the place each rightfully holds, opens new ways of speaking to one another. Recognizing truth as both relative and subjective facilitates plumbing the depths to a new I-and-Thou encounter that allows each to live, grow and discover even greater personal identity than could have been envisioned building walls instead of bridges.

Framing in our world and its people, has been the prerogative of ignorance and fear for too long. Seeing differences as either evil or dangerous has left too many scarred and separated. If reality is connectedness, then separation needs to be understood as something created by our consciousness. Yet there appear to be infinite examples of separated or distinguishable beings and things. The author addresses these seeming conundrums with dexterity and grace, providing the reader with an integrated philosophy that makes friends yet remains true to one's being

God and reality when understood as verbs, allow the growth that comes from recognizing our lives as fluid and transforming. This book helps the believer understand his/her place in the total scheme of things. Those who stand beyond the pale of faith in anything but themselves can chew on a perennial philosophy that has come up to us from the beginnings of all religions yet continues within each religion to its present expression. Religion and Science can find common ground when context, discoveries and language take their place under the broader rubric of Truth.

Chapter One: Introduction To Truth

I. Some historical background

Up to recent times one of the major motivations of philosophers was to discover Truth. Understanding both Truth and reality were the consuming reasons to study philosophy and a number of philosophers from Plato to Francis Bacon devised systems of thinking for doing so. They did this systematically in order to remain consistent in what they believed. Their underlying reason was that what was logically consistent would also reflect what was real, since nature itself reflected consistent patterns of behavior and nature was the given yardstick for natural truth.

The history of religious philosophy from before the birth of Christ to the present era is filled with examples of individuals attempting to know more than they might commonly encounter. Two of the major contributors to Truth in ancient times were the Greeks and the Jews. The Greeks started with simple Truths called axioms and built on these to more complex verities. The Jews or Hebrews started with the Law or Torah and attempted to make it understandable by applying it to human experiences. The Greeks believed that reality could be observed and upon discovery reveal consistent patterns. But they chose not to measure their theories but rather to speculate! The Jews introduced the whole notion of revelation as being axiomatic and thus beyond logical proofs. Proceeding from revelation as axiomatic, they explored applied Truth to the human condition.

The Christian era brought with it apologists who sharpened their verbal and writing skills in defense of the Christian faith against pagan, Gnostic and politically incorrect sectarians who saw Jesus differently. Centuries of church Fathers would culminate in creedal and doctrinal pronouncements designed to clearly spell out who God was, what Jesus' two natures were and the justification for the social institution that would become known as "The Church." While Christians celebrate Pentecost as the birth of the church, its formal birth as a politically correct institution appears with the conversion of Emperor Constantine in the Fourth Century. From that point on two major powers would vie for control; the church and the state. For almost five centuries, from Saint Augustine to Pope Gregory VII, the church and the state would confront one another as near equals. The end point of what historians would call the investiture controversy would come with King Henry IV who, afraid for his soul, humbled himself before the Pope in Italy. Until the Protestant Reformation in the 16th century, the church would be united under the banner of eternal Truth and the sole means of salvation. Not many were inclined to attempt to wrest power from mother church in the face of such pronouncements.

      With the plurality of religious opinion and the introduction of scientific discoveries came the need to create other anchors into the nature of reality. Motivated by commercial advancement and emboldened by the free air of scientific discovery, rationally liberated philosophers addressed the essential questions of knowing and being. "How do we know what we know?" became the rallying cry for those whose intellects could plumb the depths of observable facts and phenomena. "What is the nature of nature?" became the province of basic scientists whose curiosity drove them to understand the seamless robe of reality. But the scientists and later philosophers would make their entrance into the Cretan labyrinth with the only skein of thread they considered available, namely; the scientific method. Having rid themselves of what they considered religious superstition, rational humans fashioned a model with which to measure everything and everyone; a standard by which nature itself was envisioned to remain captive. The microscope, telescope, micrometer and test tube became symbols of this scientific method.

II. The Scientific Method

      A group of philosophers and scientists would become known as empiricists. The word itself refers to knowing something from sense experience. The question of: "How do we know?" was taken up by these empiricists and answered in the following manner: 1) We know what we know by observing it through any or all of our recognized senses of Sight, Hearing, Taste, Touch and Smell. <u>Sense Perception</u>

2) We know what we know by observing it together with others and confirming what we have observed by agreement. <u>Sense Confirmation</u>

3) We know what we know by being able to repeat what we have observed any number of times under the same conditions. <u>Sense Repeatability</u>

4) We know what we know by being able to formulate physical reasons for what we have observed in accordance with known physical laws. <u>Sense</u> <u>Understandability</u>

5) We know what we know by being able to break down what we have observed into basic axiomatic and verifiable principles. <u>Sense Reducibility</u>

These five methodical principles became the foundation of the scientific method and the cornerstone for modern philosophy. Religious philosophy, known in past periods as theology and the medieval queen of the sciences, was pushed to one corner of the room of public opinion and relegated to those who insisted on living with unproven, faith based beliefs. While they didn't satisfy the emotional needs of many not steeped in the scientific method or owing their livelihood to scientifically based industries and universities, they were able to solidify their posture in the world community by producing answers and products with which we have become intimately intertwined and upon which we have become dependent. The scientific method and those minions who carefully follow this philosophy represent a portion of truth and what is real, but fall short of what we now can affirm as ultimately true and personally satisfying.

III. Toward a definition of Truth

It seems obvious that everyone should agree on what one would mean by Truth. That is not the case, however. Truth is different than truth with a small "t". Truth also is different than reality, though it is certainly related. Truth is different than honesty, although in common usage, one is apt to refer to an honest person as someone who tells the truth.

Do you remember the old adage: "If a tree falls in the forest, and no one is there to hear it fall, does it make a sound?" Does it? The question of sound and an ear to hear the sound makes a difference. A tree falling will produce sound waves or vibrations in the air that continue in all directions until they lose their energy or are blocked by physical objects. It is the animal or human ear that hears and identifies sounds. A deaf person unable to hear the tree fall would say that the tree made no sound. So if no one is there to hear it fall, one could rightly say that the tree made no sound falling.

In a real sense one can say that Truth requires a person in order to exist as Truth. Truth is what a conscious person can perceive and integrate as something real and meaningful. Thus, for Truth to occur, one must be conscious and perceptive; one must be aware and interested; one must understand and consider the stimulus relevant. In addition, I propose another important element to defining Truth. That is its philosophical and biblical dimension. Truth is registered in human consciousness when it appears from its eternal origin and becomes manifest in time and space. That was the Greek philosopher Plato's understanding when he became aware of the eternal forms that find their faint reflections in the real world of limited forms. It is also the prophetic Hebrew understanding as divine revelation that appears to those to whom the Divine speaks. In other words, Truth has a divine origin and purpose. Its origin is God. Its purpose is to inform man.

Does that mean that upon accepting these guidelines one now has captured Truth? No, not at all. What these definitions provide are direction leaving the matter open to new discovery. The problem that has followed the Christian faith by way of its historical attempts to encapsulate the revelation known as Jesus Christ is precisely the unfortunate Roman tendency to define by delineating, limiting and blocking in what is essentially fluid, Spirit and eternal. Western religions from Judaism to Islam have been quick to codify what is spiritual, making it doctrinal and legal. The church, in the early centuries, took on Jewish laws, then Greek Philosophical categories and finally Roman jurisprudence. In doing so the church created an unfortunate misperception of the nature of Truth. Nailing things down so even ordinary people could subscribe to beliefs makes what those people believe of secondary importance. Truth is not repeating words, though words contain vibrations that affect persons. The vibrations are secondary to experiencing what they address. Truth must be experienced in its primacy if its Truthfulness will change lives. Like Plato's faint reflections, creeds and doctrines can only point to, not become what is life changing. In a real sense, Truth captures the one who hears and experiences it.

IV. What about "truths?"

How many times do we use the word Truth or true in normal conversation? "We hold these truths to be self evident," represents part of the words of The Declaration of Independence, a national treasure. Famous quotes that include Truth, truth and true are myriad. Common usage has made these words mean a number of things. Often, they are synonyms for what is real or valid or authentic or honest.

If Truth has a divine origin, then honesty has a human origin. While the word honesty has been loosely included in describing animal behavior, it is really relegated to human behavior. It is people who are honest or show honesty as a virtue. There are honest people and dishonest people. What does that mean? Simply said, honest people tell the truth with a small "t" while dishonest people lie. People who are intrinsically honest we call authentic; that is, they are genuine in how they come across, how they represent themselves.

Reality can most easily be understood as the totality of what is and can become. Reality is comparable to the grand matrix; the total pattern upon which individual events are written. Thus, Truth is part of reality but all of reality is not Truth until that part of what is real comes into human consciousness.

The tree falling in the forest is a real event even if no one hears it and it doesn't make a sound. But the Truth of a tree falling in the forest won't manifest as real in human consciousness until a human registers that event and holds it as meaningful and relevant. Truth is written on the paper of reality. Someone needs to see and hear that message. Truth is primarily a philosophical term. Reality is a scientific term that includes all the possibilities of real events. The matrix of reality knows about the tree's fall. It's Truth awaits discovery.

There are numerous Truths that need not have a direct revelatory point of contact, but nevertheless prove meaningful to living. Virtues fall into this category. Virtues are true and originally came into human consciousness to help facilitate direction. They are signposts which God provides to illustrate how to live in this reality. Virtues are the spiritual gifts and fruits the apostle Paul refers to in his letters to the young churches. Virtues like **peace**, **love**, **honesty**, **honor**, **authenticity**, **compassion**, **generosity**, **mercy**, **service**, **patience**, **thankfulness**, **righteousness**, **faith** and **justice** all reflect spiritual activity and divine giftedness. They are true because they have a basis in eternity. They are true because they speak directly to God's intention for creation. Judaism, through its profound prophets, focused mostly on the virtues of **Righteousness**, **Justice** and **Compassion**, considering them to be the most important for maintaining harmonious community life pleasing to God. People can learn of these virtues or practice them naturally without consciously concluding their original spiritual reality. Practicing them, however, draws us closer to what is divine within us and smooths out our interpersonal encounters. Being in sync with divine intentions always has that effect.

Something can be true because it is factual. It has been experienced by the several senses and thus registers on our collective radar. It may or may not have a positive affect on our lives. But its Truth value won't be known until it becomes meaningful. It may be true that you had an unhappy childhood, but the Truth of your life is that whatever experiences have helped shape your present disposition, attitude and happiness level, your life is divinely positioned for manifesting God's glory. The Truth of your life becomes part of a process of realization and discovery into the very heart of the Divine. Whatever stimulus has brought you to this point in time and circumstance, coming into contact with God will reveal who you really are and what you can do to fully be who you really are.

V. Is Truth objective or subjective in nature?

Primarily because of the scientific explosion we have become more aware of objective qualities. Prior to the scientific method, observing objective facts, notions and Truths were unimportant. Since the scientific explosion and the dominance of the scientific method, doing objective things has become quite important. "Objective" has become synonymous with observing without the observer's influence playing a part. It is seeing something because it is there and not because you want it to be there. Objective Truth is understood as standing alone and always being present under the same conditions. Whatever someone may feel or think or want is immaterial. Facts are facts and objective reality is what it is.

The axiomatic assumptions which intelligent people made were that:

1) There is an objective world apart from observers. Our bodies are assumed to be part of this objective world.

2) Our bodies are composed of particulate matter for particulate matter is the objective reality of what makes up this world. Energy is a qualifier of that matter.

3) Clumps of particulate matter are separate from one another in time and space.

4) Different expressions of particulate matter cannot occupy the same space at the same time.

5) Mind is a philosophical concept. The brain is material and does all thinking and feeling. In time, brain function will explain all thoughts, impressions and feelings.

6) Objective perception of the world is automatic and given time

and opportunity all contributions to the human condition will be explained in material ways as chemical, physical and biochemical activities.

7) Time is absolute. As the orderly measure of change, it runs in one direction only.

8) Human nature can be explained in physical and biochemical categories. Inner awareness falls under the heading of illusions.

9) Ethics, moral behavior, great contributions to human advancement can be explained in social/psychological categories separate from their effects.

10) In short, we live in a material world and are material beings.

The New Physics has discovered basic anomalies that alter objective perception and material assumptions. What religions have been professing for many centuries, the New Physics is affirming. This world is not material in essence, nor is one able to objectively describe events or produce genuine results based on an objective / materialistic model. Reality is subjective in essence and nature. The core of reality is mind, which many scientists are more comfortably calling energy.

However, a number are now saying that the basis of energy may, in fact, be mind. At the base of everything modern physicists are looking at is nothing they can see. There is nothing there to see with the objective eye or hear with the objective ear or touch with the objective hand. It is empty space appearing filled with things. In other words, objective events and objects are matters of limited programmed perception, not matters of reality.

In addition scientists, such as John Bell, are discovering a kind of knowing unrelated to contact or distance. Bell's theorem says, in effect, that electrons in coherent coupled pairs know what the other electron is doing even when they are separate from one another. Electron pairs spin in opposite directions to maintain balance. When one is compelled to spin differently, the other in the pair will immediately change its spin cycle to compensate. How do they know to do this unless they are connected in some way and aware of what the other is doing?

Scientists, such as Werner Heisenberg, have discovered

that the more you observe something the more you affect what you are observing. His uncertainty principle maintains that observing something changes what you are observing. It also maintains that measuring one thing will affect something else so that you cannot observe and measure atomic positions without changing atomic velocity.

The implications to Heisenberg's uncertainty principle are still being considered. The dual wavelike and particle characteristics of subatomic particles give them both an uncertainty for observation and a possible new identity, that of an event rather than a particle or wave. I have heard a noted physicist apply Heisenberg's principle to uncovering ancient diggings and altering what was uncovered by the very act of uncovering it. What is being confirmed more and more is that so-called objective experiments cannot take place. The experimenter actively participates and alters the experiment by his or her thoughts, intentions and predispositions. It cannot be otherwise.

The New Physics has compelled us to rethink our assumptions about a materialistic universe of knowable fixed quantities. The new model that is unfolding includes these observations:

1) There is no objective world apart from the observer.

2) Our bodies and everything else are comprised of energy and information as well as particles—energy that creates movement and change and information that bespeaks a mind within the energy providing direction and choice.

3) The mind and body, and all dimensions pertaining to mind and body are one.

4) Perception is learned. It is based on anticipation, awareness and predisposition.

5) We may discover that the very core of reality is consciousness or mind. Mind makes up the rules. Consensus consciousness makes up the forms. Agreement within consensus maintains forms and realities.

A Hindu Tapestry depicting hrina, a seed symbol for the Divine Mother

Chapter Two: How Do We Know When We Arrive At Truth?

I. Arriving At Truth ✓

What you and I are willing to accept as true has a great bearing on the condition of our lives. We literally think our way to where we find ourselves at some future time and circumstance. If we feel helpless, helpless conditions dictate themselves to us. If we feel unworthy the universe appears to confirm our self-image. When we get upset over some little matter, more little matters appear to make us even more upset. If we are afraid or angry at others, others seem to know that and contribute to our fears and anger. Not being able to forgive and let go of griefs and disappointments insures their multiplying on a regular basis.

Our personal truth, what we live & go through

Why is that the case? Why is it that self-fulfilling prophesies exist in the first place? Why do we experience events we don't want to see happen? The answer to each of these questions can be found in the Bible, of all places. It is also found in many scriptures around the world. It begins with freedom, the human lot and human aspiration. Without freedom there would be no sin, no unhappiness, no limitations, no mistakes, no suffering of any kind. That is because freedom comes with consciousness, or more specifically, self-consciousness. We are conscious beings who know that we exist and have an idea of what makes us happy and unhappy.

Free from Hard Wired Programs / to choose is a gift

Freedom is the fruit of consciousness. Our ancestors, Adam and Eve, ate of that fruit and discovered that they were free to know the difference between good and evil; right and wrong; limitation and plenty; happiness and unhappiness; pleasure and suffering, and so forth. It requires a brain to know and distinguish, and it requires a mind or consciousness to experience freedom. Freedom is the root cause of why we are where we are at any time in our journey. Freedom is the promise that enables us to become co-creators with God when we get it right and learn how to use our freedom well. It doesn't matter

Comes with freedom to make a choice?

Talking responsibility for what we Think & do?

All pain & pleasure disappear with loosing Consciousness … Conscious Mind provides us feel our own freedom to choose …?

whether you actually believe there was an historic Adam and Eve, their decisions are our decisions. Metaphysically and symbolically, Adam and Eve remind us about the cost of consciousness and invite us to return to the bliss we walked away from a time long ago.

Human beings developed egos long before they developed good sense. Ego consciousness, the natural result of freedom, forms self-conscious thoughts of limitation and separation. The Truth we lost was that we are not actually separated. *The Truth is that everyone and everything is connected, interconnected and interpenetrating*. That is the nature of the universe. That is the nature of reality. The Truth is that separation, the result of conscious choice, is not our natural state. The Hebrews understood this and called hell that state of separation from God. The Hebrews understood that sin was and is missing the mark; missing our identity as connected and part of an infinite creative plan of consciously enjoying what God called very good.

Normal people don't want to go to hell. Normal people don't choose to sin and pay the price. Normal people are already in hell because they feel separated, too often limited, lost, frustrated and unhappy. Normal people, with the apostle Paul are apt to say, "The things I do not want to do, I do, and the things I want to do, I don't do; woe is me, for I am a sinner." We call it normal because it's so common. Normal people face their limitations by believing that someday, in heaven, they will get whatever they missed here. Someday, but not today. The limitations, suffering and unhappiness that plague their lives will be compensated at some future point in heaven. Now they simply must endure.

We have all felt this separation and registered it in near countless ways. Yet in each religion there have been those-usually called mystics or holy men-who have transcended this sense of separation with the infinite and discovered bliss. They are far more numerous than are known and documented. We know the relatively few who have shared their experience. What happened to them? They affirmed what they truly were, in spite of their normal consciousness. They experienced a oneness that is in the biblical promise and finds reflections in the other religions as well. We could examine the mystic's path to determine how they came to recognize their oneness. That is a study in itself. We could also start on a new path by affirming our oneness with our loving God.

Whatever contributes to ending our sense of separation from the source of all good and our eternal parent, be that parent considered mother or father or totality, is good and puts us on the path to Truth. People find confirmation that a greater reality lies just past our limited perception through many techniques of spiritual unfoldment. People of every stripe, and coming from every race and culture, have discovered that they can overcome the endless darkness, misery, frustration, hopelessness, and despair by committing to the greater reality that is outside of our normal consciousness and the greater reality that is our true identity. Its not an either / issue but a both / result. However, you must start somewhere if you are to end up somewhere else.

Being on a path that works for you insures that you will be somewhere other than where you are right now. But choose a path that has been trod before by persons who have experienced oneness with the divine and that greater consciousness that stands on a higher mountain of awareness. Choose a path that reflects the ethical teachings found in all religions, a commonality that confirms their divine influence.

Unity is but one choice and a good one for those coming from Christian backgrounds because it doesn't disturb old loyalties yet awakens new possibilities. It's not a matter of discounting what you have learned. It's a matter of discovery of who you are in the totality of what is. Truth has many faces but a singular result; it transforms the seeker.

II. Misperceptions

One of the most devastating misperceptions arising out of Western religious faith is the notion of creatureliness. It is the disposition that we are creatures; that is, created beings dependent on forces outside of ourselves. We depend on the good graces of a God or fate or cosmic influence that can change our lot whenever it wants to but doesn't. The misperception that has arisen from separation is that if we claim our divine origin or spiritual identity we are open to being labeled egomaniacs from secular society and accused of idolatry from religious circles. How dare we dare to be something other than mere ragamuffins, creatures in need of daily and eternal forgiveness.

Recent Christianity has seen fit to employ the ragamuffin strategy to bring uncommitted persons into the fold of organized religion. Conversion experiences and vocal decisions for Christ, with appropriate confession of our unescapable sinfulness, have become the mode of change for many. Perhaps, many do need something to awaken them from their self-destructive paths. God certainly can use evangelists, circumstances and severe personal limitations to get our attention. Changing from one mode of perception to another often requires just the right moment of reflection and just the right stimulus to get our attention. So this is not to denigrate a way God has to change us from where we are to a point further along, where we should be.

But the message of estranged individual limitation when coupled with the reality of an unlimited, loving God still leaves many believing we are nothing and God is everything. How can nothing become a co-creator with everything? What makes it possible to be comfortable in a heavenly abode where we don't belong? The jump would be incredible and still beg the most important considerations. The Truth is that God is everything and we are part of that everything.

The greatest sin in ancient Israel was the sin of idolatry. In post-exilic times it became the sin of not observing the Sabbath. But in earlier times it was thinking that something could stand in place of God. Specifically, the Hebrew text that condemns idolatry states that it is a gross sin to put anything in front of God so as to obstruct our view of God. It was to block out the sun when it is the sun that gives you life and light. But that genuine spiritual discovery was put into place to enable the Hebrews to walk with God daily. It was never meant to decry or depreciate human identity. It was instituted to uncover human spirituality.

III. Toward Solutions That Express Truth

Claiming our greater identity moves us closer to our God, not in another direction. Recognizing our greater potentiality doesn't put anything in front of God, to block God from our view. It is religion's intention to be one with, or together with, our source. Recognizing our identity and total connectedness with our source doesn't place us in egomaniac categories because this experience doesn't separate us from others in some superior / inferior way. It unites us with others in an essential way. The many who have come back from their mystical encounters on the mountaintop affirm that oneness, that union with our ultimate spiritual identity, and the Truth of the matter is that the ultimate spiritual identity we know as God is where humanity should be.

Separation in all its forms brings unhappiness. Genuine union in all its manifestations brings bliss and blessing. Union with the Divine allows us to both see and affirm God's glory-in us and in the world. Fears and misperceptions, those elements that have held us back from building God's kingdom, fall away. Those elements that manifest God's kingdom, come into play. It may be ironic that the New Physics plays a role in bringing the much older Christian message into a New / Old focus some would call New Thought. It may seem ironic that discovering physical truths about the nature of nature has a corresponding role to discovering our true spiritual identity and God's intentions; but it is all part of Truth amidst truths that free.

Unity, the position which a growing number of people are subscribing to, presents a practical form of Christianity aware of new / old understandings of the relationship between believing and becoming.

It is practical because it offers answers to life problems. It is also practical because it offers ways to change; to better become who we were designed to be and become. Unity stands within the spectrum of faiths and positions that reject the present human condition as inevitable proposing solutions that work. In a fragmented world, Unity offers answers that address our fragmentation on both the individual level and societal level. In essence Unity incorporates those new / old truths that vitalize the faith open to ever new truths given humanity to improve the human condition. Self-limiting mind-sets are replaced with self-improvement strategies.

IV. How Do We Know When We Have The Truth?

There is the story of the Zen Buddhist student who asked his master how he would know when he became enlightened or entered satori. The Zen master whacked him about the head and replied, "You will know! You won't have to ask if you are there!" When we are living in frustration or loneliness or despair or pain or uncertainty we know that something is wrong. When things go right and we begin enjoying life, once more free of pain and frustration, we may be apt to want to know if it will last.

That's the wrong question to ask. Being in touch with God directly and being in touch with our true selves is experiential, not confessional. We know when we are in love with another human being. No one has to ask us how we know or if we are. We know when God is speaking directly to us or surrounding us with his healing and his love. We know when we are connected. Being connected, we know that we are far greater than past limiting experiences, past defining education or past anything we have at some point accepted as true, but which, in fact, isn't true at all. What we now know won't change; it won't disappear like a whiff of smoke. It's ours to keep, hold onto and share. It is an experience that keeps giving because it originates from a source that keeps giving.

Truth is transforming because Truth comes from beyond time
and space into time and space to be understood and used for the
good of humankind and creation. It is a gift like all of the
spiritual gifts mentioned by the apostle Paul. But it has a central
role in Unity because it has become the touchstone for changing
human circumstances and human consciousness. Other paths
may emphasize devotion or commitment or faith or compassion
or service or any of the gifts.

Unity emphasizes Truth and Truths because these
transform people seeking answers and people needing results.
Practicing those Truths achieves results and confirms our search.
Emphasizing Truth and truths doesn't mean that compassion,
obedience, service, faith, reason, love, devotion or spiritual
activity of any kind isn't actively present. Just the opposite is
true. One of the great misconceptions among Christians of good
intent is the idea that genuine mysticism is other worldly; not
concerned with the process of living and building the kingdom
of God. It's just the opposite. Mystics of every stripe, while
spending time on the mountaintops with the infinite, also spend
much time among the people in the valley being of service,
healing, helping, growing, doing and loving life to the fullest
because they know how.

But to do is to realize who it is that is doing it and how
the infinite plays a key role in the being and becoming. Practical
"Unity" is a way to practice experiencing God in a mystical,
healing manner. Unity is precisely practical even as Mysticism is
practical because experiencing God is the only way you and I
can be transformed from that helpless condition to that
triumphant condition. With the Buddha, we can finally say,
"**I'm Awake!**" Now life for me will change. Now I will be the
captain of my fate because the Christ within me has been
awakened. Those consensus realities or that consensus consciousness
that loves to limit, punish, impede and put down doesn't control this
consciousness anymore. The liberating Christ never wanted those who
would follow him to be stuck in negative, limiting patterns. He said as

much when he spoke those wonderful words, "I have come that you might have life, and that you might have it more abundantly." The liberating Christ becomes my liberator and all the power of the resurrection can now come to me, free me, use me and enable me to be one with that which has no limits, no fear, no down side.

We asked at the beginning of this section: "How do we know when we arrive at Truth?" We simply know it. It feels so right and it does so much. It confirms our best expectations and more. It demonstrates how incredible God really is. Arriving at this New / Old Truth means willfully letting go of our old misconceptions. It means lovingly embracing our new role as fellow heir of all that is. It means consciously becoming aware of our connectedness to God and our fellow human beings, not to mention creation in all its manifestations. It doesn't happen overnight. Allowing the Truth to transform you and me is a process that affects us and changes us over time and circumstance.

The consensus realities out of which we have arisen all have their power bases. Moving away from the limiting realities they represent involves energy consumption, but it also includes divine input because the Christ within is always ultimately triumphant with those who need this victory. You have come to this point in your journey because you are seeking answers to what you may perceive life is doing to you. Overcoming yourself is part of the solution. Trusting beyond yourself is another part that needs to be added. Knowing without doubt, because you experience without reservation, completes the picture of who you are and who God really is.

V. Openness To Truths Wherever We May Find Them

Being open to truths as you come upon them doesn't contradict the Truth of your life or the many truths that appear in time and circumstance because they are what you need when you encounter them. It's never a matter of resolving contradictions in some logical manner in order to hold onto everything. Truths may have a specific function that ends with another level of understanding. With the apostle Paul we may say that when we were children we acted and thought like children. When we became adults we put that aside.

Truth and Truths have that ability to be customized for particular times and development. They also need to appear respecting our individual psychologies. Thus, a particular Truth that helps us now does so as a result of being able to get past our preset belief systems and ego defense mechanisms in order to do its work. For another person the same Truth may appear quite different. Truths are measured by the good effects they have, not by their ability to be added to an objective logical or scientific system of empirical thought. Those truths are of a particular variety to do a particular activity. They are limited to their parameters. Truths have that fluid quality that resists being put into stone. They are alive. They have a spiritual basis. Their quality and mission allow them to enter resistant energy fields, or human consciousness resistant to letting go of what is comfortable, known and predictable, even when that consensus consciousness is also self-defeating and misery creating. Truths grow and change with both individual and societal changes in consciousness. That is their nature and speaks to divine intentionality.

Tantric Buddhist plate

Chapter Three: Characteristics of Truth

I. Being Authentic

[handwritten annotations: "What is true for me, also is true for others becomes the Truth?"]

Truth is authentic. Practicing Truths should also be authentic in what is done and how it is done. This is due to Truth's single moral reason for manifesting in time and space. Yet Truth is also many sided in its applications. Like Karma, the Sanskrit word for cause and consequence, each Truth produces an effect in keeping with its ultimate mission. Positive affirmations, consonant with the Truths they express, produce positive results, consonant with the vibrations they activate.

Affirming something positive over and over again will produce the results of that affirmation. During the process of affirming a positive vision, the opposite vision will occur. It is the universe's way of making certain that the vision you propose is what you really want with its consequent effects. The group consensus out of which you come, your ancestors, the larger group that you have identified with and given your energy to, all have some input into your vision. That is why it helps to secure others who agree with your vision and will affirm it with you. Their group energy brings it into fruition faster, overcoming those old energies that would act against it. It sounds like magic but it is simply natural causation. Being positive insures that the result will be positive. The question arises then, will it reflect the authentic you?

The universe is both moral and ethical in its ultimate direction and intention. It is also amoral in its applications and penultimate strategies. That means that reality, the greater consciousness that makes up that greater reality we know as the Divine, will work with you to achieve your heart's desires. Your volition comprises real energy pointed in a particular direction, and like a real physical force that must have quantity and direction, your affirmation must produce results in keeping with the energy and particularity you give to it.

II. Consensus Realities

The greater consciousness out of which we ultimately come and to which we are beholden, is totally authentic. But it allows us to be less authentic at any moment in our journey.

It knows that we are in the process of becoming and thus require freedom of choice to get there. The lesser consensus reality out of which we directly come, the partial expressionof the ultimate, can be less than totally authentic simply because it is less than perfect. The consensus reality we have accepted as true and feel a part of, is learning and growing even as we are. If our heart's desire is not in keeping with the awareness of that consensus reality, then we will experience resistance. Letting go of this consensus reality is truly letting go into God and trusting the Ultimate to the point that we can graduate to a new consensus reality that holds our heart's desires as justified and obtainable. Those who have experienced this know first hand what it means to go to the edge and jump off.

A simple example may suffice. When a person comes out of a religious tradition that teaches disease to be a punishment of God, then getting healed from that disease becomes very difficult, unless another consensus reality comes in between the patient and the patient"s traditional group mind and convinces that patient that healing is possible. Those beliefs and convictions that subscribe to disease as punishment stretch all the way back through our ancestors to the first one instituting this reality and claiming such a belief.

The doctor, who also comes from a particular tradition that holds a different set of beliefs and convictions, may convince the patient that their disease is quite treatable, curable and easily remedied. If the patient takes the leap of faith into the doctor's consensus reality, that patient will be cured. If his or her disease is such that the medical consensus is less than optimistic, than another consensus reality is needed that sees and knows that cures are reasonable and realistic for this illness.

Believing and trusting, in effect, means leaping from one consensus reality to another that offers answers, hope and a new vision that works for the patient in question. Believing and trusting is far more than claiming to do so. It is really doing so. Putting on a brave face won't change the outcome. Such a face is also likely to be found in other past members of the patient's consensus reality. But changing one's consciousness will change the outcome when done as a total letting go , a leap of faith into a reality that finds such cures commonplace. It seems ironic, but it is certainly true, that people suffering a grave illness would rather die with their illness, comfortably clinging to something erroneous but familiar, than change to something unknown capable of healing them.

Consensus realities are also known as group minds. They have been observed under many names. Unless you or I would become a great spiritual innovator we will be part of a consensus reality that includes all of our ancestors who shared the same aspirations and limitations we do. Some call that a tradition. But it is more than a tradition. It includes all of the energy that went into forming that tradition and maintaining it to the present moment. It is a reality with a penultimate life of its own. We are part of that reality unless we choose to leap out of it into the unknown, trusting God in everything for a safe landing.

III. The Hebrew Prophets

One of the most important characteristics of the Hebrew prophets was their absolute honesty. They came from all backgrounds and social classes. Some were quite willing to be used by God. Some were reluctant. But all of them were honest to the extreme. Some of the message they proclaimed was negative. Some of the message they proclaimed was filled with positive visions of hope. Speaking directly for God, the Almighty, they had little choice but to speak.

The prophetic voice, as it is referred to in the biblical witness, is the voice of God spoken by persons to warn and announce to the people of Israel and Judah the absolute need to return to the Lord. How the message was delivered often reflected the personality of the prophet. How the message was received often reflected the comfortability of the people. The more comfortable the people, the less enthusiastic their response to change in the right direction. The right direction, in the prophetic sense, was the most positive thing the people could do spiritually.

But the prophetic message was coupled with conditional statements that sound negative in their delivery. That is simply because the Law to which the prophets subscribed was cosmic in scope. It is promotion or an amiable mode of communication to maximize results. They weren't driven by marketing strategies. Perhaps they should have been. But historically speaking, they were driven by foreknowledge of a great and terrible day of the Lord that would create great suffering for the people. If the people had known and believed what the prophets announced, much needless suffering could have been avoided. It is the nature of a warning to sound negative as it is the nature of a promise to sound positive.

The Torah or Law that Moses delivered to the people from Mount Sinai reflects this cosmic dimension spoken of by the prophets. The Law, in effect, was Israel's answer to Karma, an absolute, unrelenting force of cause and consequence. What appeared negative in the prophet's message was the honest statement of natural consequence in a spiritual universe driven by divine intention. They weren't trying to be negative, nor were they obsessed with dysfunctional behavior. They were, to a man (and in one case woman) telling it like it was in a time and circumstance that required clear, bold statements.

The prophets saw beyond appearances. They were not impressed with riches or power. With God as their source, riches and power meant little. The only thing that counted for them was honestly relating a message that saw years into the future to circumstances dramatically opposite to their present social and political conditions. What they didn't do was tell the people what they wanted to hear. To do that would have been to confess to their God that the people hadn't heard the message meant to save them. That would have been unthinkable. The several prophets who delivered very negative messages also suffered the consequences of those messages and did so willingly in light of the consequences of not speaking the Truth.

Jeremiah, the suffering servant of God, boldly and repeatedly told the rich and powerful of his day what would happen to them in light of their greed and social misconduct. They did not care to hear about that so he suffered at their hands. In time, he was vindicated but not before he had suffered pain and isolation.

Amos and Micah boldly told the people they were called to address to change their ways, but they delivered their message once and left, later to record the incidence for posterity. They, in turn, did not suffer, but their words were remembered. The contention the prophets created was necessary for their day and situation. Their messages were born out in their time. At a future time they had the effect of aiding others to come back to God and his divine intentions.

Unfortunately, there are those who identify with the Hebrew prophets in each age forgetting that prophecy is a clear historical calling. Normal relations and regular spiritual growth call for positive messages and positive visions reflecting the power that makes for change. The prophetic messages were historical occurrences worth scriptural importance. They may be summarized by three positive statements:

1) God's intention for creation, and humanity in particular, is harmony, cooperation, and mutual respect. The Ten Commandments speak to this.

2) Man's role in the cosmic design is to be about doing just, fair and equitable actions. It is about loving, feeling and relating to others in a kind and compassionate manner that affirms connectedness to one another, while also walking along the path we know as life with the Divine in our thoughts and motivations. Micah 6:8

3) Always being aware of the Divine's cosmic intention in a moral universe that compels growth and evolution of consciousness while calling for a holding onto the verities given us to remember.

Now the prophets could have used this sort of wording, but the people would not have heard them. It takes persons willing to grow or who need what Truth offers to take advantage of positive words spoken in a rational manner. Comfortable people unwilling to change but heading in the wrong direction need more dramatic and forceful words. The prophets were called to a specific time and situation. Revelation is like that. Revelation is specific in what is said and what is to be done with what has been said.

Long ago God had made a covenant with Abraham and his descendants. Moses confirmed that covenant and made it specific with the revelation of the Ten Commandments. The people had promised to keep God's covenant even as God would keep His promises. They did not do so, and the prophets were called to remind them of that fact and to warn them of what God would allow to happen through natural law because of their apostasy. That is the context of the prophetic voice. Its relevance for today is clear. Faithfulness to the Divine's cosmic intentions are rewarded. Not adhering to promises made to God and kept have their own effect.

The prophetic voice introduced a new understanding on the world stage. From this time forward the people of Israel would know that God and God's laws were universal and universally applicable over and beyond the descendents of Abraham and the followers of Moses. By the voice of prophesy God graduated from a tribal deity to the single cosmic force behind reality.

At the turn of this last century Christians rallied around a new / old banner called the Social Gospel. Its chief proponent was a well educated and compassionately motivated man by the name of Walter Rauschenbusch, who believed that Jesus followed in the train of the Hebrew prophets. His books influenced generations of compassionate Christians. For a long time conservative elements felt the prophets were liberally minded people. The prophets were actually both liberal in their views of human beings and conservative in their admonishment to return to God and the covenant long forsaken for reasons generally motivated by greed and dishonesty.

IV. Being positive

There is an old adage that goes: "You can get more with honey than with vinegar." You can get further with someone else by agreement than with contention. It seems reasonable to believe that this is so. But why is it so if, in fact it is? It is generally so because by agreement you create a partial union of minds. If we are all connected and interconnected then each partial step toward confirming this universal Truth is reinforced by tangible results. The results may not be in keeping with God's cosmic intentions and if this is so, the results will ultimately fail. But if the results move us closer to God's cosmic intentions they will continue to last and be transformed into higher and better results toward those intentions. Cooperation is better than competition. Cooperation unites while competition, by its very definition, separates.

Cooperation examples union of a sort; a union of wills, goals, personalities, dispositions or values. Cooperation produces union and union enlarges focus.

Competitions in sporting events and contests entice participants to compete for recognition. In the process of doing so, they attempt to become better than they would have been under less than competitive conditions. Contests of any sort probably began in pre-civilization times to strengthen men. Survival was the primary reason. In time, competitions won winners fame and recognition. This, rather than survival, became important. The ancient Greeks were famous for their contests in which naked men ran, threw, and wrestled for a wreath. The winners knew they were better than the others. The win confirmed that. As a means to encourage participants to get better, either physically or mentally, competition has its place. What makes it work are the rules of the contest and the referees who enforce those rules. These two parameters insure fairness among participants. Successfully meeting a challenge is the heart of positive competitions that inspire excellence and thus promote personal growth.

But competition that promotes a sense of superiority can generate a negative downside. It's called ego power and it creates negative effects in time and space. Power itself, is the consolidation of resources, be it people, finances or influence. Material or psychological ego power divides. Spiritual power unites and draws together. Spiritual power, unlike its material / mental counterpart doesn't rest in ego consciousness. Spiritual power rests in its source who is universal and infinite.

Positive truths produce positive results. That is a matter of natural law. The *Dhammapada* or sayings of the Buddha state as much. The famous little book by James Allen, *As a Man Thinketh* , confirms the same thing. It is a matter of natural law. What you put in is what you get out. How you express it is how it will be expressed to you. Communicating positive messages and a positive vision creates a positive response.

That is because reality always acts as a mirror back to you. It reflects you back to yourself. Reality acts as a mirror simply because it is connected to you, much as your image of yourself is connected to you by reflection. The mirror quality of reality is how you and I learn and grow. So getting down on yourself or others isn't a sign of being realistic or humble, its a sign of ignorance of natural law.

People often believe they can't help being negative. In fact, they believe its always somebody's else's fault, so they can't see the effect their negativity is bringing to them. Sometimes a friend can break through. Sometimes an extraordinary experience can break through. Sometimes divine grace can break through, or the person may finally come to the very end of his or her limit to deal with negative effects he or she brings upon himself or herself. At this point they are so weakened by their self abuse, they let go and find divine grace that allows them to forgive themselves and then forgive everyone else who has appeared to violate their lives.

People who work at being positive soon discover their lives turning around. Whether positive or negative, what you project reinforces itself. If you originated in a negatively based consensus reality, it is harder to see life positively and thus harder to feel you are not fooling yourself by being positive. The Truth is, you can change your life completely and the circumstances that you encounter by practicing positive thinking. Millions attest to that Truth. It is well documented. But it needs to be practiced until it becomes habitual and instinctive if the effects are to be long term. Reality dictates genuine effort over time.

There is a difference between fooling yourself or denying your situation and developing a positive attitude about everything. Some cite religious faith as the difference. Some cite self-mastery as the difference. They play their part. The essential difference between the ego defense mechanism of denial (a form of separation) and the spiritual Truth incorporated in being positive, is your sensing the union that confirms your connectedness to God and to everything and everyone else. It is not a matter of willing yourself to do it that finally works. It is the confirmation experience of a close and loving God, coupled with the glimpse of a universe where you are an integral part. "No less than the trees and the stars, you have a right to be here. And whether it is trees and the stars, you have a right to be here. And whether it is clear to you or not, the universe is unfolding as it should." *The Desiderata*, as it has been called, is the confirmation of an enlightened person who knows positively he is essential to the proper functioning of a connected universe. His words ring true. You are important and you are never alone.

V. Organic truth

You may wonder how one can attest to everything and everyone being connected, interconnected and interpenetrating. How can one envision the universe, reality and human conduct in this light? The Truth is simple. The universe is not atomistic. The universe is not ultimately and intrinsically countless distinct, separated objects relating to one another by laws of physics and chemistry. The universe, reality and human beings are organic in nature. It is the organic nature of reality that allows this essential Truth to take shape in human consciousness.

"Organic" connotes being alive. The universe is totally alive. It is totally filled with energy. It is waves upon waves, all relating to one another and the whole. Incorporeal wave fronts touching, growing, changing. It is organic mind focusing on particulars even as waves behave as particles and energy behaves as matter and mind behaves as thoughts. In such a universe you can never truly be alone except in your private consciousness and only because you have the freedom to pretend.

The organic nature of reality, the spiritual Truth about your identity, the freedom that allows you to change, grow and become a co-creator with God, all address the organic character of who and where we are in the total scheme of things.

Islamic plate depicting the ascension of the Prophet Muhammed,
taken from the 16th century Indian manuscript

Chapter Four: Exploring Eastern Religions For Truth

I. Some historical background

Ideas we may call religious have a long history. In fact, it is safe to assume the very first religious notions came from the first people to populate this earth and forming as a community. In the earliest tribal societies, people began to differentiate according to useful functions. For instance, someone was chosen to lead. Others were chosen to either hunt for food or defend the tribe. Still others were chosen to heal the wounds of warriors sent into battle defending their land or gaining new land and trophies.

The person chosen to heal the wounded and the sick came with some unique qualifications. He or she had to be in touch with the greater reality that could save, restore or advance the tribe. That person, usually a man in those cultures, had intuitive abilities that enabled him to see spirits, forces and gods; pray to them for help, and treat wounds and sicknesses with herbs and other tried and successful remedies. That person was called a Shaman. Descendents of Shamans in China became the followers of the Way or Taoists. Descendents of Shamans in India became the Brahmin Hindu priests. Descendents of Shamans in the West became priests of the highly civilized cultures of Egypt, Assyria and Sumer. Descendents of Shamans in Northern Europe became the witch doctors, priests and storytellers of Nordic and Celtic religions. All of these Shamans existed long before Christianity arrived on the scene.

The oldest surviving religion continually in existence since its origin is Hinduism. It dates back to before 2,000 B.C.E. beginning in the Indus Valley and stretching to the Indian Ocean. It is believed that the Aryans brought Hinduism to India. More precisely, the Aryan invasion of the Indus river Valley brought the beginning of an amalgamation of the Dasas and later Dravidian religions and the Aryan religion. The Dasas and Dravidians were the original inhabitants of the land we now know as India. They already had a highly advanced but more peaceful civilization prior to the wandering Aryans who came to stay. The Dravidians and Dasas were darker than the Aryans. That

color difference was not lost on the eventual conquerors. Within a
short time a caste system based on varna or color separated people
according to their birth and ability to function in the larger society.
There were a number of Aryans who turned south as they were
crossing what is now Iran on their way to India. They are now the
present day Iranians.

Further East in China, religion was in full swing when the
Aryans invaded India, but those religions no longer exist. The religions
that developed around the Fifth Century B.C.E. and exist today are
Confucianism and Taoism. Both began as social philosophies.
Confucianism began as a reaction to the Warring States Period, a
bloody period of several hundred years during which China was
plunged into chaos and suffering. Kung Fu Tzu or Master Kung as he
was called (Latinized to Confucius), attempted during the course of his
adult life, to change the thinking of those in power. He began a
philosophy of social order designed to bring cooperation instead of
deadly competition to the land. His focus was to instill character, a
sense of social responsibility and personal honor in matters great and
small. His concepts, which he claims were taken from the writings of
the early Chou dynasty, reflect a totally interrelated social system where
each one knows his or her role.

Lao Tzu, the legendary founder of Taoism, is a shadowy figure
impossible to confirm having lived at all. But, if his later biographer, Ssu-
ma Ch'ien, told the Truth, Lao Tzu, (which means old master) lived
about the same time as Confucius. His system of thought was quite
different from that of the teachings of Confucius. Lao Tzu didn't believe
in education; nor did he ascribe to rules of order. Differentiation of roles,
a central theme in Confucius social thought, was alien to him. Rules
were unnecessary. Each one should listen to his intuition, get into the
flow of the Tao, the primordial mother of all life, and the answer to what
to do next would come. Early Taoists were often forest dwellers and
hermits. They practiced Shaman remedies for health and productive life.
Former Shamans gravitated to the teachings of Taoism. Taoism
represented a totally natural way of living with little mention of
supernatural truths. It focused on living a balanced life between yin and
yang, in harmony with nature and peacefully with others.

II. Contrasting Eastern philosophies ✓

Eastern religions differ from Western religions in a number of basic ways. To start with, Eastern religions are natural. They are natural religions, not nature religions. The distinction is simple. Eastern religions know that trees and rocks aren't gods. At the same time Eastern religions know that all of nature is alive in the same way that spirit is alive. There is one reality with many shapes and this reality is, & Shadow! by definition, natural. At times Eastern people see nature up close and personal. At such times natural shapes take on personality, an expression of the greater reality behind them. At other times they see nature as impersonal, functioning according to laws and principles no one can successfully negotiate with to obtain a request. The basis of these laws are order and direction (for Hinduism and Buddhism— Karma; for the Taoists—Yin and Yang; for followers of Confucius— Jen or proper relationships).

Eastern religions offer a way out of man's perennial dilemmas. ✓ They recognize that the human condition, if it is functioning at all, is not perfect. Life is not as it ought to be, ideally and realistically. The solution to the human condition is basically the same for each religion. But there are differences in particulars, which arose from perceptual / cultural / contextual distinctions. More precisely, different Eastern seers observed, prayed, meditated and then concluded solutions to the human condition based on the historically conditioned human instruments they were using, what we would recognize as their consciousness. Those various expressions of consciousness were themselves different with different experiences to draw upon, and so their conclusions, inspirations and revelations reflect those psychological / experiential differences. ✓

Both the problems and solutions for China, as reflected in the Eastern religions of Buddhism, Taoism and Confucianism, resemble solutions for personal and social chaos. They address family priorities and community solidarity. There is a clear need for health and life issues to be met on a "this life" basis.

In Hinduism, and the Buddhism that evolved out of the Indian experience, ending this life and its continuing reincarnations take on great importance. The issue of what is real, eternal and final supersede this life priorities. Being one with God in Hinduism now becomes being one in Nirvana for Buddhism.

III. Commonalities among Eastern religious philosophies

When we focus on what is common to each Eastern religion, taking into account their different histories, we first come to realize that the East sees reality differently than does the West. This was true from the beginning. East and West are like two faces of the same coin. The Eastern face of our metaphoric coin already feels connected with the greater reality, in fact, Eastern seers saw God, the gods and other invisible forces as part of nature. While differing on particular gods, influences and even human identifying characteristics, the Eastern experience of the oneness which is reality was and is a total relatedness.

Material and spiritual lifeforms, bodies and souls, all emerge from the primordial soup that is one reality in essence while many realities in manifestation. The one and the many is a common Eastern theme. In Taoism, this theme is clearly exampled by the first definition of the Tao, the primordial potentiality which is indescribable. Nirvana, the Buddhist answer to human suffering, looks very much like the Tao in this aspect. In Hinduism, Brahman, in its totality, beyond forms and particulars, speaks a similar language once you strip away cultural peculiarities. All of these religions experienced who we call God similarly, yet described their encounter differently. Felt Sense-Realize

Another theme running through each of the Eastern religions is the human condition. Hinduism speaks about the apparent ignorance unsatisfactory condition of humanity as the result of ignorance. To of reality overcome ignorance one must grow, learn, and master self to the point of dissolving the apparent separation. For Hinduism the goal is to be one with, as the various masters describe this all-encompassing reality:

1) Absolute impersonal Brahman, Totality, all that is.

2) Personal God as Vishnu, absolute, real, close and personal with attributes.

In Buddhism there is no personal God to join with. The Buddha did not see a personal God when he became enlightened. Rather, he saw the totality as that interwoven tapestry where all time and

space and matter form a unity. Thus, the solution to his quest to discover
a way to end suffering for humanity took the shape of this path to Truth.
What was:

1) The path to the cessation of suffering, recognizing first that
life has suffering.

2) That limitations of any sort cause suffering.

3) That the root cause of suffering is attachment or desire which
bonds persons to particulars from which they cannot extract themselves.

4) Successfully mastering the steps on this path, at which
moment all particulars vanish in one totality of undifferentiated
consciousness. This, most Buddhists call Nirvana. It is indescribable
because to describe it is to introduce symbols of particularities,
definitions and things, all of which confirm separation.

5) Knowing one's true self as no-self, beyond the illusion of ego
consciousness.

In Confucianism the solution to the human dilemma is
consciously defining a tradition that allows people to be truly human,
humane and victorious over their personal limitations. Confucianism,
the way of Kung Fu Tzu, starts with another form of personal
recognition. Kung's teachings recognize one's relationship to others. In
the course of realizing one's role in relationship to others, one develops
character, then honor, then selflessness, then sainthood. The gods cannot
touch or interfere with someone who has become a **Chung Tzu** or
superior man. That one has mastered his life, his duty, the honoring his
relationships and thus the dying with dignity. While Confucianism
encourages propriety in personal and communal affairs, including
worship and rites of passage, Confucianism is a this worldly religion.
What is to come appears inconsequential. What you do while you are
alive is all-important, what happens after you die takes care of itself.

Eastern religions define the human condition in different
categories but agree:

1) Human beings are not happy the way they are. There is a
problem.

2) The solution is both personal and corporate.

3) On the personal level each one needs to break down self
interest to being involved with other interest.

4) On the corporate level people as community need to recognize their relatedness.

5) Human transformation is the next step in a process of liberation.

6) The little self cannot see the larger picture. One must go higher.

7) Ethical behavior and spiritual perception shape the process to liberation.

8) Connecting to something greater than one's small isolated self confirms the path.

9) The greater reality, though defined differently, is benevolent, instructive and redeeming.

IV. Where is my basic identity on the spectrum of Eastern philosophies?

Many in the West have added Eastern religious practices to their lives, finding them fulfilling, helpful and transformative. Yet, in keeping with the inclusive characteristics of Eastern philosophies, many have continued practicing what they were before while encountering these strange but wonderful techniques for improving physical and mental health, adding years to their lives, finding tranquility in silence and so forth. Yoga techniques have slimmed bodies and cleared stressed out minds. Buddhist meditation techniques have generated peaceful, well-integrated personalities, centered in new and healthy ways. Taoist principles of balance and harmonizing opposites have changed many minds about meaningful priorities. All have added to the greater society to which we belong without taking advantage of us. ?

But what do they say about us? Who is the one whose life is prolonged or health improved or state of mind relieved? Who are we in the Eastern scheme of things and how does this contribute to our understanding of Truth?

First of all, the East sees human beings as beings of energy, or more precisely, as bits of energy and information. The East doesn't harbor a materialistic model of man as so many physical parts that need fixing. The East sees persons as energy coming from a central source and returning to this reality many times until finally returning to the source from which we came. For Hinduism the one who returns is the soul, eternal yet separated from its source finally to get it right and return for good. For Buddhism the one who returns is a bundle of connected energy functions called skandas. Each of the five skandas that make up what the Hindus call the soul is always changing until it manifests no more energy. Then the bundle vanishes and our true identity, an identity beyond description, stands before the door of Nirvana where there is no individual identity that needs to return.

For Confucianism, the one who is alive is part of a larger group to which he or she is responsible. Fulfilling responsibilities in this life insures a happy and well-deserved heavenly existence. The Chinese had varied definitions of who it is that enters heaven, what the soul is, and whether it started life here or came into life from a before time. For Confucianism's fellow Eastern philosophy, Taoism, we are differentiated elements of the Tao. Later Taoist seers would posit beliefs in multiple souls inhabiting single bodies and going to different final resting places.

These multiple answers to human identity suggests superstition instead of Truth. But they also may suggest multiple expressions of a single reality that allows diversity of forms while professing a unity of intention. The Truth rests in God's ultimate intentions rather than the form we take to realize those intentions. Individual identities are almost irrelevant to the Eastern consciousness. Blending with the infinite / ultimate in a manner that brings fulfillment is of vital importance. How we appear doing it and becoming this or that is secondary and subject to cultural factors.

The consensus realities out of which the Eastern religions spring reflect the different origins enjoyed by these cultures. Hinduism is more universal in its view of paths to oneness. Buddhism is more specific about not clinging to identities and desires that would prevent us from finally being liberated into total freedom. Taoism is more mystical about defining ultimate reality, of which we are a part. Confucianism is clear about social cooperation producing stabilizing, happy results. Each maintains a consensus reality that gives it forms and stabilizing cosmic conditions. Each moves human beings, however we may define them, toward an ultimate, happy, dynamic state of activity consonant with an infinite source.

V. The great underlying Truths the East has offered Humanity

When we focus our attention on the three major Eastern religions of Hinduism, Buddhism and Taoism we discover intuitive Truths that have glimpsed beyond the veil of ordinary perception, much as those from these Eastern religions have performed feats beyond ordinary abilities.

It would appear that the East has already influenced mainline Christianity in a number of cultural ways. Already people are able to envision reality as far more than any one belief or doctrine or system of thinking, as proposed by past contributors. What the East has shared with us is that the greater reality all around us is God, Brahman, Tao or the totality known as Nirvana. This all-encompassing reality is natural, operates using natural laws and principles much like the human body uses veins, arteries, and the various systems to move energy and vital fluids around the body or totality of being. This all-encompassing reality is loving, benevolent and interested in the well being of all life forms, including human beings. This all-encompassing reality stands ready to help us discover exactly who we are in relationship to him, her, it and in relationship to one another. That sounds much like some expressions of Christianity and Judaism. But the East throws in direct experience of what it means to become one with this totality, God. The East invites willing participants to experience God for themselves directly, be changed and transformed from the encounter and come to realize that in the midst of tangible diversity there is an underlying unity that defines who we are and what everything is. In short, the East promotes mysticism for everyone, somewhat like the West promotes connectedness with the Divine by the indwelling of the Holy Spirit, a direct result of First Century Christian experiences.

The second great underlying Truth the East has offered all who would experience it, is what it truly means to be a son of God; namely our divine origin. The East makes it clear that we came from the Divine, God, Tao, Brahman and that is to whom we belong. The East takes humanity out of a ragamuffin identity and places us on the path to self-discovery and full participation- less the baggage we seem to love to carry. Union, liberation and being in the flow, all express a bliss, peace, victory, confidence, power, energy, being-ness and consciousness that seems alien to us normally. We can't help but wonder if it's all a dream. Actually, the dream is what we call normal consciousness. The reality is what the Hindus refer to as **SAT**—**CHIT**—**ANANDA**, or total being, total consciousness and total bliss.

Thirdly, the East appears far more ready to explore the nature of nature sans doctrinal statements and creedal formulations that bind down and place what is experiential and flowing into legalese, separated noun-driven partial Truths that do more to divide. The East invites people to see for themselves, test the Truth of what they profess and taste to see if it is good. The East doesn't have a long history of religious conflicts, power-based religious persecutions and Roman style legal church laws. It simply records and reflects direct experience and thus keeps close to what is true.

Fourthly, the East has always attempted to be close to nature and what is natural. Consequently, the religions and philosophies that have arisen out of the East have never developed an exploitative position toward nature, life and wellbeing. A poor interpretation of the Hebrew creation account in Genesis has been all that was needed for enterprising Westerners to go full bore ahead destroying everything natural. Balance is something we lost a long time ago. The East never lost it. The East, in the person of its religious consciousness has prized natural balance, harmony and low waste living. It has been more spiritual in a truly spiritual way. The East never believed that we were our bodies, and thus never fell into the ego traps of identifying ourselves with material beings. Thus, Eastern philosophy promotes human evolution into spiritual beings ready to return and inherit what is ours from the beginning.

Fifth and lastly, the Eastern religions express ultimate Truths that supersede historical particulars conditioned by time and circumstance. These Truths are ultimate precisely because they are not based on clearly defined partial realities. Nothing is written in stone so everything is alive and changing. That doesn't mean there is nothing lasting. It means that to speak about what is lasting is to change it to being temporary. What is lasting needs to be experienced, not communicated. It is alive. It is organic in structure, growth and essence. The East has reintroduced ultimate potentiality as explaining a real aspect of God and creation.

Taoist plate symbolizing the Tao as water

Chapter Five: What Are Scientific Truths?

I. Church and science

Prior to the Age of Reason, Truths were directly attached to church pronouncements. If what was discovered contradicted what the church was currently teaching, those discoveries and those who uncovered them were considered dangerous and liable to legal prosecution. It was simply not safe to make scientific discoveries or postulate theories that ran counter to church teachings. There being only one church made the power and authority of the church formidable. Shortly after Saint Thomas Aquinas wrote his **Summa Theologia** the church adopted his theology as the standard for Roman Catholicism. Saint Thomas, along with other Catholic thinkers, had rediscovered the Greek philosopher Aristotle. Aristotle had, through the political and social encounters of Islam with Christianity, come into direct contact with Christian teachings. The church moved from Plato to Aristotle, considering their earlier affair with Plato as too irrational. The **Summa Theologia** used Aristotelian formulations to arrive at explanations for Christian doctrines.

But Aristotle, along with the other Greek philosophers, had postulated his theories based on logical deductions and not experimental facts. Thus, Galileo, a great scientist of the late Inquisition period, found himself the subject of that Inquisition and forced to recant his findings because they did not agree with church teachings based on Greek logic. In this case, Galileo had concluded that heavy objects fall as fast as lighter objects when air resistance is not a factor. A feather arrives at the ground as fast as a stone when both are dropped in vacuums. His experimental conclusions helped Sir Isaac Newton formulate his theory of mutual gravitational attraction. Even though an elderly Galileo recanted his findings on penalty of torture and death, Newton, living in by now Protestant England in the Age of Enlightenment, was able to bring forth his findings with no danger of church interference. Gravitational attraction is mutual and objects fall at a constant acceleration whatever their density.

The example of Aristotle and Newton provide a telling account of why religion should not make decisions outside of religion's domain. Each expression of Truth deserves its own opportunity to contribute to the greater knowledge of what we call real. The Truth brought forth from art, music, science, religion, government, sports, philosophy and communications media all example needs met and consciousness brought forward. The church lamented its fragmentation into many variations. It still does today. But religion that superimposes an artificial unity where diversity expresses creation, looses its Truth value in its obsessive need for conformity.

True unity is an ever open-ended search that is able to combine seemingly unlike realities, as well as extend itself in specialized areas. Truth is both **interrelated** and **evolutionary.** It represents the total fabric of what is at any moment. It also represents what will become across all moments. There are ways of understanding reality in terms of consciousness that sees relationships. There are also ways of understanding reality in terms of consciousness that sees development of singularly defined entities. By way of example, science has demonstrated that mammals share characteristics common to that class. Science has also postulated that particular mammals have evolved to their present state from other forms. Both are true and both are true of everything that expresses Truth, whether it is a discovery of science or religion or any of the other ways humans generate consciousness. Thus, we may conclude that Truth by its nature, expresses reality that is both alive, growing and organically associated with other Truths. It becomes a matter of relevance to single out one Truth over another. It remains God's need to guide humanity, and all of creation into Truths, that define divine intentionality and eventual union.

The early sciences that followed the Industrial Revolution and the Protestant Reformation, and consequently contributed to the Age of Reason, didn't fear church pronouncements. But they didn't understand the multiple facets of reality either. The early empirical scientists had envisioned a materialistic reality that found no room for spirit or mind.

II. Moving beyond Newtonian Physics

Earlier we discussed the scientific method, which became the scientific model for investigating the nature of reality. That method left out an entire spectrum of information not fitting the scientific model. Using this method, scientists could draw no correlations between mind and body. Nor could they envision a direct link between what could not be seen with the eye with what could be experimentally uncovered in a laboratory. Their methods were rigorous and simplistic by design, and phenomena were ignored until they could become part of a larger theoretical model fitting scientific methodology.

With the age of atomic physics and the contributions of such great men as Albert Einstein and Werner Heisenberg, modifications to empirical methods became acceptable. The data simply did not fit the older methods. Micro particles and micro space acted contrary to empirical logic. Yet, what was happening was both too important to ignore and undeniably visible using extraordinary instruments. At least forty important contributions have been made since 1897, with the discovery of the electron, to the discovery of gravitational waves by Huise and Taylor in 1993. Theories as far fetched as any pronouncements made by religionists have contributed to forever altering our self-limiting notions of reality. Thus, we can now look at some of these in light of our basic organic perceptions.

Overriding evidence strongly suggests that while we may feel reality limited to materially structured objects and random events, reality is both non-material and multidimensional. Spirit once more has a place in our society along with mind and imagination. What was considered simply random, and matters of probability now appear to be purposeful, intentional and spiritually driven. That's good for religion. It's also bad for clearly defined expressions of religion and secular philosophy that insist on their limiting sacred cows as beyond change and redefinition. The Truth has always been there. It simply has been covered up with rigid, legal clothing unfit for God's intentionality and creational designs.

III. This century Scientific Theories and Discoveries

While the physicists were looking at subatomic particles, physiologists were investigating human perception. Out of these experiments came some startling conclusions. The eyeball only sees straight and wavy lines. Images we swear are really people, objects and occurrences are produced by our brains, which themselves have mental patterns already stored to fit our expectations. Where the optic nerve touches the back of the eyeball there should be a black circle in our perception. There is not. The brain fills in what we expect to see in that round spot. Our expectations dominate what we see at any moment. In turn, the eye can only physically pick up a wavelength band of between .00007 cm. and .00004 cm., all the rest being invisible to normal perception. That represents an extremely small part of the spectrum of radiation producing events we are now beginning to uncover by indirect means and extraordinary instruments.

Early experiments in memory by such notables as Dr. Wilder Penfield, have concluded that the brain cells are not the repository of information. Each cell does not contain one particular bit of memory. Memory, along with mental activity, appears to swirl around the brain cells. When they are damaged normal consciousness is affected, but various psychic experiments done under rigorous circumstances, suggest that we think outside of our brain cells. The memory electrode prod experiments of Dr. Penfield confirm this. Thus, we are not our bodies. We are much more and science is coming to the same conclusion.

Most school children today know of Albert Einstein's famous equation, $E=mc^2$ But most persons who know of this equation don't know that it clearly refers to the duality of matter. Matter is both material and energy at the same time. Its material nature provides it form. Its energy nature provides it identity. Everything is essentially energy and Einstein's equation confirms this fact of nature. We are stored energy, temporarily molded to construct the physical world around us. The other part of Einstein's mathematical contribution is also of great importance. That is the theory of the conservation of matter / energy. Energy cannot be created or destroyed. It can only change its shape. When you couple Einstein's discovery with the scientific notion that we are swimming in a sea of energy, you quickly realize that we are part of that sea and part of one another. The energy that we are is part of the sea of gamma rays, X-rays, electromagnetic waves, ultraviolet rays, infrared rays, microwaves, radio waves and on and on. Parapsychologists have confirmed another piece of the puzzle. They have uncovered what the great religions have been affirming over many centuries; that is, that some part of us continues, is able to leave the material shell in which it finds itself, and is also part of a greater whole that is layered even as the lowly onion is layered.

Metaphysicians refer to these layers as the material body, astral body, soul body, spirit body and so on. Those people returning from extensive travels outside of their material bodies bring back impressions that our individual identities are also multiple, even as the universe is multiple in its diverse expressions. Yet, each of the various bodies travelers are experiencing form a connectedness to one another and to the greater whole of which they are a part. Those who are both scientifically and religiously motivated define energy as the basic identity. Scientists who have wrestled with the findings and their implications more comfortably define the basic identity that unifies all phenomenon as mind or Mind. Unlike the many who are inclined not to approve of these findings, the travelers and metaphysicians who speak about these travels do so from experience, the most basic denomination of Truth.

Werner Heisenberg once was quoted as saying, "Atoms are not things!" What scientists now call these illusive subatomic particles are dynamic events, a term specifically applied to quarks. Quarks are no longer considered as anything resembling substance. Instead, they are viewed as changing patterns confirming an inseparable cosmic web we call reality. What these most rigorous scientists are not inclined to do, except in private conversation, is to speculate on the vast implications of their findings. They resist doing so because they anticipate new findings that may change their picture. Rigorous investigation of our world always leads to new findings and new models of reality.

IV. New insights which have arisen out of Atomic Physics

Perhaps one of the most important contributions Atomic Physics has made to our new / old understanding of reality is Quantum Mechanics or Quantum Theory as it is often called. Quantum thinking moves past materiality into waves and activity. It stipulates that what appears to be material has a discrete radiation charge or quantum. All forms of radiation exhibit quantum qualities which, technically speaking, means that the magnitude of all quantum, emitted or absorbed, equals either its energy or its momentum. In non-technical language, one may say that waves either exhibit characteristics of direct radiation or direct activity. Anything which exists, exists as **form** and/or **activity**.

One of the interesting speculative ideas arising out of Quantum Theory is the mathematical probability that you or I can get into phase with a material object, such as a wall. There is a mathematical probability that you or I can literally walk through a wall without touching anything. That is the nature of waves and we are composed of waves. While quantum theory doesn't address ghosts or spirits directly, it opens the door for such high-energy beings to exist. It's simply a matter of frequency. And, as any first year physics student knows: Frequency is proportional to the inverse of wave length or $f = \frac{v}{\lambda}$ where $f =$ the frequency in complete vibrations per unit time, wavelength *(lambda)* is the distance between any two successive points in the same phase, and v is the velocity of the wave. Combine this characteristic with Max Planck's constant for photons and you have: $h \times f =$ energy (in consistent units). In the above relationship 'h' equals Planck's constant. The Bohr equation (as it is sometimes referred to) or $h \times f = \Delta e$, measures the amount of discrete energy given off when an electron relocates from its initial position in an atom. More importantly, the Bohr equation demonstrates the interchangeable nature of matter. Like Lewis Carroll's Cheshire cat, matter winks into being and just as quickly disappears from view. It's that kind of a universe!

In the Quantum Field Theory, a further outgrowth of the proven mathematics of the Quantum Theory, the entire material universe is made up of coexisting infinitely large fields of quantum particles, electromagnetic fields of photons, the nuclear force field of mesons and the gravitational field of gravitons. For many of us that is quite overwhelming. In days of old, the universe was simply a great many stars and planets spread over incredible distances. Today, we know that it is composed of a great deal more objects and forces than we can even imagine. But a significant number of distinguished people in the fields of science are beginning to see the vast multiplicity of events as stemming from a single source and exhibiting relational features.

Well-known astronomers, such as Vera Rubin, have postulated mathematically proven data to indicate that our universe is a lot denser then we can see with the eye. Vera Rubin has measured the mass of large blocks of the universe and the measurements yield far more than the stars contained in those blocks of space. There is a growing amount of evidence to suppose that energy is everywhere, filling all the presumed empty spaces. There is now evidence that the universe is filled from one end to the other, confirming the belief of an organic composition.

Belief is turning to Truth, based not on faith, but on evidence (a clear expression of experience). Scientists have speculated that this great deal of additional mass may be dark matter, a term referring to invisible particles so dense they take on properties of matter. The dark matter is interacting with visible matter and poses new challenges to those determined to pin reality down to predictable results. The dark matter also appears to act as an external membrane holding the visible universe together as an eggshell would hold its ingredients together.

Fred Alan Wolf, a noted physicist, has proposed the theory of parallel universes. Metaphysicians have said much the same for some time, referring to the many apparent bodies each of us is believed to have. The same mathematical models proposed for parallel universes fit the models proposed by metaphysicians. The same consideration for the description of separating membranes described by the Albert Einstein-Nathan Rosen Mathematical Bridge, may determine the possible existence of parallel universes, as well as describing the function of black holes, fits the models describing the various inner space layers making up the various bodies. The correlation is remarkable and begs discovery. Metaphysical conclusions based on experience are becoming the theories of respected scientists based on mathematical models. Science fiction is fast becoming science. What astrologers of past centuries held as the basic parallel realities of human events and cosmic happenings (as above, so below) are finding their way into serious scientific discoveries of the macro / microscopic levels of reality.

V. Overriding insights arising from the new physics

The special theory of relativity, as proposed by the great physicist Albert Einstein, referred to the relationship of speed to mass and time. The closer one came to traveling at the speed of light, the heavier one became and the more time literally stood still. Einstein proposed that the speed of light, a mere 186,000 miles a second, was the upper speed limit for anything material to achieve. Metaphysicians have proposed that an entire array of beings may exist who consider the same speed of light to be a base limit for their travels. Thus, angels may be explained as beings who slow down so that selected humans can encounter them.

Perhaps more important to our expansive view of Truth are the discoveries made within our collective lifetime to substantiate the overarching implications of Einstein's theories. We have now determined that reality is relative, not only to speed, but also to the observer. Gone are the notions of objectivity, held so dearly by empiricists. The energy of the one observing affects the energy of what is observed. Associated confirming examples of interrelatedness have been demonstrated in numerous experiments.

Mind, as the center of the real world, has created a unity amidst diversity of expressing particulars. All things are indeed possible in a multitudinous reality where one need only frame a key to get through the doors leading to greater possibilities. Simple complete acceptance nullifies consensus group mind limitations. The first step to realizing the Truth of this statement is affirmations repeated to the degree that the limitation has been instilled. To put it another way, self-limiting notions and feelings can be overcome by installing their opposites often enough and intensely enough so that the original consensus mind is forgotten. In a universe of relativity, where everything is indeed relative, everything is relative to mind. Change your mind and you change your reality. It may take time, because time is relative, but it will happen.

When we envision mind and minds as energy of a particular variety and capable of direction, we can also envision consciousness itself as correlated with the coherent energy present within us and around us but not limited to us. Consciousness affects matter; consciousness changes matter. The bonding forces at the molecular level may, in fact, describe agreed-to shapes and delineation that have preceded us but don't define us or our futures. Every consciousness that has made a breakthrough confirms this profound Truth about ourselves. Every climber who has reached the summit knows the shape of the mountain and what it means to only see the sky.

The great Indian Yoga/mystic Sri Aurobindo Gosh-educated in the West, knowledgeable in the new sciences, and master of the East, once observed from his spiritual mountain top that our brains are mere transmitters for the consciousness that swirls around us awaiting kindred minds, tuned to the same higher frequencies, to pick up Truths and claim them as their own. We may call it inspiration or even revelation.

Aurobindo called it receptivity to what has always existed and exists everywhere. "He who has ears to hear," said Jesus. To which we respond, "Give us ears to hear the harmony of the spheres, and eyes to see the glory of unlimited intentionality."

What the New Physics has done for us, perhaps more than anything else, has been to free us from a material perception of what is real. Atomic physics has moved us from Newtonian laws based on indestructible atoms and clearly defined physical activities to an incredible look with Alice through her looking glass. We have seen the Cheshire cat who disappears, the March Hare who gets through any hole (a reference to those electrons and other recently discovered particles who pass through seemingly solid nuclei only to appear on the other side) and the crazy Queen whose frequent shouts of "Off with her head" remind us of the black holes who swallow everything that comes near them. We live in an ever-expanding universe which not only expands in volume but expands in complexity as we begin to recognize our cosmic surroundings.

The New Physics has opened our eyes to possibilities considered miracles in past centuries. Healing is not only possible, it is an expression of God's divine will in a universe where consciousness reigns and God is king. Changing our lives around is more than wishful thinking; it is mandatory for partners with God whose basic identity is kin to the supreme consciousness who directs ants and galaxies alike. Random events have become purposeful in a universe where there are no accidents, only incidents along the way back to our spiritual source.

Humans, along with all other forms of life, are represented on an infinite spectrum of energy and waves and frequencies that stretch endlessly in all directions and dimensions. In such an expanded universe, consciousness is also expanded endlessly in all directions and dimensions. Just as physical force was defined as that which has energy and direction, so now Mind may be discovered to be the unifying Truth which has both infinite energy and infinite directions. We define and so limit our energy and direction. God does not. Nor does God define it for us. We have done that over the eons of time humanity has been evolving. The new sciences are coming to the point of being able to address religions as a kindred searcher whose aim will discover the same mark.

In Chinese lore it was the heavens, or Tien, which decided the fate of empires. In Jewish lore it is the heavens that declare the glory of God.

Chapter Six: Exploring Judaism & Christianity

I. Judaism–the basic theme of returning to God

If you want to know about Judaism, ask a Jew. More specifically, ask a Jewish scholar or Rabbi because they will give you answers that most closely fit what it means to be a Jew. And what it means to be a Jew is directly related to what Judaism means in the larger context of history and Divine intentionality.

Judaism did not start with Father Abraham leaving Ur of the Chaldees (modern day Iraq) around 2000 B.C.E., although many Christians might assume that to be true. Judaism, as a religion, began with Moses, considered the greatest leader the Jewish people have ever known. For many, he was the greatest of a string of great prophets. Most importantly, it was Moses who gave the people the Torah or Law. It is the Torah which unites all Jews from times past to the present moment. Father Abraham was the first of a nation predicted to become more than the sands of the sea. But Father Abraham did not have a religion. He had a God he discovered along the way and whom he trusted to fulfill promises made to him (Genesis 12 on).

Judaism is a story filled with very human heroes. In fact, it is a religion which tells us much of what it means to be authentically human, faults included. All of the great people whom Jews honor, from among their ranks had serious flaws, yet are remembered for overcoming them or revealing through them the God they worshipped and followed. From Father Abraham, whose faith armor was cracked, to Moses whose temper created problems, to King David who couldn't keep his hands off of attractive women, to Samson who revealed a poor judgment of character, to Jacob who swindled to get what he wanted, to Jeremiah who begged God not to send him, all reveal human traits many of us can identify with when we admit it's all right to be human.

The first book written wasn't the first book that appears in the text. The history of the Tanakh or Christian Old Testament is not the same as the history of the human race. Genesis (a Greek word) means "In the Beginning" and so named because those are the first words in the Hebrew Text. Genesis provides us deep glimpses into the divine light which shone in the writer's eyes as they pieced together what would become a holy text remembering a holy covenant between God and Israel.

Let us then start at the beginning. It says that God (Adoni/Lord) breathed into Adam and he became a living soul. Adam had been fashioned from the clay, even as the stars had been fashioned by God's own hands. But in order for Adam to become alive, God's breath needed to be breathed into his lungs. The word in Hebrew for breath is the same word for Spirit and wind. Already hundreds of years before Jesus came into this existence, the Jews knew that God's Spirit was in all humans even as He had placed it in the first human, Adam.

The great Truth, often lost, is that humans have a divine component that is the same as the eternal God. That is the simple meaning of these few words. The Hindus had taught man's divine identity about the same time in India that the Jews were realizing it in Palestine. Brahman/Atman is the Hindu realization of God in Man and Man in God. All ancient people knew the importance of breath. In China it is called Chi and connotes one's vital energy. In Sanskrit it is called Prana and means life force. In Hebrew, this vital life force which defines us over the rocks and hills is Ru-Ah. God's Ru-Ah or breath made Adam a living soul. When we realize what the ancient Hebrews realized, we will know to whom we belong because we have the same basic identity. Many centuries ago the ancient Jews knew that not only Father Abraham, but the first person created from the clay was also kin (identical) to the creator by virtue of what was deemed eternal, namely, breath, energy, life force, and spirit.

II. Central to Judaism

For many Jews the Torah is central to what it means to be a Jew. The Torah is the Law given by God on mount Sinai to Moses to transmit to the people. It was given as a covenant between God and his people. Keeping the Law meant God would keep his promise to bless his people. His Law would be a sign around their heads and arms, kept in front of their minds daily. They were not to harm another, nor take from another, nor undermine another's family, marriage or possessions. They were to honor God by their obedience, remembering God daily and totally resting while remembering God weekly.

In pre-exilic Israel, idolatry was considered the worst sin a Jew could commit. Simply described, idolatry was the sin of placing anything in front of God to obstruct your view of God. It didn't matter what that something was. It could be a representation of some power or force. It could be money, pleasure, self-interest, a sense of fear or inadequacy. It meant losing touch with God by no longer having God central to your life. In later times the Shabbat or Sabbath became the premier Law. Everything rested on the Sabbath: animals, fields, nature and people alike.

What made the Torah so important is simple. The Torah was and is God's way of direct communication, much as the Quran is for Muslims. It is the physical presence of God mystically appreciated, much as the Host or Lord's table is in Catholic circles.

God brought creation into being with a word, a vibration. Those vibrations are present in his Torah and are able to bring forth His holy will whenever the Torah is read. That's what the scriptural text means when it says: "God's word goes forth from Him and does not return empty, but fulfills the reason it was sent forth."

The Torah serves another important function. It reminds the people. Remember that God is the God of Abraham, Isaac and Jacob; the God who brought you out of the land of Egypt; the God who blesses you, forgives you, admonishes you, guides you, saves you and fulfills his promises to you and your seed. The Torah is identical to Judaism and Judaism is non-existent without it. It is the standard through every age throughout history, and Judaism is a religion fulfilled in history.

Our age has seen the entire Tanakh or Christian Old

Testament understood in its metaphysical meaning. The Alexandrian church Fathers, Clement and Origen, read the bible allegorically, Origen having distinguished three ways of understanding scripture, the spiritual or metaphysical understanding being the best and highest way. Mystical Jews read it that way as well. Cabalistic followers of the Tanakh see in every Hebrew letter meaning upon meaning, even as the Talmud and Midrash do for every word and story. Precisely what makes the Torah alive is the growing interpretations that build on one another from the first distinguished Rabbi who extrapolated the first text. Within Judaism there is this interesting mix of holding every word as sacred yet not holding every word as literally true.

III. Judaism and the Holy Name of God

One of the great truths the Jews uncovered they also demonstrated by the holy name of God. In **Judah** that name became four consonants (**Yodh, He, Vah, He**) with the vowels purposely left out so no one could name that name out loud. It could not be the butt of jokes or used to generate magical power. It was a living presence; never an object of distant regard. In **Israel** the name was (Transliterated) **El-o-him**. During the period of the divided kingdom, Israel built their own sanctuaries and created their own special name for God among the many descriptive titles. What is especially noteworthy of the name **El-o-him** is that it is masculine, feminine and plural. That means Israel regarded God as greater than a male or female or even a crowd. God would always be the royal "We," beyond a single person yet personal in nature.

While modern Judaism has moved away from the direct experience of God that characterized the stories dotting the Tanakh, direct experience still finds its way back into what it means to be authentically human. Judaism has given us an ethical standard unequal in intensity in comparison to the other religions surrounding Israel in times past. Ethical conduct was at the center of the prophetic message. Returning to the Torah would accomplish all that was needed. Ethical living is what makes us truly humane. Judaism has contributed a humane view of what it means to be in this life at this time. Judaism has also shown us the power of words. The Holy Words spoken by God carry their own vibrations and steer us back to God. Along the way, we discover who we are and why our ears need to be open to hearing that voice.

Many of the ways Judaism has contributed to our search for Truth are hidden beneath understandings we attribute to Christianity. Everything Jesus said, except about himself, he appropriated from the Tanakh or Midrash or Talmud of his day. We have that much to credit to what came before him. But we can say, beyond what was appropriated, that Judaism speaks to a kind of personal following of God through his interruption into history and human lives. The closer we come to experiencing God through his word and voice, the closer we come to understanding our relatedness and his intentionality. Judaism offers that kind of walk and encourages humankind to a moral way that holds justice and compassion and divine intimacy central to living.

IV. Christianity–salvation through a human called Jesus

Christianity came out of Judaism. Jesus characterized his own words and actions as a fulfillment of the Law, the Torah, the living vibrations of an infinite God. In the first century, Christianity was considered a Jewish sect by the Roman overlords. That is true. It was. In fact, early Christianity didn't have a Trinity. It believed Jesus to be the Jewish Messiah sent from God to redeem Israel. His death would have proven otherwise. His resurrection confirmed this belief for every Jew who saw him after his death. But Rome would interfere with all the potential Jewish believers who might have followed Jesus. Beginning in 70 C.E. Rome destroyed the rebellious Jewish city of Jerusalem and every Jew they could find. So many males were killed during the period of 70 C.E. to 135 C.E., the Rabbis changed the line of Jewish succession to pass through the mothers instead of the fathers. To that point the line of succession had passed through the males from Abraham to the First century.

Christianity then found a home in Greek thought. It was Greek thinking that addressed who Jesus must have been to fulfill

God's purposes. By the time Christianity had reached Rome and
been accepted as the state religion through emperor Constantine,
Christianity was ready to end the centuries of suffering imposed
by Imperial Rome. As a state religion it organized itself much as
Imperial Rome was organized. The same basic governmental
structure continued as the official religion of the empire. Two
emperors emerged. One was head of the unified state. The other
was head of the unified religion. One held the power to rule; the
other held the power of the keys of heaven to save.

Rome was enamored by unity, except that for Rome unity
meant conformity. Conformity, in turn, requires a legal system
that has authority to dictate what is to be believed and how one is
to act. From invitation, Christianity moved to oppressive legality.
Under the Christian emperor, the Pope of Rome and the princes
of the church determined through exact language how to describe
Jesus; who he was; what he had come to do; and what it all
meant. Every voice who testified differently than the official
proclamations of Rome was silenced. Creeds, doctrines and
official pronouncements followed upon one another until the
mysteries of this special historical event had been placed under
the rule of a social structure.

Within early Christianity there were the seeds of divine
intentionality. Unity was important, but it was the unity without
conformity. Diversity was also important, but it was the diversity
without confusion. "**Unitas sine obsequis; diversitas sine
confusione**," as the Latin maxim would put it. In that Latin
maxim the Truth lies. Jesus had come to call all people, first his
own, then all others, to an understanding of God that would not
deny them their identity but which would include a new identity;
fully children and heirs and partners with the Infinite.

Limiting, condemning and compartmentalizing elements
would enter the message as power and control took over the
messengers. Rule replaced love and authority replaced service.
When love and service returned, from reforming period to
reforming period, the original voice of a loving God could be
heard. The Christian message was not meant to be an exclusive

"them and us" membership drive. The original message was to announce a universal God calling all people to a universal Truth about themselves and about their divine Father. It would appear Christians were never good at handling power, for history is replete with examples of Christians handling it badly.

V. Christianity–The Message

The message Jesus or Jeshua bar Yoshep (as early Christian Jews would call him) brought was a message of reconciliation with God; healing of all brokenness and "disease" and a future kingdom where everyone would be considered equal before a divine parent whose love shone equally upon all. Part of his message was a call to repentance. Judaism has always had a call to repentance to Jews once every year during Yom Kippur. Jesus' call was to a repentance that would change lives by changing their direction, from feeling separated from God to being united with God. His call was for a direct experience of this connectedness with God and then connectedness with one another in mutual love and service.

Force was never in the original message, nor the original intention. Love was to win hearts and win humanity as a whole. Love is, after all, the center of all spiritual gifts. It is eternal. It acts to unite. It expresses divine unity in all that it does. Where love dominated Christian actions, positive results followed. Jesus exampled sacrifice as the mode of expressing God's intentions and bringing people into a greater fold, able to sacrifice in loving service because all of their inner and outer needs were met directly by a loving God.

Jesus taught that all things were possible to those who believe and trust God. He taught an unlimited spirituality reflective of an unlimited sense of true self and present God. Early on, the seeds for positive thinking were represented in the Gospel accounts. Early on, the church did remarkable things in the name of Jesus. With the introduction of secondary experience in the form of rational faith, creeds and public pronouncements, rational consensus mind-sets relegated commonly done miracles to rare events. Jesus, and those who followed closely in his train, knew no limits and were willing to do all things.

Christians have varied in how they understand the man Jesus; the God / man; the Christ who is a cosmic being. To the Christian, he is all of these things as we are inheritors of all of these things. That should be the language of mysticism. For many others, he is our brother, equal in all aspects of humanity while showing us our divinity. For still others, he is unique and special, beyond limitations and worthy of worship. For yet others, he is a true prophet who points away from himself to God, being himself totally transparent and thus allowing us to see God clearly. Ultimately it doesn't matter how you see Jesus, as long as you see him for what he offers by his life, intentions and victory over life's inherent limitations.

The test after this life won't be a written exam, but a life review. If it contains love and attraction for everything Jesus stood for, the soul's path will be clear and uncluttered. The soul will shoot like a rocket to its lover and friend, God; God in Christ; the source of all Truth, the Logos in particular form. While the Trinity has been inherently confusing to all but Christians, in one important aspect it speaks clearly: God is One. Unity is God's ultimate intention. We are part of that intention. God is capable of expressing divinity in any way God chooses, including fulfilling promises made many centuries ago. The end result remains the same.

There is mounting evidence that Jesus was also known as Master Jesus, for there is growing evidence that Jesus was knowledgeable in Eastern methods of self mastery. From time to time one can glimpse his mastery techniques in his healing and restoring accounts, as well as his ability to multiply natural substances to meet a need, much as his predecessor Moses had done. When he said to those who followed him that they could do even better and more incredible things, he pointed directly to the basic Truth that all spiritual masters teach; namely, that each one is capable of doing the highest and the best, once we get in touch with the infinite source who knows no limitations and offers none.

Spirit and magic have been a sticking point for many Christians who feel inclined to remain humble. Spirit manifests best as flow through. Thus, Spirit appears unlimited, even to consensus consciousness groups. Spirit neither knows limitation nor does it promote limitation. People, and those realities that are created by our mindsets, promote limitation. Jesus didn't teach limitation. He did teach focus and direction. He did encourage overcoming limitations with pure intentions and holy means. Magic, by contrast, is consolidated power. It remains in the hands of the one doing it. The one doing it also controls it. It can be used for any reason, including the most base reasons one can imagine. When we employ Spirit's help we also release unlimited power so that the event is done without negative consequences at some future time. Spirit insures the outcome, because Spirit sees ahead. Spirit cannot use its power in an inappropriate manner. Christianity shares this spiritual legacy with the other religions. The difference is that Christianity offers it to all who are willing to take the leap of faith into God. One does not have to become a master first.

The Christian texts have an inner meaning as well as an historically correct meaning. Like the ancient idea of "So above, so below," the Christian scriptures allow us to see with spiritual eyes into the inner reality that governs our world. It is not an either or proposition, but a both and proposition. Truth has this dual aspect that compels us to look deeper for soul satisfying answers to the important questions of life. Life is continuous. Knowing that, we can rest assured that all the characters in the drama are around to answer those questions that still linger.

Taoist plate symbolizing the nature of morality as relative
Story of the Farmer and his Horse

Chapter Seven: Inspiration & Revelation

I. Inspiration and Revelation–two sides of the same experience

One of the concise ways to tell the difference between Eastern and Western religions is by defining the Eastern religions as inspired by higher faculties, and Western religions as those depending on direct revelation.

Inspiration is often used interchangeably with revelation but the two are not actually identical in origin. Revelation is precise and specific. If we are speaking about Judaism, the first important Western religion, we are referring to the specific messages Moses, the patriarchs, the judges and the Hebrew prophets received from God. God spoke to these men directly using their language to communicate messages God wanted to send to his people. The Ten Commandments and other of the 613 laws of Judaism, came to Moses, not from personal inspiration, but from precise revelation. That's what the Jews believe and hold to, and that is what most Christians believe about the message Moses received on Mount Sinai.

The prophets began their call for the people to change with the clarion pronouncement, *Thus says the Lord!* In the Christian New Testament, Christians hold that Jesus, being divine, spoke God's words directly. The apostles, Paul and Peter, are held to have been directly inspired by Christ's presence or God's Spirit when they both spoke and wrote their words following the resurrection. The other words which fill the pages of the New Testament, are considered direct revelation by some, for still others inspired words given to reasonable corrections and historical editing. It is very possible that the Western view of revelation is a direct consequence of Judaism's singular defense of an all powerful invisible God who communicates His intentions by vibrations or words, and not by visions or intuitive understandings.

Islam closely follows the communication style of direct revelation. Muhammed's recorded encounters of the angel Gabriel for 22+ years, during which he received messages, are considered by all Muslims as revelations spoken to the Prophet Muhammed. The messages he received were specific words spoken for specific reasons at specific times in specific places that hold historic significance.

The existing major Eastern religions begin with Hinduism, followed by the religions of Buddhism in India and Confucianism and Taoism in China. All of these Eastern religions define their holy scriptures as inspired but not given by a specific God at a specific place in a specific time for a specific circumstance. They are messages given for all times and circumstances about truths that are by their nature eternal. They originate from an eternal source to be shared with a temporal audience. Interestingly, except for Hinduism, the other religions just mentioned didn't begin as religions. They began as reform philosophies. In the case of Buddhism, this later religion began to end human suffering. Confucianism began to establish social order. Taoism began as a metaphysical comprehension and continued as a religion predicated on principles of effecting a natural way of living in tune with Nature.

Other differences exist between Eastern and Western religions. Often, these differences reflect cultural and historic factors. Perception, language and environmental locations all play a part in both inspiration and revelation. North Africa, India and China have considerable differences in natural terrain that have influenced the religions arising from these regions. What is truly remarkable about several religions located in different parts of the world is not their terrain but their time of origination, the century 500 BCE, give or take seventy five years. During that time period, Jainism and Buddhism began in India. Confucianism and Taoism began in China. The great Greek philosophers arose in Greece. King Josiah rediscovered the religion of Judaism to jump start this ancient national faith, preparing it for the Babylonian captivity. Zoroaster's beliefs became the religion of Persia, in time to influence Judaism, Christianity and Islam. All this took place in about the same time frame but in different parts of the world.

II. Eastern Inspiration–a closer look

One may differentiate inspiration from revelation as the act of being informed without hearing a voice speaking in your language. Somehow you know something; you see it clearly in your mind's eye; it moves you in an extraordinary manner far removed from ordinary comprehension. The Ancient Hindu Rishis were moved to explain the mysteries of the cosmos; the eternal One; or true human identity in a manner we may guess at but have no concrete proof as having been employed. Those ancient Rishis, along with their Buddhist counterparts exhibit an enlightened grasp that bespeaks their enlightened state.

The writings of the Tao demonstrate a view of the nature of things; of reality itself, that only someone seeing the sum of reality at a glance could describe with such simplicity. By contrast, the writings of Kung Fu Tzu and his successors denote wisdom, but not necessarily elements of divine origin. Yet Confucius is honored as one who understood how a society could maintain itself in harmony and thus create well-being for most of its citizens. Confucianism is about morality, much as the Ten Commandments are about morality. In the case of the Analects of Confucius, the morality doesn't address an infinite source but human relations. In the case of the Ten Commandments, we discover that morality begins with prioritizing God, then respecting human relationships. In both incidences it is assumed that a higher power somehow oversees human events and delivers blessings or catastrophes as warranted.

The earliest shamans exhibited extraordinary powers precisely because they were able to demonstrate the healing arts. Shamans of every stripe and coming from every culture made it known to those who depended on their abilities that they were in touch with the invisible, the greater reality that surrounds the material world. Their relative ability to communicate with the spirit world; their varied abilities to dispense herbal cures to fellow tribesmen; their timely pronouncements anticipating rain, fruitful crops and good weather for hunting, all conspired to place them in the camp of inspired special people. How they did these things has been described by curious anthropologists. The information forthcoming suggests that dreams, visions, and sightings all played a part. Social scientists, while remaining skeptical about shaman claims, nevertheless affirm shaman successes on a far better than average basis.

III. Western Revelation–a closer look

What we may term revelation had its beginnings in Judaism. When the scribes put together the accounts of the patriarchs, they included visions and dreams incidentally, while prioritizing direct revelations. Father Abraham is told by God to leave his country and journey to a strange land. Judaism places special importance on the voice of God. Creation is brought into being with God's voice. God's breath, God's Ru-ah, gives life to Adam and he becomes a living soul. God speaks and His word never returns empty but does what it intended. All of these, and more examples, set in place the importance of God's voice which speaks words to appointed people.

Thus, revelation is hearing the divine voice, in contrast to seeing visions or having important dreams. Joseph, the eleventh son of Jacob, interprets dreams for other people and consequently becomes an important man for God during the Israelite stay in Egypt. His own dreams get him into trouble. But whenever a patriarch hears God's voice speaking to him, it is direct and specific revelation that he must obey. Each sound then becomes important. Each word has special meaning. That is the nature of revelation. Many have announced that they had revelations. Judaism offers a skeptical view of the many of these while honoring the few pronouncements it considers authentic.

Judaism accepted revelations when certain elements were clearly in place. They didn't have to all be in place, but it would help that most of them were. The first thing that needed to be in place was that the proposed pronouncement actually came true. That would indicate that it came from an infinite God who knows the future and tells the Truth. Second, the pronouncement needed to be consistent with what previous revelations had revealed about God, His nature and His purpose. At this point it could be considered authentic. Thirdly, the pronouncement needed to agree with the moral laws of Moses, for these were given directly from God's holy mountain to God's holy people. Without, at least three elements in place prophetic pronouncements didn't have much chance of being honored.

When the great pre-exilic prophets rose to speak for God, they were often rejected out of hand. That is, until their words came true. The many laws within Judaism, along with a growing oral tradition, provided ammunition for the prophet's dissenters to claim that the prophet's words were not consistent with Mosaic practices. What those early prophets gave to their times moved later religious consciousness past ritual form to spirit and substance. It revived the Mosaic laws giving them divine intentionality rather than ritualistic priority. Later, Rabbis working with existing texts, would see the prophet's words as divinely revealed, adding the prophetic messages to the authorized canon.

The prophetic voice, as it is called, attempted to revive the revelations given to the people. The prophets spoke for God when they announced, *Thus says the Lord.* God, invisible and not defined by a body, would become the voice of Judaism, then Christianity, and finally Islam. Western revelations would become the defined manner of knowing the will of the Infinite.

Christianity copied a great deal from Judaism, from the sayings of Jesus to worship practices, to the vision of the future. But Christianity moved past Judaism when it proclaimed Jesus as Lord. Jesus, thus became the spiritual opposite of secular authority. The Roman Caesars claimed to be God. Rome, obsessed with power from its beginnings, in time added its leaders to the pantheon of gods. It was a civic thing to do for many good citizens and showed loyalty to the Empire. The first century church resisted Rome's authority, claiming Jesus as rightfully Lord since his resurrection proved his superiority to any Caesar. More importantly, the first Christians were monotheists and thus rejected worshiping anyone other than the one true God. Jesus was accepted as Messiah and consequently as Lord, that is, the rightful savior sent from God. At this stage in Christian development there was no discussion of a Trinity.

By the third century the accounts which would be accepted as Christian canon, painted the one called Messiah as God Himself. The few references to what would become the Trinity were read back into the early texts. Rome, under the leadership of Constantine became Christian, and that pervasive authority Rome made famous, under the rubric of the *Pax Romana*, now would become the *Shalom Aleichem* (Peace Be With You) of Jewish tradition. Somehow, in time, the Peace of Christ would be associated with the right to kill and conquer, with sanction given by the church to do so.

Jesus was the one who would return. He now became the one who sits at the right hand of God, second person in a divine Trinity, looking much like a divine pantheon in the eyes of other monotheists. The breath of God or God's Spirit, as he was called in the Old Testament, now became the third person of the Trinity, making the group complete and one in nature. Jesus soon was given divine status by a Council of Bishops and the Roman Emperor. Revelation, relegated to properly designated texts, now was viewed as every word coming from Jesus' lips. Soon, with the official acceptance of a translated canon, revelation would further be viewed as the entire Bible. With the power of the keys, given first to Peter by Jesus, then to the apostolic succession of bishops of Rome, revelation would become those particular words spoken by the holy father, or Pope on matters of faith and morality. Thus, Western revelation developed from the inspired Torah of the first century church, to the direct sayings of Jesus, to the entire scriptures plus the special words of the Pope sitting in council with his bishops. Defined in such a way, revelation was now under the authority of the church to interpret and dispense.

Islam delineated revelation from the very beginning. Muhammed heard the angel Gabriel speak to him. After the Quran was written down for the first time and forever after carefully copied, the Quran has become the revelation of God through the angel Gabriel to the prophet Muhammed. No other revelations are accepted as such. The Old and New Testaments, though honored because of the various prophetic messages they contain, are viewed as corrupted. They are not required reading by Muslims. Muslims are required to read and memorize the Quran along with a lifetime of careful study and devotion.

IV. Inspiration and Revelation–by what authority?

The question of authority will always come up when discussing religion. Those who feel little or no sympathy for any religion will not place themselves under any religious authority. Free thinkers, as they have sometimes been called, pick and choose what they will believe on the basis of sensibility. Does it make sense? Is it true? Many contemporary free thinkers pride themselves as atheists or agnostics, displaying a certain formal respect for people or tradition or culture without seeing an implicit worth in religion outside of the human/contextual dimension.

A number of scientifically oriented people do not believe the formal teachings of a religion, particularly if it is Western, because it doesn't appear to fit the scientific method, and thus falls into the category of myth. Surprisingly, aspects of Eastern religions do fit the new modified scientific method, especially when that method is dealing with atomic physics. Eastern religions, unlike their Western counterparts, deal primarily with cosmology and metaphysics. Eastern religions can step away from rituals and traditions, not easily accepted by modern man, to address ultimate conditions, universal forms and primordial realities. A current generation of atomic scientists find themselves enamored with Taoism and Buddhism and Hinduism because these religions address the mystical perceptions evoked by both the micro and macro universes.

So the question of authority, once the sole province of the church, now needs to pass the test of sensibility. Often this test takes the shape of correspondence. That is, does the reality I detect through my understanding of Truth correspond to the Truth pronounced by the religon I am inspecting? What the current generation of scientifically conditioned men and women are discovering is that sense perception alone means little. It needs to be coupled with sweeping intuitive insights. It needs to correspond to my overall comprehension of what is real. Eastern religions, once one steps past their cultural particularities, address reality more clearly than do Western theological formulations and legal statements. Western religions require faith and personal / societal commitment. Eastern religions encourage experience for confirmation. The Christian church began with a multitude of positions and beliefs but a common experience. Soon experience was relegated to the few while submission to doctrines and creeds were demanded of the many. Modern man doesn't accept an authoritarian belief system dictating

Truth. Modern men and women need to experience religion as real, satisfying and relevant if the Truth contained in that religion is to be realized.

V. Toward a unified understanding of Inspiration and Revelation

One needs to clearly understand two things about inspiration and revelation. First, both are concerned with the mode of communication from an invisible source to a visible recipient. Second, neither one requires secular authority to be what it is.

However we receive information, we still can honor the information we receive if it helps us in some total manner. What all religions profess in their various scriptures is a positive human model of attitude and conduct. All have a version of the Golden Rule. All inspire subscribers to practice the known and accepted virtues. All define human beings as essentially equal in nature and importance. All feel that there is a higher reality which promotes a moral posture. All hold that the higher reality, be it personal or impersonal, deity or condition, has a benevolent intentionality which you can trust. All promote unity while honoring diversity. All imply that cooperation, and consequently oneness amidst multiplicity, is superior to competition, destruction and want.

For the more evolved consciousness this makes perfect sense. Too often, it is not the sensibility that offends potential subscribers to religion, but its authoritarian posturing. One needs to come to the same conclusion from experience, not oppression. One needs to be open to Truth and where it will lead. Fear and distrust are natural consequences of authoritarian oppression, whatever the announced motives. The positive intentionality of the universe, be it from a personal being the Jews discovered to be God, or from what the Buddhists discovered as being awake, works its magic through laws and energies that steer the ignorant to experience the Truth of what is and will become. The laws that govern lead us to evolve. The consequences of our actions and inactions lead us to reform. The inspirations and revelations lead us to trust beyond ourselves to an infinite source. It is not the mode that counts, but the realization of its Truth.

In a world of multiply voices, it is comforting to hold certain voices as definitive and of ultimate importance. That defines our path and one cannot get from here to there without walking on a path. The ancient Jews wisely surmised that a total being powerful enough to save them and keep his promises could not be seen in some circumscribed manner. They relied on hearing him and following his voice. Other ancients relied on their visions and inspired moments, not having a clearly audible voice amidst the many they could hear. Be it visible or audible, inspiration or revelation, whatever takes hold of you and enables you to get in touch with that benevolent reality which watches over you, let that be your guide.

Truth appears to utilize many modes of communication, including life experiences. It is wherever you find it, not limited to one or another venue. History has given revelation that important voice because it becomes specific in language and thus remains the same over time. Visual impressions change as the historic landscape changes. However, language also changes and with it the original meaning of those words. That is precisely why historic context plays an important role in defining the message. That is why personal experience ultimately defines one's direction.

Yin/Yang, Taoist symbol for reality

Chapter Eight: Universal/Ultimate/ Existential/Personal Truths

I. Truths come in many packages

Philosophers have posited their relative positions in a number of interesting categories as evidenced by this chapter's heading. A group of philosophers believe in eternal Truths that are true whatever the circumstance. Plato taught about such Truths. Other groups of philosophers believe in situational Truths, true for this or that condition and time, but not for other conditions or times. More recent existential philosophers, as these philosophers refer to themselves, express this position. Generally speaking, those who hold to eternal Truths also hold to ultimate Truths. Those who advance existential Truths also advance personal Truths.

But can Truth be both ultimate and personal; universal and existential? Truth is both, and if we understand Truth as reality that meets us in our human condition, that awakens us to something we didn't know before or knew but needed to recognize, then how we receive Truth becomes the issue, not its intrinsic qualities. Existential Truths address the moment. Universal Truths transcend the moment. Both originate in potential reality as does everything that is or can be. Truth is like the potential Tao, or Way, actualized to express this moment or clarified to express all moments. It exists eternally yet doesn't achieve meaning until the moment activates it. It is particular and general; circumstantial and universal. Like energy, which can be measured as potential or kinetic, Truth is potential or active; particular or infinite.

Truth is reality brought to a moment while reflecting all moments, when expressed in the same manner under the same circumstances. Its relevance pertains to the subject who experiences it and thus makes it personal and particular. The existential philosophers remind us that the Truth of a moment, especially when that moment is horrific, as was evidenced by the Nazi period, poses more questions than it may answer. Be that as it may, Truth is what it is and compels us to seek the answers posed by the moment.

II. The Question of Evil

For many, the leading question posed by contemporary religious philosophers is: "Why is there evil, and why does an infinite loving God allow it to exist?" If evil is eternal then God must be evil, and this doesn't make sense in a moral universe. So evil must be penultimate in manifestation and linked to the human condition. In the Eastern religions evil is linked to ignorance. In the Western traditions evil is linked to an evil being who, along with other evil beings, subjects humankind to both temptations and suffering. In modern elements of Christianity evil is linked to persons who, alienated from the divine source, do things that create suffering for others and for themselves.

Evil's ontology is limited to the human experience and not to the cosmos. It appears to have entered the human experience through human freedom. Without freedom, there is no evil. Without human consciousness, there is no element of freedom. Tracing evil back to its source, according to the Jewish witness in Genesis, one discovers evil as those decisions made by conscious humans which run counter to the divine intention. God does not intend evil, either to exist or for human beings. But an infinite God must allow freedom or God would not be infinite. Only an infinite being with infinite consciousness and infinite joy can allow freedom its place and thus separated beings their place in a multitudinous reality.

How far freedom can take separation may have already been demonstrated by history to this point. Man's inhumanity to man and nature is well documented. But it does not alter the reality that a divine being, with infinite powers, is hampered from changing historical events which example his displeasure. In place of preventing these events and thus human freedom, the divine source implements laws and forces which react to thoughts, feelings, events, decisions and social movements which run counter to the divine's basic intentionality. Hinduism calls this Karma. The three major Western religions, though arising from Judaism, refers to divine justice in different language. For our purposes we may propose that while humanity has freedom to go far afield from God's laws, those very laws will create mechanisms to bring persons and societies back to the starting point to try again.

Evil, either how it is defined in the East or in the West, is an existential phenomenon, not an ultimate reality. Divine intentionality employs evolution as its mechanism to both honor cosmic freedom and divine purpose. In the course of time evil disappears, in spite of appearances. Having announced that, one can avoid participating in evil by first describing its faces. Evil has several primitive faces which often disguise themselves in other masks. They are:

1) **Fear**– which is the feeling of separation from being connected. The price of freedom is the potential of fear.

2) **Selfishness**– which arises out of the misperception of implicit separation. The reality is that whatever one does relates to others.

3) **Dishonesty**– which arises either from fear or advantage. People lie for many reasons. Some reasons may even be necessary in the moment.

4) **Advantage**– which exhibits itself in the misperception of competition as a biological prerequisite for survival. Modern businesses are, as ancient empires were, based on taking advantage and having the advantage.

5) **Hate**– which arises out of an inner space which feels helpless, fearful, betrayed, and disadvantaged. Hate can be taught without these feelings.

III. Factors which have shaped our conceptions

Everything capable of thought and feeling, of motivation and intentionality, has an historical context. That means that whatever field of inquiry; whatever social or personal activity; whatever kind of transcendent moment you may have, all occur in time and space. For the many mystics across the spectrum of religious traditions, as well as for those unaligned persons motivated by inquiry unrelated to any particular religious tradition, there is a sense of timelessness. The ones who come back from their mountain tops attest to being beyond time and historic situation, but whatever they share, they share it in an historic setting speaking an historic language filled with historically conditioned images and symbols. One simply cannot escape the historic context, and thus, in a real sense every special experience one defines as a peak, is historically conditioned and therefore solidified for that moment.

Having affirmed that is also to affirm that Truths coming to us from a potential, unlimited, eternally defined condition, have both a real and immediate reality ready made for our moment, and a long-range reality fitting all moments. With Plato we can affirm an ideal goodness that is more real than its shadow appearance in an historic setting. Conversely, we can affirm that until this goodness, or justice, or balance, or Truth reaches us, awakens us, and changes us, it is of no consequence. Direct experience is at the heart of Truth, in all its many guises. For many centuries Christians have been content with the experience of faith, one step removed from the direct experience of the Divine, whom Christians have claimed to have faith in. With the institutionalization process in hand, the church moved from anticipating a direct experience of God or Christ to an indirect experience through an institutionalized recognition of spiritual activity called faith. Initially, Christians were easily recognized by their manner, attitude and glow. With full state acceptance, Christians were recognized by their membership, public pronouncements and correct statements.

Religions and profound discoveries begin with an experience of something out of the ordinary, more important to improving the human condition than what is present. They begin with an idea, new in its presentation, satisfying in its promises and expressing a greater Truth than present institutionalized formulations express. But over time human influences reshape that idea to make it manageable to the social and often political forces in place when the idea takes hold. Thus, the original idea changes to fit a social system which regulates its appearance.

Each major religion that has stood the test of time, endured and grown to a size capable of sustaining itself, attests to this process. What is spiritually true becomes what is humanly manageable. Truth revealed changes to a form acceptable to those altering its presentation. The power that the revealed Truth contains must be moderated by the power of those advocating its appearance. On the individual level inspired and revealed Truths can transform those called upon to hear, see or otherwise experience them. Once they move into the social context from their original historic entry, they are moderated to serve vested interests uninitiated into their primal importance. It is a major factor that explains why no religion can endure in its pristine condition. It is an important factor that explains why philosophical Truths change to accommodate future historic conditions.

Human consciousness must reflect the limitations imposed by its outside perceptions and what it has accepted as real. Because we are human, live in social conditions and become part of consensus realities that transcend our historic moments, we feel obligated to conform to what has preceded us. Both little Truths and great Truths enter human consciousness in moments of openness. To receive a fair hearing they must be accepted by situational necessity and consensus approval.

IV. The appearance of limitations

Have you ever been part of that party game that has you and others passing on an account from one person to another until the last person in the row says it out loud for all to hear? This game suggests the reality of selective perception. The story told quietly to the first person changes significantly in detail and content by the time it reaches the end of the row of participants. However profound and important the first words are, by the time they pass through a number of minds and wills they become something different. They may even change in theme and purpose. Such are the effects of human consciousness, bridled with individual intentions, feelings, predispositions and previous unhappy experiences.

Understanding that as part of the implicit human condition, it is remarkable that Truth has any opportunity to be properly relayed to others over time and cultures. But, in fact, Truth appears to possess its own kind of resilience. Part of that ability comes directly from divine intentionality that drives toward completion and openness. Part of that ability of Truth to surmount human subjective intent, is what Plato referred to as recognition. The recognition theme is included in a number of philosophies. It is now becoming part of psychological treatment. Its origin is the conviction that all Truth and knowledge is already within us. Using some method, be it hypnosis or dialectic discussion or freed up association, we remember the Truth that laid buried to that point. Whatever limitation appears, that limitation is based on readiness to see or understand. If we are not ready, no amount of persuasion will open us up to what the Truth would reveal about us or about our world.

In the Christian New Testament there is the wonderful phrase, *The fullness of time.* It refers to Jesus' entrance into human history and employs a Greek word for time different than the one normally used. The Greeks had two words to express events. One, Chronos, denoted the regular passage of change. The other denoted special events which change us. Kyros, as it is called in Greek, denotes particular moments significant for their contribution. What makes them significant may reflect social needs. Kyros events may also reflect personal awakenings incapable of being either shared or transferred to others. In the case of Christianity, the early ecclesia or gathered, saw in the Christ event a unique happening and thus referred to it in terms of a Kyros event. But whenever Truth strikes us personally, it does so as a Kyros moment, unique to us personally and therefore a personal gift from divine intentionality.

When I uncover or discover a personal Truth which I cannot verbally share or physically demonstrate, it would appear that I am limited by what I have learned. The appearance of limitation is a social appearance unless I accept that appearance as true. There are many humans on record who appeared to be afflicted with a severe limitation but who professed a great Truth for themselves. Their limitation opened something up within them that they would rather have than the termination of their perceived limitation. Whether it was the loss of one or more of the several senses (Helen Keller comes to mind) or a severe disability in thinking, reasoning, social discourse, academic understanding, physical aptitude or emotional normalcy, when that perceived limitation opened up new Truths, those so afflicted saw their discovery as both personal and important.

Discovering new Truths which appear to supersede old Truths often has the summary effect of labeling those old Truths as outdated or false to begin with. They may, in fact have not been true in the first place, such as the scientific assumption that denser objects fall faster than lighter objects. They may also still be true but, under new historic conditions, not true in the same way and for the same reasons. The package Truth comes in changes. What remains true is therefore true for all times.

V. The issue of relevance

The many ways Truth comes to us in our conscious states is indirectly related to the issue of relevance. The many shapes which Truth takes, its many variations and how it invades human life, is tied to the issue of relevance. The important question to ask then is: "Relevant to who or what?"

Relevance has finally been discovered as playing a role in test scores. Young people taking intelligence exams to rank them for colleges, score higher when they come out of cultural backgrounds that educate them in relevant subjects contained in the exams. Children, highly intelligent, but coming from Ghetto settings score poorly in exams that include questions on Greek mythology, classical literature, etc. because these subjects were not relevant to their education or background. Culture, as promoted by academics, plays a role in classifying people according to their relative intelligence when their intelligence is not the issue. Culture, perhaps more than intelligence, is the relevant factor for testing intelligence. So also, is motivation. So also, are emotional states. So, also are perceived goals. What we are willing to accept as true is related to a host of factors indirectly pertaining to the Truth we are investigating.

Western society is painfully self-centered, while publicly espousing humanitarian ideals. Western society is based on economic principles rather than civic ideals, and thus promotes personal gains above societal wellbeing. If all things were, in fact, equal, that wouldn't matter. In the short run it may not. It doesn't make a concerted appearance for public discourse and debate because it doesn't appear to be intrinsically relevant. Our subjective intent, perhaps a leftover from primordial days, is self-interest. Thus, public interest only receives due notice in times of crisis. But the Truth of the matter is that real crises take shape long before they make an appearance in society. Social concerns are always relevant in each present moment.

Vested interests promote the quiet use of power and control. Vested interests appear the most likely beneficiaries of the relative gains a social system based on economic principles will produce. But society is people. If people become stratified into levels in which only a portion have access to what makes them happy, fruitful and growth-bound, society fails.

The relevance of Truth is its experience. One can experience the Truth of something as pain or as enlightenment. As social Truth is experienced painfully, it is the result of not listening to the persistent voices that announce the need for change in direction. When social Truth is experienced as enlightenment, it is the result of being willing to see others in their context. Stratification of power and control closes off the very insights that allow Truths to make their appearance. Divine intentionality is thwarted. At some point an explosion occurs which breaks apart the controls vested interests hold and a new beginning emerges. That is one part Truth plays in the social drama.

Self-interest is based on a misperception of reality. It is based on the conviction that each one of us is unique, apart and separated from one another. If reality is organic, and it is, then self-interest is an expression of a perceived separation and therefore a form of evil. Self-interest is also the domain of a personal variation of relevancy that takes a short-term view of things. A long-term view would see the self destruction and social destruction that self-interest leads to in time. But the Truth of that reality requires an openness to becoming enlightened prior to that Truth painfully materializing in destructive events. It is the nature of Truth, as it is the nature of Karma, to finally bring us to realize cosmic intentionality contrary to any particular form of self-interest. Recognizing our intrinsic connectedness makes our social policies relevant. Recognizing our actual relatedness releases us from our self-imposed limitations.

Christian scholars posit an emphasis on the Protestant Reformation as the imbuing factor which generated capitalism, individualism and a growing appreciation in self-interest. Prior to the Reformation, society emphasized a conviction about the common good, the relative authority of church and state, and the view of a unified Christendom where belief patterns played a prominent part. The thought that any one person could rise independent of either society or religion was unheard of. After the Reformation, one needed only individual faith to achieve salvation and only personal drive, intelligence and good fortune to achieve success and consequently, great individual wealth.

Additional factors following the Reformation played a role in creating a preoccupation with self-interest. The rational explosion of empirical thought saw its counterpart in scientific theory. The scientific worldview that emerged was atomistic and fragmented with little room for nature or a connected humanity. Man was consequently disassociated from nature, the cosmos and a far off deity.

The old idea, recently resurrected, of being totally connected and existing in a cosmic living organism of multiple dimensions is mind boggling. For one raised in a 19th century world view and feeling liberated to do whatever you can get away with, formalized morality has held little persuasive demands. But realizing your implicit connectedness to other people, both near and far, related and unrelated, and nature in all its aspects, along with an infinite God from whom we originate, does affect one's view of self-interest. The nature of reality includes diversity in expression and thus individual identity. But each creative expression; each individual identity is also part of a greater whole to which we are responsible and in whom we are connected. The whole cosmos will bring us to this conscious understanding in time. Knowing it now saves a great deal of pain and concern along the way, and prompts us to act spiritually on behalf of one another. It is such a spirit and attitude that people call religious.

A Jewish covering of the Torah, or Law, 16th century preserve

Chapter Nine: Power

I. The reality of Power

For purposes of clarification it would be appropriate to first define what we mean by Power. Power is the consolidation, control and use of resources, either organic or inorganic, to affect outcomes, either present or future.

For one, or more than one, to have power infers that one, or more than one, has the ability to direct resources toward some outcome. Put more simply, a powerful person has a great deal of money, influence and people at his command, or knowledge that others want / need. A general of an army, a C.E.O. of a large corporation, a secret agent in a high-level position, a political leader—all exhibit power by virtue of their consolidated resources that they can bring to bear if they wish to do so. They may choose to act within the laws of their country or act outside of those laws. It doesn't matter. Multinational corporations have an interesting kind of power since they can, by geography, act outside of any one country's laws and still act lawfully by their own standards.

The history of power dates back to the beginning of recorded events. The oldest records we have suggest that power was used from earliest times. The one who had authority over others also had power over their lives and decisions. It was often necessary that one person be designated to give commands so that the social group acts in one accord for survival. Acting together, people could do what they could not do singularly. Just as the human body needs a head or central directing agent for the body itself, so groups need a single person or core group to direct the group. What originally was done by one, as groups grew in complexity, was done subsequently by core groups performing specialized responsibilities for aspects of the larger body. Tribal chiefs employed shamans, captains, etc. Kings employed counselors, advisors, lesser regional chiefs, etc. National bodies employed national parliaments, senates, etc. to go with the national head of the country. There has always been both a need and a desire to have leaders for whom the rest relinquish a measure of autonomous individual authority so that greater interests can be achieved. So power appears to be a natural consequence of communities.

The history of power also demonstrates a mixed bag of results. John Edward Dalberg and the Earl of Chadham both observed that power corrupts and corrupts in proportion to its extent. History supports that truthful insight. The more politically powerful Rome became, the more those under its heel felt its cruelty and not its just laws and civility. Where religions, including Christianity, have consolidated social / political powers, to that extent religions have shown cruelty and oppression. The great science writer and political commentator, Arthur Koestler, called this seemingly human inability to handle power as, *The Ghost in the Machine*. He surmised that there must be some evolutionary biological mechanism in the human organism that leads humankind to destruction, and that it is imperative this malfunction be uncovered before the human race dispatches itself into oblivion.

II. Power demonstrated in the greater scheme of things

Because power is an historic fact persistently present in the affairs of human beings and societies, understanding both its origin and its place in reality is of great consequence for both our present and future times. Power, along with other human qualities that isolate individuals from their peers and other life forms, evidences autonomy without understanding. The more persons feel isolated, misused or abused, the more they will compensate with a need to secure their lives by possessing power.

Youthful poverty can easily produce mature financial security and demonstrate social power. Prior volitional abuse by parental figures may in turn produce a need to overcome hurtful limitations by securing a position over others. Helplessness, seems to create dreams of dominance. You need only desire the dream enough and willingly sacrifice for it over time in order for the universe and circumstances to coalesce to fulfill those desires to dominate, control, rule, govern or lead others under your power. But the universe's intentionality, while allowing temporary power to exist and willing to compensate those without it, nevertheless introduces circumstances to ameliorate its use. Divine intentionality does not wish any to be helpless. The universe's intention is for all life forms to evolve materially and spiritually to oneness and universal consciousness. At the same time freedom always allows conscious beings to evolve at their own rate and inclinations.

Individual consciousness feels isolated, separate from the thoughts and physical presence of others. Power, therefore, comes from this illusion of separation. It manifests for purposes of control. If one can only control one's circumstances and those present, then the helplessness of this attitude of separation will also be controlled. The terribly poor youth with no education or means of advancement but a dream to be important, through intelligence and daring, is now a drug lord commanding billions of dollars and thousands of minions. Did the universe have a hand in this course of events? Yes, indeed! But the harm done as a result also comes back on those with the power to command these events, and consequently, other influences will come into the picture to undercut and disrupt such a massive demonstration of misused power, ignorantly created for the wrong reasons.

Our current times clearly demonstrate the consolidation of massive resources into fewer and fewer hands, and thus incredible displays of power lie just beneath the surface of public knowledge. Modern technology has played a part in this massive behind-the-scenes consolidation of power. Understanding modern psychology and applying this knowledge to steer, influence and generally affect millions of people has played a part. An increase in materialistic morality with a corresponding decrease in relational morality has played a part. The movement toward a global economy- a global influence that posits its entire ethical philosophy and rationale for action on money and the power it represents- must drive toward more having less until only a few have almost all there is.

III. Power as it is intended to be

Power has intentionality that runs concurrently with divine intentionality. In its isolated guise it fits the original description of how it appears. In its eternal guise it is but one of a number of examples of creational diversity, the example that promotes direction / activity in distinction to being / identity. To state it in more concrete terms, power is one of the various gifts and fruits of Spirit that the apostle Paul refers to without mentioning it by name. Power is a kind of responsibility that is designed to act on behalf of others, not oneself. Well-intentioned ancients and rulers of more recent times understood this as the divine right of kings and the mandate of heaven (Confucianism).

Along with the other creational, cooperative gifts, the gift of power is to facilitate improvement in living. Those influenced by this expression of power are meant to benefit from it. In philosophical terms, power is Arthur's Koestler's "holon," a point that consolidates activities beneath it while looking upward, as a single point of activity, to other points toward some further expression of unity. The Pope represents such an expression of power. Responsible for the physical and spiritual lives under his care, he nevertheless looks upward for inspiration and guidance to a source greater than he is or could become. Thus, he acts as a switching station (Arthur Clarke's term from *2001, A Space Odyssey*), channeling divine resources to the many who need them while representing the many as a single activity.

Cosmically, power is a selfless responsibility and calling. What has been entrusted has been entrusted for the sake of others, including events for a future time. Cosmically speaking, the universe determines persons and events to hold power for a period of time in order to achieve a global goal (a Greek Stoic notion). When these persons misuse, abuse, or otherwise selfishly employ their moment of power for other than the universe's intentions, suffering occurs. A chain reaction takes place starting with the first inappropriate incidence of misused power that begins to correct that misuse. The Hebrew prophets called that adjustment justice, or Mispat. It is the divine adjustment to bring people and events back to the universe's plan of unity. Misused power produces competition. Properly applied power produces cooperation. It's that simple. Misused power destroys, disrupts and separates. Properly applied power builds (including consensus), unites and improves everything.

IV. Getting from here to there

It seems hopeless, in the face of the overpowering influences present today, to envision so idealistic a view as just presented. The reality of the present world would indicate people giving up their

relative power or reapplying their resources for the common good is a
fool's dream. But the simple fact of history is that it will happen over
time. The Infinite appears to have all the time in the world. We do not.
Our time in one life is limited to years not centuries. The more people
see and understand the interconnectedness of all of life and reality, the
less examples of "old fashioned" power will appear until, like the
dinosaur of a million years ago, separated persons bent on controlling
others or dominating their environment will disappear.

　　　Is there anything each one of us can do to facilitate these
needed changes? Yes, but it should be noted that every movement plays
itself out. When it reaches a critical mass, it explodes or dissolves.
Along the way, those caught in its wake feel its impact. To avoid getting
caught in the wake of a large movement requires moving from the
reality consensus that governs this notion of power to one that accepts
the connected notion of power.

　　　The old notion of power, as it was displayed in ancient Rome,
and more recently in such examples as the multinational / multi-
billion-dollar corporations holding more power than many nations and
able to control or influence the economies and politics of many
nations, will run itself out. In spite of the creative efforts to further
consolidate money, power and corporate control, an end point for such
a global movement is already in sight. A new / old consciousness is
arising that runs counter to the present ideology. This new / old
attitude will grow in strength until it replaces the present view of reality
and power. In spite of appearance, the change is already in the world.

　　　At the individual level one needs to wish the world well,
consider others with positive concern. Most importantly, "visualize/
realize" that the "universe/God" wants you to have everything you need
and wishes to give you what you truly want. "Visualize/realize" that
since you are connected to others, their well being is just as important
as yours. If your need for power is such that others will be depreciated
by its application, you are still practicing the old model that does not
reflect God's intentions. If your needs reflect what is also good for all
others, than it will surely be yours to enjoy and use. There is an old
meditation wish that applies here. It goes like this: "May that which is
best for me and the whole world come about." Attitude is nearly

everything. The insect whisperings of the mind (a term coined by Loren
Eiseley) tend to carry us off to feelings of being separated. That is an
untrue ego ploy to be overcome.

   This modern world, with its extraordinary emphasis on
material wealth, was a while in coming to this point and it will take
awhile to come out of the dream that upholds it. Up to the moment the
Berlin Wall came down without a shot being fired, the general consensus
was that Communism could introduce us to World War Three. No one
seriously saw its demise coming without a shot being fired. The same will
be true of an economic system that visualizes people as commodity and
corporations as beyond personal responsibility for their actions. The
many corporate mergers, raising stock values while throwing people out
of work, will see a turning point (Fritjof Capra's term). The public,
believing the pronouncements that free enterprise is for everyone's
benefit, will come to realize that they are not best served by those who
serve themselves first and lastly.

   With understanding will come an initial feeling of
overwhelming helplessness in the face of unseen forces. Following this
awakening people will realize a better course of action in which all can
benefit in varying degrees according to their gifts, not according to their
consolidation of resources. The incentive for this new/old society will be
growth toward union while enjoying creation's diversity within care for
life in all its forms, including the planet that provides us shelter and life.

   For those who have already achieved this insight, our present
notions of reality and practicality appear nonsensical. It's like looking at a
drunken man barely able to stand up yet thinking himself capable of
intricate maneuvers with an automobile. We appear to live in a period
filled with the promise of waking up yet also filled with notions that lead
to self-extinction. Understanding God's intentions for providing power
for this world is a good place to start to see things as they really are. That
won't be easy, since you are likely part of a consensus reality wedded to
the old model. But nothing worthwhile is necessarily easy.

V. Some conclusions about Power

   To date, persons with certain gifts are prized more than those
without those particular gifts to share. In times past, music was such a

gift; as was art, as was philosophy. Today gifts which are apt to secure large amounts of money are prized because the greater consensus reality to which most of us belong, has outgrown artistic values to gravitate to materialistic values. Power was there all along, represented by those with certain gifts which that age prized.

Want, both motivates toward plenty, and represents a serious misreading of our essential being. At one level we avoid pain, so we do what we can to prevent it. The lack of power or helplessness, drove and still drives people to build an envelope that prevents helplessness from taking over again. Like the pearl the oyster produces to insulate itself from the grain of sand, people are driven to insulate themselves from their former conditions. But the rub is that intrinsically we are not helpless, nor were we ever meant to be. Our state of being is one of total acceptance by a universe that stands ready to do our bidding. The one thing we need to keep in the front of our consciousness is that what is true for us is also true for everyone. The more this consciousness develops, the less people will be driven to consolidate resources for their own ends.

There is always the view, hidden behind the best idealistic intentions, that to take such attitudinal steps is to fool ourselves, lull ourselves into a condition of unreadiness for life's disasters. We must be prepared, so we think, by securing every advantage we can, holding it to ourselves, and making certain no one takes it away. Our ego consciousness drives us into a competitive stance. Fears and anxieties raise their heads to provide the fuel to keep driving. In fact, they remain in place even after we have more money than we know how to spend, yet feel empty and afraid.

There are those, represented by some unknown number, who enjoy the thrill of competition and victories. If fear is at the base of their emotional states, it is not evident. Like gladiators of a former time, they take pride in what they are able to do, and thoroughly enjoy the game. They also succeed because it is the game they want, not the money that results from playing it well. As long as winning the game is what counts, losing great sums of money only adds interest, and not a sense of great loss. Their motivation is in tune with divine intentions because the

universe honors enjoyment and effort. They are also the ones
likely to share the winnings because the winnings are of
secondary importance to playing the game. Thus, it is not power
they seek, but opportunity to ply their gifts. As those gifts are
shared appropriately among all the players, the one winning can
continue to play. When those gifts become stilted
within a consciousness focusing on what is of secondary
importance, the universe sets in motion lessons designed to end
the game.

In whatever arena one has secured power, one needs to
realize that power is a divine right to further the universe's
intentions toward oneness. Power functions as a nozzle, not a
dam. When one attempts to block up the flow, the dam will
burst or run over damaging whatever is in its path. The
Truth that defines real power is the same Truth that defines
being, activity and relationships. Divine intentionality
dominates all events even as it defines all events. Freedom is one of
those events and thus, freedom always acts alongside organic
determinism. If reality is organic and alive, then we are not separated
entities able to do or say or think independently of others. Thus,
determinism is a natural quality alongside freedom of choice. It's not a
matter of one or the other. Nor is it a matter of one defining the other.
Definition lies above both freedom and determinism. Definition lies in
the field of total interconnectedness where freedom and determinism
play together.

All possibilities exist in the mind of God, and God wishes
those possibilities for us that we envision for ourselves, and which fit
divine intentionality. Having useful power, able to direct material
elements and people, contributes to God's ultimate purposes.
Demonstrating non-useful power which chooses not to direct material
elements and people in a manner consonant with God's intentions
misuses freedom and thus sets in motion deterministic elements which
drive toward justice. It doesn't matter how much power and control is
in place. It doesn't matter how knowledgeable those in power are about
human psychology and behavioral manipulation. The greater whole
acting in conjunction with divine purpose will end the misuse of such

power. However, it should be noted that the time required for such a course correction is directly dependent on the evolutionary energies already in place in human society.

Misappropriated power examples separation and separation, while permitted in time, space and freedom, cannot endure, nor multiply itself endlessly. Elements bent on maintaining separation in defiance of the whole must experience their discordant activities. Western religions call that hell. Eastern religions call that purposeful ignorance. In either case, it is self-induced, the direct result of free will, and lasts as long as individual wills refuse to respond to the invitation to end the masquerade. As the saying goes, What goes around, comes around, until the parties involved end it.

The penultimate reality of power is with us for as long as we need it. Its real purpose, in cooperation with other gifts, adds richness to existence and further examples diversity as a mechanism of creation. Power can exist alongside equality. Power can take its rightful place with individual and corporate dreams and aspirations.

With generosity it brings great happiness. But it is best displayed when evident under divine blessing, for then it reveals a distinct conduit from here to there.

Historic Christian plate symbolizing Pentecost, the birthday of the Church

Chapter Ten: Toward An Integrated View Of Truth

I. A cosmological view implicit in religion and philosophy

If you happen to ask a phenomenologist for a definition of religion he or she will likely tell you about studying something which has an ultimate perspective that focuses on what is holy and perhaps, holy other. The shapes and contents of religion vary, but the focus is somewhat constant with sidebars of healthy living, here and now happiness, and assurance of living forever.

Philosophy has historically focused on a search for what is real, meaningful and able to provide an integrated view of life. Philosophical definitions vary, as do philosophers. But from the ancient Greek philosophers forward to the present variety of empirical Linguistic Analysts, philosophers have searched for some way of seeing reality that satisfies both reason and the spirit. Since the scientific revolution which effectively replaced the firm foundation in beliefs, practical philosophers have stayed close to the scientific method, much as a baby prefers staying close to his or her mother's breasts. While the present popular variety does not satisfy the spirit, it has provided some comfort for the mind to know that one is standing on firm rock and not shifting emotional sands.

There has been a philosophical thread running the length of history from those early Greeks to the present period that transcends organized religions and classical schools of philosophy, yet is found within them. That thread may be described as the belief in the dual realities of matter and spirit (mind) which interact with one another or evolve into one another. That thread may also be described as the hierarchical progressive reality that moves from a lowest to highest expression along some continuum stretching from infinitely small to infinitely large; infinitely slow to infinitely fast; infinitely evolved to totally unevolved. That thread includes a cosmology which has a beginning, middle and ending or no beginning and no ending with cyclical activities throughout the spectrum.

Hinduism and Christianity appear to have a pronounced

interest in cosmology while Buddhism and Judaism do not. Confucianism, Taoism and Islam have Cosmologies but regard them under more existential priorities of living well now or being ready for what is to come. Cosmology is, after all, interested in beginnings. The scientific theory of the Big Bang is cosmology in scientific dress. It has its religious counterparts in the various creation stories found both in extant and living religions, and may even become part of future religious folklore for generations to come.

The cosmological view which runs through this text, and the continuum of religious and philosophical positions that have dotted the historic landscape, include both the belief and experience of infinite relatedness. That is, everything is related and interrelated and even interconnected. Greeks from Plato to Plotinus saw the universe, including man as part of a giant continuum that appeared to have distinct edges where matter ended and spirit or mind began. Plato saw matter as inferior. Plotinus saw matter as the extremities of the One from which everything originated. Augustine liked Plotinus more than he may have even let on being a converted Christian himself. It's clear that his theology, which became the orthodox view, owes much to this pagan Greek who captured Rome's heart during its pagan days.

One can trace this integrated view through the Scholastics, then through the Nominalists, then through German Idealism, and right up to current Process Philosophy and modern Hindu, Taoist and Buddhist positions. So what has been presented in these pages extends beyond the fancies of one or a few and includes generations from recorded history's dawn. In fact, it would not be that great a leap to include prerecorded history in this view. It would not be a great stretch to include pre-language humans who communicated intuitively and thus were always confirming relatedness on a psychic level. It is our more recent scientific culture that insists on separation on every level with clear and distinct edges, defining nouns and materialistic models. Ancient cultures had this Truth, among others, which church and scientific dogmas forced into exile. These truths are coming back however, along with the truths to which they point. Defined reality is a matter of consensus and consensus realities have chosen to evolve through the continuum, holding their identities in tact while limiting their potentials.

II. The meaning and Direction of Our Lives

You could argue that everything is about meaning since meaning is important at all levels of interaction and conception. So, saying just a few things about something so important appears trivial at best. What has preceded this section is all about meaning. What is now added is done to tie some things together. We are part of this incredible continuum, part of the infinite fabric of reality that includes spirit, mind and matter, as they appear to perception. Because we are, and because we are able to consciously reflect on who and where we are, in relation to the other elements open to our perception, we can alter our lives and each momentary outcome. That means the grand designer who brought us as us into existence also provided us a measure of freedom, free choice and the ability to change. In an infinitely complex living organism called the universe, having free choice is no small thing; it is, in fact, an awesome responsibility.

Our lives have an ultimate direction. They also have an immediate direction. The **ultimate** and **immediate** components to our lives are part of what Aristotle discovered in his description of forms. But they go beyond that, while reducing alternately to two components. The very next moment we have available to us contains all the past moments converging to that point. As Alfred North Whitehead so astutely discovered, each moment also contains an ultimate direction toward which it reaches. While traveling through the air, the arrow knows where it will land. What is ultimate is contained in what is immediate. What is immediate always points to what is ultimate. The two, like identical twins, seem to know what the other is about.

What is the ultimate direction of our lives? Part of it is to be one in intention, while myriad in application. The Indian notion of the drop of water returning to the ocean is part of it. To have completed the journey with all the tales and adventures to share is part of it. To simply come of age and grow up is part of it. All of these parts are ways to symbolically express a simple Truth. You and I are here, following a path, experiencing living and knowing, as long as we want to. When we no longer want to play, or when we realize that we have felt it all, we can lay it aside and take up our infinite identity without regret or desire or longing for just one more ride. The ride may include a number of human lives or trans-human lives or unimaginable forms of living. Each of us has choices how we want to travel. Each of us chooses to learn and help others learn lessons, attributes, unique creations and constructive combinations of interaction.

The universe is the teacher. God is the author, parent and caring lover who, both as impersonal law and personal friend, offers us the adventure. We introduce the limitations because we want to have a specific path leading to a specific outcome. Often our soul bodies tend to choose paths that both affirm where others have gone and conform to comfortable known parameters. The universe is ethical in the larger sense. It automatically drives toward a moral conclusion in keeping with the myriad guideposts planted in the way on all levels. But we make up the specific limitations because we choose the path and each path has its own guideposts and limitations defining it.

III. Spiritual evolution in keeping with organic evolution

From such early church fathers as Origen, to such contemporary mystics as Sri Aurobindo Ghosh, spiritual growth and human evolution play a significant part. Both Western and Eastern mystics and leaders of their communities acknowledge that what we consider as real is unfolding, changing, evolving and moving in a direction relative to time and purpose. Eastern religionists see it in ever evolving cycles that go on eternally. Western religionists see it in ever increasing quality moments that reach an ultimate destination. In either case evolution plays its part.

Since Charles Darwin's Theory of Evolution came into public consciousness with his *Origin of the Species*, people have chosen to react to its implications. More recent Western Christians and Orthodox Jews see it as just one more secular encroachment on a literal view of God and scripture.

But evolution is here to stay. It will take a number
of turns as new discoveries prove and disprove accepted notions. But
its general tenor affirms perception, understanding and human
consciousness. Unless all movement and change is an illusion,
evolution as a cosmic reality is here to stay.

If we consider this reality as ultimately one in design and one
in substance, then what we call spiritual is a part of what we call real. It
is just as real as what we perceive to be solid matter, simply of a much
higher frequency and not as prone to dissolution as complex organized
and much heavier material reality would be. The smaller and less
complex the material substance the quicker its death and the less
change it encounters upon death. The larger and more complex the
material substance the longer its life and the more transformation it
encounters upon death to more simple organic forms.

What is spiritual does not conform to simple / complex
categories. Spirit conforms to "in" and "out" of phase categories.
Individual identification points, spirits or souls or examples of
individual consciousness conform to their need to live and become
part of the greater whole which informs them of who they are and why
they are here. There is one eternal Spirit or Soul or Mind or
Consciousness that examples diversity in expression as easily as it
examples unity in intention. To use the term soul or spirit or mind or
consciousness is to refer to function and not essence. The same essence
performs different functions and thus appears differently on the scale
of perception.

Divine intention draws all forms of creation into its purpose
for being. Christianity calls that God's plan of salvation. Judaism calls
that God's redemption of his people. Islam calls that the will of Allah.
Buddhism calls that Nirvana. Taoism calls that the Tao. Confucianism
calls that Chung Tzu. Divine intention incorporates all the spiritual
gifts and fruits plus all the ethical teachings that hold to equality and
respect between life forms. The heart of Divine intention is Love which
manifests in compassion, bonding, service, uniting, appreciation, and
justice. The mind of Divine intention is freedom from restrictions and
limitations. The will of Divine intention is discovery and evolution.

Organic evolution becomes the field of activity for what is, what happens in the material / energy universe, interacting with while moving on a parallel path. What is spiritual is what provides dimension or fullness to what is real. Though we view reality as three dimensional, and more recently multi-dimensional, a more inclusive way to describe reality is two sided with one side being spirit and the other side being extension (a Descartes term). In this model spirit informs matter both at the individual level and at the all-inclusive totality level. More recent spiritual sensitives have referred to this cooperative activity as being co-creators with God. That's what we are and that's where we are going. With the great Indian mystics we affirm that there are many paths up the same mountain but one summit at the top. The top, in this metaphor, is God and the end of evolution. The ways we get to the top are surprisingly similar in their ethical guises but different in their particular loyalties and regimen.

IV. Dualism and Monism, two sides of one universe and reality

Dualism is real as much as any appearance can be real. Dualism has been with us from the beginning. Plato formulated a dualistic model in which the eternal forms were most real and perfect and separate from their physical counterparts. Christianity moved away from the oneness of Judaism when it agreed to a Trinitarian model for God and a dualistic model for Christ Jesus. Judaism has had its own form of duality. God, and everything else, to be precise. Christianity accepted this duality among others. It also felt comfortable going along with Plato and the general Greek notion of Spirit / matter dichotomy. Christian philosophers up to and including the early empiricists could not resolve their respective models of reality without also continuing some form of dualism; be it mind / body, spirit / matter, or faith / experience.

Dualism ultimately becomes a question of extension. That simply means, as Rene Descartes might describe it, we appear to have dimensions associated with our location and mobility. We take up space and we go from here to there. If we took up no space and needed no movement, extension would not be a characteristic and we would not appear to live in a dualistic world with dualistic attributes. As material beings, we have extension. From all normal appearances there is space where we are and a space where we are not. Some of us take up more space than others. Some of us travel more than others and thus appear to occupy more space than do others. Of course, Isaac Newton discovered that two objects cannot take up the same space at the same time. More recent physicists have discovered, through the mathematical model of quantum mechanics, that two objects in phase with one another can, in theory, pass through one another and thus take up the same space at the same time. The implications of that are staggering for a necessary notion of duality.

Dualism is thus a matter of perception. Just speak to the number of historic mystics about it and take a moment to see through their eyes. Those who came from Eastern traditions saw one reality in different aspects. Equality with God, total submersion into God seemed quite normal. Those who came from Western traditions, which did not allow their perception to include themselves as intrinsically worthy, saw themselves inferior to what they were united with; namely, God. "**Union**" is one of, if not the one important message of mystical experience.

Mystics saw one reality in which their part was either undifferentiated or inferior. Genuine mystics are the front line troops of reality and their experiences, along with the experiences of the many sensitives, penetrate the veil that appears to separate the different worlds of perception.

V. Life Is Worth Living When We Reach for the Ring of Truth

The average working person might wonder why philosophers spend their entire lives searching for Truth. Many might wonder why a few would be so committed to discovering reality- that deprivations, social limitations and seeming dead ends would not simply cause them to give up and live in their comfortable but carefully bordered consensus reality. After all, the end result is the same for each of us. There is, after all,   one way out of this existence; namely, death, barring a prophetic chariot ride or pin wheel abduction.

Breaking through whatever consensus reality enfolds you to the discovery of who you really are and what you can really do, is worth lifetimes of thoughtful, spiritual growth and struggle. Discovering the God who totally accepts you, without reservation or belief loyalties, has such a freeing affect as to warrant a close look. The message, while shrouded in complex conceptual patterns, is a simple one. True freedom comes from understanding and accepting the Truth about who you are and why you are here. True freedom is the spiritual release taught by each of the world's religions as well as those secular giants whose love of life and humanity prompted them not to accept less, but to struggle for the prize. Joseph Campbell, in his, Hero with a Thousand Faces, recognized the mythic proportions of the heroic journey that brings back what humanity truly needs. In this case, it is discovering the Truth that sets you free to be you, beyond all cultural, religious and ideological barriers.

Each of us knows limitations. Some of us come from traditions that accept those limitations as examples of humanity's fallen state. Religions arising out of the biblical witness have, as part of their source material, accounts from Genesis that confirm why people always need to struggle, suffer and live in a condition of frustration. For them, Adam's sin follows humanity right up to the present time. Furthermore, Christ's redemption doesn't offset the temporal effects of original sin. Instead, what Christ has done, as his sacrifice for humanity, insures believers a heavenly home to come. The world is, after all, intrinsically evil because the world is governed by Satan, the fallen angel who creates suffering and temptation and apostasy. And if Satan doesn't do all those things, then surely they are the direct result of creation's fallen condition. Typically, the aforementioned description encapsulates elements of traditional orthodox Christianity which has accepted some version of this scenario to explain the presence of evil and limitation in this world and in your life.

There is no way out while you and I are here. Salvation ultimately comes from faithful obedience and eventual liberation in paradise. If these classical descriptions express more than consensus realities which have formed around a central message, than you and I can only wait and hope that somehow our endurance will see a day of liberation from limitation and pain.

The new / old understanding introduced in this book offers an alternative view of who man is, who God is, and what is going on. All religions contain this view and address these questions and issues similarly within factions representing those religions. The Eastern religions appear to have gotten the big picture sooner, and with greater clarity. This age promises that the Western religions will come of age and get it as well. That is the promise. That is how we can make our lives better.

When we understand limitations as intrinsically evil and God as both the author and liberator of a purpose for creation unencumbered by suffering, lack, frustration or limitation of any sort, we will be moving in the direction of getting rid of, rather than promoting, those things we have picked up along the way. We will have transformed our consensus reality to what God had in mind from the beginning. That is unrelated to the reality of our dependence on God for all things. That is unrelated to our recognizing the significance of Christ's life and eternal victory on our behalf to bring us all back to the Infinite who manifests as Father. That is unrelated to the revelations given to Moses, Muhammad, Lao Tzu or any of the great Rishis of India. All genuine inspirations and revelations address Truth. What we have spoken of is related to Truth that changes your perception and thus changes your life. May the Truth be in you and may it set you free to be a co-creator with God.

RECOMMENDED READINGS

Biblical history and archaeology

Albright, William Foxwell. *From The Stone Age To Christianity.* Garden City, N.Y.: Doubleday & Company, 1957.

Biblical Interpretation in the Early Church. ed. by Karlfried Froehlich. Philadelphia: Fortress, 1984.

Brown, Raymond & Meier, John P. *Antioch & Rome.* New York: Paulist Press, 1983.

Bruce, F.F. *New Testament History.* New York: Doubleday, 1969.

Finegan, Jack. *Archaeological History of the Middle East.* New York: Dorset Books, 1979.

Goodman, Paul. *History of the Jews.* E.P. Dutton & Co, 1953.

Hertzberg, Arthur. *Judaism.* George New York: George Braziller, 1962.

Heschel, Abraham J. *The Prophets.* New York: Harper & Row, 1962.

Hyers, Conrad. *The Meaning of Creation. Genesis and Modern Science.* Atlanta: John Knox Press, 1984.

Johnson, Paul. *A History of the Jews.* New York: Harper & Row, 1987.

Metzger, Bruce Manning. *The Text of the New Testament.* New York: Oxford University Press, 1968.

Moscati, Sabatino. *The Face of the Ancient World.* New York: Doubleday & CO, 1962.

Pfeiffer, Robert H. *Introduction to the Old Testament.* New York: Harper & Row, 1948.

Sloan, W.W. *A Survey of the Old Testament.* New York: Abingdon Press, 1957.

Staack, Hagen. *Living Personalities of the Old Testament.* New York: Harper & Row, 1964.

Vaux, Roland de. *Ancient Israel, Volume 1- Social Institutions.* New York: McGraw Hill Company, 1965.

Voux, Roland de. *Ancient Israel, Volume 2- Religious Institutions.* New York.: McGraw Hill Company, 1965.

Books and authors in agreement with themes suggested in this text

Hick, John. *God Has Many Names.* Philadelphia: Westminster Press, 1982.

The Alpbach Symposium- Beyond Reductionism. ed. by Arthur Koestler and J.R. Smythies. New York: The Macmillan Company, 1970.

Lorimer, David. *Whole In One-The Near-death Experience and the ethic of Interconnectedness.* London: Arkana, 1990.

Ogden, Schubert M. *Is There Only One True Religion or Are There Many?* Dallas: Southern Methodist University Press, 1992.

Plotkin, Rabbi Albert. *The Ethics of World Religions.* 1993.

Robinson, John A.T. *Exploration into God.* Stanford: Standford University Press, 1967.

Slater, Robert Lawson. *World Religions and World Community.* New York: Columbia University Press, 1963.

Smart, Ninian. *The Religious Experience of Mankind.* New York: Charles Scribner's Sons, 1969.

Smith, Huston. *Forgotten Truth - The Common Vision of the World's Religions.* San Francisco: Harper, 1992.

Metaphysics

Allen, James. *As A Man Thinketh.* Old Tappan: Fleming H. Revell Company, 1977.

Beyond Space and Time-An ESP Casebook. ed. by Martin Ebon. New York: New Amercian Library, 1967.

Consciousness and Reality. ed. by Charles Muses and Arthur M. Young. New York: Outerbridge & Lazard, 1972.

Goldsmith, Joel S. *A Parenthesis In Eternity-Living The Mystical Life.* San Francisco: Harper & Row, 1963.

Johnson, Raynor. *Nurslings of Immortality*. New York: Harper & Row, 1972.
Johnson, Raynor. *The Imprisoned Splendour*. London: The Theosophical Publishing House, 1971.
Judge, William. *The Scope of Reincarnation*. Alhambra: The Cunningham Press, 1960.
Keck, L. Robert. *The Spirit of Synergy*. Nashville: Parthenon Press, 1973
Kueshana, Eklal. *The Ultimate Frontier*. The Stelle Group, 1982.
Leonard, George. *The Silent Pulse*. New York: E.P. Dutton, 1978.
Leonard, George. *The Transformation*. Los Angeles: J.P. Tarcher, Inc., 1972.
Moody, Dr. Raymond A. *Coming back-A Psychiatrist Explores Past Life Journies*. New York: Collier Books, 1970.
Moody, Dr. Raymond A. *Life After Life*. Harrisburg: Stackpole Books, 1976.
Moody, Dr. Raymond A. *The Light Beyond*. New York: Bantam Books, 1988.
Reincarnation in World Thought. ed. by Joseph Head & S.L. Cranston. New York: Julian Press, 1967.
Reincarnation: An East - West Anthology. ed. by Joseph Head & S.L. Cranston.New York: Julian Press, 1961.
Spiritual Aspects of the Healing Arts. compiled by Dora Kunz. The Theosophical Publishing House, 1985.
Steiner, Rudolph. *Reincarnation and Karma-Their Significance in Modern Culture*. London: Anthroposophical Publishing Company, 1960.
Teilhard de Chardin, Pierre. *The Future of Man*. New York: Harper & Row, 1964.
Tulku, Tarthang. *Time, Space, and Knowledge - A New Vision of Reality*. Emerville: Dharma Publishing, 1977.
Wilbur, Ken. *The Sprectrum of Consciousness*. Wheaton: Theosophical Publishing House, 1977.
Whitehead, Alfred North. *Adventures of Ideas*. New York: The Free Press, 1961.
Whitehead, Alfred North. *Process & Reality-An Essay in Cosmology*. New York: Harper & Row, 1957.

Phenomenology

Bulfinch, Thomas. *Bulfinch's Mythology*. ed. by Edmund Fuller. New York: Dell Publishing Co, 1959.
Campbell, Joseph. *The Masks of God-* four volume series. The Viking Press: New York, 1969.
Campbell, Joseph. *Hero With A Thousand Faces*. New York: MJF Books, 1949.
Croft, Peter. *Roman Mythology*. New Jersey: Chartwell Books. no date.
Eliade, Mircea. *Cosmos and History*. new York: Harper Torchbboks, 1959.
Eliade, Mircea. *The Sacred and the Profane*. translated by Willard R. Trask. New York: Harper & Row, 1961.
Frazer, James. *The Golden Bough*. New York: Random House, 1993.
Koestler, Arthur. *Janus- A Summing Up*. New York: Random House, 1978.
Leeuw, G. Van Der. *Religion in Essence and Manifestation-A Study in Phenomenology*. New York: Harper & Row, 1963.
Hamilton, Edith. *Mythology-Timeless Tales of Gods and Heroes*. New York: The New American Library, 1942.
Herzberg, Max J. *Myths and Their Meaning*. New York: Allyn and Bacon, 1931.
Malinowski, Bronislaw. *Magic, Science and Religion*. New York: Doubleday, 1954.
Mercatante, Anthony S. *Good and Evil In Myth and Legend*. New York: Barnes and Noble, 1978.
Mongrieff, A.R. Hope. *Myths And Legends of Ancient Greece*. New York: Gramercy Books, 1995.
Osis, Dr. Karlis. *What they Saw At The Hour Of Death*. New York: Avon, 1977.
Otto, Rudolf. *The Idea of the Holy*. London: Oxford Press, 1958.
Scholem, Gershom. *Jewish Mysticism*. New York: Schocken Books, 1941.
Stevenson, Dr. Ian. *Twnety Cases Suggestive of Reincarnation*. New York: American Society for Psychical Research, 1966.
Wach, Joachim. *The Comparative Study of Religions*. New York: Columbia University Press, 1958.

Physics and the New Physics

Capra, Fritjof. *Belonging to the Universe*. San Francisco: Harper, 1991.
Capra, Fritjof. *The Tao of Physics*. Boulder: Shambhala Press, 1975.
Feynman, Richard. *The Feynman Lectures on Physics*. Massachusetts: Addison-Westley Publishing Company, Inc., 1964.
Davies, Paul. *God and the New Physics*. New York: Simon & Schuster, 1983.
Koestler, Arthur. *The Roots of Coincidence*. London: Hutchinson, 1972.
Koestler, Arthur. *The Roots of Coincidnece*. New York: Random House, 1972.
Neutrinos. ed. by H.V. Klapdor. New York: Springer Verlag Berlin, 1988.
Russell, Bertrand. *The ABC of Relativity*. New York: The New American Library, 1959.
Sears, Francis & Mark Zemansky. *University Physics*. Massachusetts:
 Addison-Westley Publishing Company, Inc., 1955.
Talbot, Michael. *The Holographic Universe*. New York: Harper Collins Publishers, 1991.
Talbert, Michael. *Beyond the Quantum*. New York: Bantams Books, 1986.
The Holographic Paradigm and other paradoxes. ed. by Ken Wilber. Boston Shambhala Publishers, 1985.
Wehr, M. Russell & James A. Richards, Jr. *Physics of the Atom*. Massachusetts: Addison-Westley Publishing Company, Inc., 1960.

General references

Armitage, Angus. *The World of Capernicus*. New York: The New American Library, 1958.
Bach, Marcus. *Major Religions of the World*. Marina del Rey: DeVorss & Co., 1959.
Hopfe, Lewis M. *Religions of the World*. Upper Saddle River: Prentice Hall, 1994.
Ludwig, Theodore M. *The Sacred Paths- Understanding the Religions of the World*. Upper Saddle River: Prentice Hall, 1989.
Matthews, Warren. *World Religions*. Mineapolis: West Publishing Company, 1994.
Noss, John B. *Man's Religions*. London: Macmillan Company, 1970.
Pickthall, Mahammad Marmaduke. *Cultural Side of Islam*. Pakistan:
 Sh Muhammad Adshraf, 1969.
Redfield, Robert. *The Little Community- Peasant Society and Culture*. Chicago: Phoenix, 1963.
Early Christian Fathers. ed. by Cyril Richardson. New York: Collier Books, 1970.
Sen, K.M. *Hinduism- The World's Oldest Faith*. Harmondsworth: Penguin, 1969.
Smith, Huston. *The Illustrated World's Religions*. San Francisco: Harper, 1991.
Smith, Huston. *The World's Great Religions*. San Francisco: Harper, 1958.
Swami Prabhupada, A.C. Bhaktivedanta. *Bhagavad Gita- As it Is*. New York: Bhaktivedanta Book Trust, 1972.
The Age of Belief. ed. by Anne Fremantle. New York: The New American Library, 1954.
The Age of Adventure. ed. by Giorgio De Santillana. New York: The New American Library, 1956.
Barclay, William. *The Daily Study Bible*. -Seventeen Volume Series. Philadelphia: Westminster Press, 1958.
The New Encyclopaedia Britannica in 30 volumes. Chicago: Helen Hemingway Benton, Publisher, 1974.
The Portable World Bible. ed. by Robert O. Ballou. New York: Penguin Books, 1972.
Tierney, Brian. *The Crisis of Church & State 1050-1300*. Englewood Cliffs: Prentice-Hall, 1980.
Tillich, Paul. *A History of Christian Thought*. New York: Harper & Row, 1968.

Philosphy and beliefs

Abduh, Muhammad. *The Theology of Unity*. translated by Kenneth Cragg. London: George Allen & Unwin, 1966.

Aitken, Robert and David Steindl-Rast. *The Ground We Share-Everyday Practice Buddhist and Christian.* Boston: Shambhala, 1996.

Arberry, A.J. *Sufism- An Account of the Mystics of Islam.* New York: Harper Torchbooks, 1950.

Aurobindo, Sri. *The Life Divine.* Pondicherry: Sri Aurobindo Ashram, 1965.

Brunner, Emil. *Justice and the Social Order.* translated by Mary Hottinger. New York: Harper & Brothers, 1945.

Chang, Garma C.C. *The Buddhist Teaching of Totality.* University Park: The Pennsylvania State University Press, 1971.

Frankfort, Henri. *Ancient Egyptian Religion- An Interpretation.* New York: Harper Torchbooks, 1961.

Gaer, Joseph. *The Wisdom of the Living Religions.* New York: Dodd Mead & Company, 1958.

Grunebaum, G.E. Von. *Classical Islam- A History 600-1258.* translated by Katherine Watson. New York: Barnes & Noble, 1970.

James, William. *The Will To Believe/Human Imortality.* New York: Dover Publications, 1956.

Jaspers, Karl. *Socrates, Buddha, Confucius, Jesus.* New York: Harcourt, Brace & World, 1957.

Lippman, Thomas W. *Understanding Islam- An introduction to the Muslim World.* New York: Penguin Group, 1995.

Luk, Charles. *Ch'an and Zen Teaching- First Series.* Berkeley: Shambala Publications, 1970.

Maitra, S.K. *The Meeting of East and West in Sri Aurobindo's Philosophy.* Pondicherry: Sri Aurobindo Ashram, 1988.

Nasr, Seyyed Hossein. *Ideals and Realities of Islam.* ed. by Huston Smith. Boston: Beacon Press, 1975.

Original Teachings of Ch'an Buddhism. translated by Chang Chung-Yuan. New York: Pantheon Books, 1969.

Scholem, Gershom. *Kabbalah.* New York: Dorset Press, 1974.

Shankara's Crest-Jewel of Discrimination. translated by Swami Prabhavananda and Christopher Isherwood. Hollywood: Vedanta Press, 1978.

Shah, Idries. *The Way Of The Sufi.* New York: E.P. Dutton & Co., 1970.

Skinner, B.F. *Beyond Freedom & Dignity.* New York: A Bantam Book, 1971.

Steinberg, Milton. *Basic Judaism.* New York: Harcourt, Brace & World, 1947.

Stories of the Buddha. translated by Caroline A.F. Rhys Davids. New York: Dover Publications, 1989.

Suzuki, D.T. *Manual of Zen Buddhism.* New York: Grove Press, 1970.

Suzuki, D.T. *Zen Buddhism.* ed. by William Barett. New York: Doubleday, 1956.

Taylor, A.E. *Plato- The man and his work.* New York: Meridian Books, Inc., 1960.

Teachings of the Buddha. ed. by Jack Kornfeld. London: Shambhala Publishers, 1993.

The Indian Mind. ed. by Charles Moore. Honolulu: University of Hawaii Press, 1967.

The World of Zen- An East-West Anthology. ed. by Nancy Wilson Ross. New York: Vintage Books, 1960.

Tillich, Paul. *Systematic Theology, Volumes 1,2,& 3.* Chicago: University of Chicago Press, 1957.

Weatherhead, Leslie D. *Psychology, Religion and Healing.* New York: Abingdon Press. no date

Societal implications

Borchert, Bruno. *Mysticism- Its History and Challenges.* York Beach: Samuel Weiser, Inc., 1994.

Capra, Fritjof. *The Turning Point.* New York: Simon & Schuster, 1982.

Lenski, Gerhard. *The Religious Factor- A Sociologist's Inquiry.* New York: Anchor Books, 1963.

Rifkin, Jeremy. *Entropy- A New World View.* New York: Viking Press, 1980.

Rifkin, Jeremy & Ted Howard. *The Emerging Order- God in the Age of Scarity.* New York: G.P. Putnam's Sons, 1979.

Rauschenbusch, Walter. *A Theology For the Social Gospel.* New York: Macmillian Company, 1922.

S

6.61

CreaGod

Printed in the United States
76529LV00007B/89